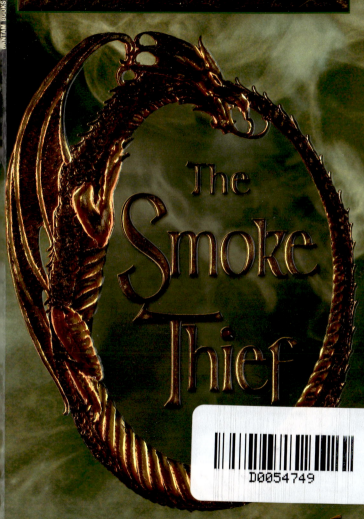

HISTORICAL PARANORMAL ROMANCE

# The Smoke Thief

D0054749

# SHANA ABÉ

BANTAM BOOKS

# Praise for *The Smoke Thief*

"A damn good read! Viewers, historical romance stories get no better than this one! It's not only highly recommended, it is extremely recommended! I loved it so much that it will never leave my possession! Awesome!"
—*Huntress Book Reviews*

"*The Secret Swan* by Shana Abé is a delightful novel that should not be missed! Ms. Abé has crafted a tale that is sure to grip readers and never let go. Once you start reading this tale of love, you won't be able to stop until you turn the last page—it's that good! Ms. Abé delivers an exciting and beautifully woven tale with a rich and fascinating plot which is layered with plenty of intrigue. *The Secret Swan* boasts excellent narration and engaging dialogue. Ms. Abé has definitely penned a winner! Readers of historical romance are sure to claim this book for their keeper shelf!" —*Reader to Reader*

## Praise for *Intimate Enemies*

"Shana Abé has created an unforgettable pair of star-crossed lovers caught in an age-old feud, while beautifully evoking the misty isle and the historical backdrop. She truly makes us believe we are part of this wondrous tale."
—*Romantic Times*

"Historical romance at its finest!" —*Jill Marie Landis*

"Ms. Abé has written another winner." —*Affaire de Coeur*

"Ms. Abé's expert writing transports the reader to medieval Scotland, where they become enthralled in an emotional romance complete with passion, drama, danger and adventure." —*Rendezvous*

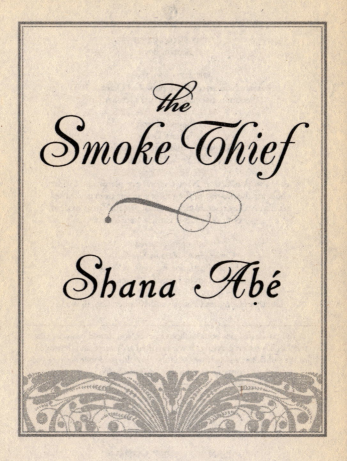

# the Smoke Thief

## Shana Abé

BANTAM BOOKS

THE SMOKE THIEF
A Bantam Book

PUBLISHING HISTORY
Bantam hardcover edition published October 2005
Bantam mass market edition / October 2006

Published by
Bantam Dell
A Division of Random House, Inc.
New York, New York

Library of Congress Catalog Card Number: 2004056634

Bantam Books and the rooster colophon are registered trademarks
of Random House, Inc.

ISBN-13: 978-0-553-58804-0
ISBN-10: 0-553-58804-4

Printed in the United States of America
Published simultaneously in Canada

www.bantamdell.com

OPM 10 9 8 7 6 5 4 3 2 1

For Mom and Dad, always and ever.

A book is just a dream, without pushing and
prodding and heaps of encouragement;
Wendy McCurdy, Annelise Robey, and
Andrea Cirillo deserve full kudos for helping
me make this dream real. Thank you!

A very special *umboogwa* to Stacey, for using up
all of her minutes on me. Ditto to Mandy!

And of course, *domo, danke,* and *gracias* to
Darren, who understood all that.

# the Smoke Thief

# PROLOGUE

Imagine a place so ripe and thick with the promise of magic that the very air breathes in plumes of pearl and gray and smoky blue; that the trees bow with the weight of their heavy branches, dipping low to the ground, dropping needles and leaves into beds of perfume. A place of white sparkling mountains and black forests and one high, ancient castle. Of diamonds that churn up raw from the marrow of the earth to lace the woods, unseen, in necklaces of ice and fire.

A place without small creatures. A place without easy sight, or breadth. A place so hidden even the sun cannot pierce the heart of it, but spreads her light across the top canopy of trees, bringing green high above and dark silence well below, and streams that flow in crystal blades over the rocks and leaves.

Jasper and quartz tumble in the streams, dusted with flakes of gold. Garlands of diamonds settle deep into pools, hidden beneath the silt.

Imagine that from this place is born a people. Special people, the sole beings of these woods.

They live and hunt apart from the rest of the world, taming the forest, carving the quartzite mountains, building the lone castle that clings in cold splendor to the bleakest side of the tallest peak.

They hear the diamonds in the earth. They sing to the clouds. They hold the dominion of thought and transformation; steeped in magic, they live splendid and aloof, and when the jealous Others begin to come, the people of the mountains and woods defend their home with a ferocity that shatters the sky itself.

But the Others do not cease to come.

Imagine blood. Imagine war.

North, south, west and east—from every direction the invaders creep, muddying the streams, numbing the earth, with the castle and its mountain the very center of their ambitions.

To the last of the people atop the peak, the future is as clear and cold as starlight. They pry up the diamonds and jasper that were pressed into the stones of their fortress. They gather their children and vanish into the smoke, blue and gray and pearl.

But they did not take every diamond when they fled. And they did not take every last child.

Now imagine...that these are not people at all.

These are the *drákon*.

For a very long while, the forsaken castle remained unbreached. There were no paths leading up the mountainside; all was sharp stone and a sharper still descent. Men and the sons of men studied it for decades, wondering at its grandeur, its absolute contempt for all things below. The scraped glacier valleys hugging the bluffs claimed many broken bodies.

Yet as with so many things held out of reach, the dream of conquest simmered like a fever through the invaders. Eventually they began to understand how to scale the mountain, how to anchor their ropes, how to hack away the stone. In this way, over years, a track was hewn.

It devoured lifetimes.

Men were small and the castle so high; there were always new battles to fight, new crops to harvest, births and deaths and fleeting seasons. The people who lived in the woods now were merely Others; they did not hear the diamonds beneath their feet, and they never traveled the clouds. The flecks of gold threading the lakes and streams were said to be the final thoughts of the vanquished gods.

The fortress began to seem more and more a mirage than a goal, ever wrapped in mist, the rough quartzite bleeding clear crystal streamers down its walls and ramparts and parapets. Eventually even the creatures who once occupied it became woven into legend, their grace and ferocity fading into tales no more tangible than the moan of the wind.

The mountains garnered a name: *Carpathians*. And the castle at the highest peak: *Zaharen Yce*. The Tears of Ice.

Time had its way. Occasionally a block from a turret would loosen and fall, striking thunder off the cliffs. The villagers below would pause and look up. Some would joke, *The gods awake.*

There came at last the day the Others finished their trail to heaven. But the olden castle held one more surprise for those first few who stepped foot inside.

Despite their uneasy jests, everyone believed it to be abandoned.

It was not.

The Carpathian Mountains slice a crescent moon across Europe and into the imaginary lines of men, jutting up through provinces and dukedoms and even kingdoms without regard for human boundaries. With windstorms and staggering heights, they remove any final weakness from civilization, savaging the frail, the unprepared; exalting only the powerful. Winter and snow and alpine flowers, meadows and opaque woods: from the most remote of these peaks a new noble family slowly began to blossom.

They were proud and very few, gaunt and beautiful.

This was the legacy the *drákon* had left behind with their castle: one son and one daughter, and from them generations of new life to dwell amid the mist and haunt the Others below, until they learned the secrets of their enemies. Until they learned, in fact, to *become* them... to look as they did, to breathe and eat and speak as they did. To plod the earth as the Others did, all the while hiding their true faces, and their true hearts.

So this is what those first invaders saw upon entering the castle, before dropping down to their knees: a handful of people, pale and stunning, with lips that smiled in welcome, but eyes that burned.

Centuries passed. The family grew. They began to command the respect of allies and foes alike, gathering towns and serfs at the flanks of the mountains to serve them. Monasteries, blacksmiths, smelts. Commerce, mines, walled cities. As the illusory borders of countries bulged with people, the family spawned warriors, and then aristocracy.

They lived in a mountaintop castle that gleamed sugar and salt in the sun, that vanished into ice with the snowfall.

They kept their dark secret very, very close.

Over time, they prospered. Their source of wealth was not merely the natural abundance of their beloved mountains, but also the absolute fealty of their people. The family had lived in The Tears of Ice for as long as anyone now could recall. They alone controlled the road winding up the mountainside. They alone controlled the mine shafts, and the smelts, and the bishops and merchants and snow-blinded passes leading to and from the many towns.

And they alone heard the diamonds in the

ground, could taste the waiting gold buried in the black, rich earth. The beings once hunted by the Others were now protected by them. They were cherished, admired, feared.

The family became known as the Zaharen, after their ice-crystal fortress, and tales of them abounded. It was said they were blessed, and that they were cursed. That they were touched by the finger of God—or by the devil. Occasionally even hints of the old legend would resurface, whispers that the Zaharen were not all that they seemed. That in the skies late at night, against the slick black shadow of the castle, sinuous monsters could be seen hunting the moon.

Only the foolish ever spoke such a thing aloud; no one risked the wrath of the family lightly.

But the truth was, for all the rumors surrounding them, the Zaharen truly heeded only one whisper: that of the stones.

The castle became filled with diamonds once more. Every hollow, every pocket from the old stones that had been pried loose from the walls was refilled. To the few Others who were invited up into the stronghold, the unpolished gems appeared stark and oddly gleaming, an uneven mosaic of drab, spectral colors lining the halls.

But when a member of the family walked by, when they touched their hands to the walls, stroking fingers, the melody of the stones would fill them like nectar. The Tears of Ice was once again steeped in music that only the *drákon* could discern.

There was one stone that was not embedded

in the walls. It was kept in a vault, in a pit, in a dungeon, left behind from the early days when that first wave of the *drákon* had fled the land. None of the Zaharen were allowed to touch it, although everyone in the family knew of its strength. It sang even from the bottom of the castle.

This diamond was called *Draumr*. Too powerful to be destroyed, too dangerous to look upon—because to look at it would be to ache for it—it was the only known fragment of earth with the potential to eclipse the family itself.

The Zaharen were, above all, strategists. They understood that the secret of this diamond was the secret of their undoing. It was forbidden even to speak its name.

Great wealth is certain to inspire great resentment, and the Zaharen were among the wealthiest families of the civilized world. It was fully believed that their treasures rivaled those of Rome herself, and that the pope fell into such envy upon his sole visit to the castle that he would not depart without a handful of cold, pure diamonds pressed upon him by the youngest maiden of the family.

She was a princess, lovely, brutally protected. Considered the living gem of the mountain, poems were recited in her name, flowers bloomed at her feet. Mortal men braved the winter passes just to glimpse her; when the pope touched her bare hand that morning, bending down to her from his mount, it was said he wept with joy.

Betrothed at birth, at the age of fifteen she was to wed a noble cousin. But on the eve of her marriage the princess was stolen from the castle. She was carried off to the slopes below, and with her the one thing in the world that could prevent her from escaping her abductor, that would keep her family from following.

*Draumr*.

The Zaharen began to fall into ruin.

The loss of the princess was a grievous blow; the lack of her recovery a worse one yet. The man who took her had wed her. There were children. There was tainted blood.

Yet when the Zaharen attempted to steal her back, to crush the mortal man who dared to defy them, they vanished utterly, one by one.

None of the Others could understand how.

This man was no one. He was a peasant, a laborer. But he had the princess and he had *Draumr*, and they were all he needed. Against knights and assassins, against fearsome beasts, the peasant began to pull apart the mightiest family the land had ever known.

Without the command of their *drákon* leaders, the armies dissolved into corruption and disarray. The prosperous cities began to empty of people.

Foreign princes smelled their weakness; new armies encroached. The borders of humankind crept closer and closer to *Zaharen Yce*. By the time the family realized they could no longer defend their castle or their lives, there were fewer than a dozen of them left.

And the half-blooded children far below, stunned under the spell of the dreaming diamond.

It was the princess who at last broke the spell. It was the princess who realized that her life was worth less than that of her kind, of her children, and so one night put a dagger into the peasant's heart and took the diamond that had enslaved her from his body.

For years, *Draumr* had sung in her head like a symphony. It had promised paradise, sweet dreams forever, and despite her resolve, she could not demolish it. Instead she crept away—far, far away—and with the diamond in her fist, she flung herself into the wet bowels of the earth.

The Carpathian Mountains are riddled with mines. Copper, gold, iron; their empty sleeves snake through bedrock and dirt.

She chose the deepest of the shafts. She made certain no one could ever follow.

Neither she nor anyone else realized that the true roots of the *drákon* had been divided centuries past, when the first of her people deserted the castle. She could not know that when she savored her last slow breath, that when she closed her eyes and took that slight, leaning step forward into black nothing, that she was merely a passage in the song of her kind, not the end note.

Because although the Zaharen had grown tainted and few, the other half of the *drákon* were green lands and an ocean away: secretly, savagely in bloom.

And their story was just beginning.

# CHAPTER ONE

Chasen Manor
*Darkfrith, England*
*1737*

The Right Honourable Christoff René Ellery Langford, Earl of Chasen, was bored.

He had decided to demonstrate this fact by slouching in his chair, his legs outstretched and his blond head turned idly away from everyone else in his father's study. One sundarkened cheek was propped languidly upon his fist; his green eyes were hooded, masked with brown lashes. He listened to his father talk with the haughty, brooding air common to either the young or the powerful.

Kit, as it happened, was both. Sixteen years old and wellacknowledged as the heir to the tribe, he endured these meetings as his duty. He did not speak. He did not bother to meet the eyes of the other men present. When he looked up from his boots he chose to contemplate the view from the Tudor windows, the summer lush hills and rich black trees. The beckoning woods.

He listened to the same debate the council had at every meeting now. He could practically predict, verbatim, who would say what.

"The safety of the tribe is paramount. We must ensure our survival."

Parrish Grady again. The man never let up. Eldest member of the council, blue-eyed, sharp-toothed. Kit was beginning to consider him his own personal nemesis, if for no other reason than these meetings crawled on hours longer than they would without him.

Outside, just over a distant hill, appeared a flock of girls. About Kit's age, white skirts, frilled aprons, straw hats with ties that dangled in the wind. A few carried armfuls of flowers. He watched them come closer.

"Naturally, Parrish, our survival is paramount." Kit's father, the marquess. "No one debates that."

"We need a full-blood female!"

"I'd say we've been doin' our best there," retorted Rufus Booke, brash and newly wed, "though mayhap you'd prefer to check our beds every night."

Kit snorted back a laugh. He felt his father's gaze flick to him, then away.

"Aye, we need a female," the Marquess of Langford agreed. "But we do not appear to have one. Yet. There are several young tribeswomen on the verge of the rebirth. We may hope one of them will complete the Turn."

"Hope," repeated Grady, derisive. "Four generations it's been, and no female to make the Turn! What will happen to us—all of us—when it becomes impossible for the menfolk as well?"

Silence greeted this. It was the great, simmering fear among the tribe, that the Gifts would be taken. That their powers would fade.

"We cannot force our fate," said the marquess, harder now. "We all understand that. We are what we are. Our more immediate concern is the perimeter of the forest. There have been signs of recent disturbance, not our own. Strangers are prowling our lands. Christoff reported horse tracks up to Hawkshead Point."

"Hawkshead? But that's not even ours! What the devil is the boy doing all the way out there? We have rules! He left the boundary!"

Again, the distinctive prickle of his father's gaze. Kit allowed himself the slightest curl of his lips.

"Let us focus on the matter at hand," said the marquess smoothly. "Hawkshead is adjacent to our boundaries. If someone has chanced that far..."

The girls had paused in a soft valley between the hills, clutching their hats as the breeze turned brisker. Sunlight showed honeyed locks flying and flaxen, strawberry blond and ginger red. Four girls, smiling and chattering amid the green. Someone loosed her flowers, and the August wind blew them into bright confusion.

Parrish Grady thumped a fist on the arm of his chair. "The boy's too wild, even for our kind. He needs to be reined in. You know it yourself, my lord."

Kit stared a little harder at the girls, his eyes narrowed.

"Thank you, Mr. Grady, but I take the responsibility of raising my son as my own."

"If he is to be Alpha—"

"There is no *if,*" hissed the marquess, coming to his feet. "You will do well to understand that right now."

Silence fell once more across the study. One of the men cleared his throat, nervous, but said nothing.

Outside, the flower girls had gone very still. The strawberry blonde turned her face into the breeze—and the other three did the same. Kit recognized them now, Fanny and Suzanne, daughters of the smith, Liza from the mill. And Melanie, their leader. Melanie, of the apple cheeks and soft petal lips. Melanie, with her quick, cunning smile. He stirred in his chair, leaning casually on his elbow to see what they did.

Sky, grass, woods...and a shape in the trees. Another girl.

"There is the matter of the runners," volunteered a new voice, George Winston.

"Aye, the runners," began the murmurs across the room, and the marquess sat down again.

The woodsgirl realized that she had been discovered. She stood frozen as well, smaller than the other four, pressed up against the trunk of a tree. Kit could make out one pale hand against the bark, fingers splayed. He could not see her face.

Very, very slowly, she began to ease backward.

Melanie had turned to the others. She was speaking. She was taking off her hat.

"...precisely as I said. We cannot risk further incidents with outsiders. We were fortunate enough to capture the Williams boy before he had gotten too far, but the next time may be the time that he—or some other hotheaded young fool—manages to evade us. I shudder to think of what might have happened had he made it past the shire. I need to have a word with his parents again. And then the game-keepers, I think..."

The woodsgirl had managed hardly a step. Perhaps she hoped the others were bluffing; Kit, however, knew Melanie better than that. With infinite care the girl slid back another step, and then Kit caught her profile. It was that lass, the scrawny one always ducking from crowds, peering out of shadows . . . what was her name? He frowned, trying in his mind to place her amid the intricate shoots and branches of the tribe families. He'd seen her mostly around the village, brown-haired, white-skinned. Timid. Mousy, even, if such a word could be applied to any member of their kin.

Melanie's group began to walk toward her and the woodsmouse froze again—then lost her nerve. She skipped back. It was all Melanie needed.

The four girls broke into a sprint.

Kit straightened in his chair, forgetting his father's meeting. Four against one was hardly sporting, especially as the prey was so much younger than the hunters. The mouse vanished from view, swiftly followed by the others. He had glimpses of gowns flashing through the trees, and then nothing.

Calm settled back upon the forest, unbroken, silent as winter snow.

Kit uncrossed his ankles, considering. He'd seen the little mouse more and more of late, now that he thought about it. Always quiet, always alone.

If she had any sense, she'd head for the river. They might lose her scent there—

"Christoff? Christoff! Are you listening, boy?"

"Aye," Kit answered, with just that trace of surliness guaranteed to send color into his father's cheeks. "The perimeter, the runners. Dire peril to the tribe, et cetera."

"How gratifying to have your attention." The marquess thinned his lips. "Perhaps, then, *you* might have a suggestion for the council?"

For the first time Kit looked around at the gathered faces fixed upon him, tanned and pale and avid eyes.

"Regarding the matter of your bride?" prompted his father softly.

Kit opened his mouth to speak. But just then the woods erupted; the young girl hurtled out of the trees in a flap of skirts and mad streaming hair, her face flushed, cutting a sharp angle across the perfectly manicured rear lawn.

Kit stood, and all the men turned.

"What the—oh—it's—"

"The Hawthorne gel," said George. "Halfling. Clara, Clareta—"

"Clarissa," supplied Kit, in a spark of memory. "And Mel," he added dryly, as the other four emerged at her heels, gaining.

"Ah." The marquess took his seat again with his back to the window. "Halfling. Well, then, no matter. Gentlemen, shall we continue?"

But Kit remained standing, watching the lass run.

She crept into the cottage kitchen on her toes but, as usual, wasn't furtive enough to fool her mother.

"Clarissa? Is that you?"

"Yes, Mama."

She ought to have known she couldn't slip in and hide; her mother's senses were far too keen for that. Or perhaps it was the draft from the back door that gave her away. Either way, she thought glumly, she was caught now.

"What are you doing, child?"

"Washing up."

She dipped her hands into the chipped basin on the counter, scrubbing, watching the water turn pink with blood. She found the dishcloth and ran it over her face, wiping off the dirt, more blood.

"Mama, would you like tea?" she called.

"Yes, dear. That would be lovely."

She set the kettle to boil and scooped the tea leaves from this morning's breakfast, still damp, back into the teapot. She tossed the wash water out over the back steps—sending a quick, nervous look around the garden first—and then refilled it from the cistern.

The kettle began to steam.

By the pot of geraniums on the windowsill was the polished tin oval she had given her mother last Christmas, hung up by a yellow ribbon. It showed the kitchen in dusky gray and always made her face into a long, funny shape that reminded her of a fish, but it was still a better mirror than the windowpanes.

Clarissa examined her reflection critically: her hair was snarled, the white tucker at her collar torn. There was dirt on her elbows and three drops of blood across her bodice. Her lower lip throbbed red and bruised.

"Clarissa, I believe the water's ready."

"Yes, Mama."

No time to change gowns. She brushed herself off as best she could, recaptured her hair and twisted it into a haphazard bun. She poured the hot water into the teapot, set it on the tray along with cups and honey and cream, and then bread with the last of the butter.

One final look into the tin oval. Better, but not best. She widened her eyes to round perfect innocence and practiced a smile—wincing at her lip—then picked up the tray and carried it to her mother's room.

Antonia Hawthorne was sitting up in bed, her ashen hair in plaits, her hands folded on her lap. It was one of her better days; Clarissa could hardly hear her breathing. Her face was drawn but her eyes ever bright as she surveyed her daughter. Her mouth took on a ruthful slant.

"Oh, dear."

With great care, Clarissa set the tray upon the bedside table, unable suddenly to look up from the butter pats.

"Tell me," her mother invited in her soft, gentle voice. She waited as Clarissa fumbled with the spoons, her face still downturned, then said more firmly, "Clarissa Rue."

"An accident. I tripped over a tree root."

"Did you?"

Clarissa tried her wide-eyed look upon the teapot, beginning to pour. "Yes. I was clumsy. I tripped, and then I rolled down a hill. You know that one just past Blackstone Fell. It's very steep."

"Yes. I know it is."

Clarissa handed her the cup, meeting her gaze. "And that's what happened."

Antonia took a sip of tea. "Was Miss Melanie there?"

"No."

"Nor the others?"

"No." Clarissa began to meticulously butter the bread.

"You must stay away from them. I've told you before. They will not be kind to you."

The bread in her hand began a watery waver; she squeezed her eyes closed and felt a tear slink down the side of her nose.

"It is not your fault," said Antonia.

Another tear fell.

"It is mine," finished her mother, still soft.

Clarissa dropped the bread to the tray, swiping at her eyes with greasy fingers.

"Come here, my sweet girl," said Antonia, and Clarissa sniffed and crawled over the covers, slippers and dirty gown and all, nestling into her mother's embrace.

She smelled of medicine and lilacs. Her heartbeat was a fluttering thrum against Clarissa's ear.

THE SMOKE THIEF     19

She felt her mother's hand lift, begin to work loose the unkempt knot she had made of her hair. Clarissa turned her head and spoke down into the pillows; her voice came out as a miserable whisper.

"Won't they ever like me, Mama?"

"No, beloved. They won't."

"But I *try* to be like them—"

"You are more beautiful, more wonderful than all those savage girls put together. You are the most precious gift of my life. I am so proud of you, and your father would have been too. But . . ." Antonia's fingers paused; she seemed to be searching for words. "When the tribe looks at you—all they see is him. And he was not one of us."

"One of *you*, you mean," Clarissa muttered.

"One of *us*. Half your blood is *my* blood, the tribe's blood. That is your heritage. No one can deny you it."

The ruffles of her mother's gown were thin and worn, crumpled beneath her cheek. She wiped away another tear.

"Keep alone if you must, keep apart," murmured Antonia, stroking her daughter's dark hair. "Someday you'll grow up to be a splendid young woman, and you'll find a man who will love you for exactly who you are, just as I did. But know, my darling, that no matter what the future brings, you will always have a place here, with the tribe."

She knew who she wanted to love her. She knew who she wanted to rescue her, to speak her name and laugh with her and defend her from the world with the sudden, blinding charm of his smile.

Christoff. Golden, lovely Christoff, with his eloquent hands and sleepy green eyes that seemed to fill her soul whenever he chanced to see her. Which wasn't often, she had to admit. There wasn't a boy in the shire to compare to him. That's what Clarissa thought. And that's what Melanie and Liza and all the rest thought too. Clarissa knew, because even though she was only twelve *and* she hadn't the full blood of the tribe in her veins, she did have one single, clever skill: stealth.

She was very good at it. Or, rather, she had been. Till this afternoon.

She lay awake in her bed and counted the stars through her window, watching Cepheus and Cassiopeia tilt across the heavens. She loved the night best. It was the time for dreaming, for imagining what might be. Tonight the nightingale was singing from her nest in the garden laurel, aching, wistful notes that looped long and then warbled fleet, like water over a streambed. The gingham drape of her curtains framed the treetops that were the eastern end of the orchard. The cottage had been built by her grandfather beside the oldest and largest of the Roman apple trees. Every spring, the air smelled like paradise.

But it was summer, not spring, and she felt too confined in her flannel nightgown and cap. She kicked off the covers but it didn't help; Cepheus still sparkled and the little bird still sang. Clarissa sat up and crossed to the window. A breeze skimmed her neck in cool temptation.

When she turned her head she could hear her mother's breathing from the other room, slow and constant. Antonia usually slept deeply, the result of the medicine or her sickness or both.

Clarissa changed quickly, finding her darkest gown, tearing off the bothersome cap. The window was already open; she climbed through it with the ease of complete familiarity, barefoot, landing lightly on the grass below.

The nightingale cut its song short and Clarissa didn't move, waiting, listening as the bird did. But after a minute her song lifted again, and Clarissa took her skirts in her hands and stole out into the night.

Freedom. It thrilled her, running a straight line down the center of the orchard, apples and cherries and pears dripping moonlight from the trees. If she ran fast enough it was almost like she could fly. She tried a few skipping hops, wondering what it would be like to feel her feet lift from the ground. Her braid slapped her back with every leap.

There was no one to judge her here, no one to smirk at her, no one to hunt her. Out here, in the wilderness, she was unique and special and stronger than any member of the tribe. She was a princess—a queen—and all the others envied her, because she was the most powerful of all. And Christoff—

He loved her. He adored her. They would fly together, just the two of them, across the earth.

In time her run became a trot, and then a walk. The grass was velvet at her feet, the dirt soft as loam. The breeze murmured through the ancient trees. Clarissa found a pear and plucked it from its bough, holding the skin up to her nose, inhaling warm, ripe summertime.

Her lip stung with the juice. But even that couldn't dim this moonlit moment. She ate her pear and endured the pain, tossing the core back to the fallen leaves when it was done.

From the top of Blackstone Hill she'd be able to see Venus rise. She had a secret hollow there, a wee deer bed pressed back in the bracken and brush. She'd been waiting patiently but there hadn't been deer on the hill since June. Tonight, still empty, it was all hers.

Clarissa found her spot, curled up with her knees to her chest, her arm a pillow beneath her cheek. From here she could see nearly all the valley, the black lacy woods and star-brushed sky. The moon hung fat and perfect over her head; she lay back and watched it drowsily, finding the familiar face in its shadows, the man in the moon . . . smiling at her. . . .

She was dreaming. She dreamed of the breeze, but it was a wind now, a deep rushing pressure against the sky. The scent of smoke, and then laughter, quick and hushed. She heard someone speaking to her. It was Christoff, saying such marvelous things about the line of her neck, her lips. . . .

Clarissa opened her eyes. The moon was gone, and so was her dream. She rolled over to sit up, sighing, picking a tuft of moss from her sleeve. And then, clear as day, Christoff spoke again.

"But I can't stay any longer."

She jerked in place, blinking.

"Oh, no, not so soon," came a new, coaxing voice. "We've hours still, pet."

She shrank back with her hands over her mouth. Melanie! Christoff and Melanie, here on Blackstone Hill! In the dark. *Not* alone.

Thank God she was downwind.

"Perhaps *you* have," said Christoff, sounding amused. "I'm expected at the crack of dawn. Another of Father's little family breakfasts."

Past the shrubs they were a starlit couple, entwined in the grass and what was left of their clothing. Melanie's hair was spread beneath her, a pretty fall of red-gold against her skin. And Christoff, much tanner than she, lean and shirtless, toyed with a lock of it, drawing it up and down her bare breasts. Despite his words, he looked in no hurry to depart.

Clarissa closed her eyes and dropped her face into her hands. A branch snagged at her braid, pulling sharply at her nape.

"Stay," urged Melanie, in a throaty tone Clarissa envied down to her toes. "Just a while longer. I promise...you'll appreciate it."

"No doubt of that." And Melanie giggled.

Silence, or near silence, and Clarissa wished she could shut her ears as she could her eyes and not hear the muffled whisper of kisses, the stir of bodies against grass. Her cheeks began a burn against her palms.

"But I can't," said Christoff after a few more minutes of this torture. She heard him stand. "We'll meet up soon, Mel."

Clarissa peeked through her fingers. Melanie, still on the ground, was stretching her arms above her head; she was half nude and not at all dying of shame, the way Clarissa would be.

"I don't know what your father could possibly say that could compare to *this*."

Christoff was lacing up his shirt. "As a matter of fact, he wants to talk about marriage. My marriage."

"Oh? Are you engaged, my lord?"

"Not yet."

"Hmmm. Not yet. But who will be your bride, I wonder?" Melanie lifted a leg, flexing her toes in the silky light. "You can only wed another Alpha. And we all know who that is."

"Do we?"

Melanie smiled up at him, arching her back, and Christoff's hands fell still. His hair was a golden dark tangle down his shoulders.

The twig at Clarissa's nape pulled harder. She reached up, very carefully, and began to work it free.

"Perhaps you'll be surprised," he said, but he didn't sound as though he meant it.

"I think not. I'm the dominant female. Everyone knows it. Besides," Melanie laughed, throaty again, "I have reason to believe . . . that you quite like me."

The twig in Clarissa's hand snapped.

Her body clenched, instant horror. She couldn't move to save her life—and she should have, she should have, because Christoff was there in a second, a swift shadow and then a hand slamming down. She was jerked to her feet, sending leaves and twigs scattering.

"What the hell?"

He had her lifted in the air by one arm, a painful grip. She dangled there helplessly with her heart strangling her throat.

"Kit!" Melanie's voice broke behind them. "What is it?"

And he looked down at Clarissa with his head cocked, frowning, his eyes alight and thoughtful.

"I fell asleep," she said stupidly.

He lowered his arm, and her feet found the dirt again.

"You!" Melanie was at his side, her gown clutched to her bosom. "You, again! You filthy little spy!"

"No," said Clarissa, "no, I wasn't spying—"

"Haven't you learned your lesson yet?" She took a step forward, her fingers knotted in the cloth. "I'll teach you to keep following me—"

"I wasn't following you! I wasn't spying! I was here and I fell asleep—"

Melanie's hand cracked across her cheek.

"Jesus, Mel, leave off." Christoff pushed between them, forcing the other girl away. Clarissa turned her head aside and worked her jaw. Her ears were ringing. She tasted blood.

"But she was *here*, Kit, here the entire time, watching us!"

He threw a green-eyed look back at her, half masked by his hair, then shrugged. "She said she was asleep."

"She's lying!"

"I wasn't lying."

"Be quiet!"

Clarissa touched the blood on her lip. "Anyway, I don't have to lie. I would have left if I'd known you were out. Everyone in the shire knows you come here with any man who'll bother to have you."

She couldn't believe she'd said it. For the space of a heartbeat there was an awful, massive silence; all she heard was her own breath, ragged in her lungs, and the slow falling drift of a leaf from the bush beside her to the ground.

Melanie opened her mouth. Christoff clapped his hand over it.

"That's enough. For God's sake, Mel, she's just a child." He glanced at Clarissa once again, his expression oddly severe, as if he were caught between anger and laughter. "Go home. Now."

Her feet moved. She began to back away from them, her gaze not on Christoff but dead-still Melanie, who had pulled his hand from her face and was following her retreat with terrible eyes.

Her lips formed soundless words: *I'll get you.*

"Besides," said Christoff, stuffing his shirt into his breeches, "what do you care what she says? She's only a halfling, after all."

Melanie's laughter pealed in her ears all the way home.

The Morcambre Courant
Saturday, March 28, 1742

Young Woman Lost to Thaw

Mistress Clarissa Hawthorne of Darkfrith, Durham, has been Lost and presumed Perished by Drowning in the River Fier. Mistress Hawthorne was knowne to be in the Habit of strolling alone along its banks.

A shawl of Rose Poplin and cap of French Biscuit Lace were discovered. Savage rents in the Poplin indicated the Peril of Dangerous Animals about. The River Fier and its Woods were once knowne to be thick with Wolves and Other Beasts, although vigorous Hunting has well reduced their numbers.

Mistress Hawthorne was the only childe of the Widow Hawthorne and was to have reached her Eighteenth Year on the very day of her Loss.

Let us learne a Valuable Lesson from this unhappy Event, and keep our young flowers of English womanhood safely indoors during this spring thaw, tending Hearth and Home in the Tender Manner by which they will most Naturally come into full Blossom.

# CHAPTER TWO

Letitia, Duchess of Monfield, felt very fine indeed.

Her soirée was coming off particularly well. She had guests of the highest calibre circling and chatting round her table; she had shrimp and roast figs and Spanish sack; she had a freshly snared husband not yet in his cups. She had the envious looks of all the other ladies present, and several excellent young noblemen vying for her attention. Most wonderfully of all, she had the Monfield gemstones.

Letitia was exquisitely aware of them, the tiara, the necklace and bracelet and heavy long earbobs, all newly secured through her marriage to the duke. She had posed with them and paraded in them alone in her chambers for weeks in anticipation of this evening, her first significant dip into society as a hostess. Her wig of rolled curls had been specially constructed for the tiara, the better to display the flare of blue and white above her smooth brow, the tide of diamonds and sapphires that sparkled in the candlelight like, she knew, raindrops against the sun.

The sapphires rather matched her eyes, she thought, and could hardly repress her delight when the Comte du Lalonde put his lips to her ear to say so himself.

*"Je suis aveugle,"* he breathed, his accent rasping her skin like lovely, raw silk. "Your Grace carries the stars and the night as her crown, and still she outshines them both. Your very gaze shames them to sorrow, I vow."

Letty lifted her chin and smiled. She had chosen her favorite for the soirée with great care, and he had yet to disappoint. Despite his youth and Continental ways, the comte was quite the most comely fellow here, far fairer than her own dull, fat Ambrose. The boy's looks—the dark eyes with such incredibly black lashes, the sweet willful mouth— were a perfect complement to her own delicate features.

They sat together on the chaise longue by the bay window, her silver *robe à la française* a pale match to his gray satin waistcoat and breeches: a pair of splendid creatures, she thought happily, framed in a splendid moment.

The duchess made a show of tapping her suitor's shoulder with her fan. "My dear comte, have a care. You will have all the gossips tattering."

He leaned back, those long lashes lowered. Really, he was so *very* pretty, with his rouge and lace and bright laughing eyes. She'd been quite charmed by him the moment they'd been introduced. Why, was it only a fortnight ago? How astonishing—it seemed ages past. Perhaps it was because she'd seen him so often since: whist at Sophie's, Vauxhall Tuesday last, that amusing little weekend at Therese's in Suffolk. . . .

Perhaps, perhaps, if Ambrose kept drinking tonight . . .

"Not for the world would I tatter Your Grace's reputation. It is as precious to me as my own." –

"You presume much, sir."

"By your gracious word, *madame,* I will depart."

The comte looked up at her again, a corner of his mouth faintly quirked. Letty brought her fan to her lips. It would not do to let the boy gain *too* much confidence. He was a comte, yes, but *she,* after all, was a duchess.

"By all means, stay you here. It is I who shall depart." And with that, she rose in a magnificent stir of hoops and skirts, footmen bowing after her. When she tossed the comte one last, coy glance from over her shoulder, he was still smiling.

"Prime bit of flesh, that."

The comte spared a look at the gallant who had come to idle next to him, quizzing glass in one hand and port in the other.

He stood, straightening his cuffs. "If you say so."

"I?" drawled the gallant, lifting his glass to inspect the comte. "Why, my dear fellow, you've only to open your eyes, or at least your ears, to catch the shower of compliments that fall upon Her most de-*lect*-able Grace."

The comte had a new smile, razor thin. "I assure you, sir. My eyes and ears are well open."

From across the room the duchess turned, finding the two men together, observing her. Her fan twitched up, and she pirouetted away.

"You know," laughed the gallant, clapping a hand upon the other's shoulder, "I do believe they are. Good show. Nice dab of flash on her too."

Lalonde did not respond. The gallant removed his hand and tried the port.

"Bit brazen of her, though, I daresay. What with all this nonsense of the Smoke Thief racing about."

Now the comte looked up. "Do you think it nonsense, my lord?"

"What? A man turned to smoke? Now, a thief, aye, there's a certain truth for you. But all the other prattle—he walks through walls, he vanishes into thin air—damme! I'd hire the fellow m'self, if it were true! Get me a good bit of blunt from m' father!" He chuckled into his port. "No, mark my words, fellow's just a common bandit. Probably even a servant. Footman, that sort."

"Probably," said the comte.

The duchess had made half a circle around the room, surrounded by beaux, drawing slowly closer to the main doors. From behind her fan she sent the comte another lingering look.

"I do believe that's your cue, old boy." The gallant swirled his drink. "Ain't polite to keep a lady waiting."

Letty was not, after all, allowed a rendezvous with the comte that night. He had managed to disappear just after the final dessert course, and despite her discreet inquiries, no one seemed to know where or when he went. *Most* vexing. But it was the only flaw in an otherwise flawless evening, and overall she remained well pleased.

Ambrose was snoring in his chamber adjoining hers. Lud, the walls clattered with it already.

She dismissed the maid, whose sleepy yawns began to overtake Letty's own, shook back her hair, and sank into the opulence of her bed. After a brief moment she rose again, crossed to both her doors, and locked them.

Ambrose might wake with any sort of bothersome idea in the middle of the night. She needed her rest.

Quiet fell upon the home of the Duke and Duchess of Monfield, broken only by the deep, snuffling snores emitting occasionally from the master chambers. The duchess's polished guests had all departed, and as the Queen Anne clock in the main hall struck two and a quarter hours, even the lowest servants were at last abed.

It was only then, from the darkest depths of the linen pantry, that a pair of brilliant golden eyes winked open.

The pantry door made no sound upon its hinges. From the dark stepped the Comte du Lalonde, divested of his wig and ornate heeled shoes. He moved on stocking feet, utterly silent, only the sheen of his waistcoat and the strange glow of his eyes revealing him.

A pair of mice watched, paralyzed, from a corner baseboard, then scurried the other way.

The oiled maple floors reflected moonlight back at him, and the comte's shadow slipped and stretched as he passed window after window. He had taken good care to memorize the layout of the mansion, but the truth was, he didn't need memory to find the duchess's chamber. The cloying scent of her perfume practically begged him along.

At her door he paused, testing the handle lightly. Locked. His lips formed that faint, droll smile that Letty would have instantly recognized.

The keyhole was empty. The comte peered through it to be completely certain, then stepped back into the hall. He began, piece by piece, to remove his clothing.

Long dark hair, a slim torso, bound breasts and ivory skin: the comte was a woman.

A tremendous snort rattled the air. The woman stopped folding her breeches, alert, but after a moment the duke settled back into his usual chirrup of snores.

With great care, she placed the pile of her clothing to the side of the door. She moved back to the keyhole and took a deep breath.

Letty slept very well. She had but one dream, and it was of smoke and mist, and how it felt so cool against her face. At first she feared she was lost, but it wasn't that sort of mist. It was gentle, peaceful. She moved through it quite tranquilly, and when she reached the end of it, it coalesced into the shape of a woman. A beautiful woman, familiar, smiling at her.

"Sleep," said the woman, and Letty did.

The sun was sinking to a horizon threaded with clouds, sending warm lazy rays to gild the trees and demure paths that formed the southern boundary of Vauxhall Gardens. Carriages rolled by with sweating horses and clinging footmen; flower girls carried their baskets over one arm, singing songs of damsels and posies. On a corner of the green a band of chimney sweeps had a rough game of trap-ball going that resulted in more than one bloody nose, and someone, somewhere nearby, was baking pork pies.

"Shocking," said one of a pair of fashionable young ladies seated upon a bench. She lifted her newspaper closer to her nose, scanning the print by the waning light.

The spectacular loss of the Monfield gemstones was included in all five evening editions of the London papers.

"Indeed," agreed the other, smoothing the pleats of her

petticoat. "They didn't even mention the bracelet. And it is particularly fine."

The first woman lowered her paper. "You know that wasn't what I meant, Rue."

"Wasn't it? Oh. I suppose then you were referring to the midnight duel in which the valiant duke fought off the thief before being overcome by the fellow's kick to his nether regions. That *is* rather shocking, I concur. I can't imagine how anyone could reach past that royal belly for a good kick."

"Rue," said the other woman, but her gray eyes were narrowed with mirth.

"Plus, it was *well* after midnight. My legs were beginning to cramp in that minuscule closet."

"Rue."

"Yes?"

"A lady does not gloat."

Rue spread her fan open across her lap, webbed lace dyed the precise shade of summer apricots. She spoke more softly. "I am no lady, Mim, as you know."

"You are. In your heart, you are. I know plenty who do what you do, and spill blood to do it. You don't. Or won't."

Rue closed the fan again and smiled. "What a romantic you've turned out to be. The truth is, you're far more of a lady than I."

"I?" Mim glanced around them, then lowered her voice. "Oi'm jest a simple lass from th' East End, Oi am. Dontcha calls me no loidy."

"Charming. Mim from East End. It nearly rhymes."

Mim straightened. "And Rue from . . . nowhere at all, it seems."

Rue met her gaze, her deep brown eyes level, her gloved

hands now motionless upon her lap. Mim was struck, not for the first time, by her companion's clear and relentless beauty, a deception of porcelain pale skin, black satin brows and lashes, and lips ever the color of roses. She wore powder and paint but Mim had never seen anyone who needed it less; everything about this woman she knew only as Rue spoke of genteel elegance, of exotic femininity.

She would have made a stunning courtesan. But perhaps that was why she was so very good at her job.

"Haven't we been friends long enough by now?" asked Mim.

"Are we friends?"

"Associates."

"I am from nowhere, Mim. You were absolutely right."

"Bugger."

Rue looked away and up, silent, watching the changing clouds past the brim of her hat.

"Very well," huffed Mim, rustling her paper. And then, testily: "You're doing it again. I always wonder what you're looking for up there."

"Dragons," said Rue promptly, and the other woman was startled into a laugh.

"Well . . . that one does somewhat resemble a . . . a rabbit, I think. And over there, above the trees, we have a teapot. Perhaps it's a chocolate pot. That's all I see."

"Yes. That's all I see as well. Shall we go? I'd fancy a stroll."

They stood, gathering the paper and parasols and fans, the fine graveled path crunching lightly beneath their feet. They walked in silence for some time, passing a courting couple with a harried little maid trailing behind, and then a pair of leering dandies, who smiled and bowed quite deep.

Rue, Mim noticed, behaved exactly as a gentlewoman should: she ignored them completely.

"By the by, Mistress Rue from Nowhere, ladies do not refer to their legs, either."

"*Ladies* sound frightfully boring to me."

"Aye. That's rather what all the gents tell me."

"How glad I am, then," said Rue serenely, "not to be one."

The path began a turn, leading them through a knot of nannies and skipping children. Their shadows swept before them, the violet dusk shades of two wide-skirted women, arm in arm.

Mim asked, "Exactly how fine is that bracelet, anyway?"

"Twelve carats of diamonds, nineteen of sapphires. Top notch."

"I believe I might be able to find a new situation for it."

"I thought you might."

"But the set will have to be separated. Especially the larger stones."

"I know."

The sun had vanished fully, softening the sky, splashing lustrous gold across the royal blue clouds.

"Poor duchess," sighed Mim. "But I suppose she has more."

"She does. And I mean, really," added Rue, watching the clouds, "who wears a tiara to a soirée?"


Number 17 of Jassamine Lane, in Bloomsbury, was by no means the grandest nor the meanest of the rows of red brick and gabled houses, but one as comfortably middle class as all the rest. It had green shutters and the same four narrow, street-level windows as nearly every other residence on the block. Perhaps its only noticeable distinction was the door, made not of wood but of painted steel, shaped to fit the frame with absolutely no gaps around its edges.

True, the windows were seldom cracked and the curtains remained drawn, but that might be easily excused by the sooty London air, which begrimed whatever it touched.

And true, too, that the mistress of the house was hardly ever seen, but she was rumored to be elderly, or infirm, or perhaps a little mad. In Bloomsbury, infamous retreat of the city's artists and performers, such eccentricity was barely worth mentioning.

That mysterious lady approached Number 17's steps just as the last candle lantern down the street was being lit, responding with a nod to a collier's cheerful, "Evenin', miss."

The steel door latched gently shut behind her.

Her sanctuary, her haven. Rue purchased it six years ago and had spent a great deal of effort and money since making certain of its security. Every opening had a secondary means of blocking it, from the windows to the keyholes to the chimney. She had memorized the scent of each room, the familiar creaks of the walls and stairs and floors. She had made this place hers, hers alone, and was a part of every corner, every peg hole and crevice.

Because despite its soot, London was a foggy place. Many things could hide in the fog. Rue should know.

She placed her fan and reticule on the entrance table, weighing the dark.

The rooms inside were far more richly furnished than might be expected for the neighborhood; it was her only open concession to the secret life she led. She enjoyed luxury, and her surroundings revealed it—sumptuous woods and imported fabrics, exceptional art and the finest furniture.

All, at the moment, decidedly unlit.

She never kept her home bright by normal standards, but usually her abigail took care to leave an oil lamp burning by the door.

Her heels clicked down the hall as the gloves were removed, and then the hat. She tossed them to a chair in the parlor—also dark—then glanced into the drawing room. But the only illumination to be seen was coming from the dining room, and she paused in the doorway there, taking in the chairs and mahogany table, the giltwood mirror above the mantel reflecting the candelabra in an infinity of slim dancing flames.

On the table were laid out the five evening newspapers, plus two others she hadn't yet seen. Rue leaned over them with her palm against the wood, browsing the headlines.

"Where is the maid?" she asked quietly, without looking up from the papers.

"I gave her the night off," said a voice, just behind her.

"Again?"

"We don't need her. I can manage without her."

She turned, finding the boy in the shadows, lean and a trace too small for his twelve years, light brown hair that never looked combed, amber-lit eyes like a night creature from a very dark woods.

Rue crossed her arms. "She is not in your employ, Zane, she is in mine. I'd appreciate it if you stopped sending all the help away." She frowned, looking him up and down. "And where is your new livery?"

"It itches."

"Then wash it."

"I ain't got—"

"*Have not* got."

"—time to wash it. I've been out, you know."

"I do know. But you need to wear the livery, especially

when you are here. Otherwise, you draw attention. The maid and the cook have uniforms; you must as well. We are an exceedingly proper establishment."

He offered her his most innocuous smile.

A mountain of combs and uniforms would not alter him: Zane was a street urchin, clever, untamed. She had found him one winter night two years ago in an alleyway, bleeding to death from a knife wound to his ribs. She had passed by him, silent as the air, but he had lifted his head anyway, and then his hand to her.

He had seen her. He had found her eyes. And because he had done that—because, somehow, he could—she went back to him.

Skinny, smelly trouble. That was her first thought. She didn't need trouble in her life. She didn't need another risk to plague her, she had too damned many as it was. Rue had been doing very well for some while, and no little part of that was because she knew how to keep to herself.

Yet in that reeking alley she had hesitated, and then crouched down before the child. She had examined his pasty face, the dim pale eyes that pleaded with hers and the lips that tried to speak.

He had *seen* her.

She touched her fingers to his cheek and decided, on impulse, to take him home to die.

She was not someone accustomed to acting on her impulses. The few times she had, great changes had swallowed her life. Zane, as it turned out, was no exception.

He had been too stubborn to die. He had flopped back on her new Hepplewhite settee, smearing a great deal of blood across its dainty lemon stripes—and lived.

The settee had been regretfully dispatched, but Zane, her dogged waif, had dug in. He was weak and malnourished and a misfit. He had no manners, no grace, and a great deal of rude wit. He screeched like a banshee whenever she ordered him to bathe.

And yet . . . Rue remembered how it felt to be small, to be alone.

She had granted him a bed in the attic, assigned him chores—which he hardly ever performed—and so sealed their unlikely, uneasy alliance.

He knew what she was. He never said it, never asked. But he knew.

Boy and woman studied each other now in the thin yellow light. Even with the sweet smile he looked like nothing so much as an underfed elf. She wondered how he managed it; she knew for a fact he routinely ate enough to fatten three grown men.

Zane gestured to the table.

"Did you see what I brun—brought?"

She shook her head, turning back to the papers. "I've read these."

"Not that one. Nipped it from The Spotted Dog. Last week's news, but I thought you'd like the bottom-right bit."

"At least your reading is coming along."

"An' I washed my face last Sunday," he said virtuously.

She picked up the paper, turned it over and found his story.

*Rare Langford Diamond to Be Displayed at the Stewart*

For an instant her heart stopped.

Langford. Diamond. *Here.*

There had to be a mistake. The tribe would never—

"What d'ye think, my lady?" asked Zane, at her elbow. "A diamond an' all. Is it good?"

She looked up and caught her own reflection in the mirror across the room, marble pale, dark-eyed. Her wig was a silver cascade to her shoulders; candlelight threw a halo against her face.

"Have the maid wash your livery when she returns," Rue said, and took the paper with her as she left the room.

# CHAPTER THREE

In the hills and vales of Darkfrith there lived a saying: *Kiss the sky, kiss the ground, and all the world shall come unbound.*

All the children of the tribe knew it, learned it in verse and in song; they grew up with its lesson, courted, wed, and then passed it down again to their own children.

But someone, it seemed, had taken the verse a bit too well to heart.

A runner.

"Smoke Thief," said Rufus, slapping the newspaper down in front of Christoff with a flourish. "He's back again, our lad."

The dining hall of Chasen Manor was nearly empty, the main meal long since finished. The fire was low in the hearth but still snapping. Servants moved through the chamber in hushed efficiency, clearing plates and flatware with the barest of tinkling clatter. They had yet to approach the ring of dishes around the head of the table; between the cold fried parsnips and the remains of a stuffed pheasant were a scattering of papers, periodicals, and Kit's own scribbled notes, written in impatient black strokes.

He leaned back in his chair, pushing a hand through his loose hair, remembering too late the ink on his fingers. He had no tolerance for wigs or powder or queues. Out here, in the country, no one minded anyway——at least, not to his face. But he'd meant to get a haircut. He always seemed to forget.

"What was it this time?"

"A tiara. Necklace. Right from under the nose of Monfield."

Kit inspected the nib of his quill. "Really. Did the duke get a look at him?"

"Well, he must've, hadn't he? Says he fought the fellow. Dueled with him."

From across the room by the fire came a sigh; Kit barely suppressed his own.

"I find myself constantly surprised at the mendacity of the press." He turned the paper around with one finger so he could read it. "Dueled with him. Indeed. He'd not be around to boast about it if he had."

"Dunno why you'd be surprised still," commented George, ensconced in his favorite chair over by the hearth. "You've dealt with enough of their nonsense yourself since inheriting the title."

"True. Perhaps I've been hoping for their reform."

"Not likely." Rufus took his own seat. He lifted his boots to the table's edge, caught the look Kit slanted him, and dropped them to the floor again. "You're one of their favorite sports. *Marquess of Langford Attends a Ball. Marquess of Langford Escorts Lady So-and-So. Marquess of Langford Scratches His Arse.*"

"I hadn't seen that last one," said Kit mildly.

"They do enjoy you," remarked George, his palms spread over his belly.

"All they enjoy is fresh blood."

"And you're it, my lord."

"I *was*." Kit tapped the headline. "But it appears I've been upstaged."

Smoke Thief. For the past three years Christoff and the council had been following his exploits, ever since the *Evening Standard* had dubbed the fellow with that most telling appellation. Logic dictated he'd been operating much longer than that, but despite Kit's social connections and a good deal of silver greasing palms, no one anywhere seemed to know much about him. He was fodder for the press, an outrage to the wealthy, and a hero to the common class. He took only jewels, and only the best of those. None was ever seen again.

He was the most serious threat to the tribe this century.

For countless years they had lived in near perfect silence, echoes of an older time, of ancient spells and hybrid magic. No one knew the tribe's true origins; those memories were lost ages past. Some said Russia, or Romania, the impenetrable black forests of Europe's farthest hills. Some of the folk claimed farther still, that they had leapt to life from the middle earth, had been heaved out into the sky with the lava and white-hot diamonds, and taken their first breaths amid the clouds.

They were hunters, peerless, apart. They were smoke and fire and claw: *drákon*.

But there had come Others in the old place, mortal men, and then persecution. The tribe had fled their homeland, taking with them the last of the diamonds, their source and inspiration. But in every place they touched, the tribe—the fabled hunters—became the hunted. They were attacked in their homes, in their sleep. They were burned and bludgeoned and tortured; legends speared to earth, one by one.

Kit could well imagine that, the mortals who feared them most rising up, slaughtering the innocents. It had kept him wide awake too many nights as a child.

They had learned to exist in disguise. To fight the Turn and walk among the Others, to live as they did. Secrecy was the key to survival and the *drákon* excelled at it, so much so that the ones who could complete the Turn—could transform from man to beast and back again—grew fewer and fewer over time.

Finally, after years of wandering, they had ended up here, in the green hills of northern England, where the mists still stroked the earth and where smoke and clouds could mingle as one. For fifteen generations, Darkfrith had allowed the tribe to quietly thrive.

Kit glanced again at the article before him, the bold printed lines. A man formed of smoke, who passed through walls and windows as if they were not there, who frightened maids and eluded constables and made off with the *ton*'s choicest gemstones—he shook his head. There could be little doubt it was one of their kind. If the thief had wanted to advertise his presence to them he could have hardly chosen a better way.

Perhaps he was growing careless. Or perhaps . . . it was a taunt.

Every now and then one was born who could not stand the life. Who could not bear the rules of the shire, the secrets, the glory. If pushed far enough that person would run, and the tribe would have to mobilize to bring him back.

It had been that thought, more than any other, that tethered young Christoff to this place. The humiliation of being caught. The futility of trying to flee his fate.

The fire snapped and popped, flinging sparks against the grate.

Kit lifted the newspaper and read aloud the duke's description of the thief: "*Swarthy, tall, and moste Foul of Face, with coal-black hair and a Scar upon his Cheek.*" He looked at the other two men. "Sound like anyone we'd know?"

Both George and Rufus shook their heads. The tribe ran to fair, with blonds and redheads aplenty, a very few brunettes. Kit couldn't even recall a tribemember with black hair, not in his lifetime.

Another lie, just as he'd thought.

"Are the family lists complete yet?" he asked George.

"Aye, my lord. We've gathered the names of every possible successful runner for the last forty years. Not many men, I'll tell you that. Six at most, and all were thought to be very much dead. Four apparently lost to fire—you remember the blaze that leveled the tavern in '33—one to drowning, and one bloke to, ah, wolves."

Kit raised his brows. "Wolves?"

"That's what his son said. Stirling Jacobs was his name. Liked to hunt at dawn. Liked a challenge. Known to venture out beyond our boundaries. Bones were found, possibly his. That's all."

"How old would this man be now?"

"Let's see . . . nearing eighty, I'd say."

Kit gazed at him over the mess of china and papers.

"Your instructions were to consider *everyone*." George shifted in the chair, uneasy. "And I've bloody well considered everyone."

"All right." He pushed back from the table and stood, restless, his mind working the puzzle, turning over the pieces. "And the other man. The drowning. What of him?"

"How old would he be, do you mean?"

Kit nodded, staring out one of the windows. Against the night sky he could see the reflection of the fire, the plump smeary shadow that was Sir George, and the more distant one of Rufus.

"Twenty-three, thereabouts," said George, after a moment. "He died young."

"His body was never recovered?"

"Not—entirely." George shifted again. "There was a hand. It wore his ring—"

"Gads," interjected Rufus, revolted.

"—and his coat was found in the reeds down by Aberthon."

Something was bothering Kit. Something was missing. It circled the back of his mind, a distant thought, too elusive to catch. Something about the river.

"A man could live without a hand," said George significantly, into the snapping silence. "He could still steal too."

Yes. He could.

Kit closed his eyes, pondering the mind of the thief, the careful game he played with the press and the law. What sort of person would he be?

Intelligent, without doubt. He had to have figured a way to openly infiltrate the *ton*'s finest houses, to walk their rooms. The *drákon* could not manifest anywhere they could not see.

Brazen. Anyone who fled Darkfrith truly threw their fortune to the winds. The punishment for running was usually imprisonment. Or death.

Cunning. Until recently, no one had missed him.

Defiant. He'd allowed the press to lionize him and still kept stealing.

And lucky. Because he'd done the one thing Christoff himself had never managed: he had cast off the shackles of his birthright.

"I'm leaving tomorrow," he said to the black glass panes.

"Tomorrow? But that's three days early—"

"I assure you, Rufus, I know how to count. I want to be there sooner than the papers reported. You and the rest will follow on schedule with the diamond."

"The council—" began George.

"They won't like it, I know. But they will accept it. From me."

Another rule. No member of the tribe left the shire without permission from the council. Except, of course, the Alpha.

He waited, not turning, listening to the fire mutter.

George scraped back his chair. "Aye, my lord."

"Do you truly think it will work?" asked Rufus. "Will showing the diamond at the museum draw out our Smoke Thief?"

"It will. He'd never come here for it. But he'll consider London his domain. He won't be able to resist."

"A great risk," said George evenly. "Letting it leave the shire. The council had a point in that, my lord."

"It must be the true stone. You know that. He'll be able to discern an imitation at once. And there will be many of us, and one of him. The Stewart Museum is large enough to allow any number of us to filter through the crowds."

"Aye, my lord."

Behind him, the servants—tribemembers, all—were taking advantage of his standing, quickly clearing the last of the meal, ghosts in the glass who threw him hurried looks and vanished as noiselessly as they had come.

Kit had grown used to those looks over the years, part fear, part awe. As if he were a creature beyond even them. As if he were—indomitable.

He thought of all the times he'd wanted to run himself, to escape Darkfrith. He looked out at the stars thrown across the cold sky and envy of the thief speared through him bright as pain—just a flash, and then he smothered it.

"He will come for the diamond," he said, very quiet.

*I would.*

He crouched, nude and alone, at the highest edge of the pitched roof of the manor, letting the night wind lift his hair, his skin chilled, his muscles flexed: as fixed to the earth as the stone gargoyles that snarled from Chasen's battlements. The stars were closer here but never close enough; Christoff stood and leapt from the roof.

For an instant he fell. There was a real terror to it, blood-pumping, heart-screaming energy. But at the last second he Turned, and the rushing ground became a blur and the wind pushed him up, up into the sky.

He was free.

Kit soared above the land, the manor shrinking, the details of the ground blending to dark and woods and pinpoints of light. There would be others out on this moonless night—his hunters, his guards—but he sensed them before they did him, and so skidded over them, too swift, too wild for them to follow.

Not that they would anyway. They knew well enough when to let him be.

He rode the winds better than anyone, fathomed the secrets of the night, where to go, how to hide. He had been stealing out like this from the very moment he could, that first night of his transformation. At ten years of age he had been the youngest of the tribe ever to survive the ordeals of the Turn. But he had survived it. And with the stars as his echo, Kit could fly.

Far Perch, that elegant London manse, was deserted.

He had expected it, of course, but still found the blank windows and ungarnished front steps disconcerting. His mother had kept urns of roses by the doors, ruffled coral buds scented of spice in the summer and in winter pruned down to sticky stalks. How strange; he had forgotten that until this moment. His father, as Kit recalled, had them torn out after her death.

The urns were empty now, lacking even a cobweb to tremble in the breeze. He touched a finger to one of the limestone lips, bronzed skin against pitted white, then dropped his hand. The knocker connected with the door once again.

No one answered. He had retained his father's elderly caretakers—not *drákon,* no one from the tribe could be left loose in the city for so long—but it seemed they couldn't hear him. It was a damned big house.

Or perhaps they were out.

No one had come for his stallion either; he'd had to stable him himself in the back.

Kit reached for the key ring in his pocket and unlocked the double doors.

"Hello?"

Old Stilson did not appear. Neither did his wife. Kit glanced behind him, to the stylish square of buildings and trees and cobblestones that flanked the mansion, then stepped into the vestibule and closed the doors.

He hated London. It felt stifling to him, contaminated by clogs of humanity and machinery and the low sullen sky. As the Marquess of Langford, he had adjusted to the smaller miseries of city life, the smells and sharp noises, the constant tumult of the streets. He knew how to walk and talk and smile when he should, yet there were always those mean, invisible moments when Kit feared he might crack apart—desperate just to get away, just to find a clear, clean spot to breathe. But there wasn't such a place. Not here.

Their kind did not do well in cities. Yet London, brilliant, suffocating London, was a necessary evil. If all went well, he'd be gone again in a sennight.

He had no idea how his father had managed it all those years. The old marquess had built the mansion in Grosvenor Square—and named it too, in what had to be the only stroke of whimsy in his life—had fulfilled his duties as a lord and even, when bidden, attended the king. To do otherwise, he had told Kit, would be to invite speculation. None of them needed that.

For years, Kit had avoided the mansion. Whenever London called he had found inns, clubs, places without spirits or silently accusing rooms. But this journey was unique; instead of disguising his presence he was advertising it, and so his father's house became another necessity.

He stalked through the abandoned halls, opening doors, pulling sheets off furniture, stirring up dust and memories.

Ah, yes. Far Perch.

Here, in the blue parlor, his mother had often sat with her embroidery, all lace and starched ruffles, her lips pursed in concentration, her needle flashing.

Here, at the balustrade of the main staircase, six-year-old Christoff had once knocked out a tooth whisking down its waxed turns.

Here, the bedroom where his younger brother had been born and—hours later—had died, taking their mother with him.

And here. His father's library, a gleaming chamber of Kidderminster rugs and rubbed oak, and books with their bindings uncracked, frozen behind glass. A perfect gentleman's retreat.

His lips curved at the thought, and he turned away. Without the sconces lit, the walls and marble floors threw a faint, pale glow; Far Perch seemed hungry to him, eager for warmth and touch.

Well, he understood hunger, at least. He trailed his hand down the wainscotting as he paced his father's room, tracing the wood grain through the pads of his fingers.

Perhaps he shouldn't have ridden ahead of the others. Perhaps he should have sent notice to the Stilsons that he was coming sooner than expected. At the very least, they would have taken off the sheets for him.

But he had wanted time alone in this place. He had wanted a chance to settle in privately with the memories, to find his peace here in the city without the constant, prying eyes of his kith and kin upon him. And, truth be told, he had hoped to stay a trick ahead of the thief.

Six years had passed since the death of his father, but Kit felt his wraith as strongly as if the marquess were still seated stiff-backed at his desk, lecturing his sullen teenaged son.

*Protect the tribe. Find the runner. Do what you must to bring him back.*

"I will," murmured Kit to the white-sheeted desk.

Outside, the trees sparkled with leaves; at least the windows had been scrubbed. He was leaving the library, preparing to finish his haunting of his childhood home, when he first felt it.

A ripple of warning down his neck, a familiar scent. Smoke. Clouds. His head lifted and he swiveled, very carefully, to the window nearby, resting a hand against the curtains. His senses flared.

One of them. One of the tribe, very near. The runner.

He remained in shadow, waiting, searching for the man—if he could get him today, if he could capture him here, so soon . . .

But there was no runner, at least not in the leafy green open. There was only a parasoled lady and her livery boy, passing slowly by the house.

"Oh, I say, Mama! Isn't it grand?"

The boy tugged at his mother's hand in excitement, pointing past the crowd to the pedestal holding the Langford Diamond, a purple-prismed glimmer against pillows and glass.

"Here you are, little man. Up you go!" The boy's father hoisted him to his hip, earning the disgruntled looks of the museumgoers around him.

The Stewart had seldom experienced such a crush. News of the Langford Diamond was enough to bring out London in force: there were Cits and housemaids and gentry, all shoulder to shoulder in the excitement to see the stone. Much had been written of the unique colored diamond—*larger than the king's scepter! heavy as a cricket ball!*—but no one alive outside the Marquess of Langford's family was known to have actually seen it. Until now.

The museum curator stood by the pedestal with a look of exulted horror on his face; he wrung his hands and begged the mob to keep a civil distance.

The hired guards were more effective, and far less polite. They fondled their pistols and grinned evilly at anyone who would meet their eyes. Even a pack of sailors edged back from them.

Rue watched the drama unfold from the heated expanse of the atrium balcony, a stained-glass dome above and a sea of bobbing heads below. The Langford Diamond was a win-some twinkle from here, but little else. It might have been a fine work of paste, for all anyone this high up could tell.

But for her. She kept her breathing steady and her hands on the rail in front of her, but the lure of the diamond pulled at her. She *felt* it, in her blood, in her pulse, as all of the tribe could. It was their nature to connect to the stones. And this one—*ninety-eight carats, shaped as a teardrop,* re-cited her mind—had been cherished by the *drákon* from the beginning of their time. It even had a name: *Herte.* The heart of the tribe.

So they would be here with it. They would not be far.

It was a trap, and a shrewd one. She'd always known they would come for her sooner or later; she had been fervently hoping for later.

But Rue wasn't taken yet.

A bead of perspiration slipped down her neck, became a tickle in the gauze handkerchief of her bodice. It was hotter than July up here.

"Blast it all, I can't see the thing," muttered the man pressed against her right, to his companion. "Bloody tourists. Let's go."

She inched closer to the railing as they departed, her feet tucked between the engraved wooden posts, her sea-green skirts flattened with their hoops into a silken train behind her. From the main doors below came an updraft, still warm but mercifully there. She took a deep breath amid it, feeling the curls of her wig lift from her brow.

"It's magnificent," remarked a woman coming to stand at her elbow, fanning herself in leisurely strokes. "Quite worth the price of the ticket. But there's really no market for such a thing."

Rue tilted her head in acknowledgment, not looking

away from the stone. She wasn't surprised to encounter Mim here; she had learned, over the past nine years, that nothing brought out the underworld like a spectacle.

"Much too singular," Mim continued quietly, also facing ahead. "A violet diamond. Even recut, it would draw attention."

"You're right."

"And the museum is too well guarded. I've examined that for myself."

"Again, I agree."

The fan slowed. "And there is the fact of the marquess, of course. Is he here?"

Rue's fingers tightened over the railing; she forced herself to let it go. "Heavens, how would I know?"

"Simply follow the trail of swooning women," suggested Mim wryly. "I saw him once at Drury Lane. The rumors are perfectly correct, for once. A poet's mane of windswept gold, ice green eyes that jolt straight through you. I swear every hair on my body stood on end when he strolled by. He is glorious."

"And ruthless," said Rue, before she could stop herself.

"That was my other point. You would not wish to aggrieve someone who has killed three men in duels and sent two others to the gallows merely for attempting to lift a bit of coin from his pocket."

"No," replied Rue. "Certainly not."

" 'The fairest face, and the blackest heart.' Who said that of him, do you recall? It's on the tip of my tongue. . . ." The fan grew slower still, then snapped closed. "Ah. The Baroness von Zonnenburg, I believe. Just after he broke it off with her."

Rue said nothing. Mim glanced at her at last.

"I wonder what you're doing here, my friend."

"Admiring a pretty stone. That's all."

"Well, luv, if you decide to do more than just admire it, I suggest you think twice. Ta."

"Ta."

Mim, in her easy way, disappeared back into the crowd.

Down below, the little boy and his parents had been drawn off from their coveted positions before the diamond. For an instant a splinter of lavender light struck Rue's eye, blocked in a trice by someone new.

She brought a hand to her face, rubbing away the light, then lowered it again. She began once more to scan the many, many people for the members of her tribe.

He was here.

Christoff felt the presence of the thief like a rising charge in the air, the distinct frisson of energy just before lightning slivered the sky, white heat encompassing everything and nothing at once.

He recognized that same charge from the mansion four days ago. It was a different sensation from any other *drákon* he knew, stronger, more refined. The man must have amazing powers; Kit had known the moment the runner entered the museum.

The problem, it seemed, was in pinpointing him.

He had scattered his guard throughout the building, wandering in pairs and alone. They squeezed by onlookers with open eyes and canny senses, listening, waiting. Everyone knew what was at stake. With their instincts rubbed raw, they had felt the shiver of the thief too.

Kit moved less effortlessly through the people, stopping to greet those who recognized him, not bothering to hide. He was known in these circles and would look a fine fool incognito; let the others drift and watch. George and Rufus and the entire council prowled the floor. Kit himself was bait, just as the diamond was. And as much as he enjoyed the hunt, he hoped, very much, that his prey would strike soon.

He looked forward to the fight.

From the corner of his eye Christoff caught a flash of gloved white, high above. A gentlewoman stood at the balcony railing with a hand pressed over her face, scalloped skirts the color of sea foam and a profusion of lace cascading from her sleeve. He thought for a moment she might fall; she wavered there, and he was already moving to the stairs—but she recovered. Her hand relaxed to her side.

She wore a wide-brimmed hat with one long, plumed feather that masked her eyes, curving down to brush her cheek. He had a glimpse of her lips, dusky rose against very pale skin, and her wig, artful curls. Her face was turned away.

Unlike everyone else around her, she wasn't looking at the diamond. She was, instead, watching the museum doors.

He shot a look over his shoulder at the entrance. Sir George loitered there, a fine country squire in his embroidered coat and brass buttons that stretched tight at the seams. He was fiddling with a ticket stub in his hands, but broke it off as he noticed Kit's gaze. He took a step forward, a question in his glance.

Kit looked back up at the woman. And now she was looking at him.

Liquid dark eyes, delicate black brows, that complexion, those lips. The snowy curve of the feather caressing her chin: Aphrodite carved from alabaster and jet.

They stared at each other and Christoff felt, astonishingly, that frisson rise to pass through him once more.

The air crackled between them.

Sweet Jesus. It was she.

The runner was a woman.

Even as he thought it she turned away from the railing, unhurried, slipping past one man and then another, a graceful figure in sea green that vanished from view.

Kit began to push through the crowd, his mind buzzing. A woman, it was a *woman*—not the thief after all, because a woman couldn't Turn, but still one of the tribe, a female here in London. How the hell could it have happened? Why hadn't the council known?

People spoke to him, touched him on the shoulder, but he shrugged them off and kept moving—*polite, polite, don't cause a scene*—looking back once to George, who was trying to follow.

The stairs were easier to navigate; most of the onlookers were crowded against the banister. He moved swiftly up them, focusing on her energy again, searching—finding her.

There. She was heading toward the staff stairwell, the narrow closed door by a Flemish tapestry he had made certain was locked and bolted before the show.

Gawkers thronged between them. He lost her, found her again.

In the space between two red-coated ensigns he saw her hand close over the latch.

Damn—there were too many people up here. Kit began to shove his way more roughly through the mob, keeping the teal-banded crest of her hat in sight.

"Blimey, mate—"

"Oh, it's you, Langford. Watch your step—"

"Well! What a rude man! Did you see, Winifred, he pushed right into me—"

She had released the latch—still locked, thank God—and was walking again, circling, looking for another way out. There wouldn't be one; Kit had the place memorized. She had nowhere to go—

The last group of women standing between them folded out of his way. Kit was at the runner's back, his blood singing, his breath coming between his teeth. She began to turn toward him.

He reached out and grabbed her wrist.

Ah. He felt it as a shock, a snap of connection between them, and if he had any doubts at all they scorched away in that instant, with the fine bones of her wrist in his hand and the full force of her power surging through him.

She twisted in his grasp—the sinewy strength of *drákon*—but he didn't let go; she stepped back, her arm stiff against his, and looked up into his face.

One of them. Of course she was one of them, more radiant, more vital than mere mortal folk, with her velvet brown eyes and flawless features. Dressed in silk and frothing lace, she was as dainty a lady as could be—but she met his gaze fearlessly, assessing, her expression cool but her eyes alight with something like fury.

The last of the air left his lungs. By God, she was beautiful.

Who was she? He'd met every member of the tribe, certainly every female, but she . . .

Wait . . .

The noise of the museum, the heat, the stench of unwashed bodies, all began to recede.

A little girl. A running child, alone in the trees.

A silver-lit face, pinched with fear.

The river. A drowning.

"Mouse?" Kit said, incredulous.

"What?" Her voice was theirs too, low and lovely, pitched to serenade the stars.

He found her name. *"Clarissa."* And she sucked in her breath.

Someone knocked into him from behind, apologized, but he barely heard it. They stood there face to face, their arms locked together, their chests almost touching, a lovers' pose that was truly a silent war of pull and resistance. Through it all she kept her chilly composure; only the quick, hard pulse in her throat betrayed her. That, and she was panting a little. The feather ruffled and stirred at the corner of her lips.

He was close enough now to catch the more human fragrance adorning her, faint lilies, purely feminine. Arousing.

Her gaze flickered past him and she saw what he already knew, that George and the others were moving in. Her fingers closed into a fist. She glanced again at the staff door.

"Don't try," Kit murmured. "Please. I don't want to hurt you."

She gave her hand a sudden jerk but he was ready for it, using the recoil of her own force to pull her nearer, his other arm wrapping around her waist. He turned his head to hers and dropped his voice.

"Be reasonable. You can't escape."

Her response was a whisper against his cheek. "Watch me."

The powdered curls of her wig tickled his jaw. Her skin was warm, burning warm beneath her winter paleness, and her waist was small and her skirts rustled against his legs. Clouds and flowers and the charged hum of lightning; Christoff felt her so keenly it was like the blade of a knife scratched over his nerves, a sensation at once both exquisite and terrifying. She was as fixed as stone in his grip, wreathed in lace and lilies, and all he wanted to do was laugh in exhilaration.

A female, a *drákon* who lived in the open—

His ears caught the scant, tinkling sound of breaking glass. A din roared up from below, yelling, shouts. The loose clusters of people surrounding them began to surge forward to the railing. He planted his feet and steadied them both as the babble of nearly four hundred museum patrons separated into words:

"Stop! Stop him! He's got the diamond—"

"Thief! Stop! There, he went there—"

Pistols fired, women screamed, and all hell broke loose.

In the split second before they were trampled, Kit looked back at Clarissa Hawthorne. She was smiling up at him: gorgeous, dazzling victory. Before he could move, she Turned to smoke in his grasp.

He was left standing at the brink of the bolting crowd, holding up an empty gown.

# CHAPTER FOUR

On the day that she died, Clarissa Rue Hawthorne had turned seventeen. It had been a late March morning that dawned with a blustery cold that felt more like winter than spring, spreading ice in black feathered plumes across the River Fier, a crystalline sparkle of clouds pushing across the bleached sky.

Hers was the only birthday in the tribe that day, but still one little celebrated. She passed a quiet breakfast with her mother—tea, sausages, jammy marmalade over crumpets—and cleared the table when it was done, as there was no one else to help.

After breaking her fast, Clarissa went for a walk along the river. Her mother would think nothing of it, as her only child was often drawn to the wild rambling parts of the woods and downs. In this aspect, at least, she was very much like the rest of the tribe.

Her cap and new rose poplin shawl—a birthday present—were not found until the next evening, tangled in the brambles, stained red with her blood.

Rue regretted that shawl. She still did. God knew how

many pennies her mother had pinched in two to afford it. Wrapped around her on that clear crisp morning, it had felt so clean and pretty and new—*new*—and when the time came she had had to force herself to rip it, to wipe her blood upon it.

But it had been necessary. It had to be done.

Rue now had shawls for every occasion of every day. Silver-threaded gossamer, heavenly cashmere, Irish lace painstakingly knotted by the most pious of nuns; every stitch and shimmer fit for a princess. But none ever seemed as valuable to her as that plain rose poplin had been, warming her shoulders beneath the brand-new sky.

She crouched on the balls of her feet in the grit of an abandoned bell tower, sweeping her hand through dust and the soft curling underfeathers of pigeons until she located the hollow knothole in the floor. Rue hooked a finger into it and jerked at the plank; it came free with a wooden squeal. And her bag was still there, wedged tight into the crawl space, layered in grime but still buckled closed. She reached for it with unsteady hands.

It had been years since she had felt fear like that. It had been years since she had last looked into Christoff Langford's eyes, and the same strange confusion of pain and hope and wary pride had come back to her the instant he had touched her. She'd made a mistake in going to the museum. She'd grown too confident, too certain in her disguises and abilities.

Now she knew better. She wasn't infallible. Damn him.

She opened the bag, shook out the gown and apron and petticoats she'd once neatly folded away. Plain worsted wool, drab as the dust, it was clothing designed to render her invisible in the London streets, a housemaid's second best, perhaps. There was also a pinner for her hair, stockings, shoes, a spare key for her house, and coin for a coach. She had bags like this scattered throughout the city, tucked away in the skeleton tips of dilapidated buildings, steeples, empty attics—wherever common people feared to tread. So far not even one had been discovered, except by the occasional family of mice.

She dressed as the sun vanished into a wedge against a line of blood-red rooftops. The maid's gown flushed to pink with the very last of the light. It would be dark soon.

They would hunt for her in the dark.

She wished now she'd thought to pack a looking glass. The tower was filthy with neglect; her fingers were smudged with dirt. Rue stared out at the looming night and tried to remember if she had touched her face since she'd arrived, but could not.

She should remember that. She should be more careful.

She wiped her hands on the apron, then crammed the bag back into the hole and reset the plank. In all the time she had known of this place, no one had ever bothered to haul away the cracked chapel bell, not even for scrap. It gaped above her like a wide-open mouth, waiting to swallow.

"Don't be a fool," she whispered to herself. She scuffed her feet across the floor, rescattering feathers, then lifted the latch to the trapdoor and crept down the stairs. It would be hours yet until she could go home. She'd wait in the vestry, where at least the air didn't carry the metallic odor of bronze and doom.


"She must be secured."

They sat in a grim circle around his father's table, the

twelve members of the council and all the others Christoff had brought to London too, blank-faced men standing with their arms crossed behind the high empty chairs, motionless in the shrouded dusk of the dining hall.

The standing men were his guard; they would not sit. Not within the council circle, and not without his invitation. Kit was not, at the moment, much inclined to grant it.

He'd had the sconces lit but not the hearth. Their flames threw smoky gold against the jade-silk walls, flashing color that managed to hide more than it revealed. But he did not want too much light. He did not want them to see his face. He could only imagine what they might find there.

The sun was setting; he felt it, as they all did. Their time was rushing close, an anticipation for the night that roiled like noiseless thunder through the chamber. The air felt warm and thick, as though there were a storm brewing, though Christoff knew that there was not.

If she were a man, they would be bound this night to kill her. But a woman . . .

"Secured," Kit murmured, from his seat at the table head. "Captured, you mean."

"Of course it is what I mean," hissed Parrish Grady, still insufferable after all these years. "She must be found at once! She must be brought to heel!"

"She took the diamond," said another man, affronted, and a chorus of grumbled disbelief followed his words.

The diamond. No one had yet said aloud what they were actually thinking: that Christoff, their brash, uncivilized marquess, had brought it here; that Christoff, with his constant indifference to their God-almighty rules, had lost it. He should be considering ways to assuage them, to convince them this was all but part of his plan. But ringing his thoughts, around and round, were a pair of cat-dark eyes and that smile, sweetly mocking.

None of them saw who actually made off with the stone. Everyone had been concentrating on Clarissa, on closing off access to the balcony, when the glass case was shattered and *Herte* snatched. The lady had been, Kit was forced to acknowledge, a most effective distraction.

It meant she had an accomplice, a mortal. Most of the spectators had scattered with the gunshots, but those who remained described a hooded man rushing to the podium. Some claimed it was more like a boy.

Either way, she was in concert with another male. The very thought of it sent a spear of irritation through his gut.

She had known the *drákon* would be expecting her, so she had sent her emissary instead, one who wouldn't smell of them, wouldn't be suspected by them. And then...

"She can Turn," said Kit quietly, and all the councilmen stilled. He looked up at them, picked them out with narrowed eyes, one by one. "Our Smoke Thief. She's *drákon,* the only female we've got who can Turn. I would like to know... how she escaped us until this moment."

And to a man, the councillors glanced away, their gazes slipping from his to the mute green shadows.

"I remember it," said a voice at last, well behind the others. The standing guard began to spread apart, shifting through the dull colored light to reveal one man alone, older than the rest, caught against the wall between two massively framed oils. It was a captain, a veteran, one of the few Christoff had inherited from his father.

"I remember," said the captain again, heavily. "Antonia's daughter. Aye. I was there when they found the girl's things."

Kit, regrettably, was not. He'd done the math and realized

that when Clarissa Hawthorne had staged her own death he must have been down at Cambridge, ostensibly acquiring those connections of the *ton* his father had so desired. She'd disappeared in the March of his final year; he had occasion to remember that. There'd been a Frost Faire that month, because even so late into winter the River Cam held thick with ice. He'd escorted Miss Helen Shimbleton to the Faire, because she had ebony ringlets and notoriously free hands.

He remembered, quite clearly, how her cheeks went bright with the cold. How he'd given her his overcoat, and she'd given him a kiss.

And back home in winter-held Darkfrith, young Clarissa had been tearing apart her own clothing, leaving it to the scrub and muddy snow.

She must have been cold too.

He supposed he'd been given an accounting of it all at some point, but he couldn't recall even that. He had forgotten all about her, that mousy brown-haired child. Just as had everyone else.

He thought of her now from the museum, of her face and voice and that soft lily scent, and felt the wake of something deep and primitive slide through him, darkly erotic . . . an echo of her. Of what was to come.

"Bitter morning, it was," offered the captain. He held rigid against the wall, so flatly austere he might have been lifted from one of the paintings. "Antonia was right worked up."

Kit felt a flicker of interest. "You knew the mother?"

The man hesitated, then shrugged. "She was comely. A widow." Another shrug; he dropped his gaze to his boots. "Didn't live long after that, anyhow."

"How many men searched for her?" Christoff turned back to the council. "A halfling girl. How many men?"

Parrish Grady curled his fist upon the table. "A score."

"More like a dozen," corrected George, with a hard look at Grady.

"No matter," snapped Grady, "if she wasn't there to find."

"But you didn't know—"

"No one knew! By damn, why are we even discussing it?" He jerked around to glare at Kit. "She's here now, she has the diamond, and she can Turn. We'll find her and return her to Darkfrith, where she belongs. She is a danger. She *must* be contained." He leaned forward in his chair, his wig cast yellow, his mouth wrinkled to an evil pucker in the light. His eyes were small and burning. "You know it as well as I, my lord. As well as I."

Kit tilted his head, studying him.

"Sun's down," muttered one of the guardsmen by the windows.

"Then it's time." Grady made to push away from the table, and the rest began to follow.

"No," said Kit.

Grady paused with his palm pressed flat against the tabletop; all the other men froze. "What?"

"No," Kit said once more, very polite. "Be seated. All of you."

"Why are we wasting—"

"Be *seated*."

Even his old nemesis knew to obey that tone. It sliced across the room slick as steel, resounding into silence. The guard at the window let fall the drapery, a soft stir of cloth that barely touched the air.

He could almost feel his father's ghost, watching, waiting.

Christoff remained silent until they were done, until the last of them had sunk into nervous attention, staring at him through the gloom.

"I claim her," he said. "I will hunt her alone."

Grady twitched. "But—"

"I claim her," he repeated, silkier and more deadly than before. "She is mine. And if you have issue with that—any of you—I invite you to tell me now. We'll settle it here. I will not abide insubordination."

Reckless, red-faced, Grady shot back to his feet. Kit was on his own in half a heartbeat, his arm slashing out, a streak of metal flashing across the table.

The stiletto struck deep into the wall mere inches behind the other man's head, the hilt of carnelian and worked gold an ominous blur against the silk.

Silently, weightlessly, the outermost curl of Parrish Grady's wig drifted down to the dining table, settling feather-light against the dark wood.

No one else moved; no one spoke.

"I beg your pardon," said Kit cordially into the hush. "Was there something you wished to say?"

Grady looked down at the severed lock, then back up at Kit. His throat worked, though no sound came out. Slowly, in awkward motion, he resumed his seat.

"Excellent." Christoff sent a cold smile around the room. "Anyone else?"


It had been the right thing to do; he knew that. The discovery of Clarissa Hawthorne had ignited what would soon become an inferno if he didn't act to control it now. By her Gifts, by her very existence, she became the Alpha female, and thus his. But her beauty, her daring, her life beyond the tribe—when he took her back to Darkfrith she'd be no less extraordinary than the sun rising through the night. Every man in the shire would sense her, covet her. Parrish Grady had been an inconvenient beginning to the challenges. In Darkfrith there were any number of hotheaded men he could think of who might move against him, if Clarissa was the prize.

The *drákon* did not woo and wed as the Others did; their dance was more primal, the outcome more fixed. Driven by instinct as well as passion, when mates were chosen, it was for the course of a lifetime. Young lovers were permitted a leniency that husbands and wives did not share; any attempt to disrupt a marriage of the shire was considered a mortal offense. Once Clarissa was taken, she would be taken forever.

He'd been right to start here, this night, to show them what was to be. He was Alpha. And she *was* his. He felt it to the marrow of his bones.

Christoff stepped alone out of the mansion, breathing deep the damp dark air, smelling horses, and sewage, and the sugar-sweet nectar of the jasmine that hedged the stone walk. He moved out of the glow of the candle lantern nearby and paused to close his eyes, concentrating, stretching his senses.

The animal in him, always so close to his skin, instantly awoke: bright-eyed, predatory, sinking tooth and talon into his heart. He felt its black hunger rising, glittering through his blood, and welcomed the power that flooded him.

Clarissa.

He alone had the strength for this. He alone knew her like this, had her imprinted upon him from just the bare minute they had spent together in the museum, pressed so close.

He brought her back to him. He summoned her face, the feel of her waist against his arm. Her words upon his cheek.

Kit filled his lungs again.

Tobacco, charred cotton from the light. Roasting meat, desperate beggars, gin from a tavern. The Thames. Cattle, garbage. Vermin, feral dogs. People and people and people and mind-clogging people—and then—

Lilies. Oh so distant, intangible, a faerie scent buried in the choked London air. Lilies, and her.

Christoff opened his eyes, faced the western wind, where she was.

Behind him, inside Far Perch, the council and the guard waited.

He'd have her soon. All he had to do . . . was breathe.

It was a plain house, deceptively so, set back from the street by a small green stamp of grass and a crabapple sapling in a wooden pot by the door. He eyed the sapling—and the door—for quite a while from his hidden location in the alley across the street, letting hackneys with their swaying lanterns rattle by, examining lone riders on cobs and servant girls with baskets over their arms hurrying home through the night before the doors were locked against them.

Not a single creature glanced his way, not even the panting terrier on a leash, galloping behind a bored footman. Kit knew how to blend into shadows as stealthy as any bandit; he was a hunter, the best of his kind. And this was her home, he was certain of it.

The country mouse had indeed escaped to the city.

There was a lamp burning in the front hall; he could see its dim life past the curtains of the parlor. He could smell the pale, oily tang of its smoke. There was not a sliver of light, however, to be seen from the doorway itself, not even by a hair. And there was no movement from within. No human shades cast from that lamp. No footsteps, no voices.

Kit leaned his shoulder against the brick wall of the house—nearly identical to hers—that concealed him, and considered that. She might not be there. Or it might be a ruse, a clever artifice meant to throw off pursuit. . . .

But no. If he hadn't known it by the scent—nearly heady here, delicate flowers overlaid with *her*—then the lack of light through ordinary cracks and seams would have betrayed her just as readily, though admittedly not to the untrained eye. She knew her weaknesses, because she knew the tribe's. But still . . . perhaps his city mouse wasn't quite as thorough as she thought. . . .

It was a very dark evening, but not dark enough to eliminate all risk. Ordinarily he'd never take such an open chance, but he could hardly just walk up and knock on her door.

Kit slipped deeper into the shadows of the alley, shed his clothes, and Turned.

It was the Gift of the *drákon* to hold this shape, to dissolve the human self and allow the beast to begin to win. He was transparent, rising, smoke that lifted and swept around her house, seeking, seeking—all he needed was one small crack, one forgotten hole—

Yet there was none. He went over it all twice, searching as swiftly as he dared before he was noticed, but she had outdone him here as well. The chimney, the red bricks, the cream-painted hinges of the windows, all tightly sealed. He was forced to give it up, to take his shape back in that dank alley across the way and stand there, staring, torn between frustration and admiration.

Very well. She desired convention. He would offer it to her.

In the end, the Marquess of Langford was reduced to

strolling across the pebbled street and applying his knuckles to her door, after all.

Sidonie heard the first knock from the kitchen, where she was up to her elbows in dough for the Welsh pudding she was helping Cook prepare for supper. Madam tended to dine late, even by city hours, but the household staff had long ago adapted to her schedule. They were well fed, the three of them, they were well clothed; and as for the maid and the cook, they were amply paid. Sidonie had come from the workhouse before Madam Hilliard had hired her, and the corners of Fleet Street before that. She was not a woman inclined to question too closely the doings of her widowed mistress.

The knocking came again, more insistent.

"Curse that boy, where is he?" groused Cook, straightening from a stack of skinned onions and leeks. "Always underfoot when he should be out, never in when he might be of the least use—" She rolled her eyes at Sidonie. "Go on, then, before whoever it is starts a fuss."

Sidonie wiped her hands on her apron, casting one final glance at her dough, then hurried out of the kitchen.

Perhaps it was a delivery; she'd have to direct them to the back. Perhaps it was Zane, forgotten—again!—of his key, who should also use the back entrance but seldom did. Or it might be fine young Thomas Fitzhugh, with his twinkling eyes and lingering glances, come from the icehouse—though it was too late for ice, surely. . . .

As soon as her feet hit the wood floors of the hall, the knocking ceased, but Sidonie rushed forward anyway, slapping out her skirts, pushing back a strand of red hair from her cheek just as she pulled open the heavy metal door.

Her hair sucked forward again, tickling threads escaping her cap as the night wind drew the heated air out from behind her.

It wasn't Zane, or Thomas. It was a nobleman, his gloves in hand, no hat, standing casually on the stairs before her with the barest glow from her lamp falling warm upon his features. Even a full step below he was taller than she, done up in a tailored russet greatcoat and brown gleaming boots, a leather bag at his feet. His hair was loose past his shoulders, thickly blond—long and unpowdered, as if he were a tinker, or a pirate—but there was no mistaking his aristocratic air, nor the cut of that coat.

He was the most comely man she had ever seen.

The lord looked at her askance from crystal-green eyes, then offered her an easy, rakish smile. A hint of beard glinted copper along the line of his jaw, disreputable.

Sidonie felt her heart dissolve to her toes.

"Is your lady about?" he asked, smooth as chocolate.

"I . . ." The wind kicked back, cooling her cheeks, and Sidonie blinked. "No, sir. Milord."

"No?" There was amusement in his tone but it was quite gentle, as if between them they shared some wonderful secret.

"Your pardon, sir." She dipped a short curtsy. "She is out."

His gaze moved past her to the darkened hallway, then back. His handsome smile never faltered.

"Mistress Hawthorne is expected soon?"

"Oh—no, sir," said Sidonie, now flustered. "Mistress Hawthorne? This is the residence of Madam Hilliard."

But instead of the consternation she'd expected, the lord's smile only deepened. "I see. Well, perhaps you'll accept my card anyway." And he held it out most gracefully, flicking it up from nowhere to rest between his two fingers.

"Of course, milord."

"Thank you. Good evening."

"Good evening, sir."

Sidonie had to fight to push the door shut again, struggling with its weight, and in her distraction over the wind and the lord's final, slanted smile, she never noticed the second calling card that slipped between the door and the jamb just as she got it closed.

Kit let his gaze linger on the little crabapple tree, dotted with glossy red fruit, as the abigail's footsteps faded off. He then pressed his palm to the door, easing it open, put his card back into his coat, picked up his bag, and silently entered the house.

It was still an hour to daybreak before she dared to venture home, walking along the near-empty streets with her head bowed and the skirts of the maid's gown gathering grime at the hem. Finding an empty coach before dawn was well near impossible.

She had remained in the ruined chapel as long as she could bear, curled up in the only remaining pew that didn't list. There were rats in the walls that kept scratching near her head. Whenever she nodded off they seemed to spin into a rabble, squeaking and scabbering across the old plaster.

The vestry was cold, and uncomfortable, and she desperately wanted the safety of her bed. She had waited as long as she could. She had tucked her legs beneath her and dug her fingers into the worm-chewed wood and tried not to sleep, because in her nightmares she kept getting captured, over and over, surrounded by the *drákon,* pinned to the earth, smothered by them, unable even to scream. . . .

The early edge of morning now hung gray and raw around her, sending a low, wet fog creeping across the sidewalks. Rue watched her feet kick into it, how it opened and swirled and closed up over her shoes again. She kept her pace steady, her hands to herself. She was no one special, just a servant on an errand, moving quickly and modestly with her eyes on the ground—but her ears, her heart and throat and all the rest of her being trembling with awareness and fatigue.

The first of the fish hawkers were beginning to appear, heaving along their heavy baskets. Dairymaids walked, sleepy-eyed, through the mist, butchers with rust-stained aprons, washerwomen. A pair of young shoeblacks arguing over dice nudged into her, pushing away again without missing a word.

And they were all only people. Not any of Them.

At the edge of Bloomsbury she paused, stopping by a greengrocer's gate, bending over a bed of pansies as if to remove a pebble from her shoe. When she glanced up and around, not a single person was looking back at her, not even the grocer, setting up his stalls in the leaden light.

Well, to hell with it. Rue lifted her chin, her confidence ebbing back. She'd been in worse spots than this before and she always pulled through. She'd been careful, she'd been deft, and after nine incredible years she was still free, despite all the rules and threats of the shire.

She was free. And she had every intention of remaining that way.

Kit Langford was probably already wed, in any case. The

papers didn't know everything, certainly not when it came to Darkfrith.

It was too early for even Sidonie to be up; Rue cherished her late hours, and so did her staff. It wasn't unusual for her to go missing all night. They'd have waited supper for her until twelve, then packed it up for luncheon tomorrow. Without the sun peeking yet past the horizon, they'd all still be abed.

Rue entered her home with only a brisk, final scan over her shoulder, but Jassamine Lane lay utterly quiescent in the fog. Even the watchman wasn't about on his rounds, only a pair of black-tipped pigeons, eyeing her warily from their perch upon a signpost.

The hallway was dark. Just as it should be.

There was her mail on the silver salver by the door, a stack of cards and letters, all the hallmarks of a very commonplace life. She passed by with hardly a glance; she'd deal with it all later. Tomorrow. After bed.

From upstairs came the faintest sound. She stopped at once, her heart pounding...but it was only Zane, turning in his dreams, mumbled words lost into his pillow.

He didn't realize he talked in his sleep. Perhaps one day she'd tell him.

First to go were the shoes—very damp—and then the limp pinner. She left the shoes by the stairs for the maid, crumpled the pinner in her hand as she made her way up the wooden steps to the master suite.

There was a lamp burning for her by the basin on the nightstand, its blue flame dim in the gathering light.

She dropped the pinner to the chair by the armoire, pulled the clips from her hair and combed her fingers through it, sighing. She was spent. What a hideous night.

The water in the basin held a chill; she sank to the edge

of her bed and ran a washcloth over her face, inhaling sharply, then collapsed back with it draped over her eyes, cool rivulets dripping down her neck to the coverlet. It felt wonderful.

She wouldn't leave the house; they'd never find her here. She'd sleep for days ... for weeks. . . .

But she didn't want to fall asleep like this. Rue pushed herself back up with another sigh. The maid's gown was deliberately simple, some plain lacing, a few hooks. She didn't need assistance to unfasten the bodice, and then the panniers and skirt, shrugging out of everything to let it drop to the rug. The gown lay there, puffed brown and dirty white, softly leaking air between the folds. She stepped free, kicking it to a corner.

She'd give it to Sidonie—no, to charity. She wanted never to see it again.

In her corset and chemise she crossed to the bureau, opening the top drawer for her nightrail—

—and lifting up instead the gown she'd abandoned in the museum yesterday, sea-green silk and exquisite lace.

Rue stared down at the colors spilling over her hands, her mind a sudden, horrified blank.

"Forgive me," said a low voice behind her. "Perhaps I should have made myself known before now."

# CHAPTER FIVE

Clarissa Hawthorne whirled to the window behind her—a window Christoff knew to be closed—and pulled from the folds of the curtains a rapier, and a serious one at that: the polished edges gathered the light into a long, sinister sheen. She whisked it up easily, her arm flexed, her cat eyes on his, as he stepped from the shelter of her canopied bed and into the open quiet of her bedroom.

In her chemise and stocking feet she was still beautifully aloof, her hair a chestnut scroll draped along one shoulder. Her skin was pale as stone.

"I thought you'd like that back." He indicated the seafoam gown, caught in a rippling fan across the bureau drawer, where she had dropped it.

"Oh?" One elegant brow arched. "And my pumps?"

Kit gestured to the armoire.

"Thank you so much." She swung the rapier at him, a flare of silver that parted the air with a lethal *whish*. He ducked and turned, shoving the chair between them, and the steel sliced into cushions.

"Sorry about your wig, though. Lost it to the mêlée."

The rapier lifted, balanced in her hand; her gaze never left his. "That's quite all right. I have others." And she thrust again.

He leapt back. "Your own hair is prettier."

"You're too kind."

"Not at all."

They began a slow circle around the room, Kit with his hands loose at his sides, Clarissa pacing him, framed in misted light.

He said, "You're very good with the blade."

"I know."

"French master?"

"Italian."

She lunged and pinked his arm; the linen of his sleeve began to flower with blood. With his next breath, she had the point at his chest.

She held motionless there with her left hand out and her hair now tumbled, her body a taut, leashed line from the *patinado*. The tip of the rapier was the barest prick over his heart.

"I have no weapon," he said evenly.

"How shortsighted of you. Perhaps, my lord, you ought not to enter homes uninvited."

He managed a smile. "I did leave my card."

Her eyes narrowed a fraction; the blade turned against his skin. "Why did you come here?"

"Little mouse—why do you think?"

"Perhaps you're a thief," she said consideringly. "Perhaps you are, in fact, the infamous Smoke Thief, Lord Langford. I can only imagine what the press might make of your capture."

"That *would* be interesting." He kept his tone peaceful, his body willfully relaxed.

"Indeed. I hear there's quite a reward in it too."

"About sixty pounds sterling, so far."

"Splendid. I'll buy a new wig."

"Is that why you do it, Clarissa? For the funds—or for the thrill?"

Now she smiled at him, her lips lifting into a luscious pink curve. "I fear you're greatly mistaken. Clarissa Hawthorne is dead. I have a copy of her obituary, in fact. It was all terribly sad."

He lowered his eyes. Despite her veneer of calm, she was breathing too quickly. Above the drawstring of her chemise a sweet, becoming blush began to warm the flawless white skin.

She wore a knot of ribbons where the drawstring tied, a flourish of turquoise satin nestled just between her breasts. The chemise was so thin he could nearly see through it, drawn tight by the corset, a dusky hint of nipples, straining against the cloth....

With her rapier against his chest, Kit felt that dark thing within him rise up once more, eager for this moment, eager for her.

"Clarissa..."

"All I have to do is scream," she whispered, all venom and fire. "I'll have three good souls in here in an instant, defending my honor. What will you do then, Kit Langford?"

"Exactly this," he said, and Turned, so that the rapier passed through his shirt and into the empty air.

The front door slammed.

Damn, damn, oh, dear God—

She had let her temper and her fear get control of her— she'd meant to reason with him, to bargain—

He knew where she lived.

Rue looked around her room, at her rumpled bed and the rosewood nightstand and the little Renaissance etching of a shepherd girl hung up on the wall. The rapier was a cold weight in her hand.

She threw it to the bed. She ran down the stairs and Turned at the door, chasing him up into the sky.


The pigeons exploded into panic. She soared by them, through and past them, as they shrieked and vaulted from the post. Jassamine Lane shrank to a path and toy houses, miniature people never looking up. The day was brightening with the dawn and he was visible ahead of her, the smoky skill and grace she'd admired for years as a child, skimming the underbellies of the clouds.

He was fleet. So was she.

And then he vanished. She caught the spiral of vapor that meant he had climbed higher, breaking through the clouds, and so she did the same, piercing the dense layers, mingling with the cool, dirty mists, rising....

She burst free into blue sky and clean, thin air, and he was there too, still smoke—and then he Turned again, and he was *drákon*.

Emerald and azure and shimmering scales; he glanced back at her only once, nearly blinding with the sunlight, a fluent twist above the earth. His wings were deeply scarlet, holding him aloft in powerful strokes. He turned his face away and plunged ahead again.

It was a challenge, or a trick—she didn't have time to worry which. He would be even faster like this. She wouldn't be able to keep up, and it was too late to retreat now; she had too much at stake. So Rue did the thing she had never done before any member of the tribe—that she'd hardly dared even out here at the brink of heaven, all alone—and took her dragon self as well.

Ah. Her first breath was like inhaling snow, fiercely cold, sending light and energy through her entire being. For a gasping instant it chilled her in place—then she had substance once more, she had form. She lifted her head and stole her second delicious breath, bounding across the firmament, a phantom creature that matched the sun and these purer clouds: her body pearl white, her scales rimmed in gold.

The *drákon* were sleeker than the depictions that had survived in medieval tapestries and texts: no fat bellies, no lumbering gait, but living flame and speed and gilded wings that mastered the wind. No wonder the Others had rendered them so clumsy in their fables; in true life their radiance was almost incomprehensible, splinters of sky, as fatal and glorious as a hail of firelit arrows.

And Christoff, the strongest of them all, was still so far ahead.

Rue stretched thin to follow him, her wings out, leaping high to fall into a long, flat dive that tore the tops from the clouds in a swirling stripe.

She was catching up. He glanced back at her again, did a clever, writhing loop at the sight of her, then soared on, higher, higher.

She climbed with him.

The air was much scarcer here. She'd never been this high before but he didn't stop, and the blue surrounding them grew deeper, closer to indigo, and the blanket of clouds below softened into a vast ivory curve. It was getting harder to exhale. He was slowing too, at last, the scarlet wings beating swifter—without the atmosphere to support them, flying was more difficult. Yet she was gaining, less weight than he, more desperate, nearly there—and all at once he spun to face her, so abrupt she couldn't pull back in time. As she tried to veer off he leapt forward and took her by the throat, his wings folded. They twirled together and then dropped like stones back to the earth.

She arched backward, to no avail. His grip was firm and very sharp, not releasing. Rue saw clouds and sky and even the faint pricks of stars; she spread her wings, sending them into a sideways topple, but Christoff flipped and wrapped himself around her, crushing them against her back with his weight.

The wind clawed at her. The clouds rushed forth with awful mass. She tried to Turn and could not—they were too high, descending too fast, and his breath was a hot heat on her neck, and his body an unyielding coil around hers. He was trying to kill them—if she couldn't Turn and she couldn't fly, they'd streak to their deaths like comets—

Sir George stood slouched with his hands in his pockets, eyeing the stone symmetry of the floor as the men around him paced, their footsteps echoing in the high, empty chamber. The warehouse was dusty, uncomfortably cavernous for his taste. The air carried the distinctive odor of sheep's wool mixed with rodent and river sludge.

They were late, the marquess and his prisoner. The day had broken and thus far the only people traveling the streets around this building were watermen and merchants. George pursed his lips, scratched the heel of his boot idly against the floor. Perhaps Christoff had failed. It hardly seemed possible to do what he had vowed, to track her through the city by

the mere memory of her scent, to capture her unaided...
even for him....

He felt it exactly as the others did, all of them checking in
place. Above them—*above* them—raged the unmistakable
presence of *drákon*. Everyone looked up at the ceiling,
shocked.

"Holy God," said George. "Here they come."


They struck the clouds, a sudden gray smack against
Rue's skin, and then they were free of even those, plummet-
ing to the London skyline, moments from their ruin against
the wide earth.

The silver-glass snake of the Thames. Ships. Docks.
Massive buildings racing toward them—

Kit opened his wings. It jerked them up, slowed them
down, but before she could react they smashed through an
enormous roof—and it *hurt*, her back and shoulders screaming with pain, wood shingles flying—and then to a floor,
where they landed in a hard bumping roll, still latched together, colliding against a wall that shuddered but did not
fall.

She lay there stunned, unable to move; the stars in her
eyes now flashed blue and purple. She hardly felt Christoff
shift. She hardly felt it when he took her again by the
throat—more delicately now—and dragged her across an
open floor, past a doorway, to a place smaller and dimmer
than before. He laid her carefully back down.

She swallowed. She blinked to clear her vision, and then
Christoff was human again, beautifully nude, crouched before her with his fingers caught in the bright silken mane
down her neck.

"Clarissa," he said.

She shook her head, springing to her feet, and he backed away only a single step, gazing up at her, his face inscrutable.

She Turned to smoke. But the door he had pulled her through was now closed, smooth and latchless, without the slightest opening to slip through. The chamber was bricks and mortar and no windows. The granite floor had no gaps.

She was trapped.

Rue took her human shape, coalescing in a corner with her hair snarled over her body and her hands pushed flat behind her against the walls. Christoff Langford watched it happen, making no move toward her, standing tall and alone in the center of the barren floor. There was a single candle burning in a bracket by the door.

"Did you really think you were the first to run to the city?" he asked gravely, and lifted an arm to the room. "Behold. My father built this place especially for our kind."

She stared at him, panting, then brought a hand to her neck and pressed it against the ache there. When she took it away again, her palm was bloody.

Her voice came as a broken rasp. "What have you done?"

"It's a holding cell. I'm sorry." He looked away finally, his lashes lowered. The candlelight shaded his mouth into a chiseled line. "I had to get you here somehow."

She could not seem to comprehend it, the sealed room, the black shadows, the solitary point of flame. The Marquess of Langford, with his remote composure and his eyes hooded green, no human modesty, no shame. He was *drákon*, and Rue realized now that she had never seen it so clearly in anyone until this moment: not mortal, not weak, but something ancient and formidable, barely bound in the sinew and grace of a man's unclothed body.

Red smeared across his left biceps, darkening the muscled

curve. A wound. She had done that with her rapier, a lifetime past.

"Clarissa Hawthorne," he said formally, never moving. "By the laws of the tribe, I hereby bind you. Do you yield to me, and to the will of the council?"

Ritual words, and the beginning of the end. She recognized them as any child of Darkfrith would, sacred words seldom relayed above a whisper, terrible words meant for outlaws, for the dangerous few who chanced freedom. The marquess spoke them softly, even tenderly, but when his eyes lifted to hers she saw the steely resolve behind his gaze.

"I bind you," he said again. "Do you yield to me?"

Yes or no. She knew what happened to those who said no. She'd shivered with all the other silly-frightened children over the rumors, and every Hallow's Eve had listened, rapt, to the dreadful stories of the dead. Adults were ever evasive on the details, but even Antonia had forbidden her to venture past the shire falls, where the bones of the tribe's outcasts had been burned and buried.

Christoff watched her, and the blood on his arm trickled slowly lower, tracing the veins of his hand down to a finger, and still he didn't move. She followed the first drop as it fell, a crimson *plish* against the floor.

His voice grew even softer, infinitely dark. "Do you yield?"

She looked up at his face, shadowed in gold, so inhumanly perfect. "No," she said, and turned to the wall. She propped an arm up against it and leaned her forehead to the bricks. Her hair was a heavy tangle against her skin, blocking what remained of the light. She closed her eyes and waited.

For a long while, nothing happened. When at last he

stirred she was able to hold herself perfectly still, not flinching, not fleeing. He halted just behind her.

She felt his hand cover her own above her head, his fingers spreading, slipping between hers. He drew his palm lightly down the bow of her arm to her hair, smoothing it, discovering her shoulder blade beneath the mess of locks, her spine. Rue squeezed her eyes shut more tightly.

"I'm grieved to hear it," Christoff said, and with his hand on her hip he urged her around to face him. She allowed it, beyond thought, beyond fear, the only thing real and true the rough wall against her back.

He stood too near, large and utterly male. His hair, his skin, even his eyes, bright with flame: he was a seraph come to life, too dazzling and devastating at once, every rise and fall of his chest taking in the light, making it his own. His fingers remained curved over her hip.

It was as if she remembered this moment from a long-ago dream, from her girlhood, all her youthful fantasies now fulfilled in the most disastrous of ways. Kit Langford touching her, looking at her as though he knew all about her, her every secret hope and sin—as though he divined her whole life, laid before him unmasked.

His gaze drifted to her lips. His fingers tensed. Candlelight slid like a lover's touch over the breadth of his shoulders.

From outside the chamber came a distant commotion. As one they glanced toward the door, then back at each other. Possibilities seemed to spin between them; Christoff captured her chin and spoke again, very quietly.

"There's going to be a crowd of people out there, drawn to our descent and what I'm sure is a rather large hole in the roof of this building. There's going to be a constable, at least. Promise me you won't scream."

She could hear the men. She could hear them running.

"Promise," he insisted, and his hand lowered, became the lightest of threats around her bruised throat. Rue licked her lips, her thoughts tumbling—if she *did* scream, if the door opened, if she Turned—and he let out his breath in a hiss.

"Listen to me! I don't demand anything else right now. But I will not risk further exposure." Someone began to approach the closed door, footsteps scuffing over stone, and she thought, *Now, now*—but Christoff's hand contracted. The pulse in her ears became a river rush.

"Mouse," he whispered, past the rising babel in her head.

"Yes." Her lips shaped the word; she couldn't hear herself say it. But his grip relaxed. She pressed back against the bricks, fighting the dizziness, then reached up and shoved his hand from her. He let his arm drop and studied her face, speculative, as the conversation beyond the walls grew clear.

"...quite a thing! Did you or your men see it, sir?"

"No, no, not at all." A glib voice, with an affected drawl. "Something falling from the sky, you say? How astonishing."

"A handful of witnesses pinpointed it near here. Quite a mess you have! Would you mind if—"

"As I've said, constable, we're in rather a rush. You understand. We've come merely to survey the building. We've over forty ton of wool coming in with the afternoon tide, and more on the way. But the place is ruined, as you can see. Quite useless."

"The roof—"

"Aye, disgraceful, isn't it? Collapsed last week, after the rains."

The marquess had cocked his head, listening. A smile caught at the corner of his lips.

"Last week?"

"I say!" chortled the glib man. "You didn't think—but surely not!"

"Oh—er . . ."

"No, my good fellow, not a bit of falling sky made this wreck. It was wood rot, and a damned lot of it. Look at this timber! Damned shame!"

"Of course. Of course."

"We plan to bring charges against the manager, naturally. Outrageous that he allowed it to fall into such a state. Perhaps, sir, as a man of the law, you'd be willing to take a hand in this. . . ."

Rue opened her mouth on a breath and Kit's palm flashed up, firm against her lips. But the sounds beyond the room were lessened now, fewer voices, as the bystanders were herded from the warehouse. When she could no longer hear them at all, he broke away from her, turning toward the light.

She pushed her hair from her face and thought again, *Now*. But it was too late, and she knew it.

Christoff walked to the door and stood there, obviously waiting, with his head bowed and his arms crossed. The candle sent up black pincers of smoke.

Rue sank to the floor. She didn't mean to, she didn't want to, but her legs had gone curiously nerveless. Through the haze of her exhaustion the room seemed to take on a creeping, sideways reel. She thought of Turning now, the instant the door cracked, and knew she'd never have the strength to hold it. How long since she'd slept? She couldn't recall. She pressed her toes into the granite dust of the ground and saw a fleck of dried blood on her calf. Hers or his, she could not tell.

Her throat hurt.

She wondered how many *drákon* he had out there. She wondered if she could outrace them all.

A low scratching came from the door.

"My lord?"

Christoff unfolded his arms. "Here."

"They're gone. I've sent for the carriage."

"We're going to need clothing too. Hats, shoes. A dress for her. Hurry."

"Aye."

He glanced back at Rue. And for the first time she had the full sense of her own nudity, of her flesh against the unforgiving floor, and her hair slipping over her shoulders. She drew her legs up before her in a mermaid pose, wrapped her arms around her chest and met his glinting look.

"You haven't won."

"No?" He leaned against the door, surveying her. "It certainly seems that I have."

"I won't go back there. I'd rather die than go back there."

"It's been a grand chase, Clarissa. But we *are* going home."

"My home is here."

In the tarnished light of the candle the marquess lifted his injured arm, inspecting the cut, the sheen of blood, then raised his eyes to hers. The smile that came to him now shone wicked with promise from all the way across the chamber.

He said, "No, love. From now on, your home is with me."

# CHAPTER SIX

She had to be blindfolded for the journey back.

He didn't like that, but the only other option was to knock her senseless. Kit could not imagine raising his hand to her, not for such a thing, and he would not suffer any other man to touch her.

So Clarissa was blindfolded, with her wrists secured behind her back. A mortal woman never could have endured it, but the *drákon* were altogether stronger than the Others. And in truth, he had no choice: in her circumstances he knew he'd do his damnedest to escape. He'd risk life and limb and anything else for his freedom, certainly the sanctity of the tribe. But she could not Turn if she could not see; Kit trusted the same rules were true for females as for males. It was a fatal flaw of their people, but one that worked in his favor today.

He recalled that his father preferred to use hoods.

They'd had to move quickly from the warehouse, before the constable and all those sharp-eyed witnesses realized there were no other conveniently crushed roofs around. Kit had watched her dress in a gown that George had procured, a merry ensemble of sapphire blue taffeta with yellow stripes down the skirts. Without asking, he finished the buttons she couldn't reach. And then he produced the blindfold.

She looked impassively at the sash uncurling from his fist. The council and his guard crisscrossed the area beyond the door, shifting lumber, muttering plans and predictions. He knew she heard them, just as he did. It was probably the only reason she let him do it.

"I don't suppose you would stash the diamond in your home," Kit said, coming near. "I didn't feel it there."

Her gaze went to his, and there was something on her face, just a flash—revelation, perhaps—swiftly hidden behind the subtle curling of her lips.

"Suppose what you wish," she said, shrugging.

"Doesn't matter." He fixed the sash around her eyes, careful to leave no gaps. "Not at the moment. I'll come back for it."

And she said nothing. She only stood silently with her jolly striped skirts and her slight, mocking smile, her back straight and her chin lifted. He led her from the room with both hands.

He hadn't expected her to surrender her secrets so easily, not really. Not her.

Now, in the enclosed luxury of his carriage, Kit was at his leisure to ponder her, since it appeared that despite the blindfold she had fallen asleep. He sat opposite her with a borrowed boot propped against her seat and let his gaze roam. Her head had tipped to rest against the velvet-padded cushions. Beneath the bruises, the pulse in her throat beat slow and steady.

The striped gown nearly swallowed her in pleats and ruffles; she had already kicked off the shoes. The straw hat with the ribbons he'd tied so fetchingly beneath her chin—the better to hide her face—had slipped sideways, covering her ear. Soft brown hair waved free as a girl's, shining dark all the way to her waist. She seemed fragile, and lovely, and everything innocent.

He could still taste her blood in his mouth.

It filled him with regret, but deeper than that, in some dim buried place—excitement. Clarissa Hawthorne was not innocent. She was unlike anyone he had ever known before. Beneath her delicacy beat a heart as untamed as his own, he was certain of it. No one else would have had the nerve to live such a life.

And flying with her . . .

He'd never, ever seen anything so amazing as the sight of her against the blue sky. He could still feel the potency of it, the sweet jolt of looking back that second time, finding she was truly there with him above the clouds, truly one of them.

His.

The carriage was part of his official persona. It was new and sleek and well-sprung, hardly swaying along the rutted Great North Road from London. He had lowered the shades for the tollgates and the city, because even he might have a time of it explaining a trussed, blindfolded woman. But his ears told him they were finally past the outer edges; he lifted the shade at his side, looking out at rows and rows of early green wheat outlined with holly hedges. Farmers in homespun plowed their fields. A herd of goats stood pressed back against a fence, following the carriage and outriders with canny orange eyes.

Kit reached over to Clarissa, untied the hat, and tossed it to the seat. She never woke.

The air still reeked of city. But there was a more pleasing note beneath it, freshness, clean earth.

Darkfrith awaited.

On the night of her fourth day trapped inside the miserable carriage, stopping only to eat and change horses, they arrived. Even without her sight, Rue felt the difference all around her, the eventide scents, the waterfall of sounds of a place she'd pushed so far from her it had resurfaced only in her dreams.

She'd spent the time in a daze; sometimes the marquess was there, and sometimes he was not. He brought her food and drink and fed her with his own hands. She wondered if it was drugged. She slept a great deal. But when Rue came awake that last night, she knew, like a lark swept by the wind back to its birthplace, that she was in Darkfrith.

She knew the crickets that chirped from the shaggy ferns that lined the long, winding approach to the manor house.

She knew the crush of pea gravel beneath her feet as she stepped gingerly from the carriage onto firm land.

She knew the fragrance of the forest that drifted over her like a cool, cool hand, touching her face, lifting her hair.

She knew the grass and the owls.

She knew the small crackles of rushlights.

She knew the whispers, and the stares, and the gasps.

And she knew the man holding her elbow. His stride, shortened now to match her own. Rue straightened her shoulders and walked confidently into the nothingness before her. She was here, that was all. She was not defeated.

"This way," Christoff said into her ear, as though she might suddenly choose another. She heard the wooden doors of the manor creak open, new smells: beeswax, roses, pine resin, polished metal. Very faintly—onions and beef stew.

The people by the carriage would be watching her walk away. She kept her fingers deliberately relaxed at the small of her back, no hint of the bitter stinging beneath her skin, of how the marquess's satin cords bit into her.

The heels they had given her were too large. God knew if they were new or old, but when she put her foot out for her third step into the slick vestibule the sole skidded out from beneath her. She stumbled for a floating instant; the grip on her arm became a vise. They paused together, Rue catching her breath with her balance, proud that she hadn't made a sound.

"Careful," Kit warned. And then, more gently, "We're almost there."

Which of course she already knew, because the smells around her changed once again, darkened as they walked deeper and deeper into the echoing halls. She'd been inside Chasen Manor only once before, for her tribal blessing by the old marquess. It was a rite celebrated for every newborn, even halflings, or else Rue doubted she would have had even that brief, stellar moment. She had been but two weeks old.

As a child, it was one of her favorite stories. She had begged Antonia to tell it to her over and over again.

*The room was lit with candles, tens of candles, every one of them angel white.*

The temperature was definitely cooler now. The walls were closer, the hallways more narrow. There were more turns.

*You were dressed in your grandmother's lace.*

Someone was speaking from behind closed doors; she could not make out the words. As they passed, the voices quickly shushed.

*Everything was the finest, purest marble, the walls, the floors, the font.*

Christoff slowed, and so did she. She felt him turn to look behind them, perhaps at the men who followed.

*The candles melted into wonderful perfume.*

There was another door before her. It radiated coldness. Metal again. Probably iron.

*You smiled at the marquess.*

She heard a heavy grinding, a bar lifted. She heard a key fit into a lock.

*The other babies were fussing.*

The air that swept her now was stale and dank.

*But you never cried, not once.*

It tasted like desperation.

*My brave little princess.*

She entered the chamber and stood motionless as Christoff at last released her arm. She heard him conferring with someone beyond the door as she took slower breaths and tried not to give in to the urge to rip her hands from their bonds.

The door shut with a small, irrevocable click. The marquess came behind her. There was a blade between her wrists.

"Hold still, if you please."

He cut the cords. For a moment the only thing that happened was that her numbed arms slipped forward again, limp at her sides. Then the blood rushed back, a delayed agony that arced from her fingers all the way up to her skull. Rue bit her lip to stop from moaning.

Christoff stepped in front of her, taking up her hands, rubbing her skin in light circles. As soon as she could, she pulled herself free—not hastily, not clumsily, but with as much disdain as she could put into a backward tug. She fumbled with the blindfold, not even bothering with the knot, simply jerking it from her face.

She blinked at the new light, at the little cell. At the man before her, watching her with unsmiling intensity.

"I'm sure you know of this place," he said. "It's yours for as long as you require it."

The Dead Room. Naturally she knew of it, everyone did. The room of judgment, of final hours. It was said to be buried so deep in the labyrinth that was Chasen that no one could ever hear the screams.

The walls were not, in fact, painted in the blood of the doomed as she had always heard, but were instead an ordinary gray stone, heavy blocks that also formed the floor and ceiling like the solar of an old Norman castle, but without windows.

There was an oak-framed bed, a plank table, and a pair of chairs. There was a lantern on a hook by the door.

The bed was narrow, and plain. It held two pillows and a fleecy blanket the color of sand.

"Will it be rape, or will you flatter yourself with an attempt at seduction?" she asked, still facing the bed.

He did not reply. Rue looked down at her hands, opened her palms and stretched her aching fingers.

"There is no rape between a husband and a wife," the marquess said.

"Yes, well, I'm afraid I'm not going to consent to marry you, Lord Langford. You'll have to call it something else."

"You may call it whatever you like, Mistress Hawthorne. You are Alpha, as am I. By the laws of our people, we're as well as married."

"Those are not my laws. And that is not my name."

"Clarissa."

"I told you. She is dead."

"Then tell me again," he invited, milder than before. "Who are you now, if not that little girl from the shire?"

"No one at all."

"Everyone has a name." He walked closer, shape and

color through the mask of her lashes, not quite near enough to touch. "Even the lost."

"I assure you, I was not lost."

"Lost to me, I should say. If you don't want me to call you by your given name, you'd better offer me another."

She drew in her breath, held it a moment, debating. "Rue."

"Rue." He repeated it deliberately, letting it roll along his tongue. "Madam Rue Hilliard, from what I understand." He reached out now, stroked his fingers down her cheek to tip her face to his. His eyes glittered green, ice against a winter sunrise. "Wed, or widowed?"

In all the room, he was the only thing of beauty. He was hard and powerful and unfathomable, his features barely lined even after all the days of travel. His palm shaped warmth against her cheek and his dominion was there too, restrained into a mere caress. But Rue wasn't fooled. Behind his winter look there was jeopardy. There was a primal creature, only waiting to pounce.

"Neither," she said finally. "I made it up."

"Good." His hand trailed downward, following her throat. "Because I'm not a patient man, nor a sharing one. Divorces can take so awkwardly long." Lower still, to her chest. He slipped a finger between her breasts. "And this place...is mine."

She slapped him. She had never hit anyone before, never once, but it was rash and instinctive, and strong enough to rock him back a step.

"You are *not* my mate." Rue pressed against the bed, trapped, enraged. "You're not even my lover."

Christoff cradled his jaw with one hand, his fingers dark against his own skin. Then his lashes swept low, and he smiled—a faint, chilling smile, full of either irony or menace, or both.

"No," he said in that utterly calm way. "Not tonight. But tomorrow...."

"Get out."

"As you will." He went to the door, called a name. She heard the key turn in its socket. As the lock released, Kit inclined his head.

"No doubt you're weary. I'll leave you to your thoughts—Rue." At the edge of the doorway he paused, glancing back at her from over his shoulder. "You could Turn in here, of course. But trust me, it's not a comfortable fit. And you'd never get even as far as the hall."

The door closed; she was alone. No need to check the seal of the jamb. It would be solid through.

She stood in quivering stillness a moment, breathing through her nose, then spun around and struck the table with a single blow. The top cracked but did not split, so she kicked at a leg, feeling the pain of connection, feeling the wood shatter. The table swayed and toppled to its side on the floor.

Beyond the iron door, there might have been laughter.


He gave her one night.

Strictly speaking, it wasn't even an entire night, since by the time the carriage had approached the scrolled gates of Chasen it was just after one in the morning. But an hour lack didn't seem very significant to Kit, not when he lay awake himself in the dark, tossing in his bed. He might have slept; he wasn't certain. If he dreamed, it was of her anyway.

One night to settle, to let her reconsider her circumstances. One night for the council and guard to disperse back to their own beds, for the tangle of exhilaration and triumph over her capture, the worry for the diamond, to smooth themselves out in the stillness of those hours that crept toward dawn.

He'd assigned two guards to her door, his most trusted men. He left orders that no one was to see her but him, that any inquiries regarding her were to be directed solely to him. Clarissa—Rue—had walked through his halls and left already ripples of wonder in her wake: it seemed half the tribe had caught the news from his messenger, had gathered on the front lawn to await that first glimpse of the girl who'd fooled them all—at least for a while.

And in just those few minutes it took to escort her inside, Kit had witnessed the insurrection spark to life. It lit from face to face, a hunger that touched every man she glided by, that feasted on long brown hair and creamy pale skin and the mere notion of all that she had done and could yet do.

Smoke Thief. Even the taffeta gown whispered temptation, marking the sway of her hips in rustling jeweled colors.

Christoff knew that hunger full well. He knew its harsh ache.

One night, just to be fair. But after tonight she was going to sleep here, with him.


Years of existing in the shadows had trained Rue to always listen, because even the most subtle of sounds could mark the difference between success and failure, between nicking a purse of copper coins or one of gold, between captivity— and deliverance.

So Rue listened. She listened closely all night long, but she never heard a single whisper filter through the walls of her prison. She never heard even the common bumps and shuffles of the men she knew kept watch beyond that metal door.

Yet it was revealed to her, over the course of the night, that her cell was not so entirely removed from the world as it first appeared.

She had stripped from the gaudy gown and lay back on the bed with the blanket wrapped snugly around her, no nightgown, no chemise. The air kept a dull, constant chill. The mattress had a lump.

After days in the dark she craved the light, and so let the lantern burn down to its dregs. The smell of whale oil seemed to cling to the sheets and walls even after the flame died.

Sleep would not come. She closed her eyes and thought of her feather bed back in London, of her home, of her people. She worried about what they'd done upon finding the front door ajar, and the strange clothing in her room. She worried that Cook and Sidonie would involve the police, and that Zane wasn't old enough yet to stop them.

She discovered the first message by accident. She had rolled to her side, trying to avoid the bulge of the lump, and her left hand lifted and brushed the wall. But the stone surface was uneven. Faintly, lightly, it had been incised.

Rue opened her eyes and traced the lines, forming the letters in her mind as her fingers outlined them: WINGS CLIPPD. And just below it: HARTBROKE, M.A., 1689

She sat up. She felt the words again in the pitch of the chamber, the initials and date, then placed both hands on the wall, letting the stone leach away her precious warmth. It didn't take long to find another carving, this one near the head of the bed, half hidden by a post. It was not words but a figure, a thin, wavering line with two rough spread wings sprouting from the middle. A dragon, flying. Directly behind it was another, and then another, and another, each one smaller than the last. Perhaps a family. Perhaps the man who scratched this out in the last few days of his life had once had a family.

She rested back on the pillows, thinking. What had they used to score the stone? The marquess had certainly left her without a weapon, without anything sharp. She rubbed her hands absently on the blanket covering her legs, warming them again, then got up, padded warily to the broken table. With her hands outstretched she groped until she found the top, the shattered leg. It had separated into pieces; the remaining fragment of wood at the joint hung loose, exposing long, heavy nails.

She cut herself tugging the longest one free. She sucked the blood from her finger and kept working the nail with her other hand until it came out.

Rue went back to the bed, found a clear block on the wall, and began to carve.

She was waiting for him when he returned, wrapped only in a blanket, seated primly upon the bed with her ankles crossed and her fingers laced in her lap. The light from the doorway opened over her in a cool, bright rectangle; she stared straight into it, unblinking, and he wondered how long she'd been sitting in the dark.

She'd pulled her hair back into a plait, emphasizing the angles of her face, the full solemn mouth, the black-lashed clarity of her eyes. Taffeta made a discarded heap at her feet.

Kit entered the cell carrying her breakfast tray, and had to step hastily aside to avoid the ruins of the table that used to be in the corner.

"I require new clothing," Rue Hawthorne said to him.

He looked around for another place to put the tray, realized there was none, and set it on the bed beside her.

"Certainly," he said.

"And a bath."

"Of course."

He bent down, picked up what used to be the foot of the table, and slanted her a look. She returned it; very slowly her brows raised, as if daring him to comment.

"I felt quite the same way." He let the wood fall from his hand. "It was ugly."

Her gaze lowered. With her chin tucked down and her lips set in that soft, demure bow, she was the very picture of timidity—a most charming act.

God, if only he didn't know what she looked like without the blanket.

The shadows danced. Behind him, the guard was bringing in a new lantern, and Kit turned to accept it. As the door began to close he caught the sudden expansion of her chest, how she took in a bit deeper than before the last of the fresh air.

It couldn't be easy, staying in this place. It had been built, after all, for penance.

"It's going to be a fair day," Kit said casually, seating himself on the other side of the tray. "The sun is rising, the sky is clearing. There's a breeze, but it's only enough to rouse the thrifts. There's a flock of them in the north field this morning, settled in the rye. Everything's scented of spring."

She was absolutely still, looking at the bleached napkin on the tray, the sugar bowl of cornflower porcelain. In the small cast of the lantern her hair shone inky smooth, the plait like a brushstroke down the line of her back.

"And woodbine," he added, crossing his legs. "We've a lot of it flowering just now. Do you remember that?"

She pinned him with her gaze. "When will it happen?"

"What?"

"The council. When do they meet?"

"Noon," he said. "With the ceremony at four."

She paled a little; he wouldn't have thought it possible.

"The wedding ceremony," he said. "What did you think?"

Within the pallor of her cheeks two new spots of red bloomed. He smiled at that, a sharp smile that he knew wouldn't comfort her—but it did erase the last of that feigned meekness.

"I've brought you something else." He reached into his vest for the folded newspaper. He proffered it but her fingers never unclenched, so Kit opened it for her, held the front page up to the light.

"Look. I thought you'd like to see—you're still famous."

*Monsters in the Sky!* screamed the headline in thick black letters. Just under it was an illustration of two snarling fiends, truly hideous, with sticks of people fleeing frantically below.

"Infamous, rather," Kit corrected himself, still smiling. "One of the fellows who lingered to close up the mansion brought this back." He eyed the crude drawing. "I imagine we were quite a sight."

" 'Tis a miracle no one shot at us," she said in a low voice.

"Oh, but see here, someone did. One Master Eugene Sumner, a bos'n on the good ship *Rip Tide*. Indeed, apparently he's a crack marksman, as according to no less than four of his mates he managed to sink us to the bottom of the river." Kit looked up from the newsprint, thoughtful. "Perhaps he'll get a medal."

"A pity he missed."

He lowered the paper.

*"You,"* she added pointedly.

He bent his head and examined the coarse edges of the daily, folding it and refolding it in his hands. Beyond his feet the old table lay at a forlorn angle, its underside revealing a darker, less even stain than the top. It had been in the cell for as long as he could remember, certainly since his father's time. He wondered how many runners had stared down at its surface and counted the hours. He wondered if she had hurt herself breaking it, and knew better than to ask.

He said, "Tell me where *Herte* is, and I'll speak on your behalf to the council. I'll demand leniency."

"And what would that be?" she inquired, dry. "A wedding tomorrow instead of today?"

"Better accommodations, for one thing. The quarters of the marchioness."

"Freedom?"

"A measure of freedom, yes."

"A measure," she repeated, now sounding bored. "Like a hound on a leash, I gather. No, thank you."

"Rue," he said roughly, glancing up at her. "Let me help you."

"You've helped rather enough."

"Is this what you want, then?" He stood, let his hand sweep the room. "This place, this life? If you fight them, they'll do everything they can to keep you here."

"Release me," she said, watching him steadily. "You're the marquess, you have that power. I'll tell you what you want then, I swear."

He shook his head. "You know that's not possible."

"I know that you're Alpha. Isn't it so? The almighty sovereign leader of the tribe." She came to her feet as well, clutching the blanket. "Well, prove it. Break their rules. Form your own."

She had taken a step toward him with her last few words, her shoulders squared and the damned silly blanket trailing behind her over the floor like the gown of an empress. He knew she meant to goad him, perhaps even to intimidate him, but right then, alone with her in the cell, with the lantern playing light and color along her skin, with her eyes narrowed and her lips—aye, her lips—so perfectly, deeply pink and ripe...with the braid gently swinging behind her, an invitation to be undone...

He felt the beast within him stir. He felt his body go stiff with it, mere inches from hers, as the tension began to spiral and bind in a hot rush through his groin. He couldn't stop it, he didn't want to stop it. He wanted it to go on and on.

She was so lovely. Every time he saw her he realized it anew, as though his memory ever failed him; he couldn't get used to the sensation. But she was. Her very presence enflamed him, from the flush in her cheeks to the black fans of her lashes, the way her eyes held his, the way her jaw clenched. Even her bare toes, just visible beneath falling layers of wool.

She was still tinged of lilies. He wanted to taste that scent, to open his mouth over her flesh, to run his tongue along her neck, to pull her to him and rub his face in her hair until she smelled of him too. He wanted to cover her, to conquer her. To bury himself in her. He wanted it with a ferocity that shocked him, so much so that Kit had to force himself not to move, not to break, every muscle in his body turned into a solid, rigid ache.

And Clarissa had grasped the change in him, he knew that she had. She stood frozen before him, wide-eyed, a doe poised at the brink of a snare. From the very edge of his perception, he saw her hand form a fist—small and ladylike, no match for anything he could do. The beast, the barbarous dragon, saw the fist and grinned.

No one would stay him. No one would think of it.

The bed was just behind her.

Deliberately, her fingers relaxed. Her lashes fell; when she looked back at him it was with a new expression, a suggestion of something like humor in the tilt of her lips.

No, not humor, he realized. Derision.

And then, only then, did he remember what she had said to him last night. How she had spoken so calmly and how it had staggered him: rape or seduction, as if that were all it could be.

His father had cuffed Kit once after some muttered insolence—from behind, the only time he had ever struck his son—and it had felt just like this, a reeling breathlessness that cut him in two, that left him winded and speechless until his wits returned.

She turned and crossed to the bed, sat down and leaned back on her hands, gazing up at him. The blanket slipped a little, revealing an ankle, the pale curve of her leg; she didn't tuck it up again. Her face never changed.

"Noon," he managed with a sneer of his own, and offered her a curt bow. It was only as he was turning to go that he noticed the new shadow etched along the wall behind her, simple letters scored fresh into the stone:

NO REGRETS.

# CHAPTER SEVEN

The Marquess of Langford had been mistaken about the weather. It was raining when Rue faced the council, raining so fiercely it thrummed a song into the pale blue and silver magnificence of the council's private chamber, music that rolled beneath every word spoken, that accented every gesture and every shared glance.

The windows here were tall, panes and panes of fine leaded glass that diffused rainlight and hazy gray shadows across the room, that shivered, ever so lightly, with echoing thunder. The hearth lay empty, and the warmth of three candelabras hardly served to penetrate the gloom. If Rue shifted her gaze from the men seated before her, she could view in the distance the hills she used to roam, soaked in wet green like fresh paint on a canvas. She could see the soft, black clouds hugging the earth.

Despite the weather, there would be guards patrolling the grounds, and the sky. They would not risk losing her again.

She had her own special chair in the chamber, set in clear solitude to face their line of thirteen. The men had a table to shield them, but Rue had only herself, her feet pressed to the

Afshar rug and her hands in her lap. She wore a new gown, nothing quite so ridiculous as the taffeta, but heavy white satin with lavender ribbons knotting the sleeves, and petal-pink roses embroidered lavishly over the stomacher and skirts—the gown of a virgin, of a sweet, modest damsel. It had come nestled in a box, along with slippers and an assortment of faerie-lace underthings, swathed in leaves of gold tissue so delicate they fluttered open with the mere passing of her hand. A guard, a stranger, had brought the box to the cell door. The marquess himself had not bothered to come again.

She had taken one look at the gown and sent it back to him. Rue knew a wedding frock when she saw it.

Twenty minutes later, wrapped in a sheet after the swift, stolen luxury of her bath—in a tin tub, with her knees up to her chin—the guard returned with the same gown and a note, which she read while the man stared down at the soap-slicked bathwater, slowly reddening.

The note said, *This, or nothing.*

Very well. If Christoff Langford desired that she look virginal for the council, she would. It needn't impede her own plans.

The frill of lace against her collarbone had been too heavily starched; it itched mercilessly. She had to keep reminding herself not to scratch at it.

The councilman seated in the precise center of the table seemed more aged than the rest, garbed in a waistcoat of dull mustard velvet and a wig of sausage curls. His jabot had been tied very tight, cutting into the skin of his neck. He kept glancing from Rue to a stack of papers before him, fingering the pages, scowling through a monocle.

She remembered him. Parrish Grady. He had scolded her

once to tears when she was nine for plucking a stray daisy by his garden house gate.

The marquess, Rue noticed, was not seated. He stood alone by a window in a corner with his hands clasped behind his back, watching the frosted slant of the rainfall. He had not turned when she entered the room.

He was wearing white, just as she was, formal silk breeches and stockings and a long-skirted coat worked in elaborate silver and indigo thread. Even his hair had been tamed, tied back into a queue. Against the fall of sky-blue curtains, against the dark-pearled clouds, he seemed nothing less than an extension of the chamber, of the manor itself, elegantly remote, unchanging, a cool wash of shadow and storm.

"For our records," intoned Mr. Grady, with a stern look down the table at a scribe, "you are one Clarissa Rue Hawthorne, born of Antonia Reine MacKenzie Hawthorne, now deceased."

Rue sat demurely silent.

"You will grant us the favor of a response," said Grady, peering up at her.

"I am," she said.

"You are the sole offspring of Antonia Reine."

"Yes."

"Aged twenty-six—"

"Pray, don't forget my father," interrupted Rue, pleasant.

The councillors gawked at her; someone's chair creaked.

"Avery Rhys Hawthorne, of Pembroke," she said. "Also deceased." Rue looked over at the scribe and smiled. "Shall I spell it for you?"

"Er, no." The man blinked at her, as if only just seeing her there. He was younger than the others, bespectacled, well-favored. There was a smudge of ink on his cuff. "That won't be necessary. My lady."

Christoff turned, silhouetted against rain and blue brocade.

"Clarissa Rue," said Grady, with calculated censure. "Also known as 'the Smoke Thief.'"

"Yes."

"You can Turn."

"Yes."

"Since what age?"

"Since the morning of my seventeenth birthday," she said.

"Seventeen." Grady ensured the scribe made a note of it, then went on. "And since that time, you have abused this sacred ability by stealing...One moment..." He scowled down at the papers, shuffling through them with blueveined hands.

"Allow me." Rue began to tick off her fingers. "The Monfield gems. The Voroshilov emerald. The Steiff necklace—extraordinary jade. Princess Caroline of York's blue pearl choker and ear clips. Lady Wetherby's nineteen-carat yellow topaz brooch, shaped as a songbird. Lord Cranston's twelve-carat ruby stick pin. The Earl of Harrogate's starsapphire jabot pin. How far back shall I go for you? The Baroness Shaw's green garnet and diamond brooch; it was a dragonfly with amber eyes, terribly clever. The Greumach tiara. The Aberdeen tiara. Oh—and once a delightful little portrait by Bordone. The Prince of Wales really wasn't displaying it to advantage. I doubt he even missed it."

A crack of sudden lightning seared the chamber, blinding. Thunder settled into the seams of wood and glass.

Grady's voice rose over the dying rumble. "And in this capacity, you also stole the heart of the tribe. You stole *Herte*."

"No," said Rue, with every evidence of regret. "I did not."

Parrish Grady dropped his monocle. "*What* did you say?"

She leaned forward in her chair, holding the man's eyes, allowing at last a measure of the anger that burned inside her to rise. Kidnapped, imprisoned, hauled before these men like a disobedient child expected to meekly take its punishment; her wrath hardened in her veins, transformed into a black well of resolve.

"I said, I did not steal your diamond. But I know who did. And I would be delighted to take you to him." She glanced once more at Christoff, now watching her openly with a new tension to his mouth, as if he knew already what she was about to say.

"For a price," she finished, and relaxed back into the chair. Rue crossed her legs, let her left foot swing lazily in the air and smiled again, this time directly at the marquess.

She could count the seconds it took them to collectively fathom her. Three, two, one—

"How *dare* you!" erupted Grady, standing. "Impudent chit! You would have the nerve—"

"Wait, wait," another was saying, his hand on Grady's arm. "Let us—"

"—dare to threaten this council—"

"—she said she knows—"

"—*someone* took it—"

"—has it hidden—"

"—just reason with—"

"—allow her to—"

The tribe's fearsome council were all on their feet now, arguing, a few beginning to shout. But Rue never took her gaze from Christoff, who remained apart and silent, examining her from under his lashes. When someone began to pound the tabletop he finally moved, a predator unfolding from its contemplation of a meal. He stalked to the end of the table and lifted it easily up into the air, letting it slam back to the rugs with a muffled *bang*. It loosed all the papers and the scribe's cloisonné ink pot, which hit the floor and wobbled into a half circle, ending up near Rue's feet. Several of the men jumped back.

"Hold your tongues and let her speak."

The council stood dumbstruck. The ink from the pot began to bleed across the rug. Rue tapped it with her slipper to send it rolling again.

"You were saying?" Christoff prompted her, courteous.

"It's quite simple." She matched his tone. "I lead you to the runner who stole *Herte*—and it *was* another runner— and in return you let me free. No imprisonment, no marriage. None of you, none of the tribe, ever troubles me again."

"Impossible," snapped Grady. "You cannot possibly think we would agree to such a thing."

"Then farewell, diamond."

"Now, see here—"

"Quiet," barked the marquess, and to her hidden surprise Grady heeded him, retreating back into his seat with pale-knuckled fury. The other twelve men followed. Most seemed stunned, ending up in chairs no longer near the table. Two or three inched forward again, but that was all.

Rue kept her heels hard against the rug, resisting every urge to leap up, to flee. She was cold despite the heat of the candelabras, despite her outer calm. She was cold inside unto freezing and could only hope that the icy smile she kept in place hid it well enough to fool them all. For days she had anticipated this moment, had planned it out in her head, imagining every sort of reaction from the council, how she'd counter each objection. She had but one card to play, just this one; without it she was truly as powerless as they had thought. She needed all her resources to make it work.

But she did not think she was fooling Christoff. Not with that narrowed green look he sent her.

"And who is this other runner?"

Rue allowed her smile to grow into a smirk.

"It's a trick," said a red-haired man flatly. "There's no other runner. We've gone over the lists, my lord. She's the only one."

Christoff inclined his head. "Rufus has a point," he said, very reasonable. "No one else is missing, save you."

"You're mistaken."

"We're not mistaken," insisted the red-haired man. "You're working with a human, that's all it is."

"No."

"Tell us the name of the runner, then. Just his name."

Rue lowered her eyes. The rain whispered and rolled around them.

"Force her," said Parrish Grady in a thin, strained voice. "Force her, Lord Langford, or we will."

"She is under my protection," Christoff said at once, shifting to brace an arm against the back of her chair. "Need I remind anyone of that? Please, step forward if you harbor even an ounce of uncertainty. There is nothing I enjoy more than clarity."

No one came forward. No one even rose from his seat. From the edge of her vision the marquess was all white and glimmer, like a shaft of candescent sun dividing the gray dusk of the room.

Rue lifted her face. "The *drákon* you want has been feed-ing off my reputation for some while. I know where he travels, I know who he knows. I know how he thinks. He tends to steal smaller things, less noticeable things. He prefers—a darker sort of lifestyle than I. But he is out there, I promise you. He has *Herte*. And you won't find him without me."

"I believe her," said the scribe. Everyone turned to him, and he flushed. "Why would she lie? When the truth can be proven?"

"Why, indeed," murmured the marquess with a slow, burning look down at her.

"If you don't agree to my offer," Rue said bluntly, "I'll go to my grave with the secret, I swear it. You'll have me, but you'll never have your diamond again. And know this as well: I won't stay here willingly, no matter what you decide."

Kit never dropped his gaze. He stared at her as if to see through her, as if he could rouse the truth from her with just the will of his mind, his eyes feral and pale, a strand of golden hair just brushing the high, pristine folds of his cravat.

"Men have died for less than this," said a councilman at the end of the table, almost incredulous. Rue tore her gaze from Kit's.

"Yes. But none of them held the key to your precious bauble, did they?"

She stood, arranging the white-and-rose skirts as serenely as if she were at a *fête champêtre* and not in mortal judgment of her life. "Perhaps you'd like to consider my proposal." Rue offered a small curtsy to the council, and then a deeper one to the marquess. "Shall we say—until four o'clock?"

She drew away from them all, one step, another, moving toward the carved and gilded doors where the guards who had escorted her to the chamber stood watching. Behind her came only the ballad of the rainfall striking glass and hills and vales; she walked forward as if she had the full right to do so, and the men at the door actually looked at her, actually began to budge—

"A moment, Miss Hawthorne," said the marquess.

Rue paused and turned again, smooth-faced, her stomach in knots.

"I imagine we can settle this now." He gave a gracious nod to the council. "Gentlemen, I suggest a compromise. Allow Clarissa Hawthorne and me to return to London for a period of time—say, a week. We hunt the other runner. If we find him, and the diamond, Miss Hawthorne gets her wish. If not, she returns to Darkfrith and takes her rightful place among the tribe."

"A week isn't long enough," she said sharply.

"A fortnight."

"That's hardly even—"

"No," said Grady at the same instant, "what are you about? We can't let her—"

"Pardon me," said Christoff, with his terrible, gentle smile, "I don't believe you're thinking this through. We require *Herte*. We require the runner. I'm certain Miss Hawthorne will agree to keep the existence of the tribe a strict secret, should she return to her former life." He cocked a brow at her and Rue quickly nodded. "But we have no such guarantee from this other fellow. He's a rogue threat."

"But why use *her*?" demanded one of the men. "We can keep her here and hunt the runner ourselves."

"By all means," retorted Rue. "Do it, if you think you can. Comb the largest city in the kingdom for one remarkably sly thief. Find him in the alleys you don't know, in the gamehells and gin houses you've never heard of. Find him before he sells *Herte*, before it's recut into a series of marvelous little gemstones, its fire destroyed. No doubt all the rage next year will be tiny violet diamonds for ladies' hats and snuffboxes."

"He wouldn't . . . he'd never. . . ."

"Of course he would," said Rue. "I would."

Oh, heavens, she knew what she risked. This was Darkfrith, and the *drákon* followed their own laws, far more ancient and ruthless than anything English society could conjure. If they sensed her fear she'd never leave that miserable cell again. She would stay trapped in marriage, in body, in heart. Even if days from now, years from now, they allowed her out into the open, she'd still be bound to a man who did not love her. And every time she looked at him it was as if some slender thread of her self came undone; she saw Christoff and in him all her old dreams, so vain and juvenile they could make her weep.

But she was not that girl. Not any longer.

Rue focused on the windows. She imagined the rain, she breathed the rain, cool and constant and strong.

Her hands began to tremble. She hid them in the folds of her skirts.

The marquess was facing Grady, but she knew his next words were addressed to her. "To be clear: you would trade this runner's liberty for your own?"

"Without hesitation."

"And you are aware of the consequences of lying to us, Miss Hawthorne? That if we discover there is no other runner, that you have taken *Herte,* the repercussions would be most . . . unpleasant?"

"Yes," she said past stiff lips.

"Very well. Gentlemen, a vote, if you please."

If she had doubted him before, if she had ever imagined that the Marquess of Langford did not hold power over the tribe and all the men in this room, Rue had no doubts now.

No one else spoke; they exchanged glances, most skeptical, a few still incensed. But they were considering what she had said. They were weighing it, measuring their dogma and creed against one outlawed woman and the lord who stood behind her. And their diamond, an icon sparkling just beyond their grasp.

The scribe had gathered his quill and sheets of paper and was staring down at them blankly.

Grady rubbed his chin. "If—*if*—we do this thing, we shall require more men than just you to accompany her, Lord Langford."

"More men will spook the thief."

"A company of a dozen or so will do."

"No," said Kit.

"Your guard, at least."

"No."

"My lord—"

"Just us. Just her and me."

"Five men," said Rue. She turned to Kit. "You'll need servants. It would look odd without them."

"Five," agreed the marquess, after a moment. "And fourteen days."

"Very well," said Parrish Grady. The rest of the council seemed to shrink smaller in their chairs, settling in, releasing pent-up sighs. Grady alone remained adamantly taut; he drummed his knuckles against the table before him. "And at the end of that fourteenth day, Mistress Hawthorne, be most assured that there shall be no further bargains."

Rue tipped her head and curtsied a third time, sinking so deep as to touch her knee to the floor.

"Very pretty," observed Christoff under his breath, but she did not glance up at him again.

---

He couldn't help but watch her leave the chamber. He tried not to gape at her; he had been trying the entire time not to gape, but the runner, Clarissa Hawthorne, drew his gaze like the only dab of color in a bleakly silvered day, and Nick Beaton found himself drifting back to her every time his attention wandered. Which was too often.

There was something about her, some ineffable quality beyond the soft glint of her lower lip, or the single chocolate lock of hair that escaped her coiffure to her shoulder, something even in the way she cupped her hands in her lap, her wrists bent, feminine and slight. When she spoke...when the light hit her just so, when the wind sighed and she glanced up at him, through him, with those incredible brown eyes...

He'd lost minutes. He'd had to sort through the echoes of words in his mind to scrawl them out on paper.

Nicholas was a dutiful man. He'd been scribe for the council for these three years, the same assignment his father had held before him, and his father's father, and he had never taken his office lightly. Yet in his distraction his thumb had smudged the final sentence of the official meeting: the scripted *e* in *vote* had a tail to it now, drawn long and plumy across the page. He frowned at his thumb, rubbing the black smear by his nail until it faded against the whorls of his skin.

He had ceased scribing after that. By their laws, the Alpha could quash a vote but not call for one, and all the men knew it—even if the girl did not.

But she was gone now. Nick rose and found his ink pot, salvaging what was left inside of the precious liquid. He took off his spectacles, wiped them clean on the sleeve of his shirt, sharpened and dipped his quill, blotted, and glanced up at the marquess.

Christoff Langford was standing with his arms crossed, watching the footmen stationed beyond the doors swing them gradually closed. The runner's footsteps down the hallway were soft, nearly silent, dimming quickly into the rhythm of the storm. It was much easier to follow the guards' staccato clip.

But they would wait, all of them, until they were certain she could not overhear.

The marquess began to shrug out of his old-fashioned coat, draping it across the chair where Clarissa had sat.

"Well?" said Grady.

Langford took the seat, lounging back with informal ease. "A fortnight will motivate her, I imagine."

"You actually believe you can control her in London?"

"She won't run again. She won't think she has reason to." He lifted a sleeve of the coat crushed behind him, examined the tracery of thread that made the cuff glitter. "Whatever else happens, she'll be working to find *Herte*. It's what you wanted."

"And at the end of your fortnight, my lord? She recovers the diamond—or simply produces it—we capture this fantastical other runner. . . ." Grady shook his head. "Your 'compromise' may have tempered her for now. But you know we'll never leave her there."

Lord Langford sent him a half-lidded look that would have made Nick's blood run cold, but Councilman Grady only stiffened in his chair.

"At the end of the fortnight, sir, with or without the runner *or* the diamond, Rue Hawthorne will be returning to Darkfrith, as my bride." Langford's fingers made a short, hard tattoo against the arm of the chair; he slanted his look to Nick. "Feel free to write that down."

# CHAPTER EIGHT

She wanted to go to the orchard cottage. He'd received the request by one of the guards while still trapped in the council's meeting. He thought briefly of refusing her, but she'd left in a fair humor and he didn't want to risk souring what was left of his plans. Kit granted her wish, sent along two extra men and the polite warning that he'd join her very soon.

Yet soon wasn't enough. The council jabbered on with their notes and ponderous motions as he stared out the windows and watched her stride through the rain across the rear courtyard and then the lawn: no cape, no cap or shawl, just her hair unraveling and his mother's white wedding dress, its train of ruffles flattening the grass behind her. She was flanked by four men. Kit counted nine more at her periphery, drifting along as if she towed them all with long, relentless ropes.

Just before she vanished from his view, someone new detached from the woods, a woman in a red hooded cloak. He recognized her gait before she reached the first guard, a deliberate saunter that used to fill him with an almost unbearable hotness; Kit had never before realized how practiced it was, Melanie's walk, how coy and certain, just like her glances.

She'd waited for years. She'd waited and waited, even after he told her not to, even after he had made it clear to her—painfully clear—that they were not going to wed.

It had enraged his father. Melanie had been indisputably the Alpha female, and the fact of their betrothal was always widely assumed. But he'd never loved her. He'd never really even liked her, beyond the welcome relief her body offered his. Even still, Kit hadn't fully known why he kept refusing her. He only knew that it sent his father into apoplexy and made Melanie's claws doubly sharp.

She'd surrendered three years ago, well after his father had died, and married the silversmith's son. She must have finally realized that without the old marquess, Kit would never be coerced.

Now he knew why he'd denied her. Now he knew.

Rue stopped and turned, apparently waiting for Mel to catch up. They stood facing each other in the last tamed space before the meadows, one fair, one beautiful dark. He leaned forward with a new intensity. He couldn't imagine what they had to say to each other, but he knew Mel well enough. If she went to all the trouble of lying in wait, it wouldn't be for naught. If she tried to hurt Rue, if she harmed her in any way—

The rain shifted, pelting the glass. He was reaching for the lever to raise the sash when, without warning, Rue's arm slashed up. She had Melanie by the throat, stepping forward and actually lifting the other woman from the grass with one hand. He caught a flash of preternatural gold eyes—another Gift; only a very few of the *drákon* displayed such an ability—and Melanie had clutched both hands against

Rue's, struggling, kicking her feet in a wild froth of cloak and skirts.

None of the men intervened. Rue dropped Mel to the wet ground and walked away from her, rounding the corner of the green without looking back.

Kit released the lever. A ritual challenge, an undeniable victory; within hours everyone in the shire would know that Rue Hawthorne was, without question, the new Alpha. All in all, he decided, he couldn't have arranged it better himself.

There were cobwebs in the eaves. They shouldn't have bothered her as much as they did, but Rue kept glancing up to find more of them, tattered specters draped in the corners of her childhood home, dangling from doorways, floating above curtains, stretched like open fingers between the old geranium pot on the kitchen sill and a small china figurine of a lamb, its tail in the air.

The tin oval was just where she had last seen it, hanging on the wall by its ribbon, feathered with dust, spotted with age.

Rue did not mind the dust; according to Quentin, one of her guards, the cottage had been vacant since Antonia died. But the empty cobwebs . . .

Even the spiders were gone. Only ghosts lingered here.

She turned away from the tin mirror; she didn't want to see herself in it.

Someone had taken away the needlepoint chairs, but the walnut floor, the gingham valances, even the quilts on the beds—all that was the same, just the same as the day she had left.

How well her heart knew this place. It hadn't been all

misery and persecution, certainly not here in her mother's house. Within these plain, strong walls she had known love, the scent of vanilla pudding on the stove, games of draughts, vases of wildflowers, larksong, laughter, hugs. . . .

After her official death, Clarissa Rue had crept back twice for Antonia. When the pain and the confusion of that birthday morning had cleared from her mind, when she had found her feet and a single cramped room in a boarding-house in Wapping, she had returned to Darkfrith to beg her mother to come to London. But Antonia was ever wise; after the joy of their reunion she ultimately refused to go, knowing they could not both safely vanish from the tribe. Rue had spent the night arguing with her about it, lying with her on the bed, their heads together on the pillows, until her voice went hoarse and the sky grew striped with dawn. Antonia never wavered. They both wept their good-byes.

A half year later, Rue tried again. But by then the consumption had won. All she could find of her mother was a simple marker in the shire's cemetery, farther down the hill than most, the last stone in a row that ended with Antonia, Rue's grandfather, her grandmother. She'd left gentians on the three graves.

Water was making a slow trickle through a cracked pane in her old bedroom window, slinking down the glass to form a pool on the sill. Rue touched her fingers to the fracture, looking out at the lush, bent grass and rows of storm-drenched trees.

Quentin and the other three guards remained in the parlor. She'd asked to be alone in here. There was nowhere to go, after all. Even in the orchard she counted six new men looking back at her, hunched against the weather.

It was a wonder they'd let her out at all. She hoped it was a positive sign.

The second plank down the hall from her door had a loose joint and a squeak; she heard that, and only that—he was as hushed as the breeze otherwise. She turned her head without looking at him, speaking to the floor.

"When do we leave for London?"

The marquess entered the room, bringing with him the darker scent of rain mixed with sandalwood. "After supper."

She closed her eyes a moment, relief and something more, bittersweet, waking through her.

"Are you weary?" he asked indifferently. "We could wait a day, if you like."

"No." She wasn't enamored of the thought of climbing back into that carriage for another long ride, but better to get it over with. Better to move on, out of Darkfrith, before any one of them had occasion to change their minds. "After supper is fine," she said aloud.

"While the trail is yet hot," Christoff said, still neutral.

"Quite."

"Was this your room?" He walked forward, his cloak a sinuous flare against the faded quilt and bed hangings.

"Yes."

"It seems pleasant."

"It was."

He approached the window. The raindrops beading his shoulders began to slink down the ebony folds of the cloak, spattering her skirts.

But the wedding frock was already ruined. There had never been a road or even a lane to the old cottage, only the broken hint of a dirt path, choked with bindweed and lichen. The storm had rendered the length of it into mud that had sucked at her every step.

"Rue," said Christoff abruptly. "For the herb, or the emotion?"

"For the flower."

"Of course." His lips turned up. "Late-blooming." When she didn't respond he touched the cracked pane just as she had, his hand a shadow against the glass. "I wonder if you might satisfy my curiosity on something."

"Yes?"

"What did Melanie say to you, back there on the lawn?"

She wasn't astonished that he knew; perhaps he'd been watching. Perhaps he only heard of it from the guard. "She inquired if I was still a filthy spy. I, in turn, inquired if she was still a whore. There seemed to be no point in further conversation after that."

"So I saw."

"Oh." She lowered her gaze to a pale rose on her skirts, careful threads fashioning a careful pink bloom, a budding of mint-green leaves so pretty and perfect they reminded her of sugar candies.

"Will you tell me something else?"

She nodded without lifting her head.

"Why did you feign your death? Why did you run?"

Rue turned her eyes to the little pool on the sill, and then to her watchers, stationed amid the trees. The Romans had tilled the soil for apples and chestnuts and pears, but Darkfrith had spent centuries creeping back to herself. Beyond this grove, beyond the men, the formal lines of the orchard tapered into forest, a dense, towering darkness that enclosed the village, alive with streams, rich with mist and bracken and fragrant layers of leaves. For some reason, Rue remembered the forest more clearly than anything else. More clearly even than this house, or the man standing beside her.

The marquess didn't ask again, only waited with the rain and the sandalwood and quiet all around.

"Because of you," she said finally. When he didn't respond she chanced a sidelong glance at him. He was studying her, not shocked, merely quizzical, the planes of his face underlit with storm. She gathered her nerve. "I left because I did not wish to be wed to you."

His smile returned. "Good gracious, was I that insufferable?"

"I . . . fancied myself in love with you."

"Ah," he said, and her gaze slid from his.

"Asinine, of course. I didn't know you. You didn't know me—you never even noticed me. But I knew what it meant, that I could Turn. And even as a girl, I didn't want you like that."

He faced the window again, tracing the zigzag splinter shining in the pane. "Like what?"

"Forced. Either of us, forced."

He let his hand fall, looking out at the trees. Through the veiled light she stole a longer moment of him: the strong profile, the firm lips, his hair very damp, careless strands that clung to his cheekbone with the deeper, honeyed glint of ale.

"All that effort," he mused, "merely to avoid me. How gratifying."

He did not sound gratified. He sounded sardonic, as though she had told him something so small and unimportant he'd already half-forgotten it. And it hurt, more than she thought it would. "It wasn't only you, Lord Langford. It was this place, these people. This life. I want nothing to do with it."

"It's a bit late for that, Rue. Whether you like it or not, we are your blood."

"*Half* my blood."

"Aye," agreed the marquess, sober. "Although 'twould seem you've gotten the better half by far. All beauty, none of the beast."

She blinked at that, and crossed her arms.

"How charming! Had you planned that for long?"

"Only since this morning." He shrugged, unabashed. "I'll do better in London."

"Please, don't bother."

"I'm afraid I can't help myself. I'm charming by nature." And he looked back at her now in utter and wicked innocence, snaring her in a world of sharp, splendid green.

She lost her breath. She lost the room, and the moment. She thought of telling him more, of how he had been the single star of her girlhood, of how she had watched him steal the hearts of all the other maidens of the shire, giddy geese knocked over like lawn pins with just the flicker of his glance, of how she had waited—and waited—for her own chance to tell him *no,* meaning *yes* . . . but that day had never come.

"I'm sure it's won you all manner of toadeaters," Rue said instead.

"It serves a purpose." Kit jerked his chin at the window. "You seem to have a few toadies of your own."

She hesitated. "Those aren't your men?"

"No, mouse. I believe they're yours."

In the trees, in the rain, the *drákon* stood motionless, faces she couldn't quite make out, sopped in water, smeared with leaves. There were more of them now, ten—eleven. Only standing. Only staring.

"Our marriage would protect you," Christoff said softly.

Rue drew away from the glass. "I don't believe I care to

wait until supper to depart, Lord Langford. I'd rather leave here at once."

He made a bow. "Come with me," was all he said, and in a sweep of black and honey gold left the chamber. She shot another glance out the window, then walked after him.

He didn't take her to the carriage house. He felt the moment she realized they weren't headed there, the break in her pace that dragged, for a scant second, at his arm under her hand. Yet when he looked at her she held her composure, everything sweet and docile, as if they were enjoying nothing more than a balmy evening stroll around the manor grounds.

She'd refused his cloak. Rain glistened on her skin, pulled her hair into heavy locks. Her breath formed wisps of frost; she was a goddess washed in cold spring.

As they walked up the drive, faces began to appear in Chasen's windows, following her, him, the guard. He knew they were watched; they would always be watched here, and he wondered if she had guessed that much as well. Probably.

London began to seem somewhat more palatable.

The pair of hounds from the stables loped around the corner of the rose garden. The larger one spotted them, ran panting and grinning across the lawn to leap at Kit with muddy enthusiasm. He shoved it aside, then rubbed its ears; the dog bounced free and danced a circle around them both, smacking them with its tail. With an air of experience, Rue snapped two fingers. The hound responded with another leap, but she caught its front paws with both hands, staggering back a step.

It gave a joyful yip. In the distance the other dog answered, not coming near.

"Yours?" she asked as it writhed in her grip, trying to lick her wrists.

"Somewhat." He pushed it from her. "Go on! Go home."

The hound gave a few more barks, prancing back and forth between them, then hared off again toward its companion, kicking up water and sod.

"I've never seen dogs at Chasen," she said, watching them vanish into a hazy coppice of willows.

"No. There's just the two."

They were, in fact, the first. The *drákon* did not mix well with other animals, in the same way that lions did not mix with lambs. There were wild birds in the trees, and mice tucked away in barns, but that was very nearly all. Darkfrith had no squirrels, no hedgehogs, no foxes or rabbits. No cats or cows or chickens or pigs. An occasional deer braved the woods for the abundant green, flitting through like ghosts before vanishing to safer grounds. The tribe kept horses because they had to, and a single flock of sheep in the hills for appearances—but the sheep had to be herded by the children. They panicked too easily when adults wandered near.

Twelve years ago his father had opened the vein of silver that marbled through the east valley. Yet by force of nature, most of the *drákon* were farmers. They traded for their meat.

Rue sent him a glance that might have held surprise. "Why are they here?"

"Lost, I suppose. Or feral. Or just dumb."

"But why are they *here*?"

"They persist in staying," he said, shaking the mud from his hands. "Rather like ill-mannered relations."

"And you let them." Her voice shaded into emphasis, not quite a question. Her sudden intensity, her velvet brown gaze; he very nearly felt uncomfortable, held in that look. Kit decided to turn the situation around.

"Would you love me again if I said yes?"

She tilted her head, examining him. "I'm merely attempting to ascertain your level of gullibility. In my business it's called 'sizing the mark.'"

"And?"

"And..." She looked down at her own palms, wiped them on the sodden gown, and trudged on. "I suspect that you're a very good actor, my lord."

He laughed, catching up. "That *was* my dog."

"Really. What's its name?"

They were at the double doors to the manor. Before he could reply they opened; they were enveloped in a rush of tepid air and prismatic light from the rock-crystal chandelier. He gestured for her to go first, then followed, both of them trailing muck along the glossy white floor.

The footmen bowed themselves into shadow but Kit dismissed them anyway, if not the guards, still trailing faithfully behind—the council wouldn't be quite that accommodating. When he offered his hand Rue accepted it, pretending, as he did, not to notice the many figures lingering along the halls. At the foot of the grand staircase he paused to unfasten his cloak, draping the mess of it across the banister. Rue only lifted her hand over it as she passed, her fingers skimming the brass as they climbed.

The longcase clock in the drawing room struck the hour, followed a half beat later by the bracket clock in the music room, and then another, and another, a fair cacophony of chimes that layered song over song throughout the manor, until the last one died into tinkling silence.

Four o'clock.

"The dog's name is Henry," Kit said.

Her tranquil expression did not change. "You named a female dog Henry?"

"Henrika," he amended, with hardly a pause. "I believe there's some German on her father's side."

Rue pressed her lips together, fighting her smile, fixing her eyes on the stairs instead of the marquess's droll, laughing look. She felt his hand turn over in hers; he gave her fingers a quick squeeze.

Oh, danger. Already it was happening, the thing she most feared: his smile, his attentions, even the smooth motion of his body next to hers, sending her senses into a spin. It would be far too easy to fall into his thrall, to believe there might be sincerity beneath his practiced facade, that he might actually care what she thought or felt or...

But he didn't. He was Alpha, that was all it was. The Marquess of Langford was a creature of instinct as surely as she; he was driven by that and nothing more. She would not make the mistake of dreaming it could ever be anything more.

*A fortnight*, she thought firmly. *A fortnight, and it's done.*

He led her to a door, not one of the elaborate paneled ones of the parlors or bedchambers but a servants' door, small and inconspicuous, with a corkscrew of stairs rising steeply above.

"Where are we going?" she asked, not entering.

"You'll see."

"I'd prefer to know first."

"Don't you trust me?"

"No."

"Well, it's not the Dead Room," he said, unruffled. "Isn't that enough for the moment?"

And it was. After climbing and climbing they emerged to a gently sloping rooftop: the southern edge of the family wing, with the glass Adam dome arching above the tiles, and eight soot-stained chimney tops marking a massive square around it, two of them breathing woodsmoke.

Perhaps the storm had lightened, or the dome shielded them from the worst of the winds, but the rain was softened to a drizzle, almost caressing. The clouds rolled above them in deep shifting hues of midnight and purple and coal.

Rue took a cautious step out onto the tiles, pushing a lock of hair from her eyes. "I thought we were leaving for London."

"Indeed."

She looked at him and he at her, his brows slightly raised, his mouth holding a faint, expectant curve.

"No," she said, and gave a startled laugh.

"Why not?"

"You're mad!" She glanced behind them to the guards, still crowded on the stairs, and then back at him.

"It's a nine-day ride by carriage," Christoff said. "Assuming that this time you'd prefer to travel at a more human pace. Nine days of travel leaves only five of your fortnight in London."

"The fortnight doesn't begin until we're there!" she said, outraged.

"Sorry." His smile deepened. "The council's decreed otherwise."

"That is not—"

"Nine days in the carriage, or, if we leave now..." He squinted up at the sky. "I expect we'll be there in about... six hours. Give or take. I've never done it before, of course, but I'm sure we'll discover the way."

Like her, he still wore his wedding clothes, but without the cloak or even his coat he was becoming rapidly sprinkled with raindrops. No powder, no wig or gloves; the marquess grinned at her, unrepentant, as the linen of his shirt turned translucent, sculpting his body in fine pale lines.

Rue clutched her skirts, inching over to the nearest chimney, and then to the watery curve of the dome. But there were no hidden listeners, only the unending trickle of rain against the wet bricks. "Is this a trick? Some new device of the council?"

"No, mouse. It is my own device. The council doesn't know."

"It's daylight!"

"It won't be by the time we get there."

"Lovely! We simply arrive in London, two everyday *dragons*—"

"Or," he said mildly, "two perfectly unclad people." He spread his hands, his hair loosened gold, his eyes clever green, his smile growing wider. "Come now. Do you mean for me to believe that you don't have some sort of provisional shelter in the city? A professional such as yourself, a master thief, without emergency recourse?"

"If I did, I wouldn't show it to you!"

"Very well. We'll go to Far Perch. I know a hidden way in. You can wear something of the housekeeper's."

She shook her head, speechless—but against her will she had a sudden vision of what it would be like, flying with him in the cold, blue brilliance of sunlight, no longer enemies. Soaring, side by side.

He came to her lightly, easily, as if the tiles were not both pitched and slick with water. Cordially, like a lover's greeting, Kit tipped his head to hers and put his lips to her ear.

"Who was it who said to me, 'Break their rules'?"

Before she could respond, he brushed a kiss across her cheek, so fleet and cool she hardly felt it, then backed away, tugging at his cravat.

"Quentin," he said, never taking his eyes from her, "kindly inform the council that Mistress Hawthorne and I are leaving posthaste for London."

The first two guards in the stairwell emerged from their darkness, one behind the other. "My lord?"

"We shall see you there."

"But, sir, you cannot—"

"Quentin," said Christoff in a different voice, chilled and very soft.

The guard faltered, one hand spread against the open door, then bowed. "As you wish, Lord Langford."

"Thank you. My lady?"

The marquess lifted his palm to her, a man held in wind-tousled grace, waiting; still as the eye of a tempest was still, inexorable force only momentarily at bay. The heels of his shoes rested at the very, very edge of the rooftop. If the wind changed, if he lost his balance—

Beyond him were only trees and sky, the dark-misted storm sweeping emerald hills up to heaven.

"You are mad," Rue said again, but she found herself moving toward him. His fingers closed over hers; he raised her hand to his mouth and held it there, warming her skin with his.

"I prefer the word *dashing*."

She huffed a breath, almost a laugh.

"Oh, and one more thing." Above their locked fingers he granted her a new smile, this one slow and blazingly sensual. "Little brown-haired girl . . . I *did* notice you."

He Turned to smoke. She watched his clothing collapse to the tiles, silk and velvet soaked instantly in puddles. One shoe teetered a moment before tumbling, end over end, from the roof. Rue looked once more at the men behind her, then up to the violet-swirled clouds. She stepped away from

Chasen's edge and Turned as well, for the second time in her life following Kit Langford away from the earth.

She had grown up watching the men of the tribe flying across the starry skies, or streaking home at the brink of day, after the moon and before the sun, when they swept like zephyrs along the heavens, the wind a distant hiss against their wings. Christoff was so often among them; she'd made it a game to pinpoint him amid their numbers, and so Rue knew his patterns, the scythe elegance of his wingspan, the dark gleam of his scales, the way he'd speed high and then diminish into a dive, as hawks did, a hunter who could spear his prey with the delicacy of a single deadly talon.

He was waiting for her in the clouds. He was dragon already, stirring great plumes of gray with his wings, burnished with the rain that had yet to fall. She Turned too, disliking at once the clammy cold, and without looking to him rose above the worst of it, punching a hole to open air at the top of a billowing black cloud, finding the sky a sheer sapphire and wisps of paler vapor above, like threadbare sheets on an upside-down bed.

She knew only west; she knew the direction of the sun. With mist still trailing the tips of his wings, Christoff swept into a tight spiral around her, never clipping her even as she stretched her neck and leapt forward to avoid him. He ended up in front, tossing a look back at her, strength and beauty in a long, twisting coil of metallic color. She thought he might have grinned. Then he tilted to the right, a slow coasting that opened his wings to their limits, pulling ahead. She mirrored him, finding the same channel of wind to carry her.

Rue was less skilled than he in this form, there could be

no denying it. She could count the number of times she'd Turned to dragon on a single hand; the crowded city did not make for safe practice. But Kit flew as if an angel had drawn a shining bright line from Darkfrith to the horizon, to London, pressed between the clouds, finding new currents when the old ones veered off, floating with no apparent effort often just beside her, his eyes narrowed, his body lean and straight.

It felt . . . exhilarating. Even with him there, it felt like liberty, like she need never touch the ground again.

The sun began to set and the entire sky kindled to flame, suspending them in wild pink and cherry and orange, colors so burning and luminous they almost hurt to behold. Every stroke of her wings shifted hues, deepening the heavens, and when the first of the stars sparked overhead—a bouquet of them, all at once—all that was left of the day was a band of intense maroon melting like hot sand into the edge of the world.

In the dark he glimmered with starlight. When they altered directions the swelling rush of the wind filled her ears, but when they glided, when they rode the wings of the air itself, she heard only *him*. The whispered resonance of his flight, respiration, heartbeat. Quiet. As if the cosmos had never held anyone but them, as if above and below, in all the black glittering solitude of the universe, there would never be anyone else but them.

And they glided. In time the clouds began to disperse. No longer heavy with rain, they scattered into furrows, revealing the invisible tides that ebbed and pushed around them. But they flew very high, and the ground was very far; Rue saw only a sprinkling of towns, uneven splotches of light that spread faint, spidery arms into the night. A flock of geese, much slower, pointing the way south. And once the alabaster reflection of the ocean, pressed up in a ragged curve to the shore.

Kit veered away from it, and she followed.

Despite the smooth air, or perhaps because of it, Rue found her thoughts drifting, her eyelids growing heavy. She realized drowsily that she should have taken supper, that with her stomach empty and her energy flagging even the hastiest of meals would have been better than none. She didn't know how far they were from London yet. She didn't recognize anything on the blank nothing of the ground. What a strange thing, to have to guess the map of the earth. It seemed astonishing that she could even venture to try, aloft here in the soft, soft silence. . . .

She came awake with a hard bump to her chin, her teeth snapping closed, her feet making brief contact with something warm and firm beneath her. Kit—there and gone as Rue found herself in a roll; she tucked her wings in and flung them out again to control it, swooping upward until she was steady once more, her heart racing.

Kit was pacing her, hanging close. The look he gave her now was shadowed with the rising moon, but its warning was clear enough.

She needed to stop. She needed to eat, and to rest. She didn't care if they landed in a field or a cave or in bloody Covent Garden, she could not go on. Rue began a downward drift, glancing back at him to see if he understood. He plunged after her, darting swiftly below, forcing her to rise or risk entangling with him once more. She hitched to the left, irritated, but he stuck with her, flicking her with his tail when she tried to descend again.

They could not speak as dragons, not even the common whiffs and growls of the lower beasts. Silence was the price of their splendor; it was said that even the ancient Gifts required sacrifice. Too often she'd heard the village elders weave their excuses, that the *drákon* didn't need words, that in the glory of the sky their minds and wills flowed as one. It was certainly true that she knew what Christoff was demanding as he pushed at her, but Rue wished, wholeheartedly, that she could tell him precisely what she thought of him in this moment.

She bared her teeth at him. He pressed heavily to the right, crowding her until she moved just to get out of his way—and then she saw what he did, spilling into view not three leagues ahead: a winking gem of dull yellow light, spreading wider and wider, sending up heat and human scent in fat rippling waves.

She picked out roads, a jagged skyline, the rising roar of a city in full motion.

London.

Home at last.

# CHAPTER NINE

His hidden way into Far Perch turned out to be through the wooden slats of a fanciful bronze-topped cupola, with barely room enough inside of it for the two of them to stand. The only reason Rue took her shape there was because she knew if she didn't, he'd harass her until she gave in.

"Brava," Christoff whispered as she found herself pressed against a scratchy oak wall. What light pushed through the slats fell in pale stripes across them both, painting their bare skin. He shifted his feet and bent to tug at the trapdoor to the stairs, his elbow bumping her thigh. The door creaked open; there was absolutely no illumination below.

"This is your plan?" Rue hissed, pulling her hair forward over her shoulders, but he didn't even glance at her body.

"Take my hand," he said. "I'll guide you."

"I can find the way."

"Suit yourself." He began to descend. Rue watched him vanish, a tiger dropping into shadows. She looked back at the slats, exactly level with her eyes. Her body ached, and her lingering vexation with the marquess was not helped by the fact that she was hungry and naked in the dank, cramped peak of his stylish mansion. She was tired, but not so tired that she could not imagine what lay beyond the artfully tidy streets of Grosvenor Square.

"Rue." Christoff's head reappeared, his shoulders. He propped his arms along the outline of the hole in the floor and regarded her with a hooded look. "What, my love? Feeling shy?" Beneath the easy tone lurked more than a hint of mockery; he knew exactly what she was considering.

"Don't you have caretakers here?"

He shrugged. "They're quartered in the basement. Pleasant enough people, centuries old, deaf as hitching posts. After we're dressed I'll rattle the family silver by their door to wake them.

"Rue," he said again, smiling with faint, amused menace when she did not move, "do you truly think there exists a place where I cannot find you?"

"I can't stay here."

"That was the agreement."

"No, it wasn't. I said I'd come to London with you, and I did. I promise I'll—meet you here tomorrow."

He made a hushed laugh, sending a shiver up her spine. "The word of a lady. And yet, I must decline. Come along, if you please."

"I suppose it must be wonderful to always demand what you want, instead of asking for it!"

His brows lifted. "It pains me to point out that you of all people should know."

She dropped to her knees before him, the ends of her hair sweeping the floor in dusty curls. "Be sensible. What do you think the *ton* will say when word gets out that you're in residence with an unknown woman?"

"I imagine . . . they'll suppose we're wed." She caught his tiger smile, feral and gleaming. "Which we are. In our way."

"They will suppose nothing of the sort!"

"Perhaps you're right. I daresay my reputation will survive it."

She began to stand. "I'm going home."

Swifter than the light, swifter than she, he vaulted back up the stairs into the cupola, his fingers warm on her wrist.

"I'm very sorry, Rue-flower, but I see we're going to have to establish some new rules between us. Whither thou goest, I follow. If you wish to leave, I will accompany you. Your house, mine—even that secret shelter of yours you're so eager to protect. I'm not so dainty as to shun a plain floor for a bed, if need be. But we are staying together."

"If you truly believe you can find me anywhere, my lord, I fail to understand why you'd insist we never part."

"I enjoy your company."

"Alas, if only it were mutual."

He took a step toward her in the dark. "It could be."

His chest brushed hers, a fleet, electric shock to her senses. It seemed to take them both aback; she froze as he did, the striped air and wood walls suddenly much too dense, too filled with him. She tried not to inhale, she tried to hold her breath, but couldn't seem to manage it: with every rise and fall of her chest her nipples grazed him, and it was like a fierce, hot drowning in her lungs, a terrible ache that spread through her body and left her weak-kneed and foolish.

He was so warm. He was so near. A solitary band of light laid amber over the brown of his lashes and turned his eyes to jade. She watched them drift lower, a leisurely perusal of her face.

"Don't..." Kit whispered, and bent his head, his lips finding hers.

She'd never known a kiss could be so soft. In her many

disguises, in her years here in London—the comte she'd invented, chambermaids, seamstresses, once even a courtesan with Mim—she'd learned of kisses, and enough of courtiers' ways to keep them brief and coolly cerebral. A kiss was only another weapon, as useful and impersonal as a pistol or a blade.

She'd never kissed, or been kissed, with passion before, with tenderness. She'd never known what it could mean to have a man explore the corners of her mouth, to feel him drag his lips over hers, so slowly, so sweetly, that breathing no longer seemed possible or even necessary. To have his hands reach up to cradle the back of her neck, his thumbs against her cheeks, stroking as his mouth stroked, in heady, exquisite circles. Rough beard, gentle tongue. The taste of him, the musky scent. The wall behind her but the fever of him ahead, as he captured her with only his fingers and lips, their bodies never touching... and yet he drew magic from her into him, offering it back again with every languorous caress.

His hair made a gold-silk curtain between them, a haze of color. She felt light and burning, a leaf brushed by the wind beyond her measure; she remembered distantly something someone—a baron, one night at a ball—said of her: *lips like a cherry's pucker, a ripe red bite.* And she'd never fully fathomed that until now.

"Don't what?" Rue managed, her voice a thin thread of itself.

"Hmmm?" Kit nuzzled her throat. She felt his teeth against her skin.

"Don't what?" she asked again, as her own hands were coming up to his shoulders, finding the smooth curves of him there, the way his muscles felt like supple stone, yielding and not. He brought his mouth back to hers as she dragged her palms down his arms and up again, something restless waking in her, something eager and unknown.

He closed the last step between them, breathing a laugh against her temple. "Move." His body was pure, hard heaven against hers; his lips skimmed her nose, her cheekbone, her jaw—tiny, teasing kisses that turned into a groan as their bodies aligned in perfect pleasure. "Don't move, little mouse."

She shut her eyes. She pushed her hips against his and took his tongue into her mouth, letting him fill her with himself, lost to the yearning that uncurled through her body, a heavy, liquid fire that built, unbearable—as if it had only been waiting to do so, years, lifetimes, for the right touch, the right man, the right moment...

...in an empty house. In the dark. Like strangers.

Which they were.

She curved her fingers into his arms, stiff instead of soft, and Christoff felt the difference. Yet it took some while for his brain to register the fact of her new resistance; he was drowning in her, in the luscious shape pressed up against him, in the shallow wisps of her breath against his cheeks, and lilies, God, even here, even now, a fragrance that set his nerve endings alight with an excruciating combination of anticipation and soul-wrenching desire.

But her fingers actually hurt. Kit lifted his head, taking in the ivory purity of her face. Her eyes, dark and startled.

"Not here?" he murmured, unable, just yet, to withdraw from the silken bliss of her body.

"Not ever," she said in a voice that belied the dewy, star-eyed look.

"Rue," he began, but the pressure on his arms intensified. He allowed her to push him away. It wasn't far. The cupola wasn't meant to hold two people. Certainly not two unclothed, panting people trying not to touch each other. He clenched his teeth and sucked in a lungful of cool, smoggy air. It helped chill his body but not his mind; his thoughts still swam with the promise of her and him and his bed, swathed in eiderdown and French satin, just two floors below.

Kit decided to abandon caution.

"Rue-flower. You feel it. You know it as well as I. We're mated."

"We are *not* mated."

"Well, not yet." He tried a smile, winding the tip of his finger around a lock of her hair. "But I'm hoping... any moment."

She said flatly, "You are delirious." And pulled her hair free.

For no other reason than the sudden emptiness of his hand, Christoff came back to himself. To the rough floor beneath his feet, and the taste of metal in his mouth, and all his plans for her set to unravel with just one more careless mistake. He'd alarmed her; he hadn't intended to, and she'd never admit it, but it was as obvious to him as the knot of her fingers and the quick, nervous blink of her eyes as she gazed up at him.

In a way, this was far more her world than his. If she bolted now he'd have the devil of the time convincing her to come back to him willingly.

He turned to the trapdoor. "You may be right. I'm famished. There's usually something passable in the larder." And he descended the steps again, leaving her before he did something truly irreparable. At the bottom of the garret landing he paused, listening; she hadn't Turned, but she hadn't moved yet either. He counted a full minute before one delicate foot was placed upon the top step, followed by its mate. Kit released a breath he hadn't realized he was holding.

"This way," he said once more, quietly, and found the second crook in the stairs, the one that would lead down to the third floor of the mansion. She followed this time, silent as smoke.

His house was filled with wraiths of furniture, almost everything shrouded from tip to floor in heavy sheets. Christoff gave none of the gloomy pale shapes a second glance; he passed by dead clocks and marble busts and what must have been a spare bed crammed in an upper hallway with equal indifference. On the second floor—more gracious, with portraits along the walls and a frescoed ceiling of gods at a feast, grapes and chalices and cherubs—he went straight to a door on their right and vanished into the chamber beyond, never once looking back.

She knew him unclad, by sight and now by touch. She knew the taut, contained edges of him, the color of his skin by both starlight and candlelight, the crisp, enticing sprinkle of golden hair on his chest. The feel of him below, the rigid urgency of his sex, a hot thrust against her belly. His kisses, his caresses, his ungentle demands: she knew these intimate things. It frightened her that she wished to know so much more.

But he had faded into the dusk of his mansion. The room he'd entered was nearly as dark as the hallway, the four windows sealed with shutters and long, wine-colored shades. It was a corner room, jumbled with the discards of fashion, chairs and dressers and folding screens, cupboards and statues, some with the sheets pulled askew. He slipped between a pair of fat Oriental vases to one of the taller ghost shapes and whisked off the cloth, dispersing a shower of grit.

Rue covered her mouth not to cough. He'd unveiled a satinwood armoire inlaid with lapis and malachite, a brass key resting in its lock. The twin doors opened with a strong waft of cedar. Kit gestured her forward; inside Rue ran her fingers over layers and layers of ravishing, useless gowns.

She lifted the edge of a petticoat gleaming with garnets. "None of these will do."

"Why not?"

"Aside from the fact that everything here is approximately a quarter century out of fashion, these are ball gowns."

"Of course," drawled the marquess. "You're quite right. No doubt you prefer to visit the kitchen *en déshabillé.*"

"We are trying to blend in, Lord Langford."

"I don't imagine Mr. Stilson and his wife are quite such sticklers to propriety—but if you wish, we shall endeavor to find you something else."

"I have my own garments at home."

"Yes. But we're here now, aren't we?" He began to circle the room, tossing aside more sheets. "I believe there's a trunk in here somewhere that held spare livery for the staff. I used to raid it as a boy. Very useful for stealing out of the house."

"Listen—I'll just wear something of yours."

He glanced up at her, framed against a red-wine window. She could not see his look, not with the streetlight behind him, but she could feel it.

"What an interesting notion," he said. "You, in breeches."

She felt her skin begin to burn. "I've done it before. Often."

"No doubt." Outside a carriage rumbled past, the horses' hooves striking an iron-sharp counterpoint to the lighter jingle of harnesses and bells.

"Well?"

"Sorry," he said. "I was just trying to envision Stilson's face when he catches sight of you."

"I'll put my hair back. Introduce me as a man."

He laughed, mirthless.

"It will work," she said indignantly. "It always works. I've gone out in society a score of times as a man. A hundred times."

"Society," muttered Christoff, brushing past her to reach the doorway, "must be far, far more beef-witted than I even thought."

But he did not have to introduce her. The kitchen's larder yielded a practical meal of smoked ham and rye and hard yellow cheese—his guest had turned up her nose at the pickled cucumbers, and at the jug of salted cod—and when it was done Kit had finally ventured to wake Mr. Stilson and his good wife, informing them through their door that he was in town for a short while, that he had brought with him an old Cambridge confidant, and that he had recently realized they were due for a holiday, which they could take as soon as they wished. They had a daughter in Cornwall; he'd be delighted to pay the fare there and back.

At that point Stilson had opened the door, unshaven but with his stock neatly tucked and his wig straight, his blue eyes beginning to water in the open glare of Kit's candle. Perhaps his years of stern employ under the old marquess had taught him not to question odd orders, or hours. He thanked Christoff for the offer and said that, with his lord's leave, he and his dame would be off in the morning.

Rue, out of sight back in the kitchen, made a ladylike snort. Kit hoped he was the only one who heard it.

"How well you do that," she commented when he reappeared. She was seated on a stool by the chopping block, tearing a heel of bread into pieces by the shadow of the lamp he'd left her. There was always spare clothing in Far Perch for its lord; she was dressed as a nobleman now in buckskin and bleached lawn, but the effect was generally ruined by the fact that everything he owned was several sizes too large on her. The shirtsleeves, even rolled, flopped around her fingers; his breeches reached her shins. She looked like a schoolmaid in costume for a play, no matter how darkly keen her glance back at him.

He brought his candle to the block. "Do what?"

"Master people." She popped a piece of bread into her mouth.

"Oh. Yes, I've been trained in the finer arts of mastering from a tender age. Although I've discovered it's quite helpful if you have a hand in someone's salary as well."

She was gazing down at the bread, her hair sliding in a pretty waterfall over her shoulders. Lamplight lent her face and throat a tropical, sun-kissed glow.

"How many men have you killed?" she asked without looking up.

The chopping block was webbed with scars, a crisscrossing of lines that marked generations of salads and minced meats. He found a splintery groove and rubbed it with his thumb. "Three."

"And how many of those *drákon*?"

"Three."

Her lashes lifted. "I'd heard five."

"Well," he shrugged. "People do enjoy a good slander."

"Were they runners?"

He didn't answer. He didn't have to. She picked up another piece of bread and slowly plucked it into crumbs.

"Will you tell me his name now?" Kit asked. "We're together on this, after all." She was quiet, frowning at her hands, so he added, "I'm here to help you, Rue, but you're keeping me at a dangerous disadvantage. Knowing his name—his family, his history—may hasten the hunt."

"Is that truly what you want?" She dropped the last of the bread to the block, dusting her fingers clean. "To help me?"

"Of course."

"Because I cannot but think that this situation is not particularly to your advantage in any case, Lord Langford. Perhaps you'd rather have a wife, not a diamond."

"I assure you," he said carefully, "that I want the diamond."

"And me?"

"Yes," he admitted, blunt. "And you. I won't lie about that. I've wanted you from the moment I first saw you in the museum. Before that. I wanted every part of you from the first time I felt you, your presence. I want you in the sky, and against the earth. I want to kiss you again, I want to touch you, I want to feel you in my arms and I want to hear you gasping my name when I'm inside you. I want all that, and I want it badly. Every time I look at you, I want it. So you're going to have to become used to that, Rue. It won't change. But I won't push you into anything that you don't want either. And I *will* help you find *Herte*. I give you my word."

Her cheeks had flushed from rose to nearly ruby; her lips pinched together, as if holding back words. She was staring down at the block, her lashes very long, very dark, against her heated skin.

He had to lock his hands behind his back to stop himself from reaching for her.

"I don't know his name," she said, after an endless, aching moment.

"What?"

"The thief. I don't know his name. I never said I did." Her eyes flashed to his. "But I can still find him, and the diamond."

He stared at her, silent.

"Daybreak's only a few hours off. I'd like to get some rest before that." She swiveled on the stool to face him squarely. "I'm not sleeping with you."

"No," he said, and turned away to pick up the lamp. He cupped it with both hands, keeping his gaze on the flame. "Gentlemen guests at Far Perch are assigned their own chambers."


He dreamed of blood. Not masses of blood, not gore, but the deathly elegant suggestion of it: a red crescent of dewdrops, spattered over snowy linen; the scarlet brilliance of a puddle soaking into a sawdust floor. The slick, hot syrup of it between his fingers. The coppery stink, burning in his nose.

The smell haunted him most. He turned his head to escape it and awoke to a painful sting at his throat.

Kit opened his eyes.

*Where is she?*

The voice was high and thin and directly by his left ear—also the location of the blade pressed up hard against his jawline.

"Where is she?" the voice demanded again, whispery words nearly spilling over one another in fury. "Tell me, you bastard! I'll kill you!"

Options flitted through his mind: this person was small, this person was young, it smelled like an urchin, the blade felt like a dagger or a dirk. He could break its arm or its neck, he could Turn and crush it from behind or more simply rip off its head—and the only thing that kept his body motionless in the bed was the realization that the creature was obviously speaking of Rue.

"Zane," she said then, a single word that broke like a calm dream through the chamber. "Please do not kill the Marquess of Langford."

The blade vanished. Kit sat up, using the sheet to dab away his blood, watching as the creature slinked across the darkened room to where she stood in the doorway. She lifted an arm to it, taking hold of its shoulder before it could throw itself upon her. She wore one of Kit's dressing robes, belted into loose paisley folds.

The urchin—a boy—was covered in black. Kit suspected most of it was filth.

"How long did it take you?" she asked him conversationally.

"Two days. Sooner if that twit of a maid hadn't took up all the clothes for laundry. *Laundry,*" he spat in disgust. "An' she never told me till it was done. Found his card. With the waistcoat an' all, it ticked up. I've been watching this place ever since. Late tonight, though. Business."

"Yes. Lord Langford." She directed her gaze to Kit. "May I introduce Zane, surname unknown. He is my—"

"Apprentice," said the youth, thrusting the dirk into his belt.

"—domestic," she finished firmly. "Apologize to his lordship."

"Never mind that," snarled Kit, swinging to his feet. "Just get the hell out."

The urchin actually jerked a step toward him, kept in place only by Rue's hand, still curled over his skinny shoulder.

"I'm not bloody leavin' her with *you,* you son of a—"

"Zane." Her voice cut like sugared ice through his. "Obey me or, as the marquess said, get out."

She released him. The boy shifted in place a moment. Kit very nearly felt the vibrations of his wrath, the face wan and pointed, a shock of tawny brown hair probably crawling with nits. But the child controlled himself; the bow he swept Kit was as polished as could be. She must have taught him that.

"Beg pardon," he muttered.

"I'm afraid my hospitality does not extend to children who attempt to murder me in my sleep," Kit said anyway. "You have found your mistress. Now kindly retreat to whichever gutter spawned you."

"One minute, my lord." Rue turned to the child. "What news?"

He threw a distrustful glance at Kit, but answered readily enough. "Spotted Dog's been raided. They nabbed Old Jinx and Nollie, but word is she's out tomorrow. Turk's Head is still taking numbers, but Pig and Poke ain't. Fat Paddy took one between the ribs last night."

"And of the Langford Diamond?"

"Naught," said the boy.

Rue nodded, as if this were something she had expected. "Go home, but keep your ears open. What did you tell Cook and Sidonie?"

"That you was visiting family. In Dartford, if they ask."

"They believed you?"

"Dunno. But they quit blathering about footpads and cutthroats after that."

"Good. I'll be by later this morning to straighten things out. But"—she paused, then sent a dispassionate look to Kit—"I won't be staying."

The urchin, too, turned his head and looked dead at him, with hostile yellow eyes. It might have been comical—the lady of the manor with her bristling lapdog at her feet—but for the damp cut on Kit's neck and the rather softly fond way she'd pronounced the boy's name.

It was ridiculous to feel his stomach tighten over a whip of a beggar child. Ridiculous to attempt intimidation by walking up to them both—taller, bigger, certainly cleaner—until the urchin had to tip back his head to keep eye contact. In a single fluid move, Kit had the dirk in his hand. The boy twitched in surprise, but that was all.

"Nice work. Burke and Boone, I believe."

"Aye. Stuck a bloke for it."

"Certainly you did." He inspected the blade, the silky length of hammered steel, the dim dark line down the edge that was his blood.

"How did you happen to come into my home . . . Zane?"

"Parlor window. Cheap lock," the boy added, malicious. "Shoddy work, that."

"I'll look into it." Christoff tugged loose the filthy shirt, deliberately wiped the blade back and forth on the material until the blood smeared off, then slapped it back into the urchin's palm. "In the meantime, you may exit the same way. Now."

The boy hesitated, his fist curling around the hilt.

"Go," Rue urged, still soft, and at last he nodded, flashing her a final glance before trotting off into the shadows. She raised her voice after him. "Don't take anything."

Zane never answered.

"It appears I need a watchdog," Kit remarked, listening to the footsteps that slapped remarkably lightly against the marble floors of his mansion.

"It would be of little use." She paused, hearing, as he did, the almost silent creak of the downstairs window opening. "He has a unique way with animals."

"Hardly shocking, I suppose. He seems more animal than not."

"A quality your lordship surely recognizes."

He gave a narrow smile, lowering his gaze to the pale V of her chest that the robe revealed. "Surely."

He could have predicted her reaction: she took a step back, caught herself, then lifted her chin. Maddening, captivating Rue, defiant and curious at the same time, a contradiction of ladylike gentility with the secret cunning of a warlord. Who stole and lied and defied a roomful of powerful men just because she could, who trusted in wet dogs and stray children with knives. Who wore her privacy like a cloak, and kissed like she knew the darkest fissures of his heart, like she knew *him,* and always had.

"Does he know what you are?" he asked. "Your little mongrel?"

Her chin tilted higher. "Yes."

"That's a perilous secret, mouse. Should the council discover it—"

"Zane would never betray me," she said instantly, defensive.

He was silent a moment, weighing his thoughts, weighing risks and scenarios and outcomes. In the end he said only, "Let us hope not."

If he had to kill the boy, she'd likely not forgive him.

In just the short while he'd been awake, the light in his room had changed, easing from muffled black into pewter, faintly brushing the bed and wing chairs and mantel with gray. He could see her eyes more clearly, the tint of her lips, the green and rust paisley print with its braiding of king-fisher blue. . . . The sun would follow soon.

He was fatigued. He must have slept only an hour or so, and felt it. But beyond the call of sleep, beyond the threat of the urchin and the small, constant disquiet over the dia-mond, Kit found he wanted nothing more than to take Rue's hand and lead her back to his empty bed, to feel her bare and wonderful against him there. And why not? She was here, he was here . . . the sheets were already warm. . . .

While his mind drifted forward into his fantasy—the robe sliding off her shoulders, the stroke of her hair against his chest, the lily heat of her skin—his hand reached out. Like the fit of a familiar glove their fingers slipped together and she allowed it, her focus turning distant, distracted.

In his mind they were already beneath the covers, and he was already tasting her skin—

"It is Friday," Rue said.

He closed his eyes, willing himself not to move. "Is it?"

"And dawn."

—she was beneath him, her arms around him, sliding her foot up his calf—

"So our fortnight begins. And I know just where to begin it."

He opened his eyes.

She asked, "Have you ever visited the establishment of Madame Leveillé?"

It was one of the most infamous brothels in London, a place so exclusive it became something of a Holy Grail among the Cambridge set, most of whom couldn't even broker an introduction.

Kit had been invited twice.

"No," he said curtly, which actually won him a smile.

"Neither have I. But I know a comte who's quite familiar with it—and its proprietor." She looked down at their hands, then, almost as an afterthought, pulled hers free. "We'll start there."

# CHAPTER TEN

They hired a coach to the House of Leveillé, two lace-bedecked gentlemen emerging in the late-morning coolness to the gray, imposing silence of Threadneedle. Rue let the marquess pay the shot.

It was still too early for fashion; the people who traveled the street now were either bank clerks or men like what she pretended to be, the blue-blooded tip of society, moving lazily along the sidewalks that led to and from this place.

She was the comte now. She felt more comfortable in these clothes, like a second skin that fit her to the last stitch. Her peruke wig, her velvet coat of cyan, the rapier and seamed stockings and pocket watch, the gold signet she'd had commissioned for her finger—she knew this person nearly as well as her true self. Whether the marquess liked it or not was irrelevant.

She had not allowed him into her home. He had agreed to remain outside until she was ready, until the servants were busy and she could slip out again. And even then, he'd only looked her up and down with flat green eyes, taking particular note of the blade at her hip, saying nothing. He'd walked off and found them the hackney.

As the coachman was counting change, the plum-painted door to Leveillé's opened. Rue kept her head down and watched without watching as a nobleman emerged from the golden shadows of the interior, accepting his gloves and cane with exaggerated care from a doorman. He was younger than the usual sort she encountered here; as he skipped down the puddled stairs he staggered twice, his hat cocked back and his coat unbuttoned to display a vest of vivid orange and yellow stripes. The hot reek of brandy struck her long before the lord himself made it past. Rue smiled to the pavement. The House of Leveillé poured only the best.

The fresh air seemed to grip him. The man moved more quickly to the nearest intersection, where a shiny black landau rolled up to meet him.

There was no hint of the true nature of the business that took place behind Madame's door, but the royal-crested carriages tended to remain at a circumspect distance anyway.

Christoff finished with their coach. She heard the driver's low "chut-chut!" as the horses bounded forward, the steel rims of the wheels grinding against stone. Still she waited, her eyes cast down, and so had an excellent vantage of Christoff's left shoe clipping into view: the fine-grained leather buffed to splendor, the heavy sterling buckle studded with topaz that would fetch more than a barmaid would make in a decade.

She could live for three months on that buckle. The house, the servants, food, coal, and transport: three months. And she'd wager that he had scarcely even noticed it strapped to his shoe.

Rue spoke in an undertone, lifting her gaze to his. "From

this instant, I am the Comte du Lalonde, an aristocrat with holdings in Corrèze and just enough income to waste as I please. I gamble, I drink, and I enjoy women."

His face held a particular taut gravity, an expression that might have masked pensiveness or amusement or anything in between.

"It is imperative that you not forget any of that while we're here. Don't call me by my true name. Don't treat me as a woman."

"I'll try to remember. Comte."

Amusement. She narrowed her eyes.

"If you're not going to take this seriously, you might as well leave now."

"Not without you."

"Then at least be useful. If you look at me like that while we're in there, people will wonder why we're bothering with whores at all."

His gaze darkened, his mouth flattened to a line. She'd offended him. Good. He'd been staring at her all morning when he thought she couldn't see, his features whetted, his eyes ferocious . . . like he would eat her, like he would devour her. But beneath his look was something even worse. Beneath it was something that flickered and caught in her chest, tenderness and recognition and a sparse, empty ache that seemed to penetrate her very being.

It made her stomach fluttery and her heart constrict. It made her slide back into the memory of his kisses, of his taste, lingering like autumn honey on her lips.

. . . *I want to hear you gasping my name when I'm inside you* . . .

Better to have him angry. She could banish those memories then.

Rue pulled off her hat, flicking the silvery blue curls on

her shoulders into alignment. "I won't introduce you. Just stay with me and try to appear..."

"Yes?"

"Less forbidding. You are here for pleasure, Lord Langford."

His lips curved into that bare, familiar smile; he looked as affable as a wolf in a cage.

*"Très bien."* She turned to lead the way up the stairs.

The majordomo and all the doormen knew the Comte du Lalonde. She had not visited often, but they were paid to remember faces, just as they did cloaks and canes; she was met with formal bows, the marquess just behind her. They were escorted into an empty drawing room in the front of the mansion and politely left alone.

"How very conventional," said Christoff, lifting a painted figurine of a stag and hare from its place on a *secrétaire*. His gaze raked the chamber. "I had hoped for velvet on the walls and a hookah, at the least."

"I'm sorry to disappoint you." She stood beside the pink chintz settee with a hand on her rapier, watching him cross to the windows. He dimmed against the panes, a shadow man prowling amid gauze curtains and plaster friezework of fleur-de-lis and ivy. A gilded vase was crowned with plump, creamy tulips in the corner; he stirred their perfume as he passed.

"Your runner is a patron here?"

"Perhaps. He'll know about it, in any case. But we've come to see someone else."

Kit tapped a tulip with one finger, sending a tremble through the petals and stem. "You move in rarefied circles, *Monsieur le Comte.*"

"When I must."

A new set of doors opened, the ones that led deeper into

the mansion. A woman slipped into the room, advancing to Rue with her hands outstretched. She might have come straight from an evening at court, with her prim, silk-tissue gown that glistened with burnished bronze thread, milky opals at her throat and ears and wrists—but for her hair, which was deeply red and completely unbound, floating behind her in rippling curls.

"Comte du Lalonde," greeted Mim in her most cultured voice. Rue accepted both her hands, bowing over them.

*"Chérie."*

Mim turned to Christoff. For an instant Rue detected a splinter in the other woman's careful veneer, the slightest flare of emotion behind the clear gray eyes—but when Mim spoke, it was in her usual practiced tones. "And you have brought a friend, I see! Welcome, my lord."

The Marquess of Langford inclined his head, not smiling but at least with a shade less of that wolfish aspect than before. He seemed not entirely unmoved by Mim's painted charms, dropping his hand from hers neither too quickly nor too late. But he gazed at the courtesan with what seemed to Rue to be something more potent than mere curiosity. She felt a rush of annoyance, and quickly quenched it.

It didn't matter to her whom he liked. Mim was beautiful, and it didn't matter.

"It has been too long," Mim said, transferring her smile back to Rue. "Do come along, my lord. Please, both of you, do come inside."

Rue offered her arm. Mim accepted it, her touch as cool and light as the air. Together they walked into the connecting hall, Christoff pacing behind.

He had anticipated velvet and hookahs, well, now he was getting a nearer taste of it. Beyond the decorous drawing room, the House of Leveillé transformed itself into a more exotic creature, as the windows vanished and the only illumination spilled from frosted-glass sconces in shades of ruby and oyster and gold. The ceiling was draped not in velvet but stiff bombazine; paintings on the walls showed pale moments of men and women coupling amid darkly rich harems or palace chambers.

Behind the closed doors they passed came occasional hints of what lay beyond: a woman's laughter, hushed and then cut short; the small, brittle splash of liquid against crystal or stone; frantic breathing; the whispered aftermath of opium; a bass viol, unaccompanied, stroking out a passage of deep, resonant notes.

The opium made her dizzy. She tried to hold her breath until they were past it.

Mim turned her head. "Will you take breakfast? Champagne? No? Never mind, then; perhaps we'll find something else to tempt you."

They entered the heart of the building, a rectangular chamber filled with sofas and chairs and fat pillows and a harpsichord in one of the corners, being played very softly by a girl with caramel skin and sloe-black eyes. There were fewer men here than Rue had seen previously, only five— two she recognized—being teased and petted by a chorus of women. But it was morning. Most of Mim's customers would be in rooms already, or gone home to their wives.

The girl at the harpsichord glanced up as they walked in. Her hands lifted from the keys; she rose and swept toward them with an unhurried poise.

"*Gaétan,*" she said, smiling, and pressed a short kiss on Rue's mouth. She spoke in French, linking their arms. "Have you just come? How I've missed you."

Rue answered in the same language. "And I you, dear

one. I've been out of town, but see—I've brought you a tri-fle from Calais." She lifted a round gold locket from her vest pocket, lavishly scrolled, draped from a royal-blue ribbon. The girl—the name she used here was Portia—danced back and clapped her hands, effectively gathering the attention of the room.

Rue knew how it must have looked to those wine-sotted gentlemen; she knew how she hoped it looked. But it oc-curred to her in that moment that Kit Langford was truly her wild card. He could make the moment or ruin it, and it was imperative that he not ruin it.

Yet he seemed impassive, almost bored, standing with his weight on one foot and his hands behind his back. He ap-peared to be gazing at a couple on the nearest sofa, the man with his cravat untied and his head propped against the cushions, the woman with her hands curled around his arm—and then Kit's gaze shifted to hers. His eyes burned sharp, sharp green.

"But is it empty?" demanded Portia, with a comely little pout. "I must have a lock of your hair for it!"

"Of course!" Rue dropped the locket in the girl's palm and gave a half smile to Mim, switching to English. "In fact, I think we must see to it right away."

Mim nodded to the marquess. "And your friend?"

"There is room in the locket," said Rue, "for two locks of hair, I think."

"Very well. Portia, you'll find the third chamber pre-pared."

*"Oui, madame."*

She took Rue's hand, and then Christoff's, leading them both to an arched doorway past the harpsichord. Someone had gotten up to play in her absence. As they walked away, a new tune began to float lightly, disembodied, down the hall-way, rebounding against the floors and walls.

Portia stopped before a varnished door, opening it for them both. Rue went first, recognizing the shapes of the walls, the cluster of furniture, the chemical-sweet aroma of cosmetics and cologne and, beneath them both, bleach.

The marquess closed the door. Portia sent him a swiftly veiled look, one Rue had seen a thousand times over, grow-ing up in the shire, then moved to the bed. With her skirts in her hands she climbed atop the mattress, reaching for a carved wooden rosebud in the cornice that lined the walls. There came a click, and a groan; in a puff of stale air the se-cret door beside the headboard slid ajar.

Portia stepped down from the mattress and over to the opening.

"Thank you for the locket," she said to Rue with a shyer, more natural smile.

"It's nothing."

The girl dipped her head and disappeared. The door slid closed again.

Rue had been in this room on no less than seven occa-sions, and each time it felt the same to her, chilled and clois-tered, almost suffocating, even with the magnificent bed with its crimson and coral hangings, the round leather table set for backgammon—surely no one ever played—and the twin mirrors on the walls placed to face each other, so that when she stood between them she saw only herself, over and over and over, diminishing down into a silver-backed void. She edged past the line of their frames. There were cabinets she had never opened in here, places she had never looked. It was enough to know about the rosebud, and that the main door was unlocked.

"You can relax," she said to Christoff, still over by the

door. "No one will hear us in here. There are peepholes but they won't be occupied."

He had noted them already, clever gaps in the floral wallpaper designed to fool the senses; places like this seldom allowed for true privacy. He listened closely to the silence. Rue was right. There was no one breathing behind the false walls, no scents emanating from them beyond dust and old rat. They were alone.

A brass chain lay coiled around one of the bedposts; Kit ran a finger along the links as he walked by. "It doesn't seem to be a room especially conducive to relaxation."

"No," Rue agreed, with a ghost of a smile. She took a seat at the table, adjusting the length of her rapier.

"Do you trust that girl?"

"In about an hour she will return to the harpsichord wearing her new locket. She'll linger another hour, but she's off at ten. She will respond to any inquiries regarding the comte with discreet details: he prefers absinthe to sherry, sugar to salt, flogging to bondage." She tapped a nail against a mother-of-pearl counter, watching him from beneath her lashes. "You needn't look so shocked. He *is* French."

"I'm not shocked. I'm merely appalled."

"Not for Portia, I hope. She's paid handsomely for her lies."

"For you," he said, and took the chair across the table. He leaned forward and very gently touched her cheek. "What a curious life you've led."

He'd meant nothing by it other than a simple gesture of communion, but she drew back as if he'd hurt her, her face going stiff. He dropped his hand to his lap and rubbed his fingers together; her skin had held that burning warmth that always seemed to spread straight through him.

"And for myself, of course," he added wryly, when she

didn't rise or speak. "Only an hour for the both of us! I fear my reputation is going to suffer, after all."

And just like last night, her face suffused. He wondered if she truly understood what he meant, his blushing thief, or if she only guessed. He wished he could tell, he wished he could ask her, but so much about her was still a mystery to him. If he asked he thought she'd either laugh or she'd lie. Or both.

She seemed confident enough in her breeches and the foppish tailed coat, and God knew she could handle the sword. But there were times when he looked at her and glimpsed someone else entirely. The woodsmouse she used to be perhaps, wide-eyed, uncertain. The bow to her mouth as she'd stared out from her old bedroom window at the rain; the way she tended to stand with one hand clasped over her wrist, feminine and unthinking; how she dared him and taunted him but kissed like a maiden, with closed lips and awe, and still it set his blood to boil.

She was proving damnably resistant to his efforts to break past her defenses. He didn't know how much longer his patience would last.

Someone was coming. They heard it together, the swish of cloth behind the walls, the small, hollow tap of high heels.

The hidden door opened. The red-haired woman of before emerged, her skirts filling the confines of the doorway.

"Dearest Rue. I was wondering when you'd appear."

Rue stood. "I was delayed."

"Indeed." The woman sent an amused glance to Kit. "And a fine delay it is. Lord Langford, how lovely to see you—and I do mean it." She perched upon the edge of the bed, baring trim ankles and an ivory mass of petticoats. "Will you forgive me? I've been on my feet all night."

"Mim runs the House," Rue said, without looking at Kit. "Among other things."

"Oh, I'm little more than an accountant these days," responded the woman congenially. "But thank you, darling."

"You know why we're here."

"I suppose I do. Although, I must say, I am surprised at the company you're keeping. You were as cool as Scottish snow that afternoon in the museum. I never guessed you knew the marquess himself."

Now Rue's gaze flicked to his. "I was unacquainted with the marquess until a few days ago."

"Really? And you're bosom friends already? How delightful."

"I need to know about the diamond, Mim. Did he bring it to you?"

The woman's eyes shifted from Kit to Rue and back, her smile pasted in place. "I have no idea whom you could mean."

Rue reached into her waistcoat. "Yes, you do. The same man who took Cumberland's black pearl and Vishney's intaglio ring. He's about Langford's height, with reddish-blond hair and an occasional limp." She produced a small leather pouch, tossing it to the other woman. Mim caught it; the metallic jangle of coins echoed in the chamber.

"There's no one else in the city he could turn to," Rue said quietly. "You're the best swagsman in the business, and everyone knows it. Unless he's already moved it abroad, he'd have to come to you."

"You know my privacy rule."

"It's important, Mim. I swear it is."

"Since when did *you* swim over to the right and proper side of the law?"

"Since me," murmured Kit, earning a look from Rue that very clearly said, *Stay out of it.*

"I'm not on any side of the law, and you know it. I just need that diamond."

"Well..." Mim rolled the bag back and forth between her palms, thoughtful. "I *have* heard that Empress Elizaveta adores those wonderfully *sparkly* stones, especially the big ones. Perhaps your diamond is on its way to Russia."

The chill in the room seemed to take on an abruptly sharper edge.

Christoff said lazily, "Somehow I rather doubt that. Don't you, *madame*? The Langford Diamond was here, in this chamber, I imagine about...three hours ago. Isn't that right?"

Mim stared at him, her expression closed, her eyes very bright.

He smiled. "Just a feeling. They come to me betimes."

It was more than a feeling. It was comprehension. It was awareness, a pulsing heartbeat through the air and the furniture and just here, at the little backgammon table, where the energy was strongest. He'd spent more time alone with *Herte* than anyone else in the tribe; it was his right as the Alpha, and Kit had full used it. He'd spent days studying the stone, memorizing it, perhaps because in the back of his mind he'd always anticipated its loss. He knew the diamond's strength and its cold brilliance, its distinctive pattern of energy that whispered like a phantom in his ear where he stood: *I was here.*

"Please," said Rue, with more emotion in her voice than he'd heard her use before. "Please, Mim."

The red-haired woman slid from the bed. "I did receive an inquiry. I declined to pursue it." She lifted a shoulder, nonchalant. "I told you before, luv, the stone's far too extraordinary. I'd have a hell of a time getting it off my hands. Much like that poor chap who took it."

"Who was it?" demanded Kit.

Her sweet smile returned. "I really couldn't say. He wasn't inclined to offer his name." She looked pointedly at Rue. "They seldom do."

He looked at her as well, finding her watching him back, her countenance stoic beneath the layers of paint, exquisite features masked with powder and rouge and kohl. But behind her dark eyes Kit thought he caught a glimpse of something raw, something bleak; it might have been nothing more than a trick of the light. He took a step toward her anyway, his hand reaching for hers.

"Thirty-one King's Court," said the courtesan, brusque. She was frowning at them both, her arms crossed over her waist. "In Chelsea. It's where he said I could reach him if I changed my mind. But that's truly all I know." She shook her head, her mouth hardening. "And the devil take both of you if you tell anyone I spilled it."


Rue said, "This cannot be right."

They peered together out the carriage window, not even opening the door.

GRAHAM'S MENAGERIE OF REMARKABLE BEASTS read the hanging wood sign that swayed over the entrance to 31 King's Court. It appeared to be little more than a skinny patch of park squeezed between thoroughfares and buildings.

"Driver," the marquess called. "Is this the only King's Court in Chelsea?"

"Aye," answered the man, muffled through wood. "This be it, guv."

There were people drifting in and out of the entrance, men and women and a few shiny-cheeked children, pulling eagerly at the hands holding theirs. A simple whitewashed stall was situated just past the sign, where a balding man in a beige greatcoat took money and handed out tickets. Beyond that, all Rue could see of the menagerie were bushes and trees swallowing up a narrow gravel path.

Something—some creature—let loose an unearthly howl that climbed and climbed into goose bumps over her skin. From the bowels of the trees a host of sparrows surged up into the sky.

Christoff rapped his knuckles against the roof. "Drive on."

Rue turned to him, grabbing the strap by her head as the carriage hit a pothole. "What are you doing? We have to go in!"

"Breakfast was a long while ago. I don't know about you, but I am accustomed to lunch." He leaned back in the seat, his pale eyes gleaming. "And I don't think it's a good idea to go in there hungry, do you?"

# CHAPTER ELEVEN

The howling had come from the bedraggled hyena. At least, Rue assumed that it had. As soon as they approached its cage it made a similar sound, albeit smothered now, as it had leapt into a wooden crate at the first sight of them and not come out since. Still it screamed and yipped, eyeing them through the slats.

DIRECT FROM THE DARKEST HEART OF AFRIKA. ONE OF NATURE'S MOST MALEVOLENT BRUTES.

"This is unbearable," Rue muttered. The hyena had the same reaction to them as every other animal in this place: noisy, unmitigated fear. It was even worse than the stench.

She spoke around the lace kerchief she held to her nose. "No runner in his right mind would even come here, much less hide a diamond somewhere in this mess."

"But that's what makes it so perfect," said Christoff, not even lowering his voice. "It was a brilliant move on his part. Think on it. You'd never visit a menagerie, even by accident."

"Not willingly."

The pair of charwomen standing beside Rue had screwed up their faces and stuck their fingers in their ears. The little boy between them mimicked their pose, elbows akimbo. He broke into laughter as the women hauled him away.

"It's useless." Rue put her hand on Christoff's arm, drawing him into a shelter of trees farther down the path. "We've lost any element of surprise at this point, if he was ever even here."

Christoff gave her a sidelong look. "Don't you feel it?"

"What?" she snapped. "The sun? The wind? The desperate terror?"

"The diamond."

She paused, looking up at him. Punctuating the hyena's howls was now a rhythmic pounding; the bald man from the gate had taken up a poker and was using it to smash the wood box while the hyena, trapped inside, screamed higher.

*"Shut—yer—mug—you—miserable—bastard—"*

"Excuse me," Christoff said to her, and walked back to the cage.

He caught the gatekeeper's wrist on a downswing, stopping it precisely in midair, then gave it a hard shake. The poker fell from the man's fingers. It clanged like a bell against the iron bars, wedging lopsided between them. The hyena cringed and whined.

In the sudden near silence Rue could hear the marquess speaking, darkly soft.

"You don't want to do that."

"Eh—what the bleedin'—"

"Listen to me, friend. You don't want to do that again."

"I . . ."

She began to move toward them. The hyena threw her a rolling, white-eyed look and took up its howl once more, echoed by what sounded like monkeys somewhere nearby.

By the time she was close enough to hear them again, the gatekeeper was slowly nodding his head.

"I don't want to do that."

"You want to clean its cage, and offer it fresh water."

"Aye."

*Straw,* mouthed Rue.

"New straw," said the marquess. "And an extra beefsteak tonight. In fact, give him yours."

"Aye."

"Very good. Don't forget."

"No."

Christoff bent down and picked up the poker, handing it back to the man. "Put this away."

The gatekeeper turned and left, not even glancing around him at the frenzied caged animals. Rue and Christoff returned to the nook of trees, and the hyena subsided into deep-throated whines.

"Impressive," she said. "Have you always been able to do that?"

"Almost always. It only works on humans, of course, and the effects tend to be temporary. What of you? You have all the other Gifts. Can't you do it?"

"Sometimes," she admitted, and he smiled—warm and breathtaking, not a smile she hoped anyone else could see.

"All it takes is practice, Rue-flower."

"Comte!"

"Comte," he agreed, inclining his head. "And speaking of practice . . ."

"I do feel it," she said, and to her surprise, it was true. She closed her eyes, reaching for that sliver of awareness, distant, elusive, dancing like a flame on the horizon behind her lids. "It's faint. But . . . *Herte* was here."

"I think it still is. Do you feel the runner?"

She tried a moment longer. "No."

"Still, one for two, not bad for our first day. Shall we venture this way, *monsieur*?"

They headed down the path, toward a pen that held a moon-eyed panther, arched back into a corner with its hair on end, hissing at them over and over. A cluster of schoolgirls pressed too close to the bars, gasping and waving their fingers at it.

"That was kind of you," said Rue under her breath. "What you did back there for that creature."

"Well, who knows?" The marquess angled a glance through his lashes at the bristling cat. "Had the world turned on a different axis, it might have been us in that cage."

The menagerie wasn't large, not by London standards, but it still took them half the afternoon to wind through it front to back. Christoff insisted they pause by each cage, absorbing the instant ruckus that would ensue, while they tried to feel the beat of *Herte* once more. And so they followed their senses like an old childhood game of Catch What You Can, meandering through the trees. Cold here, warmer there, warm, warm. Hot.

It wasn't long before Rue understood that he was leading her, that when she paused or faltered he waited for her. Twice when no one else was about he held out his left hand and showed her how to align the tips of her fingers to his, thumb to thumb, index to index and so on, the barest brushing touch that sent waves of sensation through her.

"Now," he whispered, beneath the deafening shrieks of a pair of red parrots. "Try it now."

And with his added energy something in her would flare.

Rue no longer closed her eyes to feel the power of the stone they sought. She looked at Christoff instead, into a gaze as clear as an emerald held up to the sun, green that was lucent light and crystal combined.

It even made her headache from the parrots seem less piercing.

But the diamond was not with the parrots.

With the sun sloping low in the sky they stood together before the last of the enclosures. Most of the animals seemed to have finally exhausted themselves into a stupor, but by now the menagerie was nearly deserted of visitors. The sparrows from this morning had not returned; there were long, eerie minutes of quiet but for the bustle of the city beyond the trees. Daylight was beginning to taper into evening gold, laying leaf-dapple shadows across a cramped pit filled with rocks and murky water, and yellow scum floating in long, serpentine lines.

CROCODILES said the sign before the pit. TREACH-EROUS MAN-EATERS FROM CLEOPATRA'S GREAT RIVER NILE.

One of the rocks bobbed up to become a massive head, shattering the mottled black surface of the water, opening its mouth in a huge toothsome yawn. It hissed at them, swishing its tail.

"At least it doesn't scream," observed the marquess.

"It can't be in there," Rue said, dismayed. "How could he put it in there?"

"Perhaps he threw it in."

"But *why*?"

"As a joke. As a dare. Because he didn't want anyone else to have it—I've no idea. All that truly matters is that the diamond is down there, little mouse."

It was. She felt it too. Another crocodile joined the first, angling up out of the water to snap at them, its throat vibrating with a heavy, outraged groan.

Sweet mercy. What was she going to do?

"Nothing, at the moment," said Christoff, and Rue realized then she had spoken aloud. He nodded toward the pair of workmen heading for them. "It appears the menagerie is closing. We'll have to come back tonight."

"He might have fetched it by then."

"Frankly, better him than us. If he cares to spare me the trouble of wading into a crocodile pond, I'd be grateful. But I don't think he will. I have a feeling that somewhere out there," he added grimly, "our runaway thief is laughing up his sleeve."

True to his word, in the dark hours of the nightfall the gatekeeper tossed an extra steak to the hyena. It landed with a wet slap against the straw and metal floor. The animal leapt toward it instantly, snatching the meat back to its crate while never taking its eyes from the gnarled old yew that grew near its cage, where Rue and Christoff crouched amid the highest branches that would support them.

The night hung cold and deep above. A small, crisp breeze swept flashing colors into the stars.

There were no large trees by the crocodiles, only bushes and open space.

The gatekeeper stumped off. From the yew they followed his progress back to a dilapidated cottage at the edge of the grounds. His door slammed closed.

The hyena was growling at them between bites, pinning the meat between its paws, ripping it frantically into pieces. Rue thought of the crocodiles and shivered. Kit noticed; she felt his hand on her hair, a faint stroke down her back.

When she looked at him the corners of his lips lifted to a smile, devilish. Then he Turned to smoke, sending a sigh through the leaves around them.

She followed him across the treetops to the pit, taking her shape beside his, well back from the edge. The monkeys down the path began to chatter and then to howl.

Instinctively she scanned the brush and shadows, but there was no one else near, no Others, no runner. The monkeys woke the solitary lioness, who let loose an ear-shattering roar.

Rue brought a hand to her forehead, feeling her headache creeping back.

The pit itself was little more than a muddy ditch, but deep. The crocodiles swam about seven feet below them, held back by the steep pitch of the sides and a railing of battered wood. At one end of the pit was a small, sandy beach where one of the creatures watched them edgily, breathing through its mouth. The other had to still be in the water, but with the lack of light, Rue couldn't find it.

Christoff was standing with both hands braced against the railing, looking down. Almost, almost, she was becoming accustomed to the sight of him undressed.

"I don't like your plan," she said for perhaps the tenth time.

"Sorry." He was surveying the pit, focused, frowning. "It's the best we've got. You said you can't swim. That leaves me in the water, and you guarding the shore."

Getting down to the bottom would present no difficulties, but finding the diamond in the muck would. They could not grasp it as smoke. They would have to be either in their human shape or as dragons. And the confines of the pit made it impossible for both of them to be dragons.

Rue joined him at the rail. "What if they've eaten it?"

"Let's hope not. Their lives here are wretched enough. I've no desire to injure them, even for *Herte*. We'd just have to wait it out."

"Wait it out..."

"Aye. And I believe I'd actually prefer this to that." He straightened. "Are you ready?"

"Yes."

He nodded, his gaze traveling the length of her body, deliberately, slowly, as if to memorize her as she stood.

"Then may I have a kiss?" he asked, unmoving. "For luck?"

She felt her heart pick up. She felt her face grow hot.

"You see? I'm asking, not demanding." He lifted his hands to her, palms up. "Even the most beastly of us can learn."

Rue dropped her gaze to the ground, discomfited. "I don't think you're beastly."

"Thank goodness. I was about to point out that that fellow down there has far worse breath than I do."

She laughed softly, shaking her head, but by then his fingers were curling around hers.

"Is that a yes, mouse?"

She inhaled: heat, and animal. Him.

Rue lifted her chin. "Yes."

Everything happened so gently at first, so languidly, as his hands drew hers behind his back so that she had to step toward him, so that their fronts had to touch. As soon as they did his fingers released; he smoothed his palms up her back, one hand at her waist and the other rising to cradle her head. She felt her hair bunch and slide with the passage of his fingers. She felt the cool air on her skin, and the welcome warmth of his chest and stomach and hips. His eyes roamed her face with that half-lidded intensity; she brought up a hand to the slope of his shoulder, resting it there. They stood there together in the open dark, soft and hard, while her stomach tied in knots and her hair stirred with the breeze.

She wet her lips, nervous. "Are . . . are you going to do it?"

"I am." His head tilted to hers. She felt his lips against her cheek, light, thistledown, barely there. "I just . . ."

"What?" she whispered, staring out into the shadows.

"I just like looking at you."

So when he kissed her she was smiling a little, her lips curved under his. Kit loved that curve, let his tongue travel the sweet length of it, tasting her, teasing her, but mostly just driving himself to the edge of reason. When she opened her mouth he heard himself moan, but it was faint and deep, almost inaudible beneath the thunder of his heartbeat. She was exactly as he remembered, silky, succulent. Her hands made circles across his shoulders. She leaned forward into the kiss, rising on her toes, and slowly dug her nails into his skin.

That dark edge within him began to crumble. The lioness roared again and he felt it rumbling through the air, through him, felt Rue tighten and press against him with her thighs slightly parted, her breathing growing shaky. She clung to him as he gradually deepened the kiss, taking his time with it, beckoning her, retreating, teaching her how to cling and to part, to share tongues and pleasure.

She made a feminine sound in her throat that sounded perilously close to surrender.

He honestly hadn't meant it to be more than this, a prelude to what he could give her—but desire was pumping through him in lush black waves, obliterating the last of his noble restraint. Kit had a wild thought to push between her legs and take her here, now, standing up, the two of them as ferocious and untamed as all the other creatures around them. It would be natural, it would be easy; he wanted to and she wanted him to, whether she fully realized it yet or not.

She began to rub herself against him, small, restless moves that became an extraordinary, squeezing friction against his arousal. He had to grab her hips to stop her.

"Wait," he gasped, turning his face to her hair. "Wait, Rue."

She was as flushed and winded as he was. He could do it. As soon as he mastered himself he could do it, she was ready. He felt her shivering beneath his palms. Felt her heat, the salt on her skin. Smelled her scent, lilies and woman.

One of the monkeys let out a particularly shrill scream. The crocodile answered it, thrashing and hissing below.

She took a longer breath, held it. The willing softness of her figure began to tense. Her arms dropped from his.

He did not pull her back to him, although every fiber of his being called out for him to. Instead, he shook back his hair and gave her what had to be a truly savage smile, unable even to be sorry when she shied away a step.

Kit said, "The next time we do this we have to be either clothed or in bed." And quickly, before she could tell him there would be no next time, he Turned to smoke, sinking down into the crocodile den.

The beast on the sand watched him descend, opening and closing its mouth, but at least it didn't rush into the water and try to charge him. He was safe like this, nothing could touch him—but neither could he touch anything. He couldn't even cause a ripple in this form; Kit needed solid shape for that. He skimmed the water's surface, back and forth, feeling the call of *Herte,* feeling the blunt, primitive fear of the other crocodile, nestled in the mud below him.

The pond's reflection caught a rectangle of stars and Rue, leaning over the railing with her hair dangling over her shoulders. She glanced once behind her, then back down at him.

Kit drifted higher, then Turned to dragon, digging his claws into the timbers that lined the top of the pit—there was no room in here to fly. The crocodile on the sand raised up on its feet, snapping its jaws. Kit was mostly out of its range, but the one in the water could do anything. He needed it in sight. Kit swished his tail to the surface, drew a skimming line toward the sand that broke into arrows. Nothing. He tried it again—an easy target, small, unguarded—and the second crocodile surged up like a nightmare, swifter than he'd imagined, streaming water, ignoring his tail to close its mouth on Kit's hind leg.

He Turned but not quickly enough; the crocodile snapped bloody teeth into smoke, falling back to the pond with a terrific splash.

Then Rue was there, a flash of white and gold, a magnificent dragon hanging upside down on the farther wall, her wings spread to catch the starlight. She fixed the reptiles with glowing eyes and opened her mouth to show her own teeth, slowly fanning her wings. She couldn't make any noise but she was doing a damned fine job of intimidation anyway. The second crocodile fled the water to join the first, both of them slinking as far away from her as they could, groaning and climbing over each other as they pressed against the pit wall.

He didn't have to hear her to know what she was thinking: *Hurry.*

He Turned human and instantly realized his second mistake. The pond was deep, much deeper than he'd thought.

Instead of standing in the water he sank through it, barely managing to hold his breath in time. And it was filthy.

He closed his eyes, swimming lower and lower until his hands touched silt. *Herte* sang her song and he heeded it, sifting through the mud, finding rocks and God knew what else, but no diamond.

He ran out of air. He came up huffing, spitting the taste from his mouth. Above him Rue still held position, angling a bright golden eye down at him, her wings extended over his head.

The crocodiles were paralyzed, transfixed on her, knotted into a single dimpled gray lump.

He submerged once more. This time he knew about where to go, kicking down to the deepest part of the pit, reaching into the mud and squashing it between his fingers, searching, searching—

He found it. As soon as he touched it he knew. It was cold in his fist, burning cold; he scissored up to the surface and took a great gulp of oxygen, raising his arm above his head to show her.

*Herte* blazed between his fingers, purple fire that flickered even in this dim light. With a grunt of effort he heaved it up into the air, a slow arc that sparkled. Rue caught it in her mouth. He heard it click against her teeth.

He Turned to smoke, finding his way to the trampled grass beside the pit, becoming a man sprawled out flat upon it, his arms outflung, his face to the sky.

He was wounded and out of breath, but at least he was dry. When they Turned, everything on them was left behind, even water.

A shadow draped across his torso, slender, gliding. Rue had leapt high out of the pit, suspended for one miraculous, infinite moment against the night before landing before him, her claws skidding furrows through the grass. She spat the diamond to the ground near his feet and Turned again. Smoke became woman, outlined with stars. She sat down beside him and tucked her knees up to her chin.

The screams of the menagerie reached a grievous new height.

"I wish I had food for them," she said after a moment, scarcely audible beneath the clamor.

"Try the monkeys," he said. "They're probably delicious."

"My God." She was reaching for him suddenly, her hands on his leg. "You're bleeding."

He was. It looked awful, dark liquid streaking down his calf, the bite marks of the crocodile punching lines of neat little circles into his flesh. Kit sat up. Even as he watched, the blood dribbled over her fingers, scarlet ribbons dripping off her hands.

"Turn." She looked up at him, her eyes urgent. "You've got to Turn now to control it."

"I'll still bleed as a dragon," he pointed out.

"To *smoke*," she said. "I'll meet you back at Far Perch."

"No, mouse."

"Don't be an idiot! We can't manage this here. Turning to smoke is the only thing that will help."

If he was smoke and she was dragon, she would have all the real power. She might fly away to almost anywhere in this city she called her home. She might do nearly anything. Especially since she would be the dragon carrying *Herte*.

"I will follow you," Rue said. "I swear it."

Her hands were still pressed tight over his calf, trying to stem the flow. Her lips were downturned in that familiar, endearing bow.

She had said *we*.

Kit leaned forward, scooping up the diamond and placing it in her hands. "Fly high. You're less likely to be seen that way."

"I will."

With their gazes still locked he made himself smoke, curling up into the night.

# CHAPTER TWELVE

It had always seemed to Rue that London was a city designed exactly for her, if not for her kind. From her very first years here, she had slipped easily into its rhythms, into the webwork of streets and dazzling high fashions, into gourmet food and servants and amusements like Vauxhall and the Haymarket. Her secret self had scarcely ever presented a true problem to her role as the young widow Hilliard, but despite the pleasures of her city life, there was one issue she had never managed to resolve. She could not afford to grow ill. She could not afford to summon a physician. Not ever.

The *drákon* lived and died apart from the Others for countless good reasons; in illness, their Gifts grew dangerously unpredictable. She'd heard of tribesmen gripped by fevers who Turned uncontrollably, changing from dragon to smoke to human to dragon, all the while never waking. A few demolished rooms. One man razed nearly his entire cottage, sending his wife and four children out to the winds until the old marquess had taken them in. It took a mighty disease to humble a member of the tribe, but once a fever riddled them, the consequences could be swift and disastrous.

The notion had frightened her so severely that the one time she knew she had caught the ague, she banished everyone from her house. She told them it was spotted fever and sent them off to Bath for a fortnight. She'd had the locks changed too, because of Zane. Just in case.

Far Perch made a much gloomier, if more sophisticated, prison than her own home had. Without the distant presence of the marquess's caretakers, without the council or the guards, Rue walked alone down the polished hallways, not bothering with sconces or lamps, practicing her silence as Christoff slept upstairs.

It was fairly early in the day. The fact that he was still asleep was nothing worrisome.

She had followed him here, just as she'd promised. She had delivered his diamond to him, both relieved and regretful to let it pass out of her hands. *Herte* was special, without question. Holding it was like holding a cool slice of rainbow, something so rare and magical it didn't seem possible to contain. It spread life through her blood, hummed happiness where it touched her skin. But it was not worth her freedom. So last night she'd given it back to him, made certain he washed his leg and bound it, and then retired.

It was still on Christoff's nightstand when she had gotten up this morning. She'd peered past his door to see it winking at her, a mute temptation; beside it Kit was slate shadows and a shallow, even breathing in the bed. She could just make out the spill of blond hair across his pillow.

She said his name. He did not awaken. Rue closed his door and crept off.

But she could not quite bring herself to leave. She thought of it. She actually went to the parlor window Zane had used and toyed with the latch, opening it, closing it, before drifting down to the kitchen. She found a wooden spoon in one of the drawers and snapped off the handle, bringing it back to the window to jam between the lock and the sash.

The sky beyond the glass was turning a bottomless, pristine blue. A red squirrel dashed across the road in front of her in great leaping bounds, almost flying in its haste to reach a nearby elm.

Her stomach rumbled.

She returned to the kitchen, boiled a pot of water for the tin of porridge she found, eating every bite with a shudder. She loathed porridge. But it was that or the pickles or cod.

Cook would serve her spiced sausages for breakfast. Buttery croissants. Fresh melon and juice and sweet, scalding *café au lait*.

Rue scraped the last of the cold porridge from her bowl and tossed it into a basin, along with the broken spoon. She climbed the stairs back to the marquess's chamber.

He was sprawled on his side, one arm hugging a pillow, his body sunk deep into the feathered mattress. She savored him for a slow, secret moment, the flawless contours of his face, the shape of his hand, long fingers relaxed into a curve against the linens.

It should not be possible for a man to be so beautiful. It should not be possible for him to make her feel like he did, like he wielded a sorcery that made *Herte* seem small in comparison.

"Care to join me?"

"Oh." Her eyes flew to Kit's, open now, regarding her with sleepy interest. She laughed a little, embarrassed. "You're awake."

He eased up against the headboard and pillows, his hair falling unkempt across his shoulders, the sheets slanting down to his hips. He was, of course, completely without nightclothes.

"So it seems." He rubbed a hand across his face. "What time is it?"

"After eleven."

He glanced at the shades, still closed. She moved to the windows, pulling at the draw to let light fall in blocks across the saffron and pale yellow rug.

"How is your leg?"

"Fine. Why are you dressed like that?"

She was a footman, from her fitted waistcoat to her plain woolen breeches, the brass buttons on her cuffs flashing dots in the sunlight. The only thing missing was the wig, which she never wore until she had to. Powdering wigs properly was the sort of thing that could take half the day.

It was luck, or intuition, that had her pack this particular ensemble in the case she'd brought from home yesterday. If she was truly trapped at Far Perch, she wasn't going to be trapped without a measure of her own clothing.

Rue handed Christoff the square of vellum from her coat pocket.

"The Earl of Marlbroke is hosting a masquerade this evening. He'll have hired extra help for it. It's an excellent opportunity to steal inside unnoticed."

He looked up from the invitation. "Where did you get this?"

"From your front parlor. There's a stack of them there on the mantel, unopened. Don't you ever read your post?"

Kit tapped a corner of the vellum against his lips, observing her with something that was not quite a smile. "Dare I ask why we need to steal inside at all?"

"Marlbroke," she said, and waited. "Of the Rotherham Marlbrokes. Of the fortune in South Sea pearls. Lady

Marlbroke fairly staggers with them at every event she attends."

"Ah. The runner."

"Precisely."

"What makes you think he'll be there tonight?"

She shrugged. "He likes pearls. I discovered him near the earl's town home twice last season. I don't think he's taken anything yet. But he wants to."

Christoff nodded, his head bowed, tracing the edge of the invitation with his ring finger. Sunlight threw a clear, frozen brightness into the room, reflecting off the walls and floor up against him, highlighting his jawline and cheekbones and hair. His lashes lifted; she was pinned in a green-gold gaze.

"What does he look like?"

"As I told Mim. Reddish hair, tall. Handsome."

There was a moment's pause. "Handsome?" he repeated, perfectly neutral.

She could not prevent her smile. "Extremely. Did you think he wouldn't be?"

"I had not given the matter any thought, to be frank." He dropped the invitation to the covers, lacing his hands around one knee. "Does he know what *you* look like?"

"I doubt it. We've only ever brushed paths when I was the comte."

He would know that she was female, though, Kit thought. He'd know as soon as he caught her scent. She could dress up in as many damned costumes as she wanted, she could parade in breeches before the king himself if she wished, but to another *drákon* her sex was as obvious as warm faint flowers, or long black eyelashes. Or that soft, incredible mouth.

He drew a slow breath, feeling his lungs expand to their

capacity, exploring that ache. He had never supposed her to be cloistered, not in the way of debutantes or even comely young wives—but he had supposed her to be alone. Perhaps it was naught but his own loneliness he'd envisioned on her, a shared kinship he'd derived from daydreams. But his Smoke Thief wasn't alone. She hadn't been, perhaps ever. There was another who had flown as she had, who lived as she did, in the half-light, at the rim of society. She'd even said as much to the council. Why had he never considered the implications before now?

"He never approached you?" he asked, and heard the skepticism in his own voice. "Not in all these years?"

"No." She spoke dryly. "I imagine he thinks I'm with the tribe. Perhaps a spy sent to snare him. Why else should I be allowed unfettered in London?"

"You avoid each other, then."

"It's not difficult. The city provides ample territory for us both."

Ample territory. The two of them, neatly staking out streets and parishes like the finest of cohorts, rubbing shoulders at their borders.

"His eyes are blue," she added casually, leaning against a bedpost. "Blue as mountain lakes."

"A god among men, no doubt." Kit whipped off the sheets, not bothering to cover himself as he climbed out of the massive oak bed. Rue never moved; a peculiar hard dizziness came over him as his feet hit the floor. He had to stop for an instant, balancing his weight.

She straightened. "What's wrong?"

"Nothing." He stalked toward his dressing room, pulling out a shirt, stockings, his razor and strap; he had no water for the razor; he had no exit but the one behind him. She came up swiftly, her shadow crossing his. He stood there, staring down at the worn leather strap as she crouched by his feet. He felt her fingers skim the bandages he'd wound around his calf last night.

He wanted her to touch him. He held still for it, anticipating it, even knowing what she would find.

"This wound is infected," she said, sharp.

"You can't even see it."

"I don't need to. Sit down. Let me take these off."

He dragged the shirt over his head and subsided into an armchair, watching her go to one knee before him. With her waist and breasts hidden and her chin tucked down, she almost looked the part she meant to act . . . but for the braid of her hair, sliding over her shoulder. Sunlight shifted autumn through it, a play of reds and rich browns shining along the strands. She leaned back on her heel with the loose bandages in her hands, her breath coming out in a hiss.

"It *is* infected," she said accusingly, her eyes flashing up to his. "Look at that. What did you clean it with?"

"Water. Soap. You were there."

"Well, it wasn't enough."

"I beg your pardon. The next time a crocodile chooses to dine upon me, I'll be certain not to forget my pharmacopoeia. And as fetching as I find this little tableau, you needn't fuss. It's not that bad. I'll still be able to dance with you tonight."

Her brows drew together. "Dance with me?"

"At the masquerade, love. We *are* invited."

"*You* are invited, Lord Langford. I'm just a lowly footman. Even the Comte du Lalonde isn't graced with Marlbroke's regard."

"Rue," he said, laughing, leaning forward in the chair, "it's a masked ball. People sport all manner of asinine disguises. They drink too much and talk too much and pretend they don't recognize one another as they grope their neighbors' wives. You don't have to be a footman." He captured her braid, letting the ends curl against his cupped palm. "Be a queen. Be a milkmaid. Milkmaids wear the most charming outfits."

"I'll keep that in mind." She flicked her hair free. "But if the comte isn't invited, I doubt very much the runner will be. The last time I saw him he was a tea dealer, and before that, he was a gardener. He won't be a guest, he'll be a worker. That means he'll most likely be at the house today, not tonight."

"If he's there at all."

"If he's there at all," she agreed, matter-of-fact.

He sat back again, considering her. "You know, with *Herte* in hand we're well ahead of the game. Why not take the day off?" He tried his best smile. "We could have a picnic. Visit Covent Garden. Terrify a few swans, perhaps."

"I've a better idea. On your way back from the apothecary, why don't you purchase some decent food? I won't eat porridge again."

"Dear me. Is it that bad?"

"Worse."

"I suppose," he said, "if you are a footman all day today, you won't have much occasion to dine."

"Marlbroke provides three meals a day to his servants. I won't starve."

Kit tapped his fingers against the armchair. "You've done this before."

Her smile caught his breath, almost blinding in its quick, teasing glow. "Naturally."

He wasn't going to let her go alone. He wondered if he even needed to say it, saw the lingering mischief of that smile on her lips, and decided that he did.

"The Earl of Marlbroke knows me. I cannot pass as a footman."

"No. You're going to the apothecary, remember? You need a salve for your leg."

"Rue—"

"I won't do anything without you," she said, her smile vanished. "I'm only looking for the thief. I only want to see if he's there."

"While *he* will see that *you* are there as well," he pointed out.

"Mutual surveillance. There's no harm in that."

"Mouse." He came to his feet, pulling her up to stand before him. "This is the man who decided to steal the tribe's most valuable diamond and then threw it away when he realized he couldn't sell it. Who has a great, great deal to lose by even being in proximity to another *drákon*. Who obviously risked everything for his life here, and will, in all likelihood, risk everything over again to keep it."

"As would I," she said soberly.

His fingers tightened over hers. "Damn it, you can't go alone. And I cannot plausibly go with you, at least not by daylight. We'll slip in together tonight, for the ball."

"He might not be there tonight!"

"It's a chance we'll take." He made an effort to soften his tone. "We have days yet, Rue-flower. It doesn't all have to happen this afternoon."

"No." A crease had appeared between her brows; she pulled her hands free. "I won't let you spoil this. The masquerade is tonight. Lady Marlbroke will have her pearls out of the vault by teatime at the latest. I must be there."

"It's not possible."

She backed into a ribbon of sunlight. "You swore you would help me!"

"Not help you place yourself in needless danger! Put it out of your head, Rue. We'll go tonight."

"That's not good enough." She strode to the window. For an instant—with his temper rising and the angry bite on his calf sending terse, steady spasms of pain up his leg—he thought she would Turn to smoke and just leave. The chamber was hardly secure.

But instead she stood before the glass, her hands at her sides, haloed with relentless bright light.

"Marlbroke has a daughter," she said suddenly.

"And?"

"Marriageable." She cocked a glance back at him from over her shoulder. "It's her second season. Her name is Cynthia. She prefers to be called Cyn."

"And?" he prompted again, struggling to keep the aggravation from his voice.

She turned to face him. "It occurs to me that she must enjoy having callers for tea. Certainly wealthy, eligible, gentlemen callers."

Cynthia. He couldn't place her. He barely recalled even the earl himself, much less a daughter.

"I could wait until teatime to go, I suppose." Rue made another small shrug. "It would give us the chance to get your salve first."

He stared at her, all layered in gold like a girl dipped in gilt.

A girl in men's breeches.

She was going to do it. He could try to stop her, but at the very best it would earn him her enmity. And at the worst—hell. He was tired of her hostility. He was tired of trying to woo her and manage her at once. She was too intelligent for blandishments and too independent to bow to his will just because he wanted her to.

He realized, surprised, that what he really wanted was to see that teasing smile once more.

Kit sighed. "You would need Marlbroke's livery."

"This *is* his livery." She plucked at a worsted-wool sleeve. "Cost me three pounds off some fellow who lost his position for making eyes at the earl's sniffy daughter. How do you think I know so much about his affairs?"

"Is she sniffy?" he inquired, very mild.

"She called me a jumped-up Frog behind my back, the first time we met." Rue began to peel off the coat, tossing it to the bed. "If the runner were out to steal *her* pearls, I'd probably help him."


Lady Cynthia Meir was the sort of young woman, Kit supposed, who would attract a swath of gentlemen callers. At first glance, her face held the pretty oval serenity of a medieval madonna, with wide-set, greeny-blue eyes and perfectly plucked eyebrows that winged up at the ends, lending her a look of playfulness. It might be easy to assume those eyebrows told the proper story, until one noticed her mouth: also pretty, but for when she smiled. And then Kit was reminded of Melanie. She, too, smiled like a cat with all the cream.

He was the recipient of that smile rather a lot this afternoon. She'd tucked a stem from the little posy of violets and freesia he'd brought her into her bodice, while all the other bouquets languished on a side table. He felt the damnedest fool, posed amid her green-boy admirers like a schoolmaster surrounded by smirking pupils.

She could not be more than eighteen. He sipped his tea and kept an eye out for Rue and wondered if he had ever been so young.

There were footmen passing back and forth along the hall beyond the parlor doors, murmuring voices. He'd felt Rue's presence, her lovely frisson of lightning and clouds, at times closer and then farther as she went about the house. He did not feel any other *drákon*. Not yet.

What a ridiculous plan. His sole comfort was the thought that if the runner truly did show, the instant he noticed Kit he'd likely just flee. Rue would be chasing shadows. She'd be safe.

Time dragged. His calf throbbed. He resisted the impulse to open his watch, following instead the shade cast from the pianoforte by the window, crawling gaunt across the rug. Surely the masquerade would begin soon. He watched Lady Cynthia lift her shoulders from her gown as she leaned forward to spoon more sugar into her cup. She seemed in no hurry to free her crowd of besotted swains, but if Kit could manage to excuse himself, he could find Rue and take her with him, even if it meant escaping up the chimney—

"What of you, my lord?" Cynthia glanced up at him, still holding the spoon. Kit looked at her uneasily, trying to remember what they'd been discussing. Seed cakes? The weather? This was the very thing he'd always hated most about society, dealing with giggly girls and small talk, when usually all he really wanted could be found high in the wild, open sky—or else in some dark, soft bed.

Cynthia's smile puckered into a pout. "Oh, you *are* coming, are you not? *Do* say you are. It simply won't be the same without you."

"I say," exclaimed one of the beaux, "*I'll* be there, Lady Cyn. I'll be a pirate! You can count on me!"

The lady didn't bat a lash. "But Lord Langford . . . ?"

He thought of Rue, so very beyond him in the halls. He thought of all the things he'd rather be doing tonight, every one of them involving her, than lurking about at a masked ball.

"Of course," Kit said smoothly. "I would not dare miss it."

Lady Cynthia recovered her smile. "Marvelous! But what will you come as?"

"It is a surprise."

"But how will I know you?" she protested happily, setting the spoon upon its lavish silver tray. "You must give me some clue! I insist!"

"Why, then . . . I'll be the one watching that you cannot see," Kit said, and took another sip of tea.


The theme of the mask, Rue was informed by the head footman, was the Mysterious Orient. It was unclear to her precisely which aspect of the Orient the ballroom was supposed to represent: the walls and alabaster pillars were veiled in mulberry silk with glass-beaded tassels, and the linen dressings on the punch table had scarlet-maned chimeras woven throughout. Long loops of pearls swayed from the chandeliers—all paste, she checked—and the potted plants ranged from sickly palms to enormous elephant's ears. Rose petals were to be scattered around the food platters and the pyramid of champagne glasses, and the pungent scent wafting from the kitchens was definitely curry. And cheesecakes.

The earl, a most modern man, had moved the house vault from belowstairs to above, so that the heavy safe that held his wife's jewelry was now bolted to the floor of his own quarters, discreetly concealed in the master dressing room. Rue had managed to examine it just once before, late last year. Even smoke would not penetrate its lock; anyone wishing to lift Marlbroke's pearls would have to wait until the steel door was opened. Or until the pearls were on the countess.

Or her silly daughter.

Rue did not approach the safe. As day help she had no good reason to be anywhere near the family quarters, but so far she didn't need one. She knew the pearls were still safely stowed. On her way to the wine cellar she passed a red-faced trio of maids, the three of them arguing fiercely over who had last dressed milady's best wig, and where the clutch of orchid-dyed ostrich feathers meant for it might be.

Trouble abovestairs, it seemed. If the countess was not yet in her wig, then the pearls would still be locked away. Jewelry was always reserved as the final glory.

Rue worked efficiently, as strong as any of the men, careful not to stand out in their numbers any more than necessary. But once she found herself lingering outside the main parlor, sent to polish the ormolu pier glasses framing its doors. The wedge of Christoff's shoulder was just visible to her, his waistcoat of gunmetal blue, his arm as he lifted his teacup. He was seated with his legs out and his ankles crossed, looking elegantly masculine and uncommonly relaxed. She could hardly make out the bandages she'd rewrapped around his calf beneath the stocking.

Cynthia's laughter seemed to wash out of the room with irritating regularity.

Rue exhaled hard through her nose. Lady Cynthia. For heaven's sake, he'd be better off with Mim than that nittering twit.

She stared down at her hands, the rag she was using crumpled between her fingers. Her nails were short, dirty, with dark rings of tarnish outlining the beds. There was a scratch along her left palm from carrying a chipped bottle of port. She was perspiring beneath the cheap horsehair wig and wool livery, and getting a cramp in her back from all the polishing. She felt hot, and grimy, and as far opposite the cool and haughty daughter of Lord Marlbroke as anyone could be.

She had told Mim the truth, so long ago: Rue wasn't a lady. She never would be. She could steal as many royal tiaras as she wished, but it was foolish, foolish thinking to envision her life as anything beyond that of a thief.

The marquess's ankles uncrossed. He set down his tea and leaned forward in his chair, glancing idly around him as if to take in his surroundings. Before she could pull back, his eyes captured hers, clear green attention. She nearly flushed, to be caught spying, but just then the butler strode by. Rue bent her head and applied her rag hastily to the bronze frame of the pier.

"You there, boy," said the butler, pausing to look down his nose at her. "Follow me."

It seemed the pulley used to raise and lower the ballroom's main chandelier had jammed halfway down. And that was how she came to be perched at the tip-top of a very wobbly ladder with an open flame in her hand, gently lighting each of the one hundred and twelve beeswax candles in their cut-crystal cups, when the runner walked in below her.

# CHAPTER THIRTEEN

"I tell you, I saw him," she hissed at the marquess. They were standing facing away from each other outside the stables, Rue rubbing the tarnish from her hands, Christoff apparently pretending to wait for the horse he had not brought. The dusk was stretching into a thin blue translucence around them.

"I'm not saying you didn't," he responded, hardly audible. "But I never felt him there."

"But he *was*," she began, and choked off as a pair of stable boys sauntered past, ignoring her, tugging their forelocks to Christoff. "And I don't think he noticed me," she whispered, as soon as they were gone. "He never looked up at me."

He spoke down to the dirt and straw. "Was he a servant?"

"Right, then," came a new voice, very loud, "that's it for you blokes." The head footman was herding a group of workers toward the stables, shooing them along with a lantern and gloved hands. "You'll get your pay from Hendricks—that's him over at the gate. Come on, come on. Leave them coats with Mrs. Tiverton. We've got toffs coming through in less than an hour, and they don't bleedin' need to see you lot, do they?" The man spotted Rue. "You there! Oy, you! Get along with the rest, eh?"

Rue nodded and raised her hand to hide her mouth, scratching at her cheek. "He was carrying a viola. He's a musician."

She had to walk away before she could catch Christoff's response.

She vanished into the twilight, a slight figure soon devoured by shadows and the restless flicker of the torches the stable boys were embedding in precise intervals along the drive. Kit looked back at Marlbroke's mansion, at the warm golden windows and colored drapery, the ornate plastered ceiling of the ballroom visible behind glass like distant icing on a wedding cake.

He gathered himself. He let his mind float, let his senses rise... past the stables, past the cool evening air... past limestone and mortar and bricks, to the people behind the walls, to footsteps and babbled conversation, to spices and fruit punch and the dry singe of champagne just popping open... to blood rushing, to hearts beating, and something else, something not quite right—

"Sir? Get you a coach, sir?"

Kit turned his gaze to the scruffy stable boy now standing before him, shifting nervously from foot to foot.

"A coach?" offered the boy again, remembering to remove his cap.

Kit glanced down at the cocked hat in his hands, at his gloves and stick, none of them conveniently forgotten back in Marlbroke's front hall. Beyond the stable boy someone else approached. The footman of before, closing in with a heavy stride.

"Your pardon, milord," the man said, sending the boy off with a scowling jerk of his head.

"No," said Kit, as if answering a question. "No, I'm fine. Good evening." And he strolled out the main gates like a man who knew what awaited him in the dark.

Which he did.

She was huddled with her arms crossed over her knees on the front stairs of a dark, empty doorway two blocks down. She must have surrendered her coat with the rest of the workers; he felt her first, as he always did, but just after that he saw her, her plain shirt and wig a dull paleness in the unlit night. As soon as he approached, she stood.

"Did you see him?" Rue demanded, her voice hushed.

"No."

"He's there! I know he is!"

A coach and four rushed by in a thunder of creaks and jingles and snorting horses. Kit resumed walking, looking straight ahead. She kept pace, three steps behind.

"If you won't go back with me—"

"Kindly do not jump to conclusions," he said abruptly. "I said I didn't see him. But I did feel something. I just don't know what it was."

"I do."

The night felt heavy about him, the air damp. The pain in his calf was a haze of red biting insects, climbing inexorably up his leg.

"We must go back," Rue said, and stopped walking. Kit swung about.

"We cannot Turn to smoke in there. We certainly cannot appear unclothed, or as dragons. There's only one way back into that place."

Her head tilted, her expression dubious. She was so winsome, so outrageously stubborn, that he wanted to drag her

to him and kiss her there on the open street, no matter who
might pass by.

"What are you suggesting?" she asked.

"Come with me to Far Perch. And then you'll see."

They could not be announced. The key to skulking, the
marquess had noted in his sardonic, understated manner,
was to skulk. Having the butler announce them at the ball
would ruin any chance of an ambush, and he wasn't going to
all this trouble to have some fellow in a turban shout out his
title to a roomful of people, one of whom might or might
not be the runner.

"We'll simply enter the back way," he said, throwing a
glance down the alley that led to Marlbroke's stables. "We'll
say we became lost."

"Lost? In that patch of garden back there? They'll never
believe that."

Christoff turned to her, his eyes gleaming. "Of course
they won't. But I'm sure a shilling or two will help the footmen look the other way to salvage a lady's good name. After
all, we wouldn't be the first couple to slip out of a ballroom
for a bit of privacy." His hand closed over hers, lifting.
"Keep your mask up, love. No one will know it's you."

She thought at least that much was true. Rue had tried
many guises as a thief, but none so dramatic, so incredibly
flamboyant, as this. She was festooned in emerald satin and
delicate French netting, laced up in a corset that squeezed
the air from her lungs and left her tottering in high, narrow
heels that made each step a hazard. Tiny beads of faceted jet
scalloped her skirts in layers all the way to the hem, giving
the illusion of small, perfect scales. Whalebone and wire under cloth-of-gold made narrow, folded wings fixed to her

back; they crested above her shoulders and ended in dagger points near her hips. She wore no wig or gloves; instead she was covered—from the piled locks on her head to the very tips of her fingers—in a pale, metallic gold powder, fine as faerie dust.

The Dragon Queen. And Christoff, in matching satin and powder, the beads seeding his waistcoat of silver and green: the Dragon King. Dark to his light, night to his day. Small wonder the old marquess had forbidden his wife to appear in public like this. The marchioness had commissioned the costumes for some long-ago *bal masqué* and then packed them away unworn—even the powder—until this night. Until Christoff had remembered them.

Her half mask was feathers, iridescent green and black and blue that tufted out at the ends. The handle was shaped ebony.

The marquess raised his own mask, identical to hers, and gave her a final bright look.

"I confess, as much as I enjoyed you in breeches, you hold up that gown rather well."

She studied him through the eyeholes. "You truly *have* stopped trying to be charming."

"You're the most ravishing creature in the world, sweet Rue, even when hidden behind feathers and beads. How was that?"

"Adequate, if insincere."

"Then you mistake me." He took up her free hand and pressed her fingertips to his lips, gold to gold, sending a flash of sudden, sensual warmth stealing up her arm. His voice dropped to a huskier note. "I am utterly sincere."

His eyes stayed level on hers, steady, serious, even as he kept her hand. She stared at him, trying not to feel her heart, trying not to feel his lips, so warm beneath her touch, softer than clouds.

Kit lowered his gaze; he kissed her fingers and smiled. "Poor Lady Cynthia. She'll be devastated to find she's not the belle of the ball."

Before she could respond, he draped her arm over his and drew her with him down the alleyway. Rue was forced to focus on the cobblestones to save her ankles; if one of her heels caught, she'd have to either Turn or risk her neck in the fall.

Ravishing. She gazed blindly down at the stones. He thought she was ravishing.

They came to the back of the laundry house, around the corner of the hay-scented stables to the place where they had stood together not two hours past. Torchlight lavished amber over the drive and hedges, blurred the baroque cornices of the mansion into weird shifting detail. Laughter sprinkled the air, two hundred voices chattering in one rousing mass—and beneath it all lilted the cheerful refrain of a minuet. Rue strained to distinguish the viola from the blend of strings and horns and pipes but could not.

She kept her mask up and her lashes down, feigning discretion when they ran into the first servant at the edge of the vegetable garden—a scullery maid searching for a pail—and the second, a footman who only murmured at them and bowed out of their path. As they reached the formal gardens they began to pass other couples, wine-happy guests done up in garish silks and spangles that didn't disguise them well enough in the dark.

There was a mist spreading over the sky. Behind it a half-moon had begun to rise, lonely and distant, rainbowed with haze.

Outside the open patio that led to the ballroom Kit

paused, looking up into the night, his jaw set. The people beyond the doors were a mosaic of color and motion.

"The musicians' dais is to the right," Rue said. "Against the eastern wall."

"I know." She heard him take a longer breath than before; he sent her a sideways look. "Stay close, little mouse."

"I will."

They entered the spill of Others. She was instantly assaulted with scents and light and sounds, but years of self-imposed discipline helped her to ease into it. She could narrow her concentration to specific particulars: the pinch of the shoes on her feet. The wooden percussion of the floor. The sheen of candlelight off the punch bowl. The smell of tobacco. The smell of sugar. The soft-slurred words of a lady, dressed all in rose. The music.

The viola.

They prowled the edge of the chamber, moving slowly because they had to move slowly, masks up, not speaking. Someone pressed a glass of champagne into her hand. It chilled her fingers to numbness.

And in this heightened state, she felt a change begin to slide through Christoff. Ineffable at first, just a strange, electric eddy that seemed to pull and gather all the air around them, a dry swirling of the heat and light and cold down to him. His body tightened. His stride grew longer, more even. Even his face altered; his features seemed to harden, the faint lines that marked him smoothing into polished stone. Beneath the golden powder he was radiant and remote, nothing mortal at all.

With every step his very essence shifted, the hunter in him rising, consuming, so that by the time they were in sight of the musicians he nearly crackled with black, burning energy, his arm gone to steel beneath hers, everything about him taut and primed. She held her fingers as lightly over his sleeve as she could manage; it almost frightened her, this transformation, the glamorous man stripped away to reveal the dark and silent beast that lived within. Alpha.

It frightened her, and it exhilarated her. He hadn't been like this at the menagerie. He hadn't been like this with Mim. She knew she had to search for the runner but Kit drew her gaze like a terrible flame, dark magic. She did not want to look away.

"There," he said under his breath. She followed his gaze to the musicians seated on the dais, sporting fiddles and fifes and timbrels.

The man with the viola turned his head, still playing, his face hidden behind a mask of blank velvet. His eyes found theirs. Her stomach clenched.

She had not fully considered this. She had not thought of what might actually come of this moment. Christoff was coiled destruction, he was swift ruin set to fly—

Three men, he had said. He had killed three men. And soon it might be four.

"Remain here," he said to her, his lips barely moving, and without thinking she clutched at his arm.

"Wait—"

"Langford!" A man bumbled into them, smiling, ringed in alcohol fumes. "There y'are, old boy! Cynthia mentioned you might come!"

It was Marlbroke, that pompous old toad, dressed in a long false beard and a robe of red embroidered silk, and a box-shaped hat upon his wig topped with an orange tassel. His eyes were bloodshot past his mask. "Excellent to see you, excellent! Cyn's nearby too. She's an angel; did you note her?"

Rue released Kit's arm. She inched one step back.

"Great God, what a getup! Let me guess—you're one of them Greek fellows. Apollo, that's it. Apollo, am I right?"

"Not quite," she heard Kit respond, and took another step back.

The minuet concluded. Rue looked up past the bowing dancers to the dais. The viola was placed upon an empty chair. The runner was nowhere to be seen.

"There she is! Cyn! Cynthia, my girl! Come over here, see who I've found! Oh, don't give your father that look, pet! Come over, you'll be pleased!"

Even if Rue had not known the fair Lady Cyn was near, she would have felt her approach. As the girl walked up they bumped arms; Rue became almost light-headed with the lure of the pearls Cynthia was wearing, heavy drops in her hair, around her neck, swaying from her ears. They hummed as *Herte* did but smokier, more mellow. How easy it would be in the confusion of the ballroom to slip a finger behind the choker, to loose the clasp. To catch that set of matched perfection in her fist and walk away.

Rue sidled back a third step. By either accident or design Cynthia had cut between her and Kit; she had been the lady in rose, of course, a petite, pert-nosed angel, fluffed and shirred with lace. She sported wings as well, gentle falling curves of downy pink feathers.

Christoff was accepting her hand, bowing over it. Rue turned quickly, ducking between a very tall peacock and a handmaiden in an Elizabethan headdress. She kept moving without looking back.

Lady Cynthia had that smile again. Her eyes were sparkling past the wisp of lace that formed her mask; her teeth were small and even. Kit could hardly bear to touch her.

"My lord," she purred, and some other nonsense, strings of syllables he paid no attention to. His blood was pumping very loudly in his ears. The pain spreading up his leg had become alien and unimportant; the dizziness impeded him only when he turned his head too fast. His senses stretched so sharp and fine that every moment, every breath, boiled through him like tar, slow and thick and endless. But it was always like this before the hunt. It was always like this.

His eyes were drawn to the pearls draped around the girl's white wig, a soft rich beckoning that sent a new sort of ache up his palms. Their color, their perfection: they spoke to him of Rue. The dragon in him burned to hold them.

Rue. He looked away from the girl. Instantly, without turning around, he knew that his mate was no longer beside him, that the runner had vanished as well. His heart surged. He cast his awareness outward like a net, searching for Rue even as his eyes scanned the chamber.

Someone was still speaking. The girl's voice burbled upward, ending on a shriller note, and then a shriller one still.

"Lord Langford! My lord—please—"

Kit realized that he had not released the girl's hand, that his thumb was pressing her fingers stiff into his palm, that she was trying to pull away. He opened his fingers. She drew back from him with a high, sudden arc of her wrist, her eyes much wider than before. Her smile was gone.

He inclined his head in apology and shouldered past without comment. He couldn't speak anyway, not now, with his muscles bunched and his jaw clenched so tight he had to draw the air through his teeth. Cynthia's low, sharp gasp as he walked away hurt his ears like a steam whistle hissing through his brain.

Where was she? The ballroom was flooded with Others, their scent and noise and painful colors. But there was a center to the storm, there was a place of gold composure, deep-green skirts, lily calm—there, far over there, by the doors—and with her a void—

She was addressing someone. A man in a mask and a simple gray coat. She had lowered her own mask to her skirts, they were facing each other, and through the sea of people Kit could see her talking. Her hair glinted in the candlelight like chocolate-dark flame. Her lips were ruddy gold.

The runner reached out and seized her forearm, his fingers digging into her skin. And with just that, the sight of another *drákon* with his hand upon her, hard white fingers over the pale shimmer that was Rue, the last scrap of clear will that was Christoff scorched to ash.

The beast in him exploded into life, into fury. *No one touched her, no one touched her, no one—*

He heard the people exclaiming. He pushed through them easily; they fluttered aside like paper dolls, clearing out of his way. He felt his lips drawn back. He felt the black dragon clawing up through his blood, lithe and deadly now, a savage quickening that had him panting and the need to Turn so potent his body felt like rusted iron, too heavy and clumsy to keep up.

Both Rue and the runner had turned their heads toward him, still linked. He felt Rue's gaze, the exotic wonder of her face, but Kit's focus was on the runner, the other *drákon* with his fingers smeared in gold and his eyes brilliant blue behind the mask.

Seconds before Kit reached them, the man freed her. He stepped away and gave a quick bow in her direction—she was looking back at him, distracted—and then, goddammit, the runner Turned to smoke, right there in the midst of the ballroom. A few of the women cried out.

Rue lifted her face to follow the smoke, an ashen haze twining about the ceiling and chandeliers, sifting toward the garden doors. Then she looked back at Kit. The mask dropped from her fingers. She hurried toward him.

"No," she said, reaching for his sleeve, taking hold with a grip he couldn't shake. "No, don't! You can't!"

The smoke was shifting, lowering. The doors were wide open to the night.

"No," said Rue once again, catching his other sleeve. She placed her body in front of his, her voice hushed and intense. "Christoff! You cannot—not here."

He exhaled. The dragon rose, peaking against his skin.

Rue shoved hard against him with both hands, snapping his gaze back to hers.

"*Kit!*"

Her eyes glittered, a flash of bright gold, there and gone. He inhaled again, slower, colder, suspended in a crystalline instant of vacillation, moments from release.

"By gad," exclaimed a man just behind them, with a tipsy hiccup. "Awfully foggy in here, ain't it?"

The smoke was filtering out the doorway, murk that dissolved up to the stars.

Kit looked down at Rue. At her forearm, the smudge of powder that showed pink skin beneath the gold, the imprint of the other man's hand on her clear as a brand. Behind her the runner's clothing was a heap of velvet upon the ballroom floor. People were laughing around it. Someone picked it up, shaking out the waistcoat, marveling aloud at the trick.

He lowered his arms. Rue had to let go then, and when she did he took her left hand in his right and pulled her with him the other way, not to the doors that led outside but to the ones that led into the mansion. She trailed behind with short running steps; he didn't slow to appease her.

They plunged into the deeper halls of the house, past the main staircase to a tall closed door, carved mahogany, that swept open without a sound and revealed a room of sconce-light and books and shelves: the library, quiet as a tomb. Gilt titles gave off a dull, ghostly glow of letters.

There was a desk empty of papers, and two chairs turned to face the hearth. A black japanned screen of painted flowers and birds shielded the chairs from the draft of the door. Kit towed her over to it. She let him, her brows crinkled, her fingers clasped in his. When he had her behind it he Turned, a flash of smoke to let his clothing subside, and then he was human before her, full nude, yanking her to him and closing his mouth over hers.

The powder that had covered him seconds before floated about them in sparkling wisps, sprinkling his feet and the hem of her skirts.

"No," he rasped, as she tipped her head away from his. He nipped his teeth against the delicate warmth behind her ear, imperative. "Stay as you are. Stay as you are." He ran his hands up into her hair and pulled loose the pins; soft-dusted locks fell in heavy satin across his fingers.

In the dusk of the room the golden powder lost its tint. She was reflection and light, burnished colors and pale, bright skin.

The bodice of the gown was cut low and square and barely covered her shoulders, no maidenly design, contrived for temptation. He moved his lips to her throat and inhaled deeply, trailed his mouth down the slender arch of her neck, and lower, tasting powder and her, turning his cheek to her heartbeat.

She was breathing quickly, unevenly. Her chest rose and

fell, her breasts cinched high in full, open invitation. He drew his tongue along their curves, then opened his mouth over her, tasting, caressing, pulling at the bodice until stitches popped and his fingers found a nipple. He bent his head to suckle her. She made a wordless sound, protest or pleasure, he didn't know. He didn't care. He sank to his knees on the rug and dragged her down with him to straddle his open thighs. He looked up from her breast, panting. Her fingers had left lustrous leopard spots across his arms. Her lips were swollen red from his kisses.

Kit pushed back her skirts. Without taking his eyes from hers he ran his palms along her stockings, sliding up to her garters. Her bare skin was silky just above the ties, her legs smoothly muscled; the legs of a fencer, of a sorceress. He eased back on his heels and clenched his fingers into her buttocks, lifting and guiding her, pulling her nearer so that her thighs closed around him, her weight over his and her soft curls pressed against his erection. Her lips parted. She put her arms around his shoulders, her hair crushed into perfume between them.

"What are you doing?" Rue whispered, the faintest of sounds, but he didn't bother to answer. Not with words—not when he had her dark gaze and her legs and her scent, lilies and delicious hot readiness. She shifted and her gown rustled against his skin, the false wings behind her casting off light in spare, pagan lines. The corset held her waist and back stiff but below it, oh, below, she was tender and pliant, all shivers and budding moisture when he touched her warm folds. He was balanced on his knees and the balls of his feet, she was heat and a bare, lissome tension on his lap, her cheek dipping to his and a telling catch in her throat. He stroked her again, his fingers seeking, probing. Her sheath was tight, wet velvet. She turned her face to his neck. Kit bared his teeth in a smile she could not see.

Rape or seduction. He would take either.

With one arm beneath her and the other behind her, he raised her higher and then pulled her hard back down, lifting off his heels to impale her. Her fingers jerked in his hair.

It hurt. Rue sucked in air, shocked, the sensation of burning invasion overwhelming her in waves. But he had lowered his mouth to her nipple again, was drawing on it in short, fierce tugs that sent a confusion of painful pleasure streaking through her blood—then his mouth gentled, tender kisses, his tongue lapping. Fierce again—his teeth bit and his arms bore down around her hips, pushing himself deeper inside, intensifying the burn. She twisted her fingers in his hair, a moan trapped in her chest. She wanted him to stop and she wanted him to go on. She wanted his wild, savage look and that coil of new pleasure that was unwinding through her, through the deepest part of her where he filled her and it hurt—but it didn't—

From beyond the lacquered screen came the sound of the library door opening. Distant music flooded the room.

Rue froze, mortified, staring down at Christoff, but he only glanced at the screen that concealed them and then back up at her. His lips made that devilish smile; he shook his head, just once. Silently, without evoking even a murmur from her rumpled skirts, he curved his fingers around her waist and drew her harder against him, his lashes lowering.

She bit her lip to stop the moan, her legs flexed, arrested between agony and need.

Someone was moving about the library. Someone was over by the desk. If only they walked around it to the chairs—

Kit pulled her even closer, spreading her wider, sending her heels digging into the floor. He used his hands at her waist to force her to move, slowly, slowly, in such small degrees and with such aching intensity that she felt every inch of him, her throat closed in exhilaration and anxious, blazing excitement.

There came the *chink* of crystal against crystal. The liquid purl of sherry being poured.

They rocked together, part of her ready to Turn on an instant, but another part of her, the human part of her, growing breathless and eager, stretched sore with his movements, finding that coil of pleasure of before but better now, darker, a flickering elation that licked at her from the inside.

She cupped her palms around Kit's face. He was marked with her touch, glimmer streaking his skin. He watched her with his sleepy look and that scant, clever smile.

The person beyond the screen sighed, setting the sherry upon the desk. A leather chair squeaked.

Her hands tightened; her eyes closed. She felt like someone else. She felt like her entire body was beyond her control, expanding, a desperate yearning lashing through her, and she couldn't breathe, she couldn't speak, she couldn't make a sound—

The chair squeaked again. Footsteps sounded to the door.

—but she was growing, growing, and he was deep and hard within her—

Music rushed in. Voices rang out.

—and if she couldn't breathe soon she was going to die, she was going to weep, because it was so near and she was so close, but she had to hold on—

The door shut. Kit put his fingers on her nipple and pinched. Rue shattered.

He watched it happen, felt her shudder and cry out, a low, beautiful sound that resonated all the way through him, that sent him to his own release with just one last powerful thrust. He clutched her to him and pressed his face against her chest, emptying himself into her, his seed, his life, his hopes. And she drew her arms up around his head and bent her cheek to his temple, her lips in his hair, her body a lovely, perfect bow over his.

Rue-flower, his dragon queen. His bride.

# CHAPTER FOURTEEN

The lord's house appeared dead dark, but Zane knew better than to trust in how things appeared. So he'd watched it for a good long while, crouched behind the stable doors, holding his cupped hands to his mouth to warm his face against the night. The stable was chilly and dank and impressively dismal. The hay mounded in the stalls smelled of mold. If Langford had horses there was no sign of them here, no water, no blankets or carriage, not even a few paltry flakes of spilled oats. He didn't even think there were rats.

He would have thought it damned odd but for *her*. She had never kept cattle either.

Haze was silver-plating the sky, obscuring the stars and turning the moon into an evil winking eye. It also thickened the shadows, which was fine for his purposes.

Still, he waited. He'd kept watch like this countless times before, knew how to hold himself awake through the cold numbing hours. He curled his toes inside his boots, one by one, feeling the leather scrape against his nails. He made faces, squinting, opening his jaw, wrinkling his brow. He cracked his neck, and then his knuckles, *two, three, four, five,* stretching out his arms.

The stink of the mold was a mounting pressure behind his eyes. Zane blinked the blur from his vision, staring hard at the mansion's black windows. Nothing moved. He'd been here two hours, and the stable yard and kitchen garden remained as lifeless as the house.

Good enough.

He crept out of the stable, skirting the yard to the fence and then the trees, sliding along the narrow side of the building to the front, where once again he lingered, alert to any traffic that might be passing along.

The street was empty. A white-pillared place three doors down had the second story lit, but that was all. All the other homes were shuttered tight.

In Zane's experience there were only two kinds of Quality: the ones what caroused all night like mad tomcats, and the ones what took to their beds early like wee fussy babes.

He'd wager the Marquess of Langford was the tomcat-type. He'd had that animal glint in his eye.

Zane himself neither drank nor slept; he was stone-sober awake. He stole to Langford's parlor window and pressed the heel of his palm to the weak spot of the jamb.

Nothing.

He pressed harder, glancing around and then risking a quick jump up to see if he could tell what was wrong. He jumped twice before he saw it, a wooden stick wedged against the lock.

He cursed under his breath, subsiding. He never should have told her how he'd managed it before. She'd made it clear she didn't want to hear from him until she sent word, but things were dire. He had to talk to her, and away from that bloody marquess who hovered over her like a bloody Beefeater guarding the bloody crown jewels.

He withdrew to the side of the house, but he already knew the other windows were secure. He'd tried them all before. He ran a hand over his mouth and considered what to do.

The mist drifted dead-gray above. The moon glared down at him.

Zane padded back to the kitchen door, jiggled the handle. Polished brass, fairly new, a tight keyhole; he pulled his tools from his pocket. It was better than breaking a window, but not much better. He'd be exposed like this for long crawling minutes, with the moon frosting his shadow along the porch steps and the plated light all over his back. Anyone looking out a window could see him. Grosvenor Square wouldn't be like Cheapside, or St. Giles. The nightwatch here would come quick at the first scream.

Despite the cold, he began to sweat. Dirty Clem got caught like this, busting into a house in Mayfair. Thought he was the best bleedin' cracksman, used to boast about his fingers and his picks—*ye'll never be nae good, ye soddin' whelp*—and now he was rotting in Lud Gate and Zane, his former disciple, had the picks. Not like Clem was going to use them again anyways. Not with the gangrene eating his fingers—

There. The lock released. The door sighed open. He stepped inside, closing it quick behind him with both hands.

He slipped his knife from his belt. The kitchen was very, very cold.

He knew the way to go now, down the side hall, up the main stairs, pausing at the slightest little creak—a floorboard—and distant wooden pop—the attic?—holding his breath for utter silence.

But the marquess's bedchamber was empty. So were all the others, even the one that held her things. He recognized the peach-and-blue-striped valise straight off, the short row of men's boots and ladies' shoes, all in her size, forming a neat line inside the armoire.

The house was deserted. He'd been right about Langford. Tomcat.

Zane went back to her room, smoothed a hand over the covers of the bed, took up a pillow, and held it to his face. It did smell of her, almost imperceptible. She'd come back.

He glanced around the chamber and decided upon the chaise longue far back in a corner, its cushions covered in a shiny hard satin that had him slipping for purchase. It wasn't very comfortable, which was good. He leaned his head against the padding and studied the view past the windows until the moonlight began to burn. His lids drifted closed.


They left the masquerade as they had joined it, stealing along shadows, Rue in her stocking feet and a hand clasped over her torn bodice, Christoff bothering only with his shirt and breeches, everything else bundled in his arms.

They had exited through the library window. He hadn't even asked her; he'd only opened it wide and dropped his costume and their shoes to the gravel below, a crisp *thunk* that echoed alarmingly. When she lingered behind the screen, he crossed back to her, drawing her to the open glass without words, only a quick, fervent kiss that sent all the aches in her body throbbing.

A line of light broke from the doorway; the hinges were

inching open with the new draft. Someone chuckled, very near.

Christoff Turned, gliding over the sill and down to the ground, shielded by the potted hedge of boxwood that grew between Marlbroke's mansion and the one a sidewalk away. Smoke gathered into man. He lifted his face to her, waiting.

Rue placed a hand upon the sill. She did not want to Turn. She didn't want to lose the covering of her gown, as meager as it was. She felt bruised and shy and remotely amazed. But the library door was opening farther. There were a pair of men paused just outside it, speaking of horse races.

Kit Turned again, smoke rising to encircle her, her hands and arms and hair. She'd never felt anything like it, she'd never imagined what it might be like to touch another *drákon* in this way. He was cool and blinding; she held her breath against him.

The men grew more earnest in their discussion. Their shadows fell across the entry rug.

"I'm going," she muttered to Kit, and threw her legs over the sill, rotating carefully around—the cloth-of-gold wings caught on the wood, and she lost a few of the jet beads, heard them go bouncing along the floor—easing down until her feet were braced against the limestone wall and she hung by just her hands. She let go. It wasn't far, and Kit was there to catch her, snatching her up neatly to his chest.

"Hell," he said, and put her on her feet. He looked down at his stomach, a fresh scratch welling crimson along his skin, then up at the wings. "Those things are a bloody menace."

"I didn't ask you to catch me!"

"You're so delightful when you're irrational. Of course

I'm going to catch you." He slid a hand behind her nape and kissed her again. "It's what I do."

And despite herself she leaned into him, offering herself to him with her throat arched and her heart like a drum that beat hard and close against her breastbone. He stepped nearer, breathing against her lips, his fingers spreading through her hair.

"Clarissa Rue," he whispered, making her name a hushed entreaty. "Come home with me. Let's go home."

She followed him down the line of boxwood, because when he spoke to her like that, heaven help her, she lost all logic and solid reason. She thought she might follow him forever.

But the boxwood ended at the alley and Kit still had not dressed. Instead, he bent and shoved his coat and shoes past the branches into the last pot, then tore off his shirt and breeches and did the same to them.

"We'll fetch it all tomorrow." He glanced up at her. "What's amiss?"

She didn't want to tell him the truth, that she felt like a stranger, that he was so beautiful, that the gown was her last shield. So she said, "You feel warm, and you're limping. Are you well?"

"Considering that at the moment I'm only paces away from a very brightly lit ball—aye, very well."

"Perhaps it would be better not to fly. Perhaps we should hire a hackney."

His head tipped as he took her in, his hair stirring about his face as the wind whistled down the stone gutters and cobblestones of the alley.

"Mouse," he said, and smiled. "You steal my breath. But I fear hailing a coach for you now might present a difficulty. You look soundly ravished, my love."

Her cheeks began to heat. His smile darkened; he ran a finger along the torn rim of the bodice, trailing fire with his touch.

"I vow I'm quite taken with it. I'll have to see what I can do to keep you looking this way."

The wind shifted, very cool against her face. She lowered her gaze and Turned, letting the dress and corset and stockings fall. He swept them up briskly and crammed them into the next pot, scattering leaves over the bright wings. Then he Turned too, and together they ascended up into the hazy sky.

Grosvenor Square was fairly near. She thought they'd glide there, but to her surprise Christoff kept rising, a diaphanous veil through the thicker mist, prismed with moonlight. She trailed him, curious, as he broke through the layers of condensation and became dragon, soaring against the night.

Surely his shadow was visible from below. Surely the moon revealed him, but if he knew he didn't care, because he wasn't even flying straight any longer, but circling and dipping, cutting wide, open circles around her, a streak of silvery green and indigo and scarlet, flashing eyes.

She drifted a while longer atop the mist, spreading herself thin with the moon bone-white above and the earth shifting sparks below, countless yellow flames from candles and lanterns softened through the atmosphere. Kit circled her once more, became sudden smoke that spiraled around her, drawing her upward, then dragon, flinging himself high into the heavens. At the end of her spiral she Turned and vaulted after him, her wings beating, her world an enchanted blend of warm and cold light, her body nearly weightless with the wind.

Perhaps they could be seen. Somehow it wasn't important; she felt the return of that giddy freedom. They were so high, two faraway creatures crisscrossing the moon. They might be birds, or clouds, or fleeting imagination. No one had to know.

He arced toward her, a living blade that sliced the air, rising up to fly beside her. He swept closer, and closer, then ducked under her wings to rub his jaw against hers, a swift, sweet caress before breaking off to swoop below and then above, directly above. She twisted her neck to look back at him but he was too near, so she veered left, closing her wings for the dive. Christoff copied her, matching her move for move even as he drew nearer to her back. She used her velocity to shoot upward, her wings fully opened, catching a shaft of wind that spun her in a slow tumble; he was there with her, a presence behind her, a weight. His talons found her shoulders and hips. He clutched her gently, pulling her to him. For a few wondrous minutes, as long as the wind cradled them, they were one creature, four wings, two tails, his head by hers, their cheeks touching.

She closed her eyes with the feeling. She would have laughed if she could.

The wind changed and Kit let her go. He lifted quickly above her only to ripple back down, descending to the mist, dipping a claw down into it to trace a loose, skimming curve, and then another one: a heart that flashed and dissolved back to vapor before he was even done.

He glanced up to her and Turned, piercing the center of where the heart had been, vanishing from sight.

She circled once and plunged after him, Turning only the very second before she would break free of the haze, a white-pearled dragon sailing across the London sky—

But she was smoke instead. And Christoff was too, and Far Perch was an orderly cluster of peaked roofs and chimneys and twinkling windows just below them. Kit ignored the cupola they had used before; he went instead to a window that seemed sealed, until she noted the small chink in a corner of one of the panes.

It was the window to his bedroom. They Turned together, facing each other, and he didn't grant her any time to regain her modesty. He swept her up in his arms and carried her to his bed, his lean, muscular body stretching hot over hers.

She awoke to the aroma of citrus, a faint tickle in her nose. A clean fragrance, lemony and a hint of winter orange, it lingered at the edge of the dream she'd just been having: lying on the grass on Blackstone Hill, with Christoff beside her and the afternoon sky like a blue glass bell all around. He was supple against her, breathing near her ear. His palm covered her shoulder. His legs tangled between hers.

She was in his bed, not back in Darkfrith. Rue took a moment to process that: she was in his bed. He was wrapped around her. They had made love in a library, and then again here, in this huge feather bed.

"Whatever you're thinking," he said huskily, still by her ear, "keep thinking it."

His legs slipped from hers. His palm became a force, a gentle coercion, rolling her to her back. He took a moment to stretch—she felt that, the way all his muscles lengthened and shivered before relaxing again—and then eased on top of her. His lips grazed her nose, her chin, her mouth. When he tilted his head she felt his cheek against hers, his skin a warm scrape.

"Good morning," Kit murmured. He came between

her legs and pushed into her, his face enthralled, his eyes closing.

And it did not hurt. She was sore, aye, but it already was fading, replaced by a luxurious new pleasure invading her with every thrust. He filled her and she opened to it now, knew what to expect, where they were going. He went slowly, languorous, burying his face in her hair, inhaling against her skin. Rue arched her back. He lifted his head and sucked at her lips and moved with that dark, sweet magic that gathered in her belly and spread outward, tingling. She could not get enough of it.

His weight shifted. He hooked an arm under one of her knees, drawing her leg up, leaning against his open palm while her calf rested over his shoulder. Her body tightened with the sensation. He could not go any deeper. She was pinned beneath him, captured, and the air had gone to fire.

"I trust you slept well," he whispered, less evenly than before. Rue tipped her head back, words vanished in her throat, the pillows white clouds around them.

"Rue-flower. You taste like honey." His voice roughened, his fingers clenched against her shoulder. He began to move faster. "You feel like heaven. I want to stay inside you all the time. Oh, God, I don't want this to end."

But he didn't slow. The culmination came upon her in a delirious bright spark, a blind heat that flared and caught like gunpowder, consuming her in waves and shudders.

Kit stiffened, his entire body going rigid; he let out his breath in a mighty gust, stirring her hair. Slowly he collapsed against her, a new tremble in his arms, his weight coming down heavy over her so that together they sank even farther into the mattress. He released her leg to weave his fingers through her hair.

They remained like that, locked close, until Rue had to shift her shoulders. He lifted instantly to his forearms.

"As a matter of fact," she said, "there is a sizable lump in your bed."

He kissed her chin. "I'm terribly sorry."

"I think it must have aught to do with you, Lord Langford. There was a lump in the mattress at Chasen as well. Perhaps you ought to find a new goose-plucker. I know a place...." She was looking up at him and so lost the thread of her thoughts, checked by the new light in his eyes.

"No," she said, and pushed him off her, sitting up. "You could not possibly be so reckless."

"I fear that I am. Try to consider it one of my virtues."

She abandoned the bed, going to her knees on the floor beside it, stretching her arm between the mattress and the straw-stuffed base. He propped himself up on one elbow to watch.

She found it. She pulled her hand back with *Herte* in her fist while Christoff smiled down at her, roguish.

"You hid it beneath the *mattress*? You couldn't think of a single better place than that?"

"What better place than my bed? I knew I'd be back here. I'd hoped it would be with you. Who better to guard a diamond than two *drákon*?" He laughed at her expression, swinging upright. "We were already going after the runner. No one else would think to take it."

"*Anyone* else would think to take it." She cradled the stone in her palms. "The mattress! For God's sake, you may as well have just set it out on your doorstep!"

"Frankly, mouse, I never imagined we'd acquire it so soon. I had meant to hand it to the council for safekeeping. There's not even a strongbox here, you know."

"You should have told me! I could have secured it!"

His smile faded. "Rue, it's fine."

"It is *not* fine! You risked the diamond. You risked our bargain."

"Our bargain," Kit repeated slowly.

"Yes! The diamond and the runner! My freedom!" She came to her feet, swinging her hair back, naked and uncaring. "We're halfway there and you nearly ruined the entire arrangement—if it's stolen again, I don't know how we'd track it. I cannot conceive that you would be so foolhardy! It's as if you—"

He looked at her, seated high upon his bed, splendid and still as the air, surrounded with satin covers and tossed pillows.

"—as if you planned it," she finished. "As if you planned for it to be restolen. Did you?"

"No."

"Did you?" she demanded anew, as though he had not answered. "Is that what you were after, to lose *Herte,* to have me fail?"

"No, Rue. Of course not." He climbed out of the bed, scowling.

"Then why would you—"

"I told you! There is no strongbox! The council has not yet arrived!"

"But you only had to tell me—"

"Oh, yes," he snapped, coming near, "tell you that the diamond is yours for the taking after all, hand it over to you and have you evaporate into the hills. That's a sound plan. Whyever didn't I think of it? Perhaps you might have another private little *tête-à-tête* with the runner too, just to let him know how things stand."

She felt slightly dizzy. She felt as though she stood at the edge of a cliff, with a drop far, far below her. "You don't trust me."

He ran a hand through his hair. "Trust you? Rue—trust you? You counterfeited your own death rather than wed me. You told me you'd rather die than stay in Darkfrith. I can't—I don't know how to fix that. I don't know how to mend it. Tell me." He took a step toward her. "Tell me, and I'll do it."

She couldn't answer. There was a rock in her throat, and she could not speak around it.

"Mouse," he said, and shook his head, the lines around his mouth etched deep. "Sweet Rue. I would do anything."

"I have to go." Her voice sounded very thin.

"No."

"I'm sorry, I—just for a while. I'll come back."

*"No."*

"Sorry," she said once more, and Turned, heading for the window. He blocked her, faster than she, smoke and then man, his finger plugging the small hole in the glass.

"I won't let you leave like this."

She funneled to the door, heading for the hall, but he blocked her there too, always faster, always smarter, and she wanted to scream in frustration. She wound up to the ceiling and he trailed her, twin spirals that spun and turned. However she moved he countered it; when she got close to the door he spread himself against it. She Turned to woman, very quickly, and yanked at the handle, sweeping past the opening as smoke even while he tried to prevent her.

Yet he caught her before she was through. He surrounded her, imprisoned her, just as he always had, and she was forced to revert to her human self, ready to sprint forward, but as soon as she did he was solid too, grabbing her arms, pulling her to his chest, his grip tight and unrelenting.

"Rue!"

She looked up, not at Christoff but at Zane, standing open-mouthed just down the hall.

He didn't move. He could not. He'd fallen asleep and thought he might still be dreaming but that the air was so cool it crawled along his skin. The hallway had just a single vaulted window at the very end of the corridor and so everything around them was washed in pastels and soft traces of gray—everything except her. To Zane she burned like the moonlight last night, white fire and dark-eyed contradiction, all that was beautiful and bright in his life.

She was unclothed. She was being restrained by the marquess. And she had been—they *both* had been—nothing but fumes two seconds before, solid flesh shaped from smoke like a gypsy conjurer's final rousing trick.

*What was she?*

She broke away from the marquess. She stepped toward him, heedless of her body, heedless of the swing of her hair or the outline of her figure as Langford stood unmoving behind her, his animal eyes watching them both.

"Zane." Her hand reached out. "What are you doing here?"

"I—I—came to tell you—"

He turned around and ran. He hadn't meant to but it happened, his feet pounding the slick floor, skidding to the stairs, leaping down them three at a time in his rush to reach the main doors. But the air was clouding; he landed on the foyer amid a new rush of smoke and was jerked off his feet by his collar.

He bounced and swiveled and aimed a kick at the marquess, who only lifted him high like he was a puling kitten and dangled him there with a grim, distasteful expression, his fist binding the shirt tight about Zane's neck. The breath began to choke from his chest.

"Stop!" Rue skimmed down the stairs. "Don't hurt him!"

"You said he knew." The marquess's voice was hard, whip-thin.

"He did! He does—he's never seen—" She put both hands on the man's arm. Without ceremony Zane was dumped to the floor. He bent double and wheezed.

Rue's feet moved off. He heard cloth rustle, muffled, and then the clatter of metal striking the marble tiles; she had yanked the curtains from the closest window, pulled free the rod and yards of yellow damask. It puddled around her like a river of sunlight. She lifted it, wrapped it around herself, then came back and knelt before him.

She whispered his name, the softest voice he'd ever heard. She did not attempt to touch him again. He raised his eyes to hers, defiant, despairing.

"You knew," she said. "But I never let you see, except that once. That very first time. Do you remember it?"

Dreams. That's what he had thought of that night. She had sprung from his dreams as he had pulsed between life and death. The knife wound from Clem had drained him, the blood had no longer even felt wet against his skin, and she was there. There had been smoke, and snow. She had been born of them both, white skin and that cloak of shining hair. But all this while, all these years, he was sure it had been just dreams.

"I remember," he said.

"Rue," said the marquess, still in that peculiar hard tone.

"There are things in this world," she said steadily, still holding Zane's eyes, "that defy easy words. There are things in this world worth protecting, fragile things, secret things.

Things that would do great harm should they ever be handled carelessly."

"Rue." The marquess loomed just beyond her.

"Things like magic." She touched a finger to Zane's cheek, a shock of warmth. "Things like love."

He stared back at her, dumb and helpless. The marquess set his hand upon her shoulder, his fingers marking a possessive span against her skin. Zane could see from here there was something wrong with one of his legs, that the skin was streaked red and swollen. He'd seen blood wounds aplenty in his life before her.

"Step away," Lord Langford said. "Step away from him, Rue. Go back upstairs."

Her face changed, a flash of emotion in her eyes—anger, or fear, or both. She rose and turned to face him.

"I won't let you."

"Don't make this harder."

"I *said*," something about her altered here, something grew wilder and more formidable; Zane felt it even with her back to him, "I won't let you."

"He cannot be allowed loose." For all her gathering fury, Lord Langford was chillingly rational, flat calm. "You know the laws. When the council uncovers it, they'll kill him anyway. At least I'll be quick."

*Kill him*—

"I will tear this place apart," she said quietly. "Right here, right now. I will put a permanent end to any hope of secrecy for the tribe."

The marquess said nothing.

"You might succeed, though," she went on. "You might yet slay us both. At what cost? You'll have lost me and your cherished anonymity. Will it be worth it?"

"I don't wish to fight you," he said. But Zane saw how he shifted on his leg, all tension and ready violence.

"You said you'd do anything to mend the past." She softened a little, her shoulders slumping. She lifted a hand and let it fall back to the damask. "Just now, you said that you would."

Slowly, very subtly, the marquess began to smile. But it was not a smile of mirth or joy: it was the smile of a demon, of unholy gratification. He spoke without a trace of inflection.

"Shall it be your bride-price, love? The life of this boy?"

She glanced down at Zane. He stared back at her, unable to plead with her for his heart in his throat. He thought desperately of his knife, of how he might manage to stab smoke.

"Mouse." Lord Langford took her chin between his fingers, forcing her gaze back to his. "Is this your price?"

She did not hesitate again. "Yes."

"Then I accept. I will not harm him."

Now it was Rue who was silent, Rue and Zane, who felt so sick with relief and worry that he had to cut his nails into his palms to stay standing.

"You have my word," Langford said to her.

Zane honed in on his face, on the animal there blazing in his eyes, and wondered that she would believe him. But she never moved, not even when the marquess bent to Zane and put his mouth near his ear. Zane pressed his nails harder into his palms, invisible pain.

"You are free to remove yourself from my sight. If you speak one word of this to anyone, ever, I'll consider my promise void. I'll find you wherever you are, and no amount of pretty pleading will spare you then." He straightened, raking Zane with his look. "Take your leave from the service door, boy."

And he spread his hand on Rue's back and directed her up the stairs with him, the yellow damask making a long, slippery train behind her.

# CHAPTER FIFTEEN

"I believe it's time," said Christoff, "for you to tell me about the runner."

He was dressing, taking deliberate care with it, standing before his bed with his legs apart and his London clothing strewn haphazard across the covers, *Herte* a silent starburst in the middle of the chaos. He'd pulled what he needed from his closet, barely glancing at what was there. Crisp linen, tan breeches, a waistcoat of India silk with etched silver buttons; the silk caught the light, shifting hues from sage green to citron. For some reason the changing colors smarted his eyes.

Rue was seated in a chair behind him. He could feel her gaze upon his back.

"What do you wish to know?"

"What do you think? I want to know what he said to you last night, what you said to him." He picked up the shirt. The ruffles edging the cuffs felt starched and very cool.

"Nothing useful." Her voice was subdued. "He asked why I was following him."

"And why were you?"

"Why—because he was escaping, that's why. And because you were occupied with darling Cynthia. Someone had to step in."

He pulled on the shirt. "Indeed. So you thought you'd simply confront him alone. Very shrewd."

She didn't rise to the bite in his tone, only said again stubbornly, "Someone had to."

He propped a hand against the bedpost, narrowing his eyes at the waistcoat. There was a bizarre, distant buzzing in his ears. There had been, ever since he'd seen that boy, ever since that familiar slam of ferocity and pity and blood-violence had flooded through him, the same sick wave he always felt in those final moments of a life. It was a sensation so vicious it used to make him physically ill. The first two times he'd killed, it had actually defeated him: the very instant he'd been left alone afterward, he'd fallen over and succumbed to the nausea.

Kit remembered their names, their faces. Samuel Sewell, John Howards, Colm Young. He remembered their fear. He remembered his own, that he would be weak, that he would fail, that he could not lift his hands to the task his father had set for him.

Sam Sewell. He'd been a carpenter, burly, mad-eyed. And Christoff had been just sixteen years old.

Sewell had been sentenced and shackled. He had given his oath not to Turn but had done it anyway.

The second time had been marginally easier; the man had only wept. The third easier still. Instead of vomiting Kit had gotten drunk after that one, brutally drunk. And the almost-fourth, that wan, scrawny child . . .

He would have done it. He understood by now what his role demanded of him, that for the Alpha there were sacrifices for every pleasure, and consequences for every slight deed. He knew exactly how it would have happened, how he would have moved, fleet and ruthless, how he'd strike, the distinctive jolt of the neck bones severing. . . .

A sliver of nausea lingered in the back of his throat. The buzzing would not subside.

But it was worth it, all of it, because by her own vow he had her now. Kit slanted her a look from over his shoulder. She was curled sideways in the wing chair with her head on her arms and her hair awash across her cheek, still cloaked in the hall curtain. She was white and dark and pink and gold. She watched him through long black lashes.

"What else did he say?"

"To leave him be. To let him go." She closed her eyes and opened them, by all appearances peaceful as a drowsing child. "That he hadn't wanted the diamond. That he had no desire to injure me."

Kit stilled. "He threatened you?"

"No more than someone else I know." She held him in that quiet look. "We've been allies of a sort, I suppose. I'm sure he was mostly surprised that I would corner him."

"Who is he?"

"He did not tell me, Lord Langford. No doubt he was about to, in addition to giving me his direction and handing me the key to his door, but just then you arrived. He did not seem disposed to linger."

"No," Kit said, and felt his lip curl.

She sat up in the chair, pushing back her hair. "But I did learn something of interest."

"What?"

"His right hand was made of wood."

*Wood.* His mind clicked. The man who had drowned, whose hand and ring had been found. Great God, anyone deranged enough to cut off his own hand—had George ever said who it was? He couldn't quite remember—

"It was his bowing hand," Rue continued, gazing down at the material stretched across her legs. "Ingenious, really. He had the fingers shaped to hold the bow, so he could play just like anyone else. I noted it when he first touched me."

"You will stay away from him," Kit said, beyond alarmed. "You're not to go anywhere near him again."

She glanced up at him, her brows lifted. "It hardly seems to be an issue. I've little idea of how to find him now. Especially since he knows you're pursuing him."

"Listen to me, Rue. I won't be disobeyed in this. You will stay away from him, no matter what comes."

"Fine," she flashed, rising to her feet. The curtain began to slither off to one side; she caught it up with both hands. "You win, you're Alpha, all-powerful Christoff! I bow to your infinite wisdom! Pray grant me permission to venture belowstairs for something to eat, dear lord. I find my stomach pains me." She hitched the curtain higher and marched out of his bedchamber, a wake of damask flaring past the door.

He thought to go after her. He hadn't meant to be so harsh. He wanted to be gentle with her, he wanted to catch her and protect her and adore her body and her bold heart. But without her presence to brace him, Christoff found himself leaning aslant across the bed, his hand pressing hard into the waistcoat, pulling wrinkles along the silk. The buzzing in his head was like an angry hive of bees.

She was so damned willful. She had put herself in danger without a second thought for most of her life, repeatedly, determinedly. She'd succored that wolf cub and told him her secrets and never *once* thought of the consequences—

Kit discovered that beyond his fear for her, beyond his

indignation, was a new, spinning exhaustion. He slumped to the rug, not even making it up to the mattress. He tipped his head back against the footboard and glared up at the ceiling, seeing her face instead, her flushed cheeks and the sweep of her hand as she'd left him behind in his room.

Porridge again. Rue stared down at the tin of dried flakes in the larder, her lips pursed in distaste. They'd been to market yesterday but most of what they'd bought—the pilchards, the cheese and nuts, the marzipan pastries—was gone. There was a handful of figs left, and the brick of butter had scarcely been touched. She found the bread they'd not finished, the loaf stiff already because Christoff had rewrapped it too loosely in its cloth.

She slammed the bread down upon the chopping block. She stalked back to the pantry and eyed the tin of porridge, then smacked it with the back of her hand, sending it flying to the wall.

The lid broke off. Tiny grains flung out like gay confetti.

She stood there staring down at the mess, trembling, feeling cold and hot at once.

It was over. Her life, her dreams, everything over. She'd done it herself, she'd given up *everything*—

She couldn't breathe. She felt it happen, how her lungs pinched closed, how her breath squeaked. Blue spots burst and reappeared at the edges of her vision. She dropped to her knees and pressed her forehead to the immaculate floor. She barely felt the stone.

Her life, her house, her freedom. Her future and her heart, and now she was bound to him forever, and he'd never love her as she did him, he didn't even know what love was—

She would be his wife. He'd asked her price and she had named it, fierce small Zane, and she would never walk free again, never never never. She would spend the rest of her days in Darkfrith, in the shadow of obedience to him and the tribe and all those waiting ghosts.

In time, Rue came back to herself. The floor was icy. Her hands were clenched in her hair. She lifted her head and stared blearily about the kitchen, so bright and clean it belonged to some other world. She sat back on her hips and wrapped her arms around her chest until she could make the shivers stop.

She rose to sweep up the porridge. There would be no mice in Far Perch to clean it for her.

Time shifted. He was aware of that, of how it stretched long and thick like taffy, or chopped short into blunt impressions: the blinding blink of sunlight against the ceiling. The nap of the rug beneath his fingers. He knew that he was lying flat upon it, that he had come to rest on his side and then his back. He felt sick and then not sick, very light, floating like smoke but not so focused.

He was ill. Kit perceived that. His entire leg burned with the fires of hell—it hadn't been so painful last night, but now—and he felt the sweat gathering over him, welling in the dip of his chest, dripping down his brow and groin and arms.

How had this happened? He'd been sick before but nothing like this, nothing so quick and lethal, a disaster boiling behind his eyelids.

Crocodiles. Fever. Kit realized abruptly what was about to come.

Their blood reacted to poison in particularly savage

ways. It would either kill him or not, but without question it would consume him down to the marrow. If he woke again—if he saw her again—whatever happened, he must not hurt her—

He managed, in his excruciating lethargy, to roll over to his knees, to raise himself that way. He put his good foot beneath him and held himself there, his fingers pushed hard into the rug, his head bowed. He thought of Rue. Of where she might be. There was danger and he had to protect her. . . .

He drew his torso upright. His hands found the footboard, nice solid wood, a stable comfort beneath his palms. Kit concentrated, marshaling what he found of his strength, and with great effort hauled himself to both feet, leaning heavily over the bed.

He crawled atop it. He fell upon the covers and the ironed clothes. He laughed into the sheets because he'd done it.

He was not going to die upon the floor.

*Rue,* he thought, and dropped his face to the bright satin.


She lingered downstairs. She felt ridiculous, loitering in the kitchen and then the drawing room, covered in just the drapery from his front hall because she didn't want him to hear her creeping back up the stairs.

She couldn't say when she realized he didn't have to hear her. She was standing in the sumptuous drawing room, far from the patch of sunlight that picked out the white and mauve primroses woven into the rug—like the sun was contagious, like it would burn her up—when, without even considering it, she Turned to smoke. She filtered up to the next floor without causing a sound beyond that of falling damask.

In the stateroom that she'd claimed she dressed—simple clothing because she had no maid to assist her, but still quite fine, ecru silk and wide, open skirts embroidered with plum blossoms and vines. It felt good to wear her own garments. It felt like she did not have to pretend to be anything she was not. For a change.

But Christoff did not come. She brushed her hair and considered that, slowly braiding it and winding it into a heavy knot at her nape. She picked up her cap of soft-stitched lace, allowing the ribbons to run through her fingers, but finally decided against wearing it. She disliked having her ears covered; it went against her instincts as both a *drákon* and a thief. She'd put it on later if she had to.

If she had chosen her gowns sparingly for her time at Far Perch, at least Rue had brought a full array of cosmetics: rouge and elderberries and perfume, velvet patches and scented water. She used a delicate, expert touch. No one knew her face as she did. And in the end, after at least another hour of tarrying, the looking glass showed a proper gentlewoman once more, someone she had not seen for days. Weeks. The woman looking back at her revealed nothing of the fear and confusion and desperation that bubbled beneath her smooth calm. She looked like a lady. She looked like she belonged here in this house.

Rue turned her face away. Without even trying, she was wearing a new disguise.

She stood, pacing away from the mirror. Why had he not come?

She straightened her stockings beneath the gown. She tapped her fingers on the bureau, angling a glance out past the sheer curtains to the street below. There were people out there in carriages, in sedan chairs and on foot. Stupid, normal, mule-witted people, going about their business. They had no idea of the tightly wound secrets in their midst.

Rue took a breath and left her room. She found the marquess's door slightly ajar, perhaps as she'd left it, and placed her hand upon the wood. She looked about his chamber and thought it empty.

"Christoff."

He did not answer. There was a silhouette upon the bed.

She took a step forward and then it hit her: the citrus tinge of the salve. The hot, ripe aroma beneath it, the dead quiet all around.

"No—"

She said it even as she was rushing to the bed, even as she was rolling him over onto his back, smoothing his damp hair from his face.

He was flushed, more scalding than the sunlight. His lashes flickered open.

"Mouse . . ."

"Don't speak," she said, frightened. "Move up here—can you manage it? Try. I can't lift you. There—there—just a little more." He was straining for air, his fingers clenched into the covers. She bent over to examine his injured leg.

"Oh, God. Why didn't you tell me?"

Blood, infection, that curdling smell. Why hadn't she noticed? She'd made love to him this morning, she'd felt pleasure she'd never conceived, and all this while—

"Nothing," he mumbled, turning his head. "Nothing to concern you. I'm well enough."

"You jackass." Anger replaced the fear, and with it she had the strength to pull him up properly the rest of the way in the bed, ripping the shirt apart, placing her hand over his heart.

Staccato, uneven. She stared down at him, unwilling to move, trying to force him to life, to health, with just her palm pressed upon his skin. But he rocked his head back and forth and licked his lips. She glanced away, searching for the basin and pitcher of water nearby, leaving him to pour a cup.

"Drink this."

He did, thirstily, his hands rising to wrap around her own.

"Mouse," he said again, and met her eyes. His mouth lifted into a wry curve. "Perhaps you won't have to be Lady Langford after all."

"Where is the salve?" she demanded.

"Too late," he answered softly. "Get away while you can."

"What do you mean?"

His eyes closed. "I love you," Kit said, and his body went lax. Then he Turned.

It was violent and rushing, nothing of the mastery she was used to with him but something powerfully uncontained. She felt the air suck past her in a *whoosh* of upward smoke, she could not see through it, there was an ominous rattling and thumping that shook the world, and then—he was gone.

Rue pivoted, frantic, searching the chamber and ceiling, dropping to her knees to check the floor beneath the bed, but he truly was no longer in the room.

She dashed to the window. The chipped pane now held a white cobweb of cracks. Nothing beyond it but a blanched blue sky... and there, high, high up. The sky contained a single cloud.

*Herte* glittered from the sheets. She grabbed it, stuffed it back under his mattress and Turned, shoving through the broken window to surge up into the day.

He did not follow the wind. She went after him as quickly as she dared, knowing how it must look to anyone below. True clouds did not move at will. They might be odd puffs of smoke, remnants of a fire since smothered—but they would not dissipate. He churned and whirled in unchecked motion. If he Turned again—if he became man—

And like some evil wish, it happened just as she thought it, the smoke drawing together with black purpose, his shape all at once clearly visible, a wild stream of blond hair, a comely slack form. He dropped to earth, never waking. She streaked beneath him and became a dragon—oh, heavens, here in the open pale sky—breaking his fall with her back, flipping and rolling when he bounced off her, catching him in her talons.

He was a good weight. She dipped and recovered in a reel, her wings straining to regain dominion of the wind.

From far, far below came a breaker of sound. She knew what it was without looking, the collective gasp of countless Others, their faces aimed up to the heavens.

A pair of steeples whipped by, somber gray pinnacles pinstriped with soot. Where were they? She did look below her now, past the bowed head of Christoff, his blowing hair, but the map of rectangles and half-circle streets was unfamiliar. She'd never done this before. She'd never had to fly like this as a thief, and certainly never in daylight. Her world was the city at human height—the safe night—oh, why couldn't she recognize anything—

Kit Turned again. Just like that, he vanished from her grip. She careened with his sudden loss but came out of it better this time, able to rise and circle and search for him once more.

Smoke below her, a helix so thin she wondered that it

could be him. Quickly she did the same, and hoped that all those people below rubbed their eyes and imagined their minds were playing tricks when the white dragon vanished against the blue.

Let him stay like this. She could follow him; they were so much less conspicuous.

But he did not. At a dangerously low height she saw him gather again, and this time he was a dragon, and she was too far. Still she raced toward him, still she tried. His wings spread; his eyes opened. He soared sharply upward, speeding away from her, and she veered so close to the ground she caught the screams and shouts of the people stopped in their tracks.

"Great God—did you see—"

"It's a bloomin' *dra*gon, by Mary and—"

"Miranda! Get down—"

Rue chased him as a long silvery plume, no longer concerned with natural shapes, her only goal to reach him before he tore away completely. He flew as if he had a purpose, taut and thin and his wings crooked in a hard, fixed arch that let his tail flap behind. She could barely keep up. At least they were moving fast. At least the buildings and streets and green parks below rolled under them in a shaded blur. She hoped fewer people were glancing up as they charged from ward to ward.

The sun sparked at the horizon. It was water, the Thames. And then Rue understood what he was doing—if he could.

He Turned twice more before they reached the docks, first smoke, then man, and the second time she was ready for it, already below him to let his body strike hers. She caught him more skillfully now, holding him to her as lightly as she dared, her eyes fixed on the warehouses rising up from the arch of the world like a giant's dim toys.

Where was it? It had all happened so swiftly before, she barely recalled any of it but for the smell of the river and the flying tempest of shingles.

Kit's arm moved. He raised it, reaching up to grab her leg, his fingers brushing her scales. He let it drop again, limp.

There. One of the largest buildings of them all, and the only one with a hole smashed through its roof. A flock of gulls decorated the exposed beams. They turned their heads as one to watch her descent, a hundred black polished eyes, then burst upward, screeching, blinding her in a whirlwind of wings and feathers and sharp yellow beaks.

Kit went to smoke, and so did she. He dropped into the warehouse, a man again staggering to his knees amid the rubble, and she caught him in her arms, hauling him upright.

"Mouse," he said, giving her a muddled, narrow-eyed look, but she was already dragging him to the smaller chamber, stumbling over shingles—hadn't *anyone* been back to clean this up?—stepping high with him over the stone doorway, easing him to the floor. He rolled to his side on the granite with a hoarse curse, rising up on his arms, shaking the hair from his face.

"I'm right here," Rue said to him, retreating to the threshold. "I'll be here." And she shut the door before he could look back and catch the lie on her face.

There was no lock. There was only a massive iron bar beneath the handle, which she shoved into place, sealing him inside.

She dropped to her knees, gasping, hugging herself.

Beyond the metal she heard his voice, a hollow rise and fall of dark, outraged despair.

*"Ruuuuueeeee..."*

She became smoke. She hovered near the ceiling a very long while, awaiting discovery, but although people rushed back and forth all around the warehouse, no one bothered to enter its ruin. So she lifted up and spread herself as sparse as she could manage, a mirage of a cloud drifting toward home.

Her house was contained. She knew it so well she did not have to seek out any little sly openings. There would be none. She slipped across the roof, nothing more interesting than steam rising from the wet wood on a warming day— but there had been no rain, and the day was not warm.

At least none of the other houses on Jassamine was higher than her own, not any nearby. There was a chimney sweep four roofs down; she didn't see him but his ladder and bucket and broom, propped ready against the bricks. No one else was about. Rue took her shape behind her own chimney, the one jutting up from her bedroom.

Quickly, quickly—

She dropped to her stomach, crawling head down to the gutter, leaning as far as she could over the edge without losing her grip on the roof's edge. Her hair was a long brown banner flying loose below her; she had nothing to tie it back with. It tossed and waved in eye-catching motion.

A huge ruddy tom crossing the yard below started and paused, its tail puffed, baleful yellow eyes aimed up at her. She ignored it, letting go of the roof with one hand stretched as far as she could manage, balanced on her hips, trying to reach the top pane of the window directly beneath her.

Too far. Damn it. The tom stared as she inched farther down the roof, her fingers still grasping air, and just as she was about to lose her balance Sidonie walked out of the back door, humming a Sunday hymn with a basket of clothing in her arms. She closed the door, slipping her feet into the wood pattens on the steps. The hymn cut short.

"Shoo! Is that you leaving me rats on the stairs, then? Get home, you nasty beast—"

The maid plopped the basket on the grass and the tom bolted. Rue, in trying to remain still, had leaned too far. She tipped from the roof.

Sidonie glanced up at the sound, but all she would see was thinly rising mist. She studied it a moment, frowning, but Rue allowed herself to float away, harmless, nothing worth pondering.

Sidonie lifted her basket. The laundry line was strung discreetly between two poles along the side yard; Rue heard her begin a new hymn as she turned the corner.

She swept back to her house. She judged the space and the distance, hovered a moment, and then Turned, smashing her fist into the glass, saving herself a bare instant before she would have hit the ground.

Sidonie ran up again but by then Rue was in her room, nursing her cut hand, finding her robe and covering herself as quickly as she could without getting blood on the sleeve.

She heard the back door slam, footsteps rushing up the stairs. She managed to belt the robe closed and hide her hand behind her back just as Sidonie burst into the room.

"Oh! Ma'am, I'm that sorry, I—" She stood there breathless, both hands over her heart in surprise. "I didn't know you was back, ma'am!"

"Yes," said Rue, trying to look as surprised as her maid. "I've been home just a half hour. I let myself in."

"Of course, ma'am." She curtsied, backing away. "I just—I heard a noise."

"Indeed." Rue glanced at her window, the shards of glass sprinkling the sill and floor in sharp icy bits. "Someone threw a rock. A child on a prank, mayhap."

"Yes, ma'am."

There was very clearly no rock. Rue saw the maid search for it, a quick flicker of her eyes along the bed and beechen floor before she looked back at Rue.

"You will fetch a glazier," Rue said, drawing herself taller. "But first, I need a few other things." She paused. "Is Zane about?"

"No, ma'am. He hasn't been here since yesterday noon."

"All right, then get Cook. I'm going to need a hamper of food anyway."


She could not risk taking a hackney all the way to the warehouse.

By the time they reached the wharves it was well past midday. The streets here slept deep in shadow, closed in by high, stark buildings, only a few of the tallest peaks and rooftops still glowing with light. Men moved about with their hats pressed low and their hands in their pockets. The odor of decaying fish coated everything like an oil, from the hitching posts to the brick and stucco walls.

She allowed the driver to help her from the coach, her wicker hamper over one arm. The veil draped from her hat obscured her face but also her vision; she nearly missed the last step.

"Careful, miss." He watched her find her footing on the road. "Are y'sure this be the place, miss?"

"Yes." She began to count out coins from her reticule into her gloved palm.

"It don't seem no proper sort o' place for a lady," the man continued, gently obstinate. "Ye sure this be it?"

"I am."

"Shall I wait for ye, miss?"

Rue pressed the coins into the driver's hand. "No. Definitely not."

He scratched at his wig, eyeing her, the fashionable cocked hat and white veil, the fine navy poplin of her gown. He did not even glance at his payment.

"I don't mind none," said the fellow. "Might be better, miss, me waitin' here on this corner."

Under the pretense of adjusting the hamper, Rue took a sideways step toward the pair of horses hitched to the coach. The closer one, the gray, lifted his head and shook it, giving an unhappy snort.

"That won't be necessary." She tried another step. "Thank you."

The gray clattered his front feet. The sorrel beside him gave a bounce and a little kick, straining against the harness.

"Here, now," called the man, and hurried to them. With his back to her she surged forward one last step, enough to force the gray into a scream of warning and the sorrel into another unruly kick.

"Ho! Ho now, Joseph! There, boy!"

Rue swung back, moving briskly down the main road. Behind her, the gray gave another scream. She slipped down a side street.

Around a second corner she took a moment to listen, focusing on the distant murmurs of the coachman, soothing and low, and the agitated whickering of his steeds, their shoes scraping stone. There were other people passing in the blocks between them, men with slower paces, voices that discussed flax and the prevailing winds and the price of coal from London to Hull.

The coachman calmed his steeds. She heard the reins flick; she heard them rattle away.

Rue retraced her steps. She hadn't been to this area often enough to hazard getting lost in alleyways; she'd have to walk the only way she knew.

The veil was a thin precaution. She doubted she'd see anyone she knew, or at least anyone she knew as Rue Hilliard. But if perchance a mad, nude nobleman had been discovered locked in a warehouse, better not to have her face visible to the public. She had no desire to be remembered here.

The gauze pressed filmy white against her cheeks. The hamper bumped her hip. She passed merchants and prostitutes, trying to breathe through her mouth to hold back the reek. A wheel of gannets circled above her, their cries snatched by the wind; when she looked up at them they spun away into a line to dive out of sight.

A new man neared. He moved differently from the others, a subtle slide to his step, a trait she instantly recognized. A pickpocket. Rue veered to her left, angling out of his path. But by chance the street was wide open, without even a drunken oarsman on a pony; at the last moment he moved to intercept her, as if to cross the road. She tightened her arm over the basket and kept her other hand on her purse. When he tapped into her she pushed back with her shoulder, hard, and felt him go sprawling to the paving stones.

"Oy! Look out there, miss!"

Bloody novice. Zane would have done much better. She should know; she'd taught him herself.

She listened close but the man didn't follow, only picked himself up and slapped at his breeches, cursing a shade too loudly for such a public space. A constable stood idle at the steps of the gin house nearby with a laughing girl and a drink in hand. He turned his head, eyeing the pickpocket up and down.

Rue walked on.

From three blocks away she began to hear it: the air shifting, a muffled thump, and silence, and air again. She passed by Christoff's warehouse because there was a pair of sailors throwing dice at the corner. Only when they sauntered off, bickering, did she return to the entrance.

The massive doors were sealed with a padlock and chain.

She looked around again and closed both hands over the cheap lock. It had to be merely symbolic; nothing so thin would keep out the *drákon*. She squeezed and the lock crumpled into pieces. She let them fall against her skirts, then slipped loose the chain. The doors slid back on smoothly oiled rollers.

Rue lifted her veil. Shafts of dusty daylight from the hole above picked out motes in the air, etched fire along the tips of fallen feathers and debris scattered amid the shingles. There were no sounds coming from the smaller chamber now. She approached the iron door and set the hamper at her feet.

She put her ear to the metal. She heard breathing. That was all.

The bar took most of her strength, far more serious than the flimsy padlock had been. With a grunt of effort, she freed it from the brackets, then opened the door.

At first she couldn't see. There was absolutely no light in

the cell but for what spilled past the threshold, but she felt him there, his heat, his pumping heart. She bent to find the lantern she'd brought, striking a match to flame, lifting it high before her.

Almond eyes fixed upon her from the darkness, pale eyes, fell green. An elegant head rested upon the floor, a body looped in serpentine coils, scales dipped in colors from the deepest dark oceans, shifting with each labored breath. His talons were curved into dagger points against the granite. His wings were folded into blood-red lines.

He did not lift his head. He did not move at all, only watched her with those burning eyes and that flat, deadly stillness. He showed no signs of recognizing her. He vibrated hostility, ready to strike.

Rue hefted the basket, collected the lantern and her skirts, and stepped into the chamber, pulling the iron door closed behind her.

# CHAPTER SIXTEEN

There were rats in his head. Kit felt them, their little claws pick-picking through his brain. It hurt him and it enraged him. He scratched at his ears, he shook his head until the world spun, but they would not fall out and go away.

It seemed to him they had been there a very long while, perhaps hiding, perhaps waiting for this time. They poked at him with whiskers and glowing eyes. They ate his thoughts. He wanted to destroy them with a passion that charred his heart, that held his muscles seized in rage. And he could not stop them.

*Her breath in his ear. Her body against his.*

He was cold, he was in hell, and it was frozen, it was black frost and icicles that stabbed into his joints. No matter how he moved he could not get warm again. If he tried to fly he found himself flung back to the ground. If he tried to find shelter he encountered only walls and floor and a low, moaning wind that sang a song to him about untroubled death.

*Her words, whispered. Her hands, stroking his face.*

The rats had vanished. They had evaporated in the heat,

a sultry equatorial sun—he had never been to the equator, but surely this was how it felt, this sweltering, gagging warmth, this descending ball of fire that cooked him whole, that crisped his skin and boiled his juices like a chicken ready to eat. He lay there gasping, unable to consume the air because it hurt too much, it scalded his lungs and scattered like grapeshot through his body. He could not move. He could not take another breath.

*She gave him water. She gathered blankets and sopped up his skin.*

He was on his back. He was pressed to a floor that felt cool and wonderful, that drew the fire from his skin down to the core of the earth. There was a woman leaning over him, beyond beautiful, with eyes that pierced his soul. She was near and she was far. When he could not feel her any longer he reached for her through the darkness—and found a delicate dragon instead.

*She held him down. She pinned his wings so he could not fly, and he turned his head and snapped at her.*

Bitch. She was doing this. She would keep him—him!— here in these fetters, with the rats and the sun and the sweat that kept coming and coming at him, no matter how many times he thought he'd left them behind. It was her doing. She would pay. He was Alpha for a reason, by God.

*Her hands. Her face. Her lips against his.*

And in the end, he couldn't do it. She was spirit and presence, as rare and brilliant as snowflakes in sunlight, and he could not bring himself to harm her. She lay entwined with him, white and gold and long, long lashes, and matched her breathing to his, their faces pressed together, as he slipped down the mountain and tumbled into oblivion.

————

She lingered outside the warehouse, thankful for the veil and hat, which managed to conceal her most obvious flaws: fatigue, snarled hair, the run of bruises along her cheekbone from the time Christoff had managed to flail free and strike her. A buttermilk sky—what day was it? Wednesday? Thursday?—was rapidly thickening into storm, a muggy darkness she could taste on her tongue with the rising breeze.

She watched the people passing by until she found precisely the sort of messenger she required—a river rat, no more than fourteen, unbathed, hungry, with gangly legs and sharp greedy eyes.

"Take this," she told him, and handed the child a bright half-crown. "You will find a boy named Zane at this address. Tell him his mistress bids him to come and to give you another two crowns for directing him here." She caught his arm before he could dart off. "Do not fail me. You will not appreciate the consequences."

"Aye, ma'am."

She went back into the warehouse to wait for Zane.


Two hours later her messenger returned. She heard his hesitant knock at the front and hastened to meet him, pulling a shawl over her shoulders, hauling him along with her to the side of the building where the wind cut very cool around them both, scented with rain.

"He weren't there, ma'am," the rat said, scrubbing a hand along his face. "I left yer message wit' a girl. Can I have me two crowns anyways?"


She did not know how much longer she could keep him here. It was not a healthy place, certainly not a comfortable one, despite the blankets and food she'd brought. When she went back to Christoff he was smoke—she shut the door quickly but he did not move from the ceiling, a lovely cloud hanging in plumes and thin billowing curls, never resolving, always indefinite. She sat down upon the floor beside the slender light of her lantern and just watched him, wondering if this might be his death throes.

Thunder began a slow roll outside. It swelled and cracked around them, subsiding in skin-chilling echoes.

She felt her lips tremble. She felt her eyes begin to sting. She remembered the quick grinning boy she used to idolize; she remembered the man who kissed her hands and her mouth and made her body flush hot with just a hidden glance, who could cut moonlit mist into a heart but couldn't wrap bread. Rue held her breath until it burned.

"Don't go," she said to the smoke. She stood and reached a hand up to him, not tall enough to touch, never enough to reach him, moisture leaking down her cheeks. "Don't go, I'm going to save you. I am."

But even she didn't believe it. Not any longer. He did not Turn again. As the thunderstorm broke beyond the walls she sank back to the floor, pressing the shawl to her mouth. She bent her head and willed herself not to be weak. Crying never helped.

Nothing helped. She'd tried compounds and cool compresses, she'd bathed him and held him and felt him thrash with the fever. She'd run out of the orange-scented salve and had wanted Zane to get her more—she couldn't leave Kit for so long, she couldn't bear to think of what might happen—but now she didn't have even that. She had never heard of a certain treatment for fever in the *drákon*. Perhaps there was none. Certainly nothing had cured Antonia in all those years, not herbs or tonics. The only thing that ever seemed to help were the brief, sunny days when she had ventured outside, when she could enjoy the sky and the earth.

Something hooked in her memory. Rue lifted her head, frowning.

The sky. The earth. The stony paths.

Stone.

*Herte.*

She didn't know why she stood up. She didn't know why her mind fixed on an idea so far-fetched and tissue-thin she would have laughed to hear it aloud.

But why not? Nothing else had worked.

The smoke above her boiled and lingered, never changing back to man or beast. If he died like this she didn't even know if he would leave behind bones.

Rue dropped her shawl to the floor. She left the chamber, sealed it, and Turned at three running steps.

The storm whisked her up into its folds nearly at once, sweeping her about so severely she lost her sense of up and down. Everything was dark and wet and noisy. A tremendous pressure began to rise and rise through the vapor, nearly tearing her apart. She had no body but felt the electricity mount through her, a zinging torture that would not stop. Lightning gathered into a massive fissure below; it ruptured with a roar, spearing off in wild directions. She was released, spinning, and swiftly Turned to dragon to climb above the clouds.

Only she could not. There was too much wind, and the clouds did not seem to end. She had no idea if she was going the right way or if she was being pulled out to sea. She could not see.

The electric pressure began to mount once more. Rue dove. The lightning arced above her head, fire bolts that seared her eyes. She dropped, and dropped, battered with rain. Her wings began to quiver with strain. She was not meant for this. She'd never flown like this, in such a gale. If she went to smoke she might not have enough force to push herself against the winds.

Another burst of light. All the clouds were lit in a flash of mammoth, black-walled fury. She threaded through them, letting gravity take her down, and barely missed splashing into the mouth of the Thames below.

She dipped above the water. She was thrashed by rain and salty spray—but there were lights ashore. She made her way to them, Turning only at the first clear signs of a quay, coming up against a broken awning above a black-shuttered cottage. She went to her knees and pressed her face into her arms, waiting until the panic ebbed from her heart.

A trio of men in oilskins staggered past, so close she could see the rain-pocked cheeks and beard of the nearest one. They did not notice her.

Rue Turned to smoke and made her way inland.


There were candles alight inside Far Perch. Flickering light shone visible from nearly all the windows, and it took her so aback that she materialized in a treetop across the square, clinging to the high branches like a half-drowned monkey, squinting against the storm.

A shadow crossed the parlor window. A man. Another man joined him; they stood conferring, dark coats, white wigs. Of course—Kit's guard. The five men they'd agreed upon finally arrived from Darkfrith. Great heavens, how many days had it been since that afternoon in the council's chamber? It seemed a lifetime past. She heaved a sigh of relief, so abruptly grateful she felt almost faint; she didn't have to do this alone. She could tell them about Christoff, and they would help her. They would...

Three more men moved against an upstairs window. And another two at the other end of the mansion. And another one in the drawing room.

Eight. Nine. The front parlor, with Zane's weak jamb, seemed to be the main gathering place. It had two finely arched windows in front and another that shed gold along the side of the house, all of them traced in lead filigree that lent the mansion's facade an air of magnificent, old-fashioned caprice. In minutes she counted at least twelve figures.

One long-wigged man walked up to the glass and stood staring out at the rain, his hands behind his back, his gaze aimed precisely at where Rue perched. She gripped the slippery branches more tightly, motionless behind the leaves.

Parrish Grady. She could see that it was him, even with the light behind him. It wasn't just five men they had sent, it was the council, all of them come to London, and who knew how many guardsmen besides.

They had forsaken the agreement.

*I had meant to hand it to the council for safekeeping.*

Kit's words, that morning of their argument. She shook her head with a groan, small and disbelieving. He had never meant to give *Herte* to the guards. He'd been awaiting Grady. All the rest. He'd said it out loud, and she'd never given it a second thought.

*The council has not yet arrived....*

He had known. He had colluded with them. And he'd looked her straight in the eye and lied to her with that easy, heart-stopping charm she'd always adored. He'd never meant to let her go, not at all.

She bowed her head to her wrists, precarious in the tree,

gritting her teeth. God save her from deceitful men. Now what was she to do?

She could not enter Far Perch without Kit. She certainly could not produce the diamond and then tell the tribesmen their leader was trapped in a warehouse, mortally ill. They'd laugh at her idea. No—they'd think she had made it happen somehow, that it was a trick to keep *Herte* for herself, to end any hope of a marriage. It was what she would think, if she were an arrogant, underhanded, son-of-a-bitch councillor.

She should walk away. She could. Only the marquess knew where she lived.

Rue pressed her cheek to the rough branch, closing her eyes.

*I love you.*

He'd been delirious. He hadn't known what he was saying.

But he had said it. And she had given her word to stay with him, because deep in her heart the girl named Clarissa loved him more, and always had.

The cracked windowpane to his bedroom had been boarded closed, crudely but most effectively. She misted up to the cupola. They hadn't discovered this way yet; she Turned inside the little space, quiet as she could manage, and very gently opened the trapdoor. The garret was unlit. She crept down it barefoot, not daring to Turn inside the house. They'd sense her at once.

The majority of the men seemed to be downstairs. She heard their voices, low murmurs, no agitation, not yet. They'd probably only been here a day or so; they had no suspicion yet that anything would be truly wrong....

There was a guard at the next landing, half angled to the window to watch the storm. She held her breath and crept, slowly, slowly, behind his back. A line of portraits watched her inching progress, their painted eyes gleaming black and pewter in the dark.

He never looked around. She made it down to the next level of the house, and then the next, where the master chambers lay. It did not occur to her until she reached Kit's doorway that there might be someone among their company with skills enough to detect the diamond beneath the mattress. But when she entered the room she felt *Herte*'s life like a caress. She hurried to the bed, less careful now, and pulled out the diamond.

Now what? She couldn't Turn, and she didn't want to chance going back up to the cupola. That guard wouldn't stare dreaming at the rain forever.

She crossed to another window. She opened the lock and pushed at the sash; it gave with a blast of chilled air. The bedroom door slammed closed.

Curse it. She shoved the window all the way open, leaned out, and glanced up at the clouds. The air drew hard around her. She looked over her shoulder at the man paused in the chamber doorway, his hand on the knob and his coat flapping wide.

It was the scribe. He stopped in place, staring at her. Rue stared back, then smiled, lifting a finger to her lips. She twisted around and hurled the diamond up to the sky as hard as she could, Turning instantly, smoke, dragon, managing to catch it in her teeth just as the stone reached the zenith of its arc. She flapped her wings and drove upward into the pelting rain, leaving the scribe staring up at her from the open sill, his spectacles flashing white with lightning.

She did not risk any foolishness with the storm this time. If there were people out in this mess they would not be looking up but down, minding their feet and the rivers of water that turned the city streets into floating sewage and slush. So she flew just under the clouds, ducking and weaving when the lightning threatened, panting around *Herte,* trying to see past the needle darts of rain that scored her body and her eyes.

The warehouse was a welcome relief. She landed awkwardly among the wet wood, placed the diamond on the floor, Turned, and stumbled to the closed iron door.

The lantern still burned dim inside the cell. The scent of rain mixed with clouds, with him, dark and distinctive.

She didn't know precisely what she had thought would occur. She didn't know what she should do. Christoff was still smoke at the ceiling—was he thinner now? was it her imagination?—so Rue lifted her hand to him as she had before, only this time the diamond was a small, cold fire on her open palm.

She stood there, dripping, as nothing happened.

A shiver took her. Her muscles clenched to control it; *Herte* jerked with her, a spray of colors sparking light into the corners. Water puddled at her feet.

"Please," she whispered through her teeth. "Please."

And the silky smoke that was Christoff began to gather, dropping to her palm, sliding into a corkscrew down her arm. He was very cool, long tendrils at her shoulder, and then he enveloped her body in a rush, a cloud that covered every part of her. Her shivers stopped. She closed her eyes and held perfectly still, afraid of moving. The diamond burned like ice against her skin.

She tilted her head back. She took a careful breath, released it. He smoldered over every inch of her skin, the softest caress, and she thought, *Now you're inside me. One part, one moment of you, forever.*

He fell from her body. He was gray mist that danced and changed and lifted in layers to become a dragon encircling her. She let her arm fall to rest against him, touching the diamond to his back. He shuddered, loosening; she climbed free of his coils, sliding feet first down his side, falling to her knees by his head. His eyes were slitted, following her, sinking closed as she stroked her hand along his neck.

"Be well," Rue prayed. She placed the diamond against his heart. "Come back."

Kit gusted a sigh that tipped over the lantern. She rescued it, setting it upright, and the flame licked amber across his face, vanishing into faint glimmers along the line of his body. It seemed—she hoped—he was breathing easier than before. She found the blanket she'd brought and cast it over him.

Rue rubbed her hands up and down her arms, watching him. In time, when the chill grew too keen to ignore, she dressed again in the navy poplin, wrapping the shawl about her shoulders and head like a country *frau*, huddling next to him to preserve the last of her heat. But he was still bitter cool; she fell asleep with her knees to her chest, dreaming of alpine snow.


He felt groggy, and cold. That was his first impression of life after years—aeons—away: the world was a hard arctic place, and he needed some defense against it. On top of that thought: a small something warm was pressed against him, something sweet and female and wonderful.

He opened his eyes. Everything was dark and running colors, maroon bricks and honey-buff granite, hoarfrost shadows and the girl curled at his side.

She wore blue. She slept with an arm under her head,

and her hair was ripples of warmth, glossy chestnut over her face and shoulders. A white shawl lay rumpled against her chest.

His mind struggled with a name.

*Mouse.*

*Rue.*

*Wife.*

There was a lantern by her skirts. The light was guttering, nearly gone, but it showed him the shell pink of her lips, the dusky sweep of lashes that lay soft against her skin, the tender cup of her fingers beneath her chin.

She was the most completely beautiful creature he had ever seen.

He felt a weary peace, gazing upon her. He felt as if he could sleep now and never worry about his dreams.

The light upon her increased. It warmed and brightened until he could make out each hair, each gentle lash, and the subtle darkening along her cheekbone he had first taken for shadow. The skin there was marred with green and purple and blue. She was injured. She was bruised.

A sharp new shadow lanced across the floor. Kit tried to raise his head and found that he could not. Emotion began to pound through him—she was hurt, she needed him, and the shadow had crawled to her gown. He had to protect her—

There were men all about. They crept on stealthy feet and surrounded her, muttering words in low monotone voices, glancing at him, at her, and making gestures.

She began to wake. Her eyes opened; she blinked once. He found the strength to raise his head and open a wing, but they had already rushed at her. She was dragged from him with a soft pained cry, and they had jerked a hood over her head. He opened his mouth and very nearly managed to kill the nearest man, but the bastard danced out of range at the last moment, following the others that pulled her away from Kit, out of the shadow light and into a brightness that he could not bear to look at.

Wrath shook him. He tried to climb to his feet to follow, but that was useless as well. All he could do was rage and stew, his body a sudden new enemy that would not obey him, that would not follow her and destroy the men who stole her from him.

He tried anyway. He snarled and clambered to his feet, agony thumping through his blood until the darkness towered over him in hideous silence and crashed down to roll him away.

She was smuggled out in a perfectly proper carriage, or so it had seemed. It had *felt* proper, with rattling shades and drafty windows and a left wheel that clunked and groaned at every rut in the road. But she never saw any of it, not the shades or the floorboards or the men pressed in around her. All Rue could see was black cotton. And all she could hear was the rain.

It thrashed about Far Perch, drumming hard against the windows of the room that held her, until the wind skipped directions and the low constant boom rumbled from the other end of the house. From her position on the chair they'd led her to, she picked out the heartbeats of at least six *drákon* around her. But no one spoke.

When they'd first shoved her into the carriage, she'd feared they meant to try for Darkfrith right then, despite the storm, but thank God they had more sense than that. Far Perch was closer, and certainly more convenient. No doubt the council felt they could keep an easy eye on her here, at least for the time being.

All she needed was to be left alone. Just one minute. She would strangle herself getting out of this hood if she had to, but she would do it. Somehow.

Her arms were bound again, this time with what felt like cords of steel. It was impossible to relax with her fists secured at her back and so she remained stiffly upright in the chair, listening for any sort of revealing detail that might help her. No need to guess who had betrayed her to the council; it had to be the scribe. And no need to guess who had ordered she be bound and hooded.

Parrish Grady had come to stand at the open doorway behind her. Odd how she'd not forgotten his scent, mothballs and hair powder and oversweet cologne.

He entered the room with a studied, heel-first pace, circling slowly around her chair, stopping in front of her without a word. She envisioned his face as he perused her, his eyes heavy-lidded, his narrow lips drawn up into a sneer.

At least she was dressed.

Rue lifted her head. "Mr. Grady. How grow your daisies, sir?"

There—despite her dry mouth she'd managed just the exactly right tone of offhand derision. She heard him expel his breath.

"You were granted an amount of freedom, Miss Hawthorne, unprecedented in the history of our tribe." His voice was very quiet. "You were granted liberties not offered even to our Alphas, the right to roam, the right to hunt within the city, all for a very significant and specific purpose. And how did you choose to spend this time you were given?"

"Why, by making merry, of course. I especially enjoyed

dancing the night away with the Bonnie Prince in the Tower. He's vowed to steal me off to Gretna Green, just after he takes the throne."

Someone scuffed his feet. She heard the rustling of paper.

"And did you also enjoy revealing yourself to the world?" Grady's voice, still hushed, began to shake. "Did you enjoy flying about in full daylight, proving to all and sundry that dragons are real?"

Rue hesitated. "That wasn't me."

"No? Allow me to edify you. Perhaps you'll relish a column from last Monday's *Evening Standard*: *A monstrous Whyte Dragon, with fearsome Claws and Wings dipped in pure gold, has Stolen a Man and carried him off into the Sky, to the sincere Dismay of our good City. Five Men witnessed also that it breathed a Great Fyre upon the Holy Church of St. Augustine.*"

"The *Standard* is a rag," she said after a moment. "I hardly breathe fire."

Once again the paper rustled, crisper than before. "The *Evening Standard* is merely one of seven newspapers to carry such a story."

"Very well, then, it wasn't *only* me," she revised with false calm. "I've far more sense than that. Your marquess began the whole mess; he flew off first. I was merely trying to save him. But here's a jolly idea: instead of approaching him like a reasonable soul, why don't you hood and bind him and see how well he appreciates it?"

Grady's voice took on a new shade of ire. "Do you imagine there is some humor to be found in this disaster, mistress? Do you imagine we will treat it as some girlish jest and let you by with a slap on the wrist?"

"I imagine," replied Rue, "that when the Alpha discovers

what you have done to me, there will be hell to pay, Mr. Grady."

"The Marquess of Langford is indisposed, as you must well know. Perhaps permanently so. That is a rather nasty wound on his leg."

For the first time, a beat of real fear thrummed through her. "Where is he? What have you done with him?"

"Done with him? Nothing. He appears to be fixed in a dragon state. Obviously we cannot move him. As long as he remains as he is, he is safest in the warehouse."

Her mind raced. Did they know about the diamond? If she told them, would they take it from him? She tried to remember how she had last seen him in those seconds before they'd blinded her—she thought the stone had been beneath him—

"You, however, are to be removed to Darkfrith at first light. You have proven too great a liability to the tribe. You will retire to Chasen and await your marriage there. As much as many of us would no doubt prefer you be punished in a more befitting fashion, as a breeder you are too valuable to destroy." He began to move toward the door. "Should the Marquess of Langford not survive, you will be wed to the next man in line to be Alpha." Grady paused. "Whoever that may be."

She had to modify her breathing. She had to control her pulse. They would be watching her body. They would be searching for any signs of weakness.

"Good night, Mistress Hawthorne," said Grady softly. "Rest well."


She did not sleep. She could hardly slouch, much less relax into slumber. She tried to scoot back in the chair enough so that her hands were hidden, so that the two men left in the room with her would not see how she was slowly twisting her wrists into bleeding rawness, straining to pull free of the cords.

Without her hands free she was unable to adjust her skirts. No matter how she moved they stretched the wrong way beneath her legs. It bent a crook into her spine she could not seem to straighten.

She was tired now, her body kinked and knotted, her mind reeling with worry. She let her head droop. The hood had grown damp with her breath; it smelled unpleasantly of fresh dye. She wondered if they had prepared it just for her.

Beneath the rain someone was speaking. She turned her head but couldn't make out the words; it was beyond the walls of the room. The men around her shifted. The door opened. A single footfall scraped the floor.

"The council has been convened into emergency session," said a man.

"What, now?" The fellow to her right moved. "Again?"

"Aye. Grady sent me to summon you."

"What of her?" asked the other guard.

"It will be quick. I'm to stay with her."

"I don't—"

The voice hardened. "Emergency session. Something to do with Langford. You must go now."

"All right." And both the men walked past her, creaking down the hall. The door hinged closed.

"Whoever you are," Rue announced quietly to the room, "that was a damned flimsy excuse. They'll be back soon."

"I know it."

Hands fumbled behind her neck; she bent her head again to help him free the ties. The hood loosened. He drew it up over her face, and Rue took her first clear breath in hours.

The young scribe knelt before her, his wig pushed back to show a line of blondish-brown hair, his brows wrinkled. His eyes were dark gray and fretful behind his lenses.

"I'm sorry!" he blurted. "I wouldn't have told! But there was someone else with me—he saw you as well—"

"It's fine." She stood up and walked away from him, bending over, stretching her arms out behind her. "Open a window for me, please."

He nodded, going to the nearest one. Rue crossed to stand beside him, watching his fingers work, the lock sliding free. Wind and wet air rushed at them like the breath of God; she never thought she'd be so glad to feel the rain.

The scribe was gazing down at her. His spectacles began to steam. He jerked them off nervously, rubbing them on his sleeve.

"They won't forgive you this easily," she said.

"No."

Rue smiled at him. "Thank you."

"I—well..." He actually began to blush.

Footsteps resounded through the house, far at first, pounding nearer. She spoke more quickly. "Listen. Go now to the warehouse, see what they've done with Langford. If he's sealed in the cell, let him out. Do you understand?"

"Aye."

"And then vanish awhile. When it's safe to return here, you'll know."

"Yes." He swallowed. "I understand."

"What's your name?"

"Nicholas. Nick."

She leaned forward and brushed her lips to his cheek. "Good luck, Nick."

She Turned, and a moment later so did he, each of them

rising through the rainfall in opposite directions, he heading toward the docks, and she to the heart of the city.


She did not go home. She would not tempt fate that far. So instead she retreated to one of her sanctuaries, this one the pillared and gothic-laced belfry of a most active cathedral. The spire was one of the tallest in the city, the stone streaked with age. When she checked the trapdoor, the sole evidence of human life she could find was two flights below, where the tower bells rang by ropes that fell straight down for stories. Up here, in the open dark, the only footprints that ringed the balcony of pink alabaster and slate were from pigeons. It was tightly cramped and ethereally beautiful. She sat down next to a lead gargoyle and looked out at the city lights.

It would be dawn soon. The storm was slanting off to the north.

Hopefully Nick had completed his task. Hopefully Christoff was well enough to understand what had happened, what had yet to be done.

Rue wrapped a hand around the fluted column at her side, leaning out into the wind as far as she could manage with her other arm outstretched, letting raindrops bead her skin and slip cold through her open fingers.

*Find me.*

# CHAPTER SEVENTEEN

Rue waited a day. She dressed for warmth from her hidden bag of tricks and after a while haunted the floor just below, which wasn't a floor at all but a catwalk of giant oak beams supporting the twin bells of the spire. She crisscrossed their maze with her skirts kicking up, buffeted by the wind, then sat with her feet swinging, her heels tapping, very lightly, against the enormous bronze curve of the bell right below her.

She watched the sky change colors. She watched the clouds begin to thin and lighten; all true clouds, no hint of the *drákon* stealing among them. But they would be out there. Somewhere. They would hunt her now to the very ends of the earth.

Morning brightened into day. Day mellowed into afternoon. Whenever the bells were tolled, Rue fled back to the tower top with her fingers in her ears, the booming notes rolling over her and through her and rattling her bones.

Matins, prime. Terce. Sext.

The sky was mostly blue now, with racing white clouds

and feathery gray threads from countless chimneys and smokestacks below bent sideways with the wind.

But the catwalk was better sheltered, so that was where she tried to stay. Every so often a wash of shadow-cooled air would rush upward through the spire, tugging at her hair, flipping strands up into her eyes. The bell ropes would sway in place like long rolling snakes.

She was watching that, leaning over her lap to stare as far as she could into the void below, when there came a little noise above her head, nearly imperceptible. Rue straightened, glancing up at the trapdoor. It opened into a bright crack, and then a sudden square of brilliance. She brought a hand to her face to shield her eyes as the outline of a man blocked the light.

Tossed golden hair caught the sun into a halo, more radiant than an angel's grace. An arm reached down to her. She took his hand and was lifted straight up to the little round balcony, finding her feet against the sooty puddles and stone.

Christoff did not greet her. He didn't say anything, only brought his hands to her face and kissed her, hard and open and deep. There was nothing preliminary about it: his fingers in her hair, his mouth over hers, his body a solid pressure against her chest and hips, pushing her back against a column with an urgent sound in his throat. He kissed her as if he had already thrust inside her, as if they were both nude and entwined at the top of this high, airy spire, with sky and pink stone and stillness all around.

Her heart skipped. Her blood began to pump in a dark, eager rush.

She broke it off. She pulled away from him and pressed her fingers to her lips, hoping to disguise the betrayal of her uneven breath. He let her go without protest, his hands lowering. Her hair surged into a curtain between them, the ends flicking and teasing his stomach.

"You're better," she said, and inwardly cursed herself for being so flustered.

"Better." Christoff inclined his head. "I can Turn and fly. I no longer fall over when trying to stand. I no longer feel as if the very sun is exploding inside my head. Thanks to you." His voice warmed. "You saved my life, clever mouse."

Her eyes dropped. "Credit the diamond, not me."

"It was your idea to bring the stone to me."

"A lucky guess. You might just as easily have died."

He shifted, angling away from her as if to take in the view. "But I didn't. The diamond was my guide, but you were my anchor." From the corner of her eye she saw his head turn. "You kept me there, Rue. You kept me."

She didn't reply, her gaze averted, her face downturned. Kit remained motionless, weighing the clues of her mood: the shy demeanor, the set mouth, her hands tucked beneath her apron. She didn't seem altogether pleased to see him. She had accepted his kiss but not returned it; she had clearly chosen a place where he could find her, her scent carried on the wind in whispering invitation. Yet she held herself aloof, her skirts and hair dancing merrily like they belonged to a carefree girl and not this grave and bewitching woman who would not hold his eyes.

He wanted to go to her and crush her to him. He wanted to melt this new resistance, and so had to concentrate fiercely on keeping still and apart.

She was all he had thought of, from the very moment he could think again. From waking in the warehouse cell, the wary voice at the other side of the door offering to help him— from streaking back to Far Perch, confronting the *drákon* there, the ruckus, the accusations and explanations, the hurried apologies from a very apprehensive council—through it all his blood had beat *Rue, Rue, Rue,* so loudly through his veins he wondered that no one heard it but he. It had pushed him to the peak of his limits; he was balanced there, dangerous, on that high and whetted edge, when he strode unclad into his father's study, shocking his tribesmen into chairscraping silence.

He remembered exactly what they had done to her. He remembered exactly the sound of the bar sliding into place after they'd dragged her out of the cell. He had looked at Parrish Grady standing puffed up with consequence, lecturing Christoff on discretion from behind his father's desk—behind *his* desk—and imagined with graphic, perfect clarity ripping the man's throat out. The flood of crimson gurgling over his cravat. The rusty scent. The wet, gasping sound of his death on the blue and cream rug.

Grady's lecture ended on a quavering note, as if he had literally run out of air. They stared at each other, and the older man slowly blanched to the color of boiled oats. Christoff had let the moment endure a while longer, then suggested with absolute civility that Mr. Grady take his leave of Far Perch. At once.

George had shown up, and Rufus. None of them had known where or how to find Rue. None of them had a clue but him.

The breeze murmured through the columns of the bell tower, warmer than expected for a fresh-scrubbed spring day. Rue captured her errant hair with one hand, twisting it into a rope over her wrist. Under his steady contemplation, her cheeks begin to tint.

"Did you return *Herte* to the council?" she asked, still without looking up.

"Aye."

"Parrish Grady must have been relieved."

"Parrish Grady did not get the opportunity to be anything but grateful for his sorry damned hide. I handed the diamond to George Winston and told Grady to go home before I lost my good humor and decided to carve him up like a Christmas goose. He took me at my word." Kit decided to break their impasse; he went to her, lifting her chin with his finger, capturing her gaze. "He wants you, you know. He has, from the minute he first saw you. I watched it happen."

"What of Nicholas?"

"Ah, yes, your friend the scribe." He opened his fingers; her pulse was a hummingbird against the back of his hand, fleet and warm and vital. "As he was somewhat instrumental in freeing you—and me—I could hardly return the favor by threatening to disembowel him, no matter how heartstruck he became merely speaking your name. It's going to grow tedious after a while, menacing half the population of the shire just because they're in love with you. I thanked him for his help and assigned him as Grady's escort. Two birds, one stone, that sort of thing. One by one, I stave off your suitors."

She did not smile, as he'd hoped. She only looked at him, velvet brown eyes, heavy black lashes. He touched the bruises on her cheek. "Did I do this, or did they?"

"Both, I should think. I don't have a mirror; I don't know how bad it is now. I've an idea of how it looked before."

*Sorry.* He wanted to say it, but it seemed so inadequate a word for what he was actually feeling. *I'm so sorry, I'd never hurt you, I bleed to look at you, I love you so much.* But whatever it was that kept her so austere also rebuffed even that first, simple word. She seemed stern and distant as she stared out at the rooftops, even with her winning flush.

He eased back a step to grant her room again, glancing around the narrow spire. "Nice gargoyles."

"Yes. Welcome to my . . . what did you call it before? Emergency recourse."

"Very cozy."

She crossed her arms. The movement pulled his attention to the scoop of her bodice, the demure white kerchief that folded across her shoulders and tucked over her chest. Her dress was dove gray and unadorned; the kerchief matched the apron spreading wide down her skirts. He was sure—reasonably sure—it was the gown of a milkmaid. Kit had to press the smile from his lips.

She said, "I'd offer you tea, but I'm afraid the service here is sadly lacking."

The smile came anyway; he ran a finger over the grit along the railing. "Perhaps you should fire your maid."

"Indeed. It's so difficult to find *honest* help these days."

Kit paused. "You're angry."

"You lied to me." She leveled an open stare at him now, her lips flattened, her brows drawn into a line. "You lied about our agreement. You lied about ever letting me free. I know you never meant to, diamond or no."

"Oh." He leaned back against an alabaster column. "Did the council tell you that?"

"The *council* didn't have to. I fathomed it myself when they showed up here en masse, hood in hand. Were you even going to wait the full fourteen days before hauling me back to Darkfrith?"

"*I* was," he said softly.

"Well, how generous of you. It's nice to know I'm dealing with a man of his word." Her voice had begun to tremble; she looked sharply away.

"Would you like an apology?" he asked after a moment.

"Another lie? Thank you kindly, but no."

"Good. I'd actually prefer not to lie, so here's the truth for you, mouse. I'm not sorry. I'd do it all over again if I had to—except, perhaps, the part with the crocodiles." He pushed off the column, approaching her, placing a careful hand at her waist. "I was only heeding my instincts. I needed you, I needed *Herte*. Fate had tied you together and dropped you both into my lap. I couldn't truly let you go; my blood wouldn't let me. If you want to call it ruthless or cunning or outright devious, that's fine. I don't care. It's who we are. Even you."

"*My* word is my honor," she said, low.

"I'm delighted to hear it." He bent his head, savoring the curve of her ear, the perfume of her skin. "We'll let your word be my honor as well." He drew her earlobe between his teeth, bit down gently, kissed it better. "Righteous intentions, noble deceit. Two sides of the same coin. That way we're both satisfied."

Air escaped her in an irritated huff. "I am far from satisfied."

Kit smiled against her throat. "But I'm going to remedy that." He kissed her neck, her lips, breathing in lilies and lightning, pleasure expanding through his lungs. "Right now. Forever." He took a step against her skirts, tilting her head back with his thumbs at her cheeks.

She caught his wrists, checking him in place, their lips inches apart. "Some people would say that since I saved your life, you owe me a courtesy."

"Is that right?"

"To wit, my freedom."

His smile deepened. He closed his eyes, touching his mouth to hers despite her token resistance. "You might as well have left me to die, then. I'm afraid that I can't live without you."

"You sound like a halfpenny ballad," she said rudely.

"Do I?" He pulled his hands from hers and began to work free the kerchief, tugging it loose, letting it fly from his fingers to trace the wind. "Obviously you're going to have to elevate my standards."

"A daunting task." But like a summer shower she had changed again, blue clouds to sunlight, her tone less astringent, her body leaning into his. He drew his fingers down her chest. Her skin was warm beneath his touch, warm from the kerchief, and warm from him.

"But you're already halfway there. When I do this—" Kit tried her lips again, tender, fleeting, tasting her with his tongue. "And this—" He nuzzled her neck, allowing the dragon inside a fleet glory, closing his teeth on her, hard enough to leave his mark. Her jaw brushed his temple; the air left her in a rush. "Rue-flower . . . I feel like I'm soaring."

Her hands shifted on his arms. He lifted his head and took in her face, her eyes dazed and heated—passion or pique, he couldn't tell. It didn't matter. He couldn't wait any longer. Kit heard the husky break in his voice, all pretense stripped away.

"Let me love you. Please. I swear I'll make you happy."

She gave a small shake of her head, a dreamer waking. "Why do I feel these things for you?" she whispered, her brows knit. "Why with you?"

"You know why." And he didn't let her speak again; he didn't want her to wake. He wanted her like this, lush and ready in his arms, a flame held aloft against the azure sky, firm and real and his. He covered her lips, taking what wasn't yet offered. She held frozen again, her body taut— but then she made a soft ardent sound and pulled him close, the two of them tilting together until he had her back against a column, just like before. Only this time Kit did not stop.

He took her there roughly against the fluted pillar. He raised her skirts and found her moist curls, stroking her, sliding his fingers in and out. When he couldn't take the sweet noises she made any longer, he shoved himself into her heat with a chest-deep groan, linen and muslin rucked up around them, her eager pants at his shoulder. He tangled his fingers in her hair to force her head up to his and stole the breath from her, claiming dominion over this as well, her body, her heart, pumping in and out until her throat wrung with those soft little cries at his every thrust. But he couldn't get enough of her, wanting deeper, wanting more. He had a wild thought to rip away the dress but couldn't wait even for that.

Her hair blew in ripples against the pink stone. She lifted a leg, sliding it up his, worsted stockings and slender strong muscles; she opened to him like a flower. Too much, too much: with his hands on her buttocks, Kit came in a violent blind rush; he had to have hurt her, his fingers bruising, his teeth scoring her pretty skin. But she cried out and climaxed with him, erotic feminine shudders that left him desperate for air. For her, and the clouds, and the heaven all around them.

She felt so strange. She felt alone and yet not, because she was cradled in Christoff's embrace, the two of them seated in the fancy-wrought pinnacle of the belfry, on par with only birds and bells and wind. She was nestled between his legs, her cheek to his chest. She wondered if he was cold. She was, even with her layers of muslin.

One of the four gargoyles of the tower, the one posted east, looked back at her through the railing with blank leaden eyes and a leer. Christoff's arm was a muscled weight around her shoulders.

"Do you love me?" Rue asked, watching the gargoyle.

His arm tightened; he dropped a kiss to her hair. "I do."

"I think I can lead you to the runner," she said slowly.

For a long while he said nothing. She closed her eyes, her cheek rising and falling with his calm respiration.

"It's too dangerous," he answered at last. "You're far more valuable to me than his capture. Don't say anything to the council. I'll come back and hunt him later."

"I can't," she said, painful. "I can't wait. Zane is at risk."

"...Zane?"

Rue sat up, letting her hair cloak her face. She'd dreaded this moment. She'd had to make a decision, she'd had to choose to trust Christoff or not. She'd had all day to consider it, and the time had not passed by easily. But the truth was out now. She would not shrink from it.

She tucked her hair behind her ears, meeting his gaze.

"Do you remember when I told you about the runner, what he said to me at the mask—that he hadn't wanted the diamond?"

"Aye."

"As though someone had offered it to him. Why would he steal what he hadn't wanted? Why go to all that trouble, only to toss it away to a crocodile pit?"

"Zane," said Christoff again, this time with dawning understanding. "Your apprentice."

"He knew the diamond was coming to London. He knew I'd covet it. He even showed me the notices for it. He's rash and he's canny. But he never—" She shook her head, frowning. "He's never tried anything so foolhardy before."

"Until now." Kit climbed to his feet, running his fingers through his hair. His body was sculpted clean and elegant against the blue. "He stole it for you. To give to you."

"I think so. I think he even tried to tell me, that day at Far Perch."

"What a damned stupid stunt. If he'd been caught, the council would have had him boiled and flayed—"

"As I said, he's rash. But also incredibly loyal. It's why he tracked me down after I was taken to Darkfrith. Why he waited for me all those nights."

The marquess's mouth took on an acerbic curl. "What a faithful lapdog."

"However you choose to denigrate him," she retorted, also finding her feet, "at least he accepts me for who I am. He's been steadfast and true. I will not abandon him to the mercies of the council, or the runner. Or to you."

Christoff looked back at her, surprised. "I accept you."

"Yes. Now."

"Oh, I see. This is about the past, isn't it?"

"This is about a young boy, Lord Langford. That's all."

"I accept you, Rue. Shall I say it again? I accept you. I cherish you. I adore everything about you, from the little girl you were to the woman you are today."

She flicked a hand at him, frustrated, turning away. "You're just wasting time."

"No." He caught her back to him, spreading his fingers over her uninjured cheek. "Listen. When you were twelve years old I saw you for the first time. Truly saw you. And from then on, I took note whenever our paths crossed. You were so quiet it was difficult to believe you sprang from the same messy bloodlines as the rest of us. You had modesty and grace. You didn't flirt, and you didn't give quarter." His palm slipped from her face; he took up both her hands. "If the other maidens of the shire were garish bright stars, then you were the midnight around them, silent and mysterious and all the more interesting for it. I accepted you as that, mouse. I still do."

Rue glanced down. Her fingers curled over his. "Not even a halfpenny ballad. A mere farthing."

"Alas. Nothing I say can move your heart."

She shook her head, her throat tight. "Help me save Zane."

"Does he even need saving? The child seemed capable enough."

"I think he took *Herte* to the other runner, perhaps even before he went to Mim." She remembered the courtesan's carefully chosen words, how she'd managed not to give away her secrets after all: *I did receive an inquiry....* "He's been a part of this city longer than I have, and in a sense, more completely. Zane was born here. He grew up here. He knows the belly of London in a way that even I can't conceive. I think he's known all along where the runner is— probably even what he is, just as he has with me. And when Zane realized the diamond could not be sold or even given away, that you and I were hunting it together—"

"He threw it to the crocodiles," Christoff finished. "Beast to beast. Little whelp."

"Will you help?" she asked, lifting her eyes.

"I don't suppose there's aught I could say to convince you to stay out of it?"

"No."

"Even if I promise to protect your urchin?"

"You told me your honor was no good."

"Not quite." His lashes lowered, veiling the cool clear

green with warmer brown; he spoke more quietly. "I said that *you* were my honor, Rue Hawthorne, and I meant it. I'll do what I can to shield him."

"No. I must come too."

"Damnation, mouse. Can't you trust me to handle it?"

"Can't you trust me to?"

He sighed and drew her back to him, enfolding her in his arms. "Another stalemate, I see. Life with you is going to be challenging."

"Perhaps you'd rather have a garish star," she said to his bare chest.

"No, my sweet. For all its wild ways, I love the night."


She found him by the monkeys. His back was to her; he was slouched against the railing meant to separate the humans from the caged creatures, flipping peanuts from a bag into the pen, one at a time. Shells littered the gravel at his feet. The peach-faced monkeys were dashing over one another in deft, rubbery confusion to grab the treats. For a while they didn't even notice her, standing mute in the tree dapple down the menagerie path.

One of the peanuts struck a bar and bounced back to him. Zane stooped to pick it up and placed it directly into an eager brown hand, then slouched back against the railing and began pitching again.

Rue walked up. The monkeys instantly abandoned their search for the nuts and began to screech. The boy's head lifted. She touched a hand to his shoulder and he jerked away as if he'd been scorched, whirling about with the bag in his fist.

"Come away," she said to him beneath the racket. "I can't linger here."

Without waiting for him to follow, she withdrew down the path, finding an open, empty space before an abandoned cage set askew in the mud, bleached yellow hay still heaped in its corners.

JAGUARUNDI. A SMALL YET MOST VICIOUS HUNTER.

She remembered the brawny ruddy cat in her yard and sent a measuring glance back to the boy behind her. He returned it sullenly.

"You've done a very foolish thing," Rue said. "I don't think you know how foolish."

"Why? Because *he* says so?"

"No, because I do. You've stirred up a hornet's nest of ill will, not to mention left us both open to the inquiries of the authorities and a certain element of my past I've been working hard to avoid."

"Langford," Zane sneered.

"Lord Langford is the least of your troubles." She watched a mother and son walk by, the boy chattering in a high, excited voice about lions and bears. The child was dressed in green velvet and curls; his mother smiled down at him tenderly. Rue waited until they passed. "None of us is without family, Zane, or histories. Mine have caught up with a vengeance. They're a lot of ruthless old bastards—and they're dead focused on that diamond you filched."

Zane bent his head and took a peanut from the bag, crushing the shell between his fingers. He didn't bother to deny her accusation, saying only, "I don't have it no more."

"I know," she replied gently. "But where is the man you took it to? The one like me?"

His fingers stilled.

"You can tell me," she murmured, still gentle. "I'm not angry."

"He don't have it neither."

She smiled. "I know, Zane. I have it. Rather, I did. The diamond is back where it belongs."

"You ... found it?"

She looked deliberately down the path, toward the end of the park that held the crocodiles. The boy swallowed. His wolf-yellow eyes flickered up and down her figure, just once, before he dropped his gaze again.

"I thought it'd make you happy," he whispered, and for the first time since she'd known him, he sounded close to his age.

"A ninety-eight-carat diamond! Of course it would have. You're going to make someone a wonderful husband one day, my dear. It was just ill fortune that had this particular diamond wedged in my past."

His eyes raised to hers again.

"Where is the man?" Rue persisted. "I truly must know."

He dropped a peanut into the dirt, smashing it with the heel of his shoe. "He's going to take you away, ain't he? Langford. He's going to make you stay with him. Take you back to that place with all the old bastards."

"Yes," she said.

"Did I make it happen?" he asked in a strained voice.

"No. It would have happened anyway, sooner or later." She looked down at the empty cage, seeing forest instead, seeing Chasen, and emerald hills. "It was only a matter of time."

"I'm sorry," Zane said.

She forced another smile, going to him, drawing his meager warmth close. He felt slight as a sparrow, the bones of his shoulder blades painfully gaunt. "It's not your burden, child. You were only the catalyst. If it had not been you, trust me, it would have been something else."

"I'm not a child," he said hotly, wrenching away. He glared at her with burning cheeks.

"It's not your burden," Rue repeated, unmoving. "Tell me where the man is."

He was breathing too quickly, glowering at the path with his tawny hair untied and his arms rigid at his sides. The peanuts from the bag began to dribble to the ground. He dropped the lot and kicked it into the shrubs.

"Zane."

"Lambeth. The amplitheatre."

Collins Amplitheatre. The pleasure gardens—fountains, mirrors, a display of fireworks every third weekend of the month—one of the most public and popular places in the city. Rue pulled back, staring. Zane hunched his shoulders, his face drawn into a scowl. "It's true. Says he likes the fire shows."

"All right. Go home now. You look like hell. And whatever you do, stay away from Far Perch. I'll come back when it's safe."

"With *him*."

Zane had turned his head to the dark leafy entrance of the path where Lord Langford now stood waiting, cool and handsome and every inch an aristocrat in splendid pewter-gray satin. He tapped his Nivernois hat against his thigh, never taking his eyes from Rue.

"Aye, with him. Life is constant change, my friend. But know this: I will always make a place for you, no matter where I may be." She smiled and placed her palm over her heart. "We're linked now, you know."

"I know," he said, very still.

Rue moved away, walking toward the marquess. After a few steps she stopped and looked back at the boy.

"Oh, and Zane. There are a number of fine woods just outside the city. I don't care how or if you do it, but let's be very clear—I do not want a horde of monkeys mucking up my house."

# CHAPTER EIGHTEEN

They were to arrive in stages. The guardsmen went first, rambling into the gardens in uneven numbers, disguised as sailors and footmen and chandlers, the blunt, unassuming backbone of the city.

Then came the council, ensconcing themselves in the infamous Delilah House tavern near the center of the park as a loose company of journeymen, enjoying their beer and gin at the close of the day.

And finally the marquess and Rue, taking a turn through the Collins Amplitheatre and Pleasure Gardens simply as . . . themselves. Well—Christoff was himself. Rue, done up in silk and lace and expensive Italian shoes, was not certain who she was supposed to be. Not the Smoke Thief; not the comte; certainly not prudent Widow Hilliard. She was dressed tonight as finely as any gentlewoman of the realm, her apple-green skirts hooped wide and opulent over a quilted petticoat, her wig caught up in ivory curls that draped from her shoulders down the back of her mantlet of cream crêpe. Powder and rouge covered the bruises on her cheek.

Only one thing set her visibly apart from the other noblewomen nearby: Rue wore no jewelry, not even a ring. Her sole adornment was a black velvet ribbon around her throat.

Christoff had tied the ribbon for her in the carriage. He had bent his head to hers and let his fingers brush her nape, a slow, grazing stroke of his hand up and down her spine. He had not kissed her. She'd wanted him to, even turned her cheek to his—*sandalwood, smoothly shaved skin*—but he'd only settled back into the other seat when he was done, watching her silently with hooded eyes.

He was in evening kit too, a hunter deceptively relaxed in pale gilt brocade and ruffled lawn, one arm thrown along the back of his seat. He'd helped her from the carriage with the greatest of courtesy, leading her through the elaborate wrought-iron gates of the gardens at a pace so leisurely that the Cit behind them nearly trod on her hem. Fans began to snap open, heads began to turn. Christoff only gazed nonchalantly ahead with her arm in his, taking them both into the shimmering depths of the gardens.

The amplitheatre was the sunken center of the grounds, a scoop of Roman stone hollowed out of the earth, surrounded by trees and flowers and plenty of nicely secluded alcoves for lovers, or footpads, or both. Collins was best known for its multitude of fountains and flashing mirrors—and its liquor—where anyone with a shilling to spare could stroll admiring the lights and jets of water that frequently overshot their mark. Every so often ladies gave little screams, avoiding the splashes by fleeing into their companions' arms.

It was a place that teetered on the knife's edge of decorum at the best of times. But tonight was the last Friday of a very wet April; after sunset there would be a show of fire suns and sparklers. Even members of the *ton* flocked to that.

Years ago it had proven a profitable testing ground for honing her skills, surveying, tracking, a deft touch upon a pocket or wrist. The din of fireworks offered a most effective protection against the noisy pebbled paths.

Perhaps the other runner enjoyed it for the same reasons.

They approached the outer ring of gardens, torchlit camellias and acacias and a canopy of pink Japanese *sakura* blossoms arching handsomely overhead, still misted with raindrops.

"Chin up," the marquess whispered, smiling and nodding at a passing couple. "Let them see you."

"I don't know why you think this is going to work," she replied, just as hushed. The combed pebbles were sprinkled with cherry blossoms; the fragrance marked their every step. "It would have been far better to be circumspect. He's going to discover us straight off."

"Aye. Us. But not the others."

He was banking on that. Christoff's single encounter with the runner suggested that his abilities as a *drákon* were fairly limited. Rue said he hadn't noticed her as a footman in the ballroom; Kit himself had noted a distinct lack of energy around him that night at the mask, even when standing beside the fine humming power that was Rue. So they would show the runner what he could not sense, that Christoff and his mate were out hunting in plain sight, a glaring distraction while the others closed in.

He knew the man's name now too. Tamlane Williams. Kit's father had caught him twice as a youth before he'd drowned in the River Fier.

Just like Rue.

She knew all that, in addition to the patterns and coils of

tonight's plan. But Christoff hadn't told her the rest of it—that, very simply, he wanted her here in the open with him. That if she remained beside him in this bright flattering torchlight her face would be unforgettable, her every movement tied to his. It was his second, unspoken message to Williams and every other member of the *drákon* stalking these grounds: *Taken.*

Besides, there was no way he was leaving her to her own devices tonight. At least here she was surrounded, protected, by the best of their kind.

" 'Tis a foolish scheme," his beloved whispered.

"It worked on you, my lady."

"Did it?" She sent him a sideways look. "I seem to recall escaping the Stewart rather easily."

"Only because I was too much of a gentleman to give chase."

Her brows lifted; she laughed softly. "Oh, is *that* what happened?"

"Well, more or less." Kit put a shrug in his tone. "That, and I was caught short by your beauty."

"More like by the pack of people rushing headlong over you."

"They were a trifle . . . inconvenient."

"You looked like the lone salmon swimming upstream, my lord."

"You saw it?"

"I *was* there."

They stopped before a fountain of marble mermaids and dolphins, water bubbling up from a massive carved nautilus at the top. Droplets caught the mirrored lamplight to bounce liquid fire across the stone faces and tails. He watched her watching it, her head tilted pensively, as if the mermaids held some deep dark secret she needed to fathom.

The light etched her profile in silver and gold; she was pale as the sirens, far more lovely. He found his gaze drifting lower, to the open décolletage of the gown, framed with crêpe and a short edging of lace.

She wore no kerchief for modesty tonight; the ribbons of her mantlet tied just at the base of her throat, their ends trailing down in satiny suggestion over her breasts. A delicate pink bloom had caught in the folds of the crêpe. It rose and fell with the rhythm of her breathing. Christoff found his own slowing to match it.

Crickets sang. From far away someone laughed. The fountain kept up a peaceful, flowing music that filled his ears.

"And will you be a gentleman tonight as well?" Rue asked quietly, unmoving.

"No." Kit took up the cherry blossom, crushing the petals into perfume between his fingers. "Tonight I'm someone else."

Her face tipped to his. She looked from the flower to him, her lips parting; she seemed about to speak when a blithe new voice interrupted from over his shoulder.

"Langford! Good heavens, is that really you? We'd heard you'd retired already to your damp northern hills!"

Kit dropped the flower to the path, drawing Rue to his side as he turned to face the group coming up to them. He recognized the speaker at once, and with her a throng of dandies and beaux. The Duchess of Monfield's husband, however, was nowhere to be seen.

He knew her hardly better than society had permitted. She'd been intriguing at first—intriguing in the way a fine new wine could be, piquant on the tongue, but that was all. She'd allowed him a few purloined kisses but nothing more. By their third meeting he'd wanted nothing more anyway, bored with her constant prattle of gowns and peers and balls. By the fourth he'd decidedly cut her short. Then—six months, a year later—he'd heard she had hooked her fish and gotten betrothed. Poor Monfield; Christoff didn't know him either, but he had to feel pity for any man shackled to a woman who lived solely for cotillions and haute couture.

"Your Grace," he greeted her, and released Rue's hand to bow over Letty's. "Surely you know it seldom pays to listen to rumor."

"Indeed." Letty laughed. "But who doesn't adore a good anecdote? I heard the most astonishing one about *you* from Cynthia Meir." Her eyes went to Rue, bright, assessing, her lips curving in expectation. She was covered in gemstones and frippery, drenched in that mawkish French scent she always wore; Kit saw the instant her memory began to wake. Her smile faltered. A tiny, tiny frown made a fold in her unblemished forehead.

"Your Grace," said Christoff again formally, offering another bow. "May I present Clarissa, Marchioness of Langford."

The beaux understood him before the duchess did. They stirred and hissed, but for the longest while Letty only stood there, staring at Rue. Rue stared back, unsmiling, then sank into a graceful curtsy. The fountain splashed and burbled.

"Oh," said Letitia at last, barely a shade too sleek. She took up Rue's hands. "My dear! How delightful. I had no idea. Kit, you slyboots! Is it a country match?"

"You might say so," said Christoff, his eyes on his ominously silent new wife.

"Isn't that fascinating," trilled Letty. She sent a flinty smile to Rue. "And are you not the most darling little country bride?"

"What a magnificent necklace, Your Grace," said Rue,

returning her smile with a sudden, cutthroat ferocity. "I've rarely seen such finely matched rubies. And how well they compliment your gown."

Letty lifted a gloved hand to her throat. "Well, I . . ."

"You quite light up this humdrum garden." Rue turned to Kit. "Langford," exclaimed his bride, using the precisely same lilt Letty had, "I simply *must* have one *exactly* like it."

The duchess laughed uncomfortably. "Why, 'tis a family heirloom, Lady Langford."

"*Is* it?" Her voice darkened. "Would you mind terribly if I took a closer look?"

"Dearest heart, we're running late," said Kit, pulling Rue forcibly back to him. "Forgive us, I beg you. We have an assignation we cannot miss." And before the men around them even completed their bows, he had them both walking away toward a particularly dark expanse of the gardens.

When they were far enough off, he spoke. "How much more tranquil my life would be if you were even a whit less headstrong."

"Perhaps you should have considered that before you *married* me." She kicked at a pebble. "And now everyone's going to call me Clarissa," she added grumpily.

"Only the people you don't like. Think of how much it will simplify things."

A man in a sailor's coat appeared from behind a willow down the path; as he lifted a tankard of ale to his mouth his eyes met theirs. Kit gave a scant nod of acknowledgment, and the *drákon* guard drifted back into the trees. Rue followed his shape until he was gone.

"Did you even like the necklace?" Kit asked, to distract her.

"The Duchess of Monfield has a rather reliable tendency to overdress. It's one of the reasons I befriended her as the

comte." They passed by a pavilion surrounded with can-
dytuft and budding lavender; a shadowed couple on a bench
traded whispers within. Rue never gave them a glance.
"Why did you?"

"Did I what?"

"Befriend Her Grace. Or dare I guess?"

He felt his jaw tighten, and willfully relaxed it. "We're
not friends."

"Ah." And then, "I begin to understand Melanie a little
better now."

"Is that so?"

"It cannot be pleasant, knowing you can be so readily replaced."

He absorbed the sting of that, surprisingly poignant, but
managed an even tone. "I had no idea you thought so little
of me."

"I beg your pardon." They approached a tiered fountain
of mirrors, every inch of it covered in glass. The water lifted
and fell in diamond sparkles, nearly too bright to behold, reflecting out points of silvery brilliance that bleached the colors all around. Rue spoke to the ground.

"Did you have a look at the painting in Her Grace's
boudoir? I was astonished. Watteau is so out of fashion of
late."

"I did not. As you surely must know."

"I know hardly anything, Lord Langford," she replied,
very serious, and came to a halt within one of the deeper
spots of dark. Her arm withdrew from his. "Don't you
realize that? All I really know of you are rumors and
memories—little more than witless Letty—and very old
dreams." She gave a low, unhappy laugh. "And now you're
introducing me as your wife."

Kit glanced around them. Ahead were only more

fountains and people, couples and foursomes and a rowdy knot of youths rounding the bend in the footpath. But there was an obelisk to their left, rising snowy and straight from a thick bed of ivy. He pulled her over to it, crushing vines underfoot. When they were out of sight of the others he dropped her hand.

"I've grown a trifle weary of being constantly cast as your villain, my love. I am only what I've been forged to be. Not evil, and perhaps not especially good. I care for a very few things—the tribe, my name, my position. And you. If it pleases you to roll stones into our path, go ahead. At least I know my own heart, black as it may be. I make no apologies for my past, Rue, so don't expect any. I won't demand them of you either."

He could barely make out her face. They were deep in the long, unbroken shadow, shielded from the torches and mirrors, only the faint babble of fountains and people a reminder they weren't truly alone. But he could hear her breathing. He could feel her mounting tension, drawing keen and tight.

"Stones," she muttered, after a moment. "I think they're rather more boulders."

Christoff softened his voice. "You know me, mouse. You might not entirely like what you know, and you might not like to admit it, but you do know me, as deeply and completely as I do you. It's our way. With or without a church or banns or witnesses, we are wed because we're the same. Same essence, same soul, same hell-born command. But I can't change a single second before this moment. You're not Melanie, or Letitia. Not the stars but the blessed night, remember? Just to be drastically clear: that makes you—utterly—irreplaceable."

He thought he could see her a little better, now that his

eyes had adjusted. She was still only a suggestion of a girl, doe eyes, an oval face, an expression that could have held wonder or pleasure or burning disdain.

He bent his head to hers. He touched a hand to the ivory curls at her shoulder and found her mouth, exhaling softly over her skin, his tongue slipping between her lips. She tasted of rouge and lilies and the cool-tinged sweep of evening. Kit withdrew before he forgot himself, monitoring his breath, running his palms lightly up and down her arms.

Not now. Not here. But soon—

"I don't want you to fight him," Rue whispered, gazing up at him. "The runner. I don't want you to get hurt."

"Now you truly wound me. Do you think I wouldn't win?"

"I think," she said slowly, "that you would win at all costs."

"There. You know me better than you thought."

"Christoff." She gripped his arms but said nothing more, only her fingers closing and opening over his sleeves.

"It's who we are," he said gently. "It's how we must be. You are Alpha. And because I know you, Rue, your sovereign heart—I know you understand."

She reached up and put her arms around his neck, pressing her mouth to his, pushing him back against the hard stone. She kissed him deeply, using the lessons he himself had taught her to pique his blood, her tongue and hot caresses and her teeth drawing at his lower lip. He wanted to touch her; he was afraid to. She was slight and fierce, clothed in silk that would tear like a cloud under his hands. But he wanted to. With her chest against his, her gown stiff and unyielding, her mouth all softness and heat . . . God, he wanted to.

Light sparked behind his lids. Kit opened his eyes; her

face was revealed in the dying light of a fire sun, smoking into cinders far above their heads.

Rue lifted her chin, watching the ashes sift down to the trees. Before they dissolved completely, a second firework ripped high and burst into light. From the center of the park came the sound of rousing applause.

Kit smiled down at her, running a finger over her lips to smooth out her rouge again.

"Our time has come," he murmured. "Lady Langford, shall we take in the show?"


She was jealous. Jealous of stupid, pretty Letitia, who had picked up all the little bones Rue had tossed her as the comte as eagerly as could be, compliments, flowers, courtly gossip and dances. The duchess had proven to be as shallow as a puddle. Why did it hurt that Christoff had once enjoyed that?

Because she loved him. Because Letty was all that Rue was not, fair and forward and tinkling bright. Because, in the darkest chambers of her heart, she was afraid it was still all he wanted, and ultimately he would be disappointed with what he would get. He said he knew her. How could that be, when she hardly knew herself?

She had worked hard at her successes. She had gambled large and largely won. The thought of leaving London, her home, her life, was a bitter one. But the thought of living without Kit was like poison in her throat.

He stood benignly at her side in the midst of the sizable audience attending the show. He kept his hand cupped on her elbow and looked perfectly convincing as a gentleman who had nothing better to do than admire colorless lights exploding against a very smoky sky. The smell of gunpowder fell about them like snowfall.

She tried to imitate his ease. She tried to not notice the other *drákon* in the press of bodies, faces she hardly recognized but scents, vibrations, energies—almost overwhelming. In the sudden next flash of light she saw Kit as the boy he had been once, gazing up at the stars; then the memory was gone and he was looking back at her without turning his head, taking note of her scrutiny.

Rue returned her gaze to the sky.

Fire suns, fire trees, exploding round balls that looked to her like Scotch thistles, torn apart by the wind. There was a quartet of strings playing gamely in a roped-off little square—no viola—and the booth by the rose garden was doing a brisk business in shucked oysters and beer.

In the pit of the amplitheatre, twin showers of sparks erupted into columns of tall, white-hot glitter, throwing the figures of men working there into sharp relief, their coats unbuttoned and their ears wrapped with cloth, soot streaking their hands and faces. Everyone applauded, even after the pillars died.

Fire suns. Fire trees.

The workmen sweated and toiled, passing long rockets from hand to hand, the scorched clay dais they used for the launch, the smoldering orange tip of the torch they used as a light, a procession she had seen more times than she could count—rocket, dais, torch, stand back—but she found herself watching it again anyway. There were four men doing the job of five; she wondered where the fifth might be, and then, as musicians started up a country jig and the next thistle popped, she saw the small, set face of Zane in the crowd beyond the dais. There was a man standing behind him, right behind him, with his hand on the boy's shoulder. The man was scanning the people around them, but Zane, incredibly, was looking straight at her.

Everything inside her began crumbling into a slow, sinking abyss. Heart, stomach, lungs, sloughing off into the void. In their place came fear, licking through her veins. Zane was expressionless, white face, dark face, as the rockets were lit and lit. The runner holding him—*Williams, Tamlane Williams,* circled her mind, *had she ever even seen him at the shire? Had he been kind? Had he been cruel?*—was still searching the crowd, but when Zane tried to move, she saw the man's hand press down at once and the glint of something that might have been metal at his back. A pistol, or a knife.

Rue glanced at the marquess, who was still observing the show. She lowered her lashes and pulled the mantlet closer around her and felt his immediate attention, even though he never moved a muscle.

He would do anything to win. He'd promised to protect Zane, but she knew, deep down, he'd do anything.

"I need to visit the tavern," she said under her breath; embarrassing, but all she could think of. Christoff looked at her fully.

"Come with me, if you like," she said. "But it's just around the corner there. I'll be right back."

Without bothering to reply he began to make a path for them through the people, moving easily along with her in tow. The tavern was perilously close to Zane, but it also extracted her from the thick of the assembly; the fewer witnesses, she reckoned, the better. She began to count the tribesmen they passed and had gotten to fourteen by the time they reached the pergola that marked the beginning of the path to Delilah House. Crystal lustres dangled from the crossed slats overhead, turning slowly, twinkling light.

Green leaves and tiny jasmine petals littered the lanterned walk like fallen stars. Rue stopped.

"You should remain visible. I'll meet you here."

"I think not, love."

"You still don't trust me?"

Christoff's smile was narrow and gleaming. "Not tonight. Not in the least."

"You can't follow me *all* the way in," she said, disguising the fear with indignation.

He shrugged. "Perhaps not. We'll see. You'd be surprised what a guinea will buy."

"Kit. I'll be right back."

"No, you won't, mouse. You'll be right beside me."

Damn it. She was going to have to leave her gown behind. Rue ducked her head in false acquiescence, beginning down the path. One, two, three—at five she would do it—

"My lord!"

They both turned to the new voice, the man hurrying toward them. It was the squire, the heavyset one who'd guarded the museum door that day at the Stewart.

"Rufus thinks he's seen him, my lord," said the man, lowering his voice. "Felt him, rather. Vague, indistinct. But he looks like us—"

"Where?" demanded Kit.

"He last saw him by the amphitheatre, but the chap's moving off. He's got someone with him. A child—"

Kit swung back to Rue. She Turned, no grace, no subtlety, leaving the men behind her swearing, because just then a parcel of revelers had opened the tavern doors and staggered out into the light, and it was all the delay she needed. She whipped away into the gray dust of gunpowder and smoke.

# CHAPTER NINETEEN

Fire tore through her. It was instant and excruciating, a faint dry *whomp* of air and then the rocket and raging light, worse than lightning. Golden sparkles shimmered and burned in countless black streamers; Rue rushed away from them, gathering herself, finding Zane below her in the hundreds of faces looking up, being pulled out of the light and into a thicket of exotic eucalyptus and myrtles.

Just before he disappeared, Williams looked up too, noticing her. She hoped he knew it was her, and not Kit or a guard. She recognized his scent, so surely he'd recognize hers.

Please, please, God, please—

Rue dropped down past the peeling boughs. She didn't see anyone else about, neither *drákon* nor Others. There was only the runner and Zane and the crunch of curled bark that had fallen to the grass. She materialized behind them and the man pivoted at once, yanking the boy with him, an arm around his throat.

"Your coat," she said, and held out her hand.

"What?"

"Give me your greatcoat."

Rockets howled; the sky flashed. Zane was turning every shade of red. Despite the pistol and the arm at his neck, he had leaned away to stare hard at the ground.

"He won't flee from you," said Rue, as calmly as she could manage. "Promise him, Zane."

"Aye," choked the boy.

"But I need your coat, Tamlane Williams. Now."

Still he hesitated. Rue lost her calm.

"Do you want them to come upon us and see us like this?" she hissed. "Langford will kill you before you can blink."

Williams shoved the pistol into his waistband—it was a pistol—and shrugged out of his greatcoat, tossing it to her. She slung it over her shoulders.

"All I wanted," began the runner; his voice broke. He paused, clearing his throat. "All I ever wanted was to be left alone."

"I'm sorry," Rue said, and meant it.

"Why have you done this?" Anguish threaded his tone. She'd never realized he was so young. He'd vanished after she had; they'd never openly met. But he'd been here nearly as long as she. He must have been barely older than Zane when he'd escaped Darkfrith.

Williams took the pistol from his waist and clutched the polished handle. In his waistcoat and sleeves she could more easily see the unnatural stiffness of his right hand, frozen in his glove.

"It's who we are," she said to him. His padded coat was unwieldy over her shoulders; she held the lapels closed at her chest. "We can't escape it. I lived here for nine years before they found me. But I always knew, Tamlane, that one day they *would* find me. I think that somewhere inside you, in that place that remembers the shire, you must have known it too."

"*No.*"

She let his denial die into silence. Another rocket burst. Rue remained very still.

"Let the boy go. We can talk, the two of us. We don't need him."

Williams gave a queer laugh. "I can't go back there. You must know that. They'll kill me."

"I'll speak with them. I won't let them."

"You! What could you say? I pleaded and pleaded with them. My mother begged—" His voice cracked again. The pistol began to quake. "Ah, God, why did you do this? Why did you join them?"

With his head still bowed, Zane raised his eyes to hers, holding her in that pale wolfish yellow. She couldn't tell what he was thinking but she recognized his stance. He was preparing to fight.

Rue tried a cautious step forward, willing Zane not to move. "I thought it would purchase my freedom. The council demanded at least one of us, and at the time I had rathered it be you. I regret that now. And I realize—it doesn't matter. Regret, remorse, all the fine apologies in the world." Rue took another step. "You're using a *child* as your shield. Don't you see? You can't remain here. You're a danger to yourself, and to the tribe. You need to come home."

An extra-bright explosion blanched the sky beyond the trees. Leaf shadow tilted harsh over them all, highlighting bark and grass and stones before fading down into black.

"I won't," Williams said. "You don't understand."

"Actually, I do."

"It's so easy for you! Look at you! But if you're different

there, if you're born different—if you're poor and peculiar, if you don't think like the rest of them—the things they do to you..."

"Teach them," she said. "Teach them how they're wrong."

He drew a trembling breath. "God help me. I'd rather end it here."

"If that is your wish," said Christoff, walking silently among the leaves, "I can certainly arrange it for you."

Zane lifted his head; Williams ceased trembling and Rue shattered in two. Protect Zane. Protect Christoff. Zane was closer; if she Turned she could reach him first, but Kit would come to her—

"Well, lad? What shall it be?" He had paused by the pale trunk of a myrtle, leaning his shoulder against it, an apparition of gleaming satin and gold-buckled shoes. Christoff smiled his gentle smile. "You seem a man of uncommon clear will. I feel quite prepared to respect your decision."

The runner leveled the pistol straight at Rue. She stared back at him, unflinching, as his thumb cocked back the hammer.

"Wrong decision," said Christoff, and straightened from the tree.

Williams's eyes held hers, bitter, burning blue. He squeezed them closed and then rolled his gaze skyward, Turning in a haze of pale smoke, flying up through the leaves. Zane dropped to his knees, snatching up the pistol, spinning wildly about to take aim at the empty air.

"Stay *here*, damn you," Kit snarled at Rue, and followed the runner as smoke up into the night.

"I'm sorry." Zane was standing in a pile of shredded bark with the pistol in his hand. He began to pant, his words tumbling, his voice thick with tears. "I'm sorry, I'm sorry, I came to help, he found me before I even knew he had it—"

She went to him and closed her hand over his mouth, her face raised sharply to the sky. Fireworks, more applause. The spritely final bars of a galliard from the quartet.

She dragged him, her hand still over his face, to the break of the trees, keeping them both well behind the trunks. Together they looked out at the sea of animated faces, men and women laughing and talking and drinking as the show wound up to its radiant finale.

There—that cloud there was Kit, she knew him—and there was the runner, not so sheer, not so fine. They flexed through the choking haze of smoke, winding together, never quite touching.

And then the runner Turned to dragon. The entire audience broke into a gasp.

He was turquoise and bottle-green, extravagantly beautiful, because all the *drákon* were beautiful in this form. He soared high, blowing easily through the smoke that was Christoff. Another fire sun had already been lit; it shot straight up and detonated like a Chinese bomb, freezing the heavens and the earth in cold white light, exposing the second dragon that had overtaken the first, scarlet wings, bright emerald eyes.

The people below gasped again . . . and then, in tentative pockets, began to clap.

Rue hauled Zane back with her into the thicket. "Get out of here. Hurry. Get home."

"I can't leave you!"

"Do you truly think I can't handle myself? You see those creatures? I'm one of them. Go home. Do as I say this time! Don't speak to *anyone*. Just go."

The pistol dropped to the grass. "But—"

*"Now,"* she snapped, and flung off the coat.

Zane flinched back, then turned and ran lightly away. Within seconds he was invisible among the bent lines of the trees.

The musicians began a military march, the final piece of the night. Rue pressed against a heady-sweet eucalyptus and searched the sky—she and everyone else, because the two dragons were still circling each other, high and deceptively slow-moving, fangs and claws and wings that sheared the smoke into ribbons. The workers in the pit had already aligned the final ten rockets. With their ears muffled and their gazes aimed deliberately at the ground, they wouldn't realize there was a battle taking place above their heads.

They were rushing now, anticipating the end of the night. All ten fuses of the final rockets were lit, blistering orange. They burned short and flared in a volley and screamed up together into the cloudy black firmament, arrows flying straight to the beasts overhead.

Kit dodged twice, three times. The runner did not. A trail of fire struck his wing. He twisted and plunged but Kit was right after him, all the dazzling color and glamour that the fireworks lacked, and the chorus of *ooohs* and *aaahs* from the audience rose to overpower the music.

The last of the fire suns died. Both dragons had vanished from view, lost behind the curtain of smoke. It cleared, slowly, to show lucid glimpses of stars and the sickle moon and nothing else, no hint of mythical beasts. Only dark. Only night.

The people in the gardens began a roar of approval that climbed and climbed, clapping and whistling, slapping tankards together in toasts.

"Cracking good show!" enthused a man nearby to his companion. "How the devil do y'think they did it?"

She floated above the pleasure gardens, another drift of smoke among the many, blank moonlight flashing over fountains, lamplight a dim warmth along the paths. People were spilling back into the shadows, or to the tavern; she saw a man in a straw hat carrying off her dress.

But she could not find Christoff. She couldn't even find another *drákon*. The pleasure gardens were extensive, rolling in trees and grass and that soft, buttery light, but below her all she sensed were people and small hidden creatures like wagtails and finches and mice.

The grounds were fully surrounded with a brickwork wall. The northern corner seemed especially murky. Rue glided over to it, leaving behind the fountains and ambling couples, sinking down to become fog above the long tickling grasses. She curled over a wooden turnstile and fence with a sign posted PRIVATE MATTERS ONLY, entered an enclosure where the leaves gathered unswept and willowherb and cow parsley poked their heads through old flowerbeds, and logs that had once marked out boundaries fell apart in spongy green. A weathered toolshed slumped to one side, propped up with a plank, looking only a brisk breeze away from full collapse.

She heard voices, very furtive. It was darker here than she'd anticipated, the moonlight too thin to prick through the matted trees but for a few lacy plots. She Turned, avoiding them, stepping from the path to the silent grass, winding like a cat through the brush to a stand of oaks.

Definitely voices. Men's voices. She peered around the limbs yet saw nothing but more vegetation, so she moved again, creeping from tree to tree, until at last she was at the verge of the stand. Only yards away were all the missing *drákon*, standing in a rough circle amid the wild clawing bushes.

Everyone was dressed but for Kit. She did not see the runner, not at first. But when a pair of men moved, the pale, lax shape of Tamlane Williams came clear through the weeds.

". . . the carriage round here, to this wall," the marquess was saying. "He won't be that difficult to lift over."

"Aye, m'lord."

"Have a care with him. He's already bruised up. We don't want to make it worse for him than it already is."

Rue exhaled, her cheek against the tree. Christoff lifted his head.

"What of the girl?" whispered one of the men. "Do we bring her back tonight as well?"

"I'll take care of it."

"There's an extra hood in the carriage," offered the squire.

"Aye," said Christoff, and turned his face directly to hers.

Rue drew back. She retreated as swiftly as she dared, past all the trees, becoming one with the inky thick night.


One of the panes of her bedroom window was broken, the glass rudely smashed. But more significantly, the window itself was open, letting in the murmur of wind that stirred with the coming sunrise.

Kit took it as an invitation. It was highly unlikely she'd just forgotten to close it.

He found her sitting up in her bed with her legs drawn up, the covers at her feet. She wore a chemise but nothing else; it clung to her, translucent cotton stretched over her arms and shoulders, rippled into folds across the sheets. She regarded him gravely as he took shape, her face framed with tousled hair, her eyes looking him up and down, once, before lowering to her knees. There was a vase of fresh roses upon the bureau; their scent warmed the room.

"I haven't packed," Rue said.

"So I see."

"And you owe me a gown," she went on, still to her knees. "The green was my favorite. I'd like to get it replaced here." Her lips twisted. "There's not a *modiste* in Darkfrith I'd care to patronize."

"We *are* a bit beyond the brink of fine society."

"Well I know it," she replied, dark.

He approached the roses. They were pink and coral and reminded him of her lips, so he touched one, feeling the firm silky petals, imagining, with his lashes lowered, that he touched her instead.

"Will you hate it there so much?" Christoff asked.

She didn't answer, so he lifted his gaze, first to the reflection of color and sky past her window, then back at her. She'd lowered her chin so her hair spilled forward, a dusky veil over her cheeks. Her fingers clenched, bloodless, around her bare arms.

"I didn't kill the runner," he said.

"I saw." Her hands loosened a little; she ran her palms down her shins. "The pistol wasn't loaded. I checked it to be certain."

"He still threatened you, Rue."

"In his position, would you have done different?"

"I don't know," he answered honestly. "I've never been afforded the luxury of wondering."

She didn't have a ready response for that, and it irritated her. Rue drew the chemise taut over her legs, scowling at it, freeing it again. She didn't want to look up at him, because when she did all she saw was Kit, golden Kit, nude and warmly smiling. She would make this easy for him then, because she could not help herself. He'd sprinkle her with sugared words and kisses, all her best dreams, and she'd melt like snow under the sun. But she didn't want to make this easy. He was taking something valuable from her, no matter how much he offered in return, and she didn't want it to be easy.

"Rue-flower . . . I release you."

It took a moment for the words to wind through her brain. She raised her eyes, shocked. "What did you say?"

"I release you, Rue Hawthorne." He gave her a look she couldn't interpret, cool and dim against the brighter window. "You're no longer bound."

For a moment she only stared at him. Somewhere outside, a dog began to bark.

"Is that supposed to be a jest?"

"No."

"What are you saying?" She sat up straighter, getting angry. "You're saying I'm free? I don't have to return to Darkfrith?"

"Yes."

"Oh—very amusing, Lord Langford. I am to believe the council condoned this, that after everything that's happened all those mad old men merely wish me a fond *adieu*."

"The council," he said mildly, "will do as I say. In the end, it is our nature. Besides, none of them knows where you live, and I won't tell them."

She snapped her mouth closed. The dog subsided into diminishing echoes.

"What of Zane?"

"What of him?"

"Do you release him as well?"

"My love, as difficult as you may find this to believe, I never wanted any part of your grubby street urchin. All I wanted was his silence. He's not released from that, but otherwise...yes. He's free to bloom into years of full-blown larceny, for all I care."

"He won't betray us," Rue said.

The marquess gave a very dry smile. "I'm beginning to think it wouldn't matter if he did. After last night, I doubt anyone would believe him. We've a whole city full of witnesses now, and no one seemed especially panicked about flying dragons." He looked down at the roses. "I suspect it was quite a show."

She traced a slow circle into the sheets with her finger. "I heard it said that you were a new kind of shadow puppet, projected up into the sky." She shrugged. "People will believe anything, I suppose."

"Especially the intoxicated ones." Christoff blew his breath out in a sigh. "I tried to draw him away, God knows. I tried to keep us up high. But he just..." He trailed off, his features drawn harsh.

"You weren't visible that long," she said softly.

"Is that what it was like for you?" He took up one of the roses, tapped the water from the stem, and carried it with him over to the bed. The mattress sank; he sat beside her without touching. "I heard him talking to you about the shire. Is that what it was like for you too? You felt like an outsider, like you didn't belong?"

"Every single day." *Except when you looked at me.*

His hair was long and untamed, a spill of darkened gold down his shoulder blades. The muscles of his back were smooth and flat. Rue lifted a hand, combing her fingers through the strands. His skin beneath felt deliciously warm.

Kit tore off a rose petal, let it drift down to the rug. "It won't be simple," he said. "Changing the ways of the tribe. It won't be an easy task."

"No."

Another petal. "Perhaps you might write to me. Offer suggestions."

"Perhaps."

"Rue." He shifted around to face her; she let his hair slip from her hand. "You're not really going to make me be this noble, are you?"

"I think a little nobility might be good for your disposition, Lord Langford."

"A *little*," he said with a strange, uneasy laugh, and closed his eyes. "God. You've opened windows in my soul I never knew existed. You've made me think I have a hope of becoming the man I always wanted to be." He looked down at the rose; his fingers cupped together and tore off all the remaining petals at once. They fell in painted silence from his palm. "Rue-flower—Clarissa—for better or worse, you've woken my heart. I don't think I can be a noble man without you at my side, prodding me along every day. I'm a damned stubborn fellow. Don't you know that?"

She didn't reply. He tossed the stem to the floor, frowning now at her knees, as if the stretch of white chemise across them vexed him. He touched her arm, his palm skimming her uncovered skin, then lifted her hand to place his lips upon the inside of her wrist. His kisses were tantalizing, a path of sweet little butterflies winding up to her inner elbow. Rue found that she was holding her breath.

He pressed his cheek against her forearm. "You do realize that if you don't end up marrying me, I'll turn out a sour old man, just like the rest of them. I need you to rescue me."

"Yes," she agreed. "But what about my gown?"

Christoff looked up.

"It's going to take months of proper fittings. Swatches. Plates. A gown like that is not whipped together like some fishmonger's sackcloth."

"Ah. I believe I understand." He inched closer. "A lady's toilette is not to be rushed. If you think it's going to take so long...perhaps I might just stay with you. To ensure a proper fitting. I am, if I may say so, something of an expert on your figure."

"Are you?" she breathed, lying back to the pillows, stretching out her arms.

He smiled down at her, a truer smile than before. His hand discovered the drawstring of the chemise; he wound a thin ribbon around one finger. "Aye. A most...loving... expert." He tugged the bow loose.

"And what if I were to say to you—" Rue had to stop, because he had bent his lips to her chest, his tongue brushing her skin where the chemise fell open. "Say to you," she went on, determined, "that I would want a few more gowns like it, every year?"

"I suppose someone must keep Far Perch in order." His eyes were laughing, brilliant clear green, even though his tone remained bland. "It would be a crime to let it languish empty all the time."

"I agree. And someone should also be around—periodically—to guard against the natural hazards of the city. Urchins. Purloined diamonds. Ruthless thieves."

"Little mouse." Christoff leaned up to cover her lips, abandoning his reserve, his body lithe over hers, pressing into her with his hard, eager heat. "Let them come. There's nothing there worth stealing. Everything of value in the world is here before me, in your eyes."

———

Dawn came and left, waving green and gold and ginger, but Rue wasn't awake to see any of it. Kit watched her sleep, her lovely face unguarded, her cheeks tinted with the light. He felt an aching in his heart unfamiliar to him, and quietly perused it as he stroked the hair from her forehead. It took him a good while to realize that what he was feeling was happiness, absolute, complete.

It frightened him a little. He'd never known such a thing before. It seemed fragile, elusive, as temporal as the wash of colors that had blazed through the sky.

Her eyes opened. She regarded him with her drowsy, dark-eyed look, not speaking.

"Do you think you might love me again yet?" he asked.

She smiled at him, a woman's smile, mysteriously profound. "Ridiculous man. I've loved you my whole life. Didn't you know?"

He put his face into her hair to hide his relief. "A true gentleman is loath to appear immodest. . . ."

Her laughter shook them both. "Too late for that."

He relaxed to his side and pulled her closer, her back to his chest, his arms going tight around her in a gradual, squeezing embrace. She hugged him back with her arms over his and her feet tucked up.

"Will you marry me, Rue? Truly marry me, before our people?"

Her answer came low. "I will."

"Thank you."

"You're welcome."

Her body was softly rounded. Her buttocks made a warm, tempting pressure against his groin. Her breasts were a pleasing weight between his arms, her hair lay trapped across the pillows and under his cheek. Kit bent his head to hers with a new purpose.

"This is how we'll do it."

"What?"

He nipped her shoulder with his teeth.

"Oh."

"Tonight," he murmured. "In the sky."

Rue rolled over, wrapped in a sheath of lovely brown hair, white skin, pink lips, watching him through her lashes. She smiled with slow, sensual mischief. "Why wait till then?"

And drew him back to her.

The London Town Crier
July 20, 1751

Menagerie Set to Close

The M——s of L——d has made a Private Purchase of Graham's Menagerie, Chelsea, for a sum undisclosed, citing a Desire to restore the Peace to our City. Gentle Readers may recall the Peculiar Disappearance of an Entire Company of Capuchin Monkeys June last, which have since been discovered living Feral in Rollingbrook Forest and causing a Great Deale of Havoc in the crops nearby. The M——s has vowed no further Devilment will occur, as all the Creatures are to be moved to a Secluded Location, else sent back to the Lands from which they Came, sparing no expense at the cost.

The M——s wed in April. His Bride is said to be a most avid Lover of Wild Creatures.

# EPILOGUE

The truth of the stones is this: they change the chemicals in dragon blood.

Like a drug to a mortal, a diamond or ruby or mere chip of jasper can incite visions of bliss, of torment or sorrow or unbearable desire. The structure of any stone can be echoed in the dragon heart, in their very substance; both dragon and diamond are true beings of the earth. They feed off each other. They are twin reflections of a greater whole, which is why the *drákon* collect the stones, and why a few—a very few—mortal men collect them as well.

For if the stone can change the dragon, the dragon, too, can change the stone.

In the year 1751, for the first time in centuries, two Alpha hearts united. The power of their union shivered the very web of the *drákon*. Souls trembled on invisible strings. Fates shifted. And ancient ties, long forgotten, thrilled to life.

In that year, *Draumr*, the dreamer's diamond, transformed her song. From her hidden place in the Carpathian mines, in the dark, in the cold, her beckoning rose to flare across the skies.

Neither fortune nor distance can rend a true family. Blood calls to blood.

It was only a matter of time before the English sent their own dragon princess to find us.

# ABOUT THE AUTHOR

SHANA ABÉ is the award-winning author of nine novels, in-
cluding *The Smoke Thief*. She lives in the Denver area with
five surly pet house rabbits, all rescued, and a big goofy dog.
Please, please support your local animal shelter, and spay or
neuter your pets.

Visit her website at:

www.shanaabe.com

Read on
for a preview of Shana Abé's
next novel in her enchanting *Drákon* series…

*the*

*Dream Thief*

BY

SHANA ABÉ

A Bantam Hardcover
On sale October 2006

HE COULD BE HER MASTER—OR HER SLAVE....

# The Dream Thief

# SHANA ABÉ

AUTHOR OF *THE SMOKE THIEF*

## The Dream Thief

On sale October 2006

# Chapter One

Once, years ago, Lia had asked her mother if she heard the song.

"The supper chime?" Rue Langford had asked, tucking her daughter into bed.

"No, Mama. The other song. The quiet one."

"The quiet one. The music box from your father?"

"No. The *other* song."

And Mama had gazed down at her with her lovely brown eyes, her head tilted, a smile on her lips. She and Papa were hosting a *fête* that evening for the members of the council and their wives. Her skirts were ivory and cream; she smelled of flowers and soap and the silvery dust of hair powder. She wore pearls that thrummed with a low, gentle melody, simple, like a hymn. Lia reached out and ran her fingers over the bracelet.

"I'm afraid I don't know what song you mean, beloved."

"That one...."

Audrey was already out of the nursery, but Joan was in the bed against the other wall, sulking because she wasn't yet old enough to attend the *fête*.

"She says she hears a song all the time," said Joan in a very bored, grown-up voice.

Mama's look sharpened. "What sort of song?"

"A quiet one. You know...like the wind in a meadow. Like the ocean."

Rue's expression relaxed. "Oh. Yes, I hear that sometimes too."

"You do?"

"I do. Nature plays a wonderful symphony for us."

"No, not *nature*. It's a *song*."

Rue placed the back of her fingers upon her daughter's forehead. Her skin felt very cool. "Can you hum it?"

"No."

"Does it bother you? Does it hurt your head?"

"No..."

"It's not even real," said Joan loudly in her bored voice. "If it was real, we'd all hear it. We can hear *everything*."

"It is real to your sister," answered Mama, firm, and looked back at Lia. "You must tell me if it ever starts to fret you. Come to me, and I'll fix it."

Lia sat up in her bed, wide-eyed, interested. Rue was powerful, the most powerful female of the tribe, but Lia had no idea her mother's Gifts were that strong.

"How, Mama?"

"Why, I'll love it away, just like this," said Rue, laughing as she caught Lia by the shoulders and pressed rose-petal kisses all over her cheeks.

That was how Amalia knew that her mother didn't believe her either.

When the dreams began to surface a few years after that, Lia didn't bother to tell anyone. The song, for all its persistence, held a certain sadness and distance that made it seem almost innocent. But there was nothing of innocence in the blind dreams. In them she was another person...older. Enigmatic. She woke from them flushed and panting, guilty and excited and miserable at once. She wouldn't share those feelings with anyone, not even her mother.

At first they were fragments, just voices and sentences that seemed strung together without reason. She could hear herself speaking in them, but what she said made no sense. She could hear the man's voice, but it was as though he was far away from her, talking through a rainstorm. She caught only snatches of words.

Yet the dreams had grown clearer. And clearer. And with them, a rising sense of danger, a warning that pushed down on her chest and prickled the hair on her arms.

Nothing truly terrible ever happened in the blind dreams. At the same time, she knew that somehow they meant everything terrible. She spoke of stealing and killing and the loss of her parents as if reciting a list for the village market. It was not pretend. But in that humming, welcome dark, Lia felt nothing wrong at all.

A few months past, in the gray morning hours of her fourteenth birthday, the dream had revealed for the first time who the man was.

Zane. Zane the Other, Zane the criminal. Zane,

former apprentice of the Smoke Thief herself, now the tribe's hired hands and eyes and ears in the real world, the world beyond Darkfrith.

And tonight, even though she had run as fast as she could in her hoops and heels, she had missed his carriage. By the time she'd made it past the forest break and onto the front lawn, she couldn't even see the smudgy glow of its rear lanterns. There was only the faint squeak of metal and wood and the *clip-clop* of hooves fading off into the hills.

That—and the song. Thin and eerie and sweet, it beckoned from the farthest thread of the eastern horizon. It always beckoned.

Deliberately, she turned her back to it. It haunted her days and nights; it haunted her soul; and the fact that no one heard it but her was something Amalia never liked to consider.

She found herself gazing at the warm, handsome windows of Chasen Manor, set back against the forest and lawn like a perfect painting of country peace. At the figures moving inside, supper being laid, beds turned down, evening fires stoked, everything as ordinary as could be.

Something new flashed in the sky above her head, twisting, bright as a scythe with the rising moon; it dropped swiftly into the woods.

With her arms hugged to her chest, Lia watched it fall.

She'd be called in soon. She needed a plan.


The London air hung heavy with soot and a wet, cool fog, clinging to his face like an unpleasant skin, dampening his breath. But he was used to it; in fact, he usually welcomed it, because foggy nights meant fewer shadows. In his business, light and shadow were as important as picklocks and poison and knives.

At least tonight was over. Tomorrow he'd start again, but right now he was hungry, he was tired, and he was very much looking forward to a meal and his bed—and what awaited him in that bed.

He made himself part of the night. He made his footsteps silent, his breathing imperceptible. He listened to the dark so intently it sounded like his own heartbeat, familiar and calm.

This was his realm, for better or worse. This was the place he claimed and defended, a tiny, ragged patch of safety in the midst of chaos.

And so in the back of his mind, past his awareness of the fog and the candle-lantern and the muffled thumps and groans of the city, Zane was counting off his steps.

*Twenty-two, twenty-three*... there would be an oil lamp flickering in the front window of Madam Dumont's two-story, for the wastrel son who whored away half the night.

*Thirty-seven, thirty-eight*... step over the exposed root of the elm that had finally cracked the pavement into halves.

*Forty-five.* The black cat watching from the roof of Lucy Brammel's.

*Forty-seven.* The loosened trellis the cat used to climb to the roof; Zane had pulled it free of the chimney last January to see if it would hold his weight—it wouldn't—and Lucy still hadn't noticed.

*Fifty-one.*

He paused, another reflex. Fifty-one marked his first step onto his property. Too many men relaxed when they reached their own doors. It was one of the easiest places to make a kill.

But Zane was not like other men. He wasn't like anyone else on this clean, comfortable street, and it was one of the things he appreciated most about Bloomsbury.

He slipped around to the back of his house, evading all the traps he'd set, finding the short rise of stairs through the clouded darkness, and then the keyhole to the kitchen door.

Joseph was waiting inside. He was seated at the side table eating a bowl of something that smelled like very bad eel.

"Late," he grunted, by way of a greeting.

Zane removed his cocked hat, running a hand through his hair. "Whatever it is you are consuming, I do not want it served at my table tonight. Or any other night."

The man's brows arched; past his scars and badly mottled skin, he looked pained. "It's me mum's recipe."

"Then she is welcome to my portion." He bolted the kitchen door closed once more, had worked the top buttons of his coat free and was heading for the hall, for bed, when he was halted by his front man's voice.

"Got a visitor."

"I know."

"Not Mim."

Zane slanted a look back at him. Joseph shrugged. "A girl. Put her in the parlor."

"A girl," he repeated slowly. "Are you certain?"

"Aye," answered Joseph, with exaggerated care. "I'm certain."

Zane turned again and silently left the kitchen.

His house was dark. He'd grown up with it this way and kept it as a useful habit. A house ill-lit on the inside revealed much less of its inhabitants; he nearly always preferred to see and be unseen. But Joe had apparently felt the girl in question required a great deal of illumination. When Zane stopped at the arched doorway to the parlor, he saw that every lamp was burning, plus the pair of café candelabras from the dining room. The contrast was almost like daylight: the reds and blue-greens of the Peshawar rug searing bright, the carved corners of the paintings rubbed with gilt, the gleam of the satinwood chairs eye-wateringly sharp.

The child slumped aside in one of them, head back, eyes closed, lips apart. There was a half-filled cup of chocolate tilting precariously on her lap, her fingers still curled around the handle. Her frock was girlish blue sprigged with daisies, her pumps were dirty, her hair was mussed. Limp ringlets of darkened gold fell softly against her cheeks. She looked pale and gaunt and remarkably plain, despite the beauty of that hair.

He stood there and felt, to his distant surprise, none of the anger he had expected, but instead a profound sense of relief.

To manage it he took the cup from her fingers and gave the chair a hard kick.

She came awake at once, straightening, her hands fluttering across her skirts.

"Lady Amalia. I wish I could say I was happy to see

you, but I've already endured the pleasure of the Marquess of Langford's company thrice in the past two days. What the devil are you about?"

"Father's here?" she asked, looking around them.

"Not at the present. No doubt it won't be long before he returns. I don't believe he's fully convinced I haven't hidden you away somewhere in the house. Imagine my joy," he added silkily, "at walking into my parlor tonight and discovering it to be true."

"I'm sorry. I. . . ." She trailed off, shaking her head, then covered her eyes with one hand. "I haven't been sleeping well."

"Perchance it has something to do with the fact that you've been riding in a public coach for—let me see—almost a fortnight, isn't it? That's about how long it takes to travel from Darkfrith to my door by stage. Unless, I suppose," he paused, "you flew here."

He hadn't meant it as a barb but she grimaced, just a little. Then her hand lowered; she gazed at him steadily.

"I didn't fly. You know I can't. And that's not why."

Zane didn't like that look, long-lashed, brown-eyed, direct. It reminded him too much of her mother. They stared at each other in the growing silence. Amalia's lips slowly compressed into a thin, stubborn line.

With a sigh he gave it up, lowering himself into the opposite chair. He glanced down at her cold chocolate and then tried a taste, feeling his stomach rumble. Hell was going to cut loose sooner or later, and he'd already missed supper.

The *drákon* did not take kindly to losing one of their kind. He knew that too bloody well.

Lamplight glinted silver along the scrolled edge of a tray beside him. Saints be praised, Joseph had left her food. Scones, orange cake, a dish of honeyed nuts and dried fruits—he leaned forward and helped himself to half an apricot and a sliver of cake.

"Bad dreams, snapdragon?"

"Yes." It was a miserable whisper.

"How unfortunate. I'm certain it was worth fleeing your home without a word to anyone—without, I am equally certain, permission from your almighty *drákon* council—to come here to tell me."

But she still didn't avert her gaze. She didn't even seem abashed. All her initial, drowsy confusion appeared completely vanished. She looked cool and composed and very much older than her years, even in her wrinkled skirts. Whatever it was that had compelled her halfway across the kingdom was well hidden behind that mask of mulish calm.

Very well. He knew how to wait.

She made a slow circle of the room, not drinking. "This doesn't seem much like the residence of a notorious criminal."

"No. That's rather the point."

"Is that why Mother gave it to you?"

"Pardon me," he retorted, brushing the crumbs from his waistcoat, "she did not *give* it to me. I purchased it from her, and at a damned premium price. It was all extremely legitimate."

"Oh."

"Yes, *oh*."

She set the chocolate on the windowsill. "You love my family," Amalia said, her back to him, rubbing her palm up and down her rumpled blue-and-flowered skirts.

He did not reply.

"Some of them, anyway." She glanced at him from over her shoulder. "You do love some."

"If you say so."

"You know what we are," she persisted. "You've helped us, over the years. You're ... close to my parents. You've aided the tribe."

"That wasn't for love, I assure you."

"What was it, then? Only money?"

"Money is a subject very dear to my heart, child. Do not underestimate it."

"And what of power?" she asked, softer. "Is that dear to you as well?"

"Did you venture all this way for an examination of my character, snapdragon?"

Lia turned and looked him fully in the face. She didn't like his pet name for her, and never had. It sounded whimsical, childish, when everything inside her felt strong and cold.

But she knew what he thought of her. She'd always known.

He was the only mortal tolerated by the tribe. He was the only one suffered to keep their secrets. While she and all her kind were kept trapped in the green heaven of Darkfrith, Zane was the sole living creature allowed to come and to go at will. Even her father, the Alpha, tended to inform the council when he meant to travel.

Lia was the daughter of a lord. She lived in a mansion of glimmer and light; she looked out her bedroom window every day at open skies and wild wooded hills and sometimes felt so suffocated it was a wonder she didn't open her mouth and start screaming and never stop.

The council gave lectures to the children in the village:

*Of all the world, we are the last of our kind.*

*It is our duty to remain safe.*

*It is our duty to remain here.*

*We protect the earth-bound: the young, the women, the weak.*

*We are* drákon. *Duty to the tribe above all.*

Lia understood why her mother had run away, all those years ago. If she thought for an instant she could truly do the same—

But she couldn't. She wasn't Gifted like the rest of her family. She couldn't Turn to smoke, much less to dragon. She wasn't beautiful, she wasn't brave, she wasn't any sort of reflection of the magnificence of her kind. It had taken all her meager resources just to get this far, and Lia knew her time here would be short. They'd find her soon.

There were only two things about her that set her apart from the rest of her tribe—two dark, disturbing things. And one of them was seated before her in this chamber.

Zane had not stirred from his chair. The lamps were bright and the shadows were harsh; he was sketched in charcoal and light, studying her with a half-lidded gaze she recognized from years of watching him pretending to relax at Chasen Manor, every line of his body casually elegant, his coat unbuttoned to drape the cushions, his waistcoat a satin gleam of pewter and taupe.

His eyes were paler than amber. His hair was very long and thick, honeyed brown. He was poise and muscle and tall as her father; Joan and Audrey used to keep her awake at night for years in the nursery, just giggling his name, until at last she was old enough to realize why.

Because of this. Because of his hands, so strong and tanned. His fingers, gently tapping the wooden arm of the chair in an easy, steady percussion that belied the wolf-watchfulness of his gaze. Because of his jaw, and his brows, and the handsome curve of his mouth. Because when he stretched his legs and crossed his ankles and lifted his dark lashes to fully see her once more, she was as pinned as a deer in a dragon's clear yellow sights.

She remembered the blind dream of him. She remembered the stroke of his voice—

"Forgive me if I interrupt your contemplation of my cravat," he said now, in a very different tone. "No doubt it's adorned with all manner of fascinating stains, as I've been out the past two days and nights straight searching every inn and tavern and coach yard in the city for one thoughtless, wayward miss. I find I'm a shade impatient with all these heavy silences. Why, pray tell, have you landed in my parlor?"

Lia blinked. "You—you were searching for me?"

"Your father seemed to require it."

"Oh."

"Yes, *oh*," he repeated, this time clearly mocking.

She took a breath. "If I tell you something, will you promise not to mention it to anyone else?"

"No," he said bluntly.

"What if it's important?"

"In that case, absolutely no. Look," he said, leaning forward to prop his elbows on his knees, "if it's something so dire you can't share it with your parents, then I want nothing to do with it. I'm not courting that sort of trouble. Sorry, my heart. That's the way of things."

*And tonight, my heart?*

"Do you think," she asked carefully, "that it is possible to—to tell the future?"

His eyes narrowed. "What, like tinkers and starcasters, that sort of thing?"

She shrugged. "Or, like dreams."

"Certainly."

"You do?"

Lia crossed the rug to stand before him. She felt calm, removed, after all the days of worry and heat and dread, rocked to sleep and awake in that wretched excuse of a carriage, the stench of people and old horsehair clogging up her nose. She felt a thread of her dream-self, smooth and mysterious, flowing through her veins.

With Zane still seated, their heads were nearly level. She leaned forward and pressed her lips to his.

When she drew away again his eyes had taken on a harder glow.

"Passable," he said coolly. "Feel free to try it again in about ten years. Until then, don't waste my time."

"Oh dear," came a light, feminine voice. "Am I interrupting?"

"Not in the least." Zane rose from the chair; Lia was forced to step back. In the parlor doorway stood a woman, hooded and cloaked, the slit in her mantle revealing skirts of dove silk and a stomacher of white threadwork and moonstones.

With a graceful turn of her wrists, the woman pushed back her hood. Red hair, gray eyes; her every movement carried the fresh scent of night.

Lia felt a flush of exquisite shame begin to creep up her throat.

"Who is this?" asked the woman, sounding amused.

"No one. Merely a little lost lamb."

"A lamb," said the woman, still smiling, entering the parlor. She touched a gloved finger to Lia's chin, lifting her face. "With those eyes? I think not. Rather more a windstorm descending."

Amalia pulled away. She glanced up at Zane—wolf-eyed, stone-faced, despite his languid tone—then grabbed his hand and held it hard.

"I want you to know," she said quietly, "that I will do anything to protect my family. Now, or in the future. I'll do anything at all. Remember that I warned you."

His mouth flattened into a smile. "How charming. Perhaps you'd care to inform your father, as well." He disengaged their hands. "I believe that's him at the window."

And the locked shutters blocking the broken pane began to rattle and shake.